HOLLOW TRIUMPH

Henry Mueller is convinced that he is better than everyone else, but is frustrated when he realizes that the rest of the world doesn't agree. He wants to become a doctor but doesn't have the patience, so instead pursues a life of petty crime. Upon his release from prison, Henry marries a trusting young woman for her money. Once she gets wise to the fact that the only person Henry loves is himself, she leaves him. And now it's just Henry and his put-upon friend Turk. But even Turk has his limits. He balks at murder…

Henry discovers that there is a wealthy, successful psychiatrist in town who appears to be his exact double, except for a scar on his face. Could Henry be clever enough to trade places with the doctor? Once Henry creates a scar on his own face, he is ready to try to become Dr. Viktor Bartok. Unfortunately, he first must first remove the real doctor. But how could he know where his deception would lead him, what it would cost him—and the people he would lose along the way?

Hollow Triumph

Murray Forbes

Introduction by Bill Kelly

Stark House Press • Eureka California

HOLLOW TRIUMPH

Published by Stark House Press
1315 H Street
Eureka, CA 95501, USA
griffinskye3@sbcglobal.net
www.starkhousepress.com

ISBN: 979-8-88601-049-7

Book design by Mark Shepard, shepgraphics.com
Proofreading by Bill Kelly

First Stark House Press Edition: October 2023

Hollow Triumph: Book and Movie
By Bill Kelly

Hollow Triumph, by Murray Forbes, was originally published in hardcover by US publisher Ziff-Davis in 1946. The book was also published by UK publisher Gordon Martin in 1948 and saw a French edition by Hachette entitled *Château de Cartes* (House of Cards) in 1949. *Hollow Triumph* was later reprinted in a 1953 paperback edition by Pyramid (#97) but was retitled as *The Big Fake*.

Author Murray Forbes was born in Chicago, July 20, 1905 and died in Los Angeles on January, 28, 1987. *Hollow Triumph* was his sole criminous novel, and as far as I was able to determine, his only published work. Forbes primary career was that of a radio actor playing the role of Willie Fitz on the long-running *Ma Perkins* radio show and he also appeared in the radio serials *Guiding Light* and *Today's Children*.

Forbes' novel was filmed in 1948 by Eagle-Lion with both Steve Sekely (*Lady in the Death House, Waterfront*) and Paul Henreid (uncredited) directing a Daniel Fuchs (*Between Two Worlds, Criss Cross*) script.

This essay will examine both the novel and the film, each on its own terms. The primary influence in making the movie was star and co-director Paul Henreid who, with his co-creators, created a different vision of Forbes' novel.

The Novel

After serving six years for forgery, embezzlement and confidence scams, Henry Mueller is being released from prison. The time is 1936. Henry was once an ambitious and talented medical student whose education is cut short by his inability to accept being rejected by a prestigious college fraternity. Originally, love of humanity did not motivate Henry to become a doctor; dreams of wealth and a social position much higher than his own drove his ambition:

"I'm going to be a specialist, Mama," he would say, "with a big office downtown, and rich patients who can afford to pay, and a nice home, and clothes...."

But when the Phi Tau fraternity rejects his application, Henry sees a key element of his success denied him and his wounded pride, jealousy and social paranoia enrage him to the point that he rejects the medical profession and leaves the university.

Before leaving prison, Warden Riley praises Henry for his intelligence and dedication to his work and studies while in prison, but deflates Henry's ego—swollen to enormous proportions by the warden's effusion of praise—when he remarks that Henry is a failure as human being because he lacks "intestinal fortitude":

> If you hadn't lacked guts you wouldn't have quit medical school. When you did quit school and got yourself a respectable job with an investment banking firm, you lacked the guts to stay with them and work up gradually toward a decent income. So, you finally wound up selling fake stocks, passing forged checks, and conning old ladies out of their money because it was easier, and you walked around with more money in your pockets.

Henry reels from the criticism and is tormented by this accusation of cowardice, but as is evident throughout the book, Henry's ego (and low regard for the critical faculties of others) eventually provides enough rationalization to minimize this trauma or any event that pricks his pride or his conscience. Unfortunately for Henry—and his victims—these ego-deflating events always leave a residue of resentment and bitterness.

Henry falls in with an old acquaintance, Gil Turkel, whom he engages as a partner in petty crime, with "Turk" doing most of the work and Henry manipulating a fifty percent share of the proceeds— despite making a minimum contribution to whatever enterprise they are engaged in. Turk, like many others who have the misfortune to meet Henry, fall for his intelligence, facile charm and like Turk, are flattered by the interest shown in them by this cultured man who exudes an air of mastery of the world around him.

Unlike Henry however, Turk eschews violence and crimes where there is an identifiable victim, restricting himself to gambling related offenses. When he believes Henry is playing a widowed mother (Carlotta) for her money, he bids Henry goodbye.

> "Henry, I've always liked you. … People call you an intellectual. They call me a stupe. But there's one thing I got, and that's a conscience. Sure, I like to make money the easy way, same as a

lot of other guys, but I wouldn't enjoy a penny of dough that was screwed out of somebody as fine as Carlotta and that kid of hers. A guy that would be cooking up a deal like that in the back of his mind is a low-down no-good son-of-a-bitchin' pimp!"

Henry becomes enraged and beats Turk, but their symbiotic illness plays out with victimizer and victim soon brushing it all away as they resume their respective roles of provider and parasite. Repeatedly Henry displays an uncanny talent for identifying people who will succumb to his personality; those who are not susceptible to exploitation are immediately abandoned.

Henry muddles along, frustrated in his quest for the big score, when fate deals him an ace. He is mistaken for an eminent psychiatrist, Viktor Bartok, and Henry formulates a plan that will make his dreams of wealth, power and social prominence come true. Herein, of course, lies much of the tension and suspense in this novel: Can Henry assume the identity (and responsibilities) of a famous doctor and fool everyone enough to get away with it? For Henry's ego it is a monumental challenge, but more important to Henry, he will be able to revenge himself on a society he believes has repeatedly humiliated him and worse, has penetrated his façade and revealed him for what he has been to this point, a low-life cowardly trickster.

A critical part of Henry's impersonation scam depends upon him being able to duplicate the dueling scar on Dr. Bartok's cheek. Henry performs an excruciatingly painful operation on himself and revels in his success—not for successfully duplicating the scar—but for "proving" that the world has underestimated his character:

… Henry examined the neat patch on his left cheek. He gave the adhesive a last pressure with his fingers and stepped back from the mirror, complimenting himself on his skill in doing such a neat job of cutting and stitching. His medical training had certainly helped him here. This was an incident in his life he would not soon forget. Guts? He wished Warden Riley could have watched him.

The scar, as well as all the other challenges that would be expected in assuming the identity of a famous doctor and man-about-town, present Henry with numerous difficulties. How he meets these challenges in order to successfully pull off this scam of scams was also of course a challenge to Forbes as a writer: he has to convince the reader that Henry can successfully meet these challenges and remain undetected. There are several scenes in which Henry must convince those he meets that he is Viktor Bartok and that any doubts they may have about his identity are groundless. I believe Forbes did an excellent job with this aspect of the story and all of the scenes involving someone potentially exposing Henry are convincing, as Henry proves a consummate con artist. The "Henry weaseling out of trouble" scenes are cleverly constructed, but it is Forbes' characterization of Henry's massive ego, warped intellect and will to success that make the scenes convincing.

Henry's success causes extensive collateral damage among those that trust him. As Henry begins to enjoy the rewards of Bartok's lucrative practice and wealthy lifestyle, he begins to discover that, for the first time, he has some remorse when he harms someone. A suicide deeply affects Henry, but after he pays for funeral expenses and gives some money to the victim's family, he is able to purchase "freedom from conscience" and goes merrily on his way. Is Henry a psychopathic monster completely devoid of human feelings and conscience? At the point where Henry disposes of Bartok and assumes his identity, there is every reason to believe so. Yet Henry seems to undergo a change as he feels sympathy for Bartok's patients and he works very hard to help them, studying their files and spending many hours consulting psychiatric literature relevant to their cases. But, is Henry's motivation in helping them purely ego driven because failing them or making their lives worse would represent a failure on his part and/or expose his crime? Henry is a supreme egotist and has been totally ruthless in his relationship with others, so this seems a likely conclusion, but Forbes provides enough evidence to show that Henry is not a cardboard monster and that there are some layers of complexity to his character. And neither is Forbes posturing shopworn homilies like "There is good in the worst of us" and "some good has come from all this evil", etc. Forbes avoids the "evil genius" and "anti-hero" stereotypes, but even when Henry is doing some good in the world, we see that the Henry riding a white horse and dispensing good works has a darker side. The dichotomy between Henry's evil nature and the good he is able to do is handled well: Henry, when pushed into a corner, is pure psychopath, but when not threatened, he usually feels empathy for others and is able to work hard and harness the gifts of intelligence he has to do good. And the prize for Henry is twofold: normal ego gratification; each of Henry's successes with his patient is a merit badge to his success and the not so normal rage-driven revenge on those that have doubted or rejected him.

Early in Henry's masquerade he encounters a fortune teller in a nightclub, who after reading his palm, gives Henry a scare. He at first refuses a reading, but his date questions his courage, a sore spot with Henry, so he relents and the fortune teller knocks him back with:

> You are a man with many sides to your personality. … Your hand is the hand of a genius and a conqueror. You have a multitude of gifts. Your intelligence is that of a Socrates and your powers are that of a Caesar. You have a lust for life and a driving ambition that will not allow you to rest until you have attained your goal. The brilliance of your mind is capable of doing many things, both good and bad … Wealth and power will one day be yours. In your efforts to reach the heights, you will be victorious, but fame and fortune that is ill-gotten and procured at the sacrifice of self-respect and honor can bring to its possessor only the feeling of a triumphant emptiness … I would say that had you selected the profession of medicine, you might have been a good doctor. As it is, I see that you wisely chose to become an actor.

The fortune teller has captured, in a nutshell, the driving forces behind Henry's personality and by suggesting that his profession is "actor", he has exposed Henry's scam, if obliquely. Additionally, the fortune teller has also given Henry a warning of the consequences to come. Henry laughs it all off of course when discussing the event with his date and as with any event he finds disturbing, quickly subsumes it. So at this point, Henry is still struggling to subsume Bartok and as it were, make everything that is Bartok's, Henry's.

As Henry struggles to maintain and even enhance Bartok's professional position, he proceeds to ruin a succession of people, all sacrificed to his mad ambition. Midway through the carnage he begins to feel remorse more deeply than before and becomes haunted by the people he has destroyed, but in a surprising turn, fate once again bestows upon him an opportunity that will enhance his glory and self-satisfaction and erase any doubts he may have about his self-worth. Henry is presented with an opportunity to put Bartok's theory for treating a psychological condition that today would be referred to as PTSD. He is wildly successful and receives enormous praise and recognition from his superiors. But Henry's joy is short-lived as he realizes that the credit for all his work actually belongs to Dr. Bartok, the man whose life he has taken and usurped:

Henry Mueller was non-existent. He was Viktor Bartok and he would always be Viktor Bartok. As Viktor Bartok he had won the fame he had always sought for Henry Mueller. He had achieved nothing in his own name. As Henry Mueller he could not practice as a psychiatrist. *Henry Mueller was nobody—a nonentity.* To whatever heights he would climb, it would be as Viktor Bartok! … The man that he had killed lived on to rob him of *his* glory— *his* achievements—*his* success—*his* fame—*his* entire identity. He had done away with Viktor Bartok, but ironically Viktor Bartok had also taken the life of Henry Mueller. The dead had had the last laugh!

Hollow Triumph is a nightmarish glimpse into the consequences of an entirely self-warped man stealing the life of another, but it is also an exploration of the enabling factors that allow Henry's impersonation of Dr. Bartok to be successful. Those who enable Henry and indulge his mania are duped, and it could be argued that their own weaknesses lead to their destruction, but the particularly frightening aspect of their situation, and by implication, ours, is that we are all potentially vulnerable to the Henrys of this world who can uncover our weaknesses and exploit them.

The Movie

Hollow Triumph was an Eagle-Lion production released in 1948 and directed by Steve Sekely & Paul Henreid (uncredited), with a script by Daniel Fuchs and cinematography by John Alton. The film had a working title, The Man Who Murdered Himself, and was later rereleased under the title, *The Scar*. Paul Henreid, Joan Bennett, Eduard Franz and Leslie Brooks were the principal cast members. The film is in public domain and easily available and may be viewed or downloaded from archive.org. Look for the remastered print entitled *The Scar*.

Paul Henreid was the driving force behind the project—the book having been recommended to him by its initial director, Steve Sekely—and Henreid was eager to play the lead role of Muller: playing an American gangster would be an extension of the range of roles he had been playing in Hollywood, where he was usually cast as a European adventurer, most notably, the French Resistance leader Victor Laszlo in *Casablanca*.

Henreid, as Johnny Muller, is the overwhelmingly dominant presence in the movie and is rarely offscreen. Joan Bennett has a significant role, Eduard Franz less so, playing Muller's brother Frederick, who tries to divert Johnny from a life of crime and its consequences. Changing the principal character's name from Henry to Johnny was one of the many changes the movie creators would make to the novel. While both works share common characters, plotting events and themes, the movie *Hollow Triumph* can be seen as a hybrid film—part gangster thriller evocative 1930s and part noir thriller, whose heyday was in the 1940s and 1950s. The movie opens with a heist scene and the revenge murders of some of the perpetrators and then becomes more atmospheric of mood, deliberate in its depiction of flawed human nature and features a fatal ending. Indeed, *Hollow Triumph* is usually referred to as an example of film noir as it features a character whose poor decision making, when combined with the intrusion of the fatal "finger of fate", eventually ensure Johnny's downfall. John Alton's cinematography (*I, the Jury, Raw Deal, Bury Me Dead, He Walked by Night*), set design by Edward L. Ilou (*He Walked by Night, Kansas City Confidential*) and several night scenes, including a brilliant chase scene using the Angel's Flight funicular railway at its climax, provide all the basic filmmaking ingredients of noir.

As in the novel, Johnny Muller is a recently released convict but in the movie he organizes a heist on a gambling casino that comes a cropper and Muller finds himself on the run. Through a chance encounter with a flaky dentist, played to the comic hilt by John Qualen, Muller learns that he is a dead ringer for Dr. Bartok, a prominent psychiatrist. Muller soon ingratiates himself with Evelyn Hahn, Bartok's receptionist and the impersonation is on. The script departs from the plotting events seen in the novel, but the problems inherent to impersonation and the character of the ruthless, egotistical Muller remain pretty much intact. Muller's all-consuming pride and ambition are evident, but circumstances beyond his control, rather than his own flawed character lead to his undoing. The irony of Henry Muller's dilemma in the book is portrayed in an entirely different fashion than in the movie with Johnny Muller ending up as a "victim" of fate. As in the book, Bartok, from the grave, will be Muller's undoing, but the how of it all is entirely different. In the movie, events and their consequences are more plot driven than in the book; in the novel, it is Henry Muller's character that is the beginning, middle and end for all that takes place.

The key element the book and the movie have in common is the impersonation challenge: is Henry's/John's usurpation of Dr. Bartok's identity successfully (believably) portrayed? Fiction, be it book or movie, often walks the tightrope of credibility and the creator(s) remain aloft or crash to the ground based on their ability to convince the reader/viewer that the events portrayed are possible. In my opinion, the book is more successful in achieving believability than the movie is, but I'm sure opinions will vary on this one. Through the skill of the actors and, in this case, two directors, the crew probably did its best with a script that occasionally creaks. Additionally, there is a scene at the end relating to the impersonation problem, where a scrub woman challenges Muller, but it seems very tacked on and intended to pound on the irony theme drum, rather than create any tension or suspense.

The movie *Hollow Triumph*, regardless of some plot and characterization choices, is well worth seeing for John Alton's cinematography and contains many well done scenes, including Muller's self-inflicted scar makeover and a delightfully comic scene in which garage attendant and would-be-ballroom dancer Jerry (played in deadpan style by Alvin Hammer) gives the paranoid Muller the willies, chattering about his career fantasy with Muller misinterpreting his words as insight into Muller's plans for Bartok's demise. This and John Qualen's nutty dentist add some comic relief certainly not present in the book.

Because several of the situations in the book, like suicide, abortion, etc. would have been unfilmable subjects in mainstream 1940's Hollywood, the creators of the film had no choice but to avoid those events, and their alternative of portraying the petty but ambitious gangster Bartok trying to pull off the Big Score was selected by the creators. Henreid was able expand his resume from playing European adventurer types (perhaps the switch from the common European name Henry to Johnny, the archetypal crime movie hero name of the time, was part of this) and *Hollow Triumph* was Henreid's first attempt at directing, warming up for forty subsequent directing credits, including the Bette Davis chiller, *Dead Ringer* and many episodes of *Alfred Hitchcock Presents*. Joan Bennett overcomes a tricky characterization reversal as Muller's love interest and accomplice and delivers a fine performance. Eduard Franz's character as Muller's brother is used by the script as a device to keep us updated on the earlier botched heist event in the story, but Franz brings some pathos to the story that the other characters are incapable of delivering. Jack Webb of *Dragnet* fame has an interesting bit as the killer "Bullseye" working for the robbed casino owner, pursuing Muller in the aforementioned chase scene through the Bunker Hill section of Los Angeles.

Hollow Triumph, book and movie, is a good example of creating two different stories using the same character whose nature is essentially the same, but following a differently plotted path to destruction. Would-be doctor Henry Muller's path is more grandiose than that trod by the hoodlum Johnny Muller and Henry entirely owns his own downfall, whereas Johnny is undone be a quirk of fate. In the end both book and movie tell the story of the rise and fall of a man consumed by overweening pride and ambition. Both works are completely dominated by their respective Mullers, with the differences in the plot points and the characterizations of the supporting characters between the two media amounting to, in the end, very little. Each work can stand solidly on its own creative feet.

—Mesa, AZ
February, 2023

Bill Kelly has proofread many Stark House releases since 2017 and recently has contributed introductions to several volumes, and edited two author anthologies, including the recently released *Pulp Champagne: The Short Fiction of Lorenz Heller*. Bill received a B.A. in English from Columbia University and was a technical writer and illustrator for several corporations. Bill's first exposure to crime fiction was the works of Raymond Chandler, Penguin UK editions, purchased in Singapore.

Hollow Triumph

Murray Forbes

To my brother Ben

ACKNOWLEDGMENTS

The author expresses appreciation for the valuable assistance given him by Lieutenant Colonels W. Park Richardson and H. S. Gordon, Medical Corps, Army of The United States. Also to Harry C. Coblens, M. D., for his kindness and patience in checking the medical facts in this book.

The possession which the Creator has written on our forehead, be it small or great, we shall surely attain, even in the desert; and more than this we can never get, though we be on Mount Meru, whose sides are packed with gold.

BHARTRIHARI, *The Vairagya Sataka.*

CHAPTER ONE

The warden of Mohawk Prison turned in his swivel chair, smashed the chewed butt of a cigar in the ashtray, and crossed the office toward a file cabinet. Glancing again at the parole board's order in his hand, he pulled open a file lettered M. So many cards in the M file … he had never quite realized just how many. He began to riffle through them—Machek, Mangos, Marrafino, Marko, Masyk, Mattello; Steve Mattello—199 years for a hatchet murder. We're lucky, thought the warden as the card flashed through his fingers, no trouble with him now for almost a year. McGrath, McKay, Miner, Mitropolous, Moberg, Monaco; Frank Monaco awaiting sentence of death in the electric chair December 14. Too bad for Frankie, sighed the warden, he won't live to see this Christmas. Guess the world won't miss him much. Shot it out with a copper in an east side tavern. Press decided to make a crusade out of it … One card less in the M file.

Warden Riley squinted at the card in front of him. "Henry Mueller, alias Henry Miller, alias Henry Milton, alias Henderson Mills, alias Milton Henry, alias Henry Milford. Forgery, embezzlement, confidence game. Arrested June 16, 1932; indicted by grand jury on charges of fraudulently obtaining $3,600 from some elderly spinster at Middleton, N. Y.

"Born, Essen, Germany, March 11, 1900. Came to United States at age of two. Parents, Karl and Greta Mueller, both deceased. Education, Pittsburgh Public School; Fulton High School; Standish University, four years pre-medical school; two years medical college; studied diligently to become doctor; withdrew from Standish University in 1922, took job with investment banking firm selling stocks. Stayed two years with investment banking firm. Went west to California, became associated with Pacific Irrigation Company, which went bankrupt in 1926. Next heard of cashing forged checks in several midwestern towns. In 1928 appeared in Tulsa, Oklahoma, affiliated with oil company selling stock in non-existent oil wells to southwest communities. Fled back east when fake promotion scheme was discovered; no trace of whereabouts in 1929-1930. Later forged checks in Albany, Buffalo, Yonkers, and New York City. Apprehended in Middleton, N. Y. Convicted and sentenced to Mohawk Prison, October 4, 1932."

Quite a career, mused the warden. He certainly got away with a lot, but it finally caught up with him. Too bad; with his education, he might have amounted to something.

Warden Riley glanced again at the letter in his hand: "… and so after reviewing the case of Henry Mueller, No. 147963, it is the opinion of the parole board that he be recommended for release. This prisoner has fifty-one months of good behavior credits which would reduce his sentence to five years and nine months. Therefore, his release would become effective July 12, 1938, or any time thereafter at the warden's discretion."

Fifty-one months of good behavior credits. Henry Mueller had been an ideal prisoner. He was not only a trusty, but also head accountant in the prison office. A good accountant too. His books were always correct and he ran the department with dispatch and efficiency. He had even installed a new system of bookkeeping that cut expenses by two-thirds. Warden Riley had to admit that he was impressed, and so were the other officials. In fact, they looked upon Henry Mueller as a rather unfortunate victim of circumstances, and his case was set up for review long ahead of many others equally deserving. The warden wasn't sure he approved. Mueller's polite, ingratiating manner, his suave and educated approach, had earned him the respect of his superiors and the resentment of his fellow inmates. But Henry Mueller was out for Henry Mueller. The quickest way to freedom was by being a model prisoner in every way, obeying orders, working diligently, being humble, affecting an attitude of complete remorse. It wasn't too hard, and if at the same time he could show the prison how to save some money, Henry knew that the parole board would hear about it.

His brain was always working, and it was not an ordinary brain. It refused to stand still just because he was incarcerated behind iron bars. The state had no control over his mind. They could sentence and confine his body, but not his brain.

Henry had adopted a philosophy that carried him through the rigors and strain of prison life and fortified him with an unswerving faith. Somewhere he remembered reading: "The body may be beaten and placed in chains, but an unfettered mind constitutes the greatest single dynamic force at man's disposal." He never forgot this passage.

Among several thousand prisoners convicted of crimes ranging all the way from petty to grand larceny, from rape to murder, Henry Mueller played the part of a lost and confused soul. He had nothing in common with his companions—nothing, that is, but an unsuccessful brush with the law of the land. He knew it, and so did they, and they didn't like him any more than he did them. "The Genius," they called him; "The Brain," "The Bookworm,"—because he was never seen in an idle moment without his books.

The prison library had become his refuge; he read one book after another. Not fiction—that didn't interest him—but books on philosophy, psychology, psychiatry … especially psychiatry. He wanted to know what it was that made people tick, to explore the recesses of the human mind and fathom the mysteries of life—the emotional, the physical, the mental, and the spiritual forces that controlled the brain and the soul. Why was one man different from another? Why could one cope with the problems and obstacles of life, while others groped about blindly in the dismal darkness of failure and frustration? What made some ambitious, energetic, powerful, while others lapsed into laziness, chronic indifference? Why were there the haves and the have-nots, the brilliant and the stupid, the successful and the unsuccessful?

These were the eternal questions over which Henry Mueller pondered. This was the source of his insatiable thirst for knowledge; to absorb all he could about life's eternal question mark. And to answer the questions he asked himself. Why was he superior to other men in so many ways? What combination of genes had given him his intellect and the will power that raised him above even the bad luck that had got him into prison? He read and pondered, and read some more. Little wonder the rest of the prisoners resented Mueller. The stuff only a crackpot would read, they said. But Warden Riley knew that Henry was no crackpot. To the warden, Henry was an interesting example of a man who had completely lost himself somewhere on a detour. A detour that had taken him off the road of decency and self-respect, a detour that was somehow his own fault. But the warden could never quite be sure about that, or explain how he knew it.

Now Mueller was a social outcast, denied the rights and privileges of associating with his fellow men; imprisoned in a building built of concrete and steel with heavy bars on the windows and a high stone wall. The only touch of color to remind him of the outside world was a patch of green grass and a small flower garden outside his window.

This little strip of color in a world of monotonous grays and blacks gave new life, new hopes, to many of the broken spirits—men who had lost all identity, who had become numbers instead of human beings. Henry seldom noticed it, but on the few occasions when he looked up from his reading, it sometimes reminded him of another garden where he used to dream and study for hours at a time. Another garden with soft, cool, green grass on which to stretch out. That garden, too, had in its background a large stone building that housed many people—only those people were young, and gay, and carefree, and laughter was heard ringing down its great corridors. No high wall surrounded it—no towers with watchful guards—no machine guns— no disillusionments—no hollow sunken faces with eyes that looked, but did not see. These were eager faces with hope and faith written on them; faces that expressed a challenge to the future—faces that said, "Here I am, world, ready for anything you have to offer!"

Henry's had been one of those faces.

It was a long, hard road that Henry had chosen to travel back in those days when he was a student in the medical school of Standish University. A scholarship had taken him through his first semester. From then on the going was tough, attending classes by day, studying nights, washing dishes in the school lunchroom, sweeping out dormitories, and doing general janitor work. In addition, Henry was able to pick up a few extra dollars by instructing the other students. That was the part he enjoyed—instructing, because it gave him the feeling of being somebody, somebody of importance. Sure, they were rich men's sons, but so what? He was smarter than they were, he had more on the ball, they were coming to him for help, for tutorings, and they were paying him for it.

Henry had a special knack for absorbing all he read and all he was taught in class. It had always been that way, through grade school, through high school. His marks were always excellent. Wasn't he an honor student, a valedictorian at twelve, and didn't he graduate from high school with top honors in his class, making the full course in three years? Of course he did, and he was only fifteen at the time. Mama and Papa Mueller were so proud of their son. Papa wanted him to be a lawyer, but Mama wanted her boy to be a doctor.

"Ja, he will be a good doctor," she would say, and Henry would smile in complete agreement. He thought he would make a good doctor, too. But not like old Dr. Bauer who had his office upstairs over the corner drugstore, and who had treated everyone in the neighborhood for the past thirty years. Half the time Dr. Bauer took nothing from his poorer patients. That was not the kind of doctor Henry wanted to be. "I'm going to be a specialist, Mama," he would say, "with a big office downtown, and rich patients who can afford to pay, and a nice home, and clothes...."

"But the important thing is to be a good doctor first, and then those things will come later, *mein Kind*," Mama would say. "Is that not so, Papa?"

"Ja, ja," Papa would mutter between puffs on his old Meerschaum pipe. "A good doctor is more important than fine clothes."

"But fine clothes are important too, Papa," Henry would answer. "You've got to make a good impression if you want to have a practice that amounts to something."

A good impression ... that was one thing to which Henry had always given a great deal of thought. Everything he said, everything he did, was aimed at that. He was forever worried about what people were thinking of him ... how he was impressing them. That worry had always been a part of him. He studied diligently to impress his classmates and teachers. He delighted in seeing them impressed and startled at his always correct answers. He enjoyed hearing himself referred to as "the Child Prodigy" and "the Boy Wonder." They were titles that suited his vanity—and Henry was vain. Vanity was so much a part of his physical makeup that it dominated his personality.

At Standish Henry wanted terribly to be a Phi Tau. He felt that his entire future happiness depended on his being accepted. To make this most exalted of all fraternities would be compensation for the other things he lacked—wealth and background. Being a Phi Tau, he'd feel like one of them; he would *be* one of them. Henry waited anxiously, breathlessly, for his acceptance.

His ego never recovered from the blow it received when the Phi Taus failed to pledge him. Henry wasn't just hurt. It was more than that; it was a deep and penetrating wound that never healed. It was the first social rebuff he had ever experienced in his life. Henry fought back the tears until he was alone and then threw himself down on his bed and wept bitterly in a crisis of dramatic self-pity. If only he had had wealthy parents and a background to boast of, he would have made it! What a lousy, stinking world. He found himself suddenly hating everybody in it. His mother, his father, his neighborhood, his background ... everything. He built up a resentment for the Phi Tau members that increased with each day. The goddam snooty sonsofbitches! He'd make them crawl in the dirt some day! It was a promise he made to himself that became an obsession with him. Henry felt that fate had singled him out to bear the cross of class discrimination, that he had been dealt an undeserved blow. Within a month he had built up a first-class persecution complex that became so completely welded to his personality that it defied all attempts by his own circle of friends to pry it loose.

Henry's little group comprised the radical element at Standish. All of them had certain little resentments and prejudices against the rest of the world, but Henry carried the biggest chip of all on his shoulders. Where the others had complaints against humanity and the injustices and inequalities of man and were interested in the betterment and advancement of peoples and races, Henry was concerned only with injustices and inequalities to Henry. Gradually his personal grudge against society became more important to him than studying medicine. It seared itself into his soul and left an ugly scar. Over and over again it taunted him. He was one of the have-nots of this world— he might as well face the truth. But he didn't have to go on being one of them. He could always do something about it. He didn't have to go on taking the snubs of these rich bastards with their shiny roadsters, and their sport clothes, and their dates with the most popular girls on the campus. Not that he gave a damn about the girls; in fact, he hated them for their shallow beauty and their empty-headed giggles. He never realized that his own personality was responsible for his own unpopularity with the co-eds. He thought it was because he didn't have a car and money. He didn't know that after one date, a girl would invariably say to her roommate, "Henry Mueller? All he talks about is himself. Never again."

Months went by and Henry retired more and more into his shell. He became a confirmed introvert. He lived in his own private little world, nursing his own private little grudges, using the small group of Mueller sympathizers and admirers for his audience when he felt like spouting off about the cruelties of mankind. He buried himself in books and became a student of Freud and Karl Marx. Extracurricularly, he studied psychopathology, became fascinated with the subject. In his second year at medical school, Henry was almost as well informed on the theory of psychoanalysis as are most men with a medical degree and a complete course in neuropsychiatry behind them.

Then Henry Mueller began to psychoanalyze himself. He was a dominant personality, he told himself, born to be one of the haves, not one of the have-nots. He was an intellectual with a prolific mind and a glib tongue. He didn't have to take the guff and the snobbery of these so-called idle rich. He was not only their equal, he was far ahead of them. He felt he was destined to be a leader, not a follower; a master craftsman, not an apprentice. He was one of those rare geniuses that every century produces. He was sure of it. There was nothing he wasn't capable of accomplishing once he put his mind to it. He had the drive, the force, the ambition. All he needed was the opportunity. The opportunity for what? He had the answer all ready. The opportunity to make money! Money was power and power was life.

With money he could do anything, have anything. He could have everything the Phi Tau members had, cars, clothes, girls—well, the girls weren't important at the moment; he could do without them. But they were so easily impressed by those things, and Henry had to impress somebody. It was necessary to his own self-importance; it was vital to the existence of his whole mental structure. He became terror-stricken at the thought of having to spend two more years at Standish with only the prospects of being further belittled and ridiculed. The persecution complex, imaginary though it was, had actually taken hold. His ego, his former attitude of superiority, had given way completely to an inferiority that sprang into full growth the day he failed to make Phi Tau.

There was still time, he knew, to regain whatever it was that these jealous, parasitic lice had tried to squelch in him. They were jealous, he told himself, jealous of his personality, his intellect, his looks—everything. All they had was money and rich parents. They were golden spooners, that's all. But though he wouldn't admit it even to himself, his jealousy became the motivating force that decided him to leave Standish. It descended upon him one night like an avalanche, crushing logic and reason. Yes, money was power, and power was life, and life was racing by every minute. Life doesn't stand still and wait for medical degrees and physician's licenses! Suddenly a shingle seemed so futile and far off. Two more years of medical school; then a full year of internship—that would make a total of three more years; then the certainty of long lean years of trying to build up a practice. It might easily be eight to ten years before he could expect to make any money at all.

All at once, it became crystal-clear in Henry's mind. Medicine was not for him. He wasn't cut out for a doctor, there were too many of them anyway, and people didn't pay their bills. What a lousy profession! Nothing particularly glamorous and exciting or adventurous about being a doctor. A humdrum, monotonous routine of peering into people's throats, looking at coated tongues, smelling bad breaths, testing urine specimens, listening to the complaints of fat women whose bodies you wished you didn't have to examine. No, thanks! That's not for Henry Mueller.

Strange that he had never thought of it that way before. But now he knew it, he was sure of it. He wasn't meant to go through life carrying a little black bag, and going out in the middle of the night in zero weather to take somebody's temperature! If he could be a neurologist or a psychiatrist, that would be more interesting, and the fees would be better. But it would require at least five more years of training at mental institutions, still making a total of nine or ten years of work and study with little or no income. That would be even worse! He had to get going, and he had to get going soon. Money was power, and power was life, and life was racing by. He had to get into something that would pay better dividends and pay off soon.

Henry's mind became a turbulent sea of thoughts that night as he paced his small room, poised on the brink of the gravest decision of his life. When the first streaks of daylight began to filter in through the half-drawn shade, it revealed a bed that had not been slept in. There were empty cabinet and dresser drawers that had been hastily and awkwardly pulled open and left sticking out grotesquely. Wire and wooden clothes hangers were strewn about the floor, a few were still swinging crazily from the closet rod. Torn papers and notes filled the waste basket and overflowed onto the floor. A rabbit's foot that had hung over the door was missing. On the small writing desk lay a note addressed to Dean Walter Munson, marked "Personal."

Henry Mueller had arrived at his decision.

CHAPTER TWO

Warden Riley pushed a desk button. "Bring Henry Mueller to my office," he told the assistant who answered his ring. The door closed, and the warden settled back in his large swivel chair which gave the usual short squeak as he pushed himself back and crossed his long legs on top of the old-fashioned roll-top desk. For a long moment he thoughtfully fingered the card that he had withdrawn from the file.

"The warden wants to see you, Mueller!"

Henry Mueller looked up from his ledger to see the warden's assistant, Jim Scanlon.

"What's up, Mr. Scanlon?" he asked politely as he laid down his pen and blotted the neat figures on which he had been working.

"I have a pretty good idea," replied Scanlon brusquely, "but it ain't up to me to tell you. Come on!"

Henry followed Scanlon through the prison office past other trusties who pretended to be absorbed in their work, but who watched this little procession through eyes that flashed under beetled brows. Soon the grapevine would be at work, even beyond the prison.

It made Henry Mueller feel important once more to know that he was again in the spotlight; to know that the convicts in other prisons hundreds of miles away would soon be informed of his release. He knew it must be about his release that Warden Riley was sending for him. It had to be. It couldn't possibly be anything else. Riley had told him in their last chat, six weeks before, that he was doing everything in his power to bring the case before the parole board. Henry's hand squeezed the rabbit's foot in his pocket a bit tighter and he walked with a confident step.

"Good morning, Henry," came a jovial greeting from Warden Riley as the door opened.

"Good morning, Warden," Henry replied, assuming an air of confidence as he stood before the warden's desk.

"That'll be all for the moment, Jim," Riley dismissed his assistant.

A second later the two men were left alone—one still standing at polite attention, and the other fully reclined in his big swivel chair, puffing leisurely on his cigar.

"Sit down, Henry," said Riley as he opened the lid of a cigarette box on his desk. "Smoke?"

"Thank you, Warden, I don't use them," replied Henry as he pulled up a large leather chair and sank gratefully into the well-worn seat. His heart was pounding and he tried hard to hide his anxiety.

Riley smiled and his Irish blue eyes twinkled. "That's right, I forgot, you're a man of few minor vices."

"Oh, I wouldn't say that, sir," retorted Henry, feeling more at ease; "it's just that I never cultivated the taste for them."

"Lucky for you," chuckled Riley. "Sometimes I wish I could cut down on these damn cigars. But I guess it's a little bit late for me to start breaking old-time habits."

His nervousness made Henry snatch at any conversational lead. "Habits are easily formed," he replied somewhat pompously, "impossible to lose. It requires a great deal of mental and physical control to break a habit, particularly if it happens to be one of the pleasure variety. The mind and the body can easily become slaves to the pleasure senses, and it then becomes a long and difficult—" Henry stopped abruptly. "I'm sorry, Warden, I didn't mean to go off on a long dissertation...."

"That's all right, Mueller, you're very interesting."

"Thank you, sir." Henry smiled with inner satisfaction. It was good to have someone appreciate his words. It gave him a firmer grip on himself, and he felt a surge of confidence. His brain had not become stagnant. He was still very interesting. The warden interrupted his momentary reverie.

"I've got some good news for you, Henry."

Henry straightened up in his chair and his pulse quickened. This was what he was waiting to hear. He was going to be released—be free—it had to be that, it couldn't be anything else.

"News from the parole board?"

"Yes, Henry, I received a letter from them this morning about your case."

Henry stirred in his chair and leaned forward.

"It seems they're quite satisfied with your conduct and they've recommended you for release. You've got fifty-one months of good behavior to your credit. That's a very good record. You'll be a free man next Tuesday."

Henry found it difficult to contain himself. He had expected his freedom; the moment Jim Scanlon had spoken to him he knew he was a free man. He had paid his debt to society and would soon walk out of Mohawk as Henry Mueller, a citizen and taxpayer—free to go wherever his will took him—to breathe the fresh air and feel the warmth of the sunshine. But now that he heard the words from the warden's own lips, it was as though they were a bolt from the blue. The tears flowed freely, and Henry made no effort to hide them.

"I'm sorry, Warden," he apologized as he pulled a handkerchief from his pocket. "It's … it's just that …"

"No apologies necessary, my boy," Riley assured him gruffly. He too was deeply moved. "It's always good to be able to free a man who deserves it." The warden turned toward the window to give Henry a moment to collect himself. When he turned back, his words might have been addressed to a colleague or a friend.

"After being here at Mohawk for twenty-two years you get to know a lot of things, and a lot about people. I've even read quite a few books myself on psychology...." The warden saw that Henry's self-possession was returning. With renewed enthusiasm he continued: "Maybe that's why you and I hit it off so well right from the beginning. We had a common meeting ground. Remember that first conversation we had when you came here—the one we give all the boys, about what is expected of you, that you were here to work and to behave yourself, that you were here to pay a debt to society for your crimes and that eventually you might be restored to the world as a useful citizen *if* you could adjust yourself to prison life?" Henry smiled faintly. He remembered, all right. The warden went on, "You did adjust. Some of them never do. Some palookas come in here nursing a grudge, and stay here for half a lifetime just waiting for the day when they can get even with somebody. I'm sorry for men like that. They're hopeless."

"Yes, I know just what you mean, Warden," said Henry, now quite composed. "I've seen a lot of men right here eat, sleep, and dream one thought, *to get even*. 'Bugs' Bonnelli in my tier is like that—he's always dreaming he's hacking the stool pigeon that testified against him into little pieces. Some nights he scares the other guys half to death, laughing and shrieking. He imagines he's devising every conceivable form of torture for his poor victim."

"Yes, I know about Bonnelli." The warden uncrossed his legs and leaned forward, fingering the letter opener on his desk. "We've had him examined time and again by the state alienists and even outside psychiatrists, and they've never found him insane."

"No, of course not," replied Henry, warming up to a subject upon which he considered himself an expert, "just the other day I was reading about that particular type of thing. It's called dream psychosis, and it's a definite form of schizophrenia wherein the person develops dream hallucinations. These hallucinations are impelled by the conscious mind constantly dwelling on something that eventually becomes an obsession, which in Bonnelli's case is a revenge complex, and this in turn affects the subconscious mind to the extent that in his dreams Bonnelli finds himself giving complete vent to his restrained emotions. Vengeance is a horrible thing."

The warden stopped playing with the letter opener. "Mueller, you amaze me," he exclaimed. "I bet that was quoted word for word. What a memory you have, man! You've got a real mind."

Henry felt an urge to be modest for the first time in his life. "Thank you, Warden Riley," he said with more than a hint of emotion. "But I'm afraid I don't deserve it. Sure, I've read a lot, but you know people. Mine's book knowledge—yours is real. You know how to treat men like human beings, not just case histories from court records. You've clapped a few of the boys into solitary once in a while, but even the worst bums in this prison think the world and all of you, and there's not a thing any of us wouldn't do for you!"

There was a long silence after Henry finished speaking. The warden had stopped smoking and his cigar had long since gone out. Finally, he took a deep breath and his words were soft, and a huskiness in his voice gave full indication of the effect Henry's sincerity had had upon him.

"Henry, that's the nicest thing that has ever been said to me in twenty-two years. I'll never forget it!"

Henry lowered his gaze in embarrassment. Then Riley continued, "By the way, Henry, what do you intend doing when you leave here—any plans?"

"No—that is, nothing definite. I'd naturally like to get into something—something I'm fitted for."

"You know, Henry, I have a lot of confidence in you, and shouldn't think you'd have much trouble making a success out of anything, once you put your mind to it. You know a man with your education and intellect need never have turned to crime. I've often wondered what it was that caused you to leave school. Do you mind telling me?"

Henry fidgeted rather uncomfortably. "I … I suppose it's the old story—had to get going and make some money and I guess I didn't want to wait ten or fifteen years to be a successful doctor. I … I just made up my mind, that's all!"

The warden scratched his chin. "Too bad, too bad. Doesn't sound like you either, Henry. Always thought you'd have a lot of ambition and initiative. There's only one thing you're lacking—"

Henry looked puzzled. "What's that, sir?"

"Intestinal fortitude," replied Riley, looking at Henry with an enigmatic smile.

"Intestinal fortitude?"

Riley's expression changed, his eyes narrowed and he looked straight ahead of him, straight into Henry Mueller's eyes. "Yes, *guts!*"

Henry winced. The words didn't sound so complimentary now.

"Guts? I … I don't understand, sir—"

"Yes, you do, Henry, you understand very well what I mean. Intestinal fortitude is an expression you probably have come across many times in your psychology books, but I like to use the word *guts*. It's not as high-class sounding, but you and every one of my boys know what I'm talking about. I've watched you and studied you for almost six years. Sure, you've learned to adjust yourself to prison life, and you behaved and did your work and never gave anybody any trouble. And you've earned your freedom, but that has nothing to do with what I'm about to tell you. I want you to accept this not as friendly advice, but more as fatherly advice. I hate to see you go through life defeating your own purposes. When I said before that you lacked guts, that's exactly what I meant. If you hadn't lacked guts you wouldn't have quit medical school. When you did quit school and got yourself a respectable job with an investment banking firm, you lacked the guts to stay with them and work up gradually toward a decent income. So, you finally wound up selling fake stocks, passing forged checks, and conning old ladies out of their money because it was easier, and you walked around with more money in your pockets. So you ended up in prison and almost six years of your life were spent paying for your crimes. Six years that you couldn't see yourself spending learning to be a doctor! Not much of a percentage, was it, Henry?"

Henry squirmed about uneasily in his chair, "No, I guess not," he mumbled. The conversation had suddenly become acutely embarrassing.

The warden went on. "Henry, you're just too damned egotistical. You are smart—but not as smart as you think. And there's a deep-seated feeling of inferiority in you, too. Tell me, when you were in college, didn't you feel you had to have money in your pockets in order to be on a par with your friends?"

Henry hesitated and wet his lips with his tongue. He swallowed with difficulty and did not answer. The warden insisted, "Isn't that right, Henry?"

"Yes," Henry's reply was slow and came grudgingly. "But where does that come in? I never thought of myself as being egotistical!"

"No?" Riley's eyebrows arched. "Suppose I tell you that you're one of the most hated men in this institution!"

Henry blanched and his surprise was unmistakably genuine.

"Does that startle you? It shouldn't. I'm sure you've known it for some time. And it isn't because they're jealous of you, either. They hate you because they think you're an egotistical heel! I'm sorry to be the one to tell you that, Henry, but I think you should know. It might straighten you out after you leave here."

Henry bit his lip with nervousness. He felt more uncomfortable every minute. Not that he gave a good goddamn what the other men thought of him. Sure, he had always looked down on them—what did he have in common with a bunch of stinking lousy cut-throat bums with no sensitivities, no ideologies, no feeling for the finer instincts? They were hard and brash and toughened by years of living by the law of the gun. They were without souls; they weren't fit companions for Henry Mueller! He had nothing in common with them. Henry found it easier to lie to the warden than to try to explain his indifference.

"I'm honestly sorry, Warden," he said, feigning a humbleness that he did not feel. "I always tried to get along with the men and I thought they liked me."

Warden Riley was not fooled. "You know better than that, Henry. Let's not try to kid one another. I squashed a plot that was hatched out by some of your cellmates to give you the works. They put it this way: 'We'll smash that intellectual face, but good!'"

Henry sat rigid with hatred burning in his eyes. So they wanted to beat up on him, eh? The jealous bastards! They were jealous, just like all the rest. Everybody was jealous of him—even the warden … to hell with him and his fatherly advice—he didn't need any fatherly advice from wardens or anyone else! Christ! Who did this guy Riley think he was anyhow, a man or a school boy? Lecturing him on the values of prison prestige! He didn't care who liked him or disliked him. He wasn't interested in the opinion of the lousy bums, and as far as he was concerned, they could rot here forever. He wouldn't be around!

"Well, Henry," said the warden as he rose from his chair, "I think that'll be all."

Thank God, Henry thought as he also stood up; this was getting boring!

"You can go back to your work now, and make arrangements to leave here next Tuesday. You should be a very happy man at this moment, Henry. I'm counting on you—don't disappoint me." The warden extended his hand and Henry took it, grasped it firmly. For a second they looked into each other's eyes, then Riley spoke a final word of counsel. "Think over what I told you, Henry. You'll find it does matter what other people think of you, sometimes."

"Thanks, Warden," Henry said. Thanks for nothing, he thought. The door closed behind the prisoner, and Riley stared after him for a long moment. What was there about this man that made him such a paradox? Why did he like Mueller when he should dislike him for his irritating ego, his superficial smile, and his obvious insincerity?

Warden Riley found no answer to these thoughts. He could arrive at only one conclusion. *Henry Mueller had enough charm and magnetic power to be either a very successful man or a very successful criminal!*

CHAPTER THREE

Henry faced the big iron gate at the entrance to Mohawk Prison. He felt like Ali Baba as he saw the mass of iron twenty feet high and weighing perhaps eight tons obey the touch of an electric pushbutton. Stepping forward a few paces, he tried to look back, but the closing of the big gate abruptly shut off from view the familiar grounds and building that had been his only world for six years.

With a glance at his watch, Henry saw that it was fifteen minutes to eleven. Better hurry along; don't want to miss that eleven o'clock bus! He walked rapidly and soon reached the highway. Automobiles were roaring by, heedless of the SLOW signs posted on either side of the road.

Henry waited for a break in the traffic, and then darted across the highway toward the sign marked BUS STOP. He had been standing there less than half a minute when a car which had been parked a hundred feet or so down the road began to move slowly forward. It came to a stop in front of him.

"Like a lift, mister?"

Henry look up, puzzled. "Well, thanks, I ... Turk! Gil Turkel—you old son-of-a-gun. Where did you come from?"

"I was parked a little ways down the road," replied Turk, "waiting for you to get on the ground. I've been there since eight this morning. Get in."

Henry eagerly opened the car door and a second later found himself rolling along, happy but bewildered.

"Gosh, Turk, it's good to see you, but how in the world did you ever find out—"

"Oh, you pick up things when you're around," he replied casually, "News travels fast, you know."

"Awfully nice of you to come way out here to pick me up, Turk, I certainly appreciate it."

Turk slowed down for a crossing. "Oh, that's all right, Henry," he said nonchalantly, "I kind of thought you'd be glad to see an old friend."

"Oh, I am," Henry assured him. "It's a very pleasant surprise, believe me. In fact I'm flattered. I thought I'd been completely forgotten."

"Not by me, Henry, you know I wouldn't forget. We were too good friends for that. We had too many swell times together. You ought to know I wouldn't forget." Henry slouched down further in his seat, smug and serene in the knowledge that he still had admirers, that he had not altogether been deserted. He broke the awkward pause that followed Turk's declaration of devotion with "Nice little car you've got here. Did you ..."

Turk quickly broke in. "Nope! I bought this from a dealer—got the bill of sale and everything. Want to see it?" He began to fumble through his inside coat pocket with his left hand.

Henry laughed. "No, never mind, Turk, I take your word for it. Don't be so touchy."

Turk seemed hurt. "It ain't that I'm touchy, Henry. I just didn't want you to think ..."

"I didn't think anything, Turk. I'm glad things are breaking for you. In fact, from the looks of things, you must be doing pretty well."

"Oh, I pick a winner once in a while," said Turk as he reached in his pocket and took out a pack of cigarettes. "Have one?"

"No thanks," Henry replied. "Remember me? No vices!"

"Oh yeah, I forgot."

For a few minutes, Henry studied his companion out of the corner of his eye. Strange, he thought, this combination of Henry Mueller and Gil Turkel. He had run across Turk in a hotel lobby in Cleveland, and they struck up a friendship which was as weird as it was unexpected. Turk was a small-time gambler, racetrack tout, and petty racketeer. He never seemed to get himself in any scraps with the law, and his police record was surprisingly clean. In fact, his only arrest was in Chicago in a bookie joint that was raided when Turk happened to be present. He was booked on a disorderly conduct charge and was later released along with the other patrons. Of course, that didn't mean that Turk never pulled anything, but he always managed to keep his fingers clean.

Henry had taken a great liking to this newly discovered friend. He found Turk and his racetrack jargon, his admitted lack of education, and his free and easy off-the-cuff manner a source of great amusement. Turk, on the other hand, found Henry the complete antithesis of himself and a very desirable companion. It took only a few minutes of conversation for both to find that they had a common bond and a common interest—to make money without having to expend too much energy.

Together they worked as a team, and each profited by the other's individual talents. When they found they needed a suave and educated approach to facilitate a new transaction, it was Henry who took over. On the other hand, when the situation called for a bit of good old-fashioned sleight-of-hand and down-to-cases method, it was always Turk who came through with flying colors. Turk got the dirty work to do, but he never seemed to mind. His affection for Henry, perhaps the only educated person he had ever known, was deep and sincere. He admired Henry and respected him. There was nothing he wouldn't do for him and the money angle became secondary. He looked up to Henry for counsel and always took his advice in blind faith. This relationship fed Henry's overweening ego and made him feel smug and content. A stooge who complimented and flattered him was vital to Henry's existence. It was the fuel that kept alive his egocentric personality. Henry felt no particular love for Turk. His attachment was purely that of king to jester. He felt that Turk was amply repaid by what time and attention Henry gave him. Turk took all this in his broad stride. He had swallowed many a bitter pill during their two-year association. He took the crumbs of Henry's affection uncomplainingly, and although their "take" was always on the basis of a fifty-fifty split, it was the only thing that Henry ever gave in equal share and he did that because it was a form of insurance. He got his percentage even if Turk did all the work on some jobs.

Because of Turk's long association with the gambling element, with underworld characters, and the various illicit forms of earning one's livelihood, Henry quickly learned the ropes, and soon the pupil became the teacher. He improved on all of Turk's ideas, and even went a few steps beyond. Turk, who was a distinct conservative, often cautioned Henry against his flamboyant schemes and his pretentious ambitions. "Better to take less and be safe," was Turk's motto. Henry chose to disregard this warning with his usual disdain for anything commonplace. He was sure that his personality, his knowledge of psychology, and his prolific tongue could manage any situation. He knew the right buttons for everything, all he had to do was push them.

For two years, Henry and Turk were partners in a one-sided friendship. Henry managed to stay within the law only because of Turk's watchful eye. But Henry began to chafe at the bit and long to break away from an association which he felt had become a hindrance and a liability. He wanted to give his personality the wide scope it needed. He had outgrown Gil Turkel; he had learned as much from him as he possibly could, and he had no further use for him. Turk was no longer a source of amusement to him. The king no longer needed the jester.

It was a blow to Turk when Henry told him he was going on alone. He swallowed the news with an outward display of calm and reserve. He wasn't surprised; he had expected it for weeks. It had been a pretty lean season and the pickings at the tracks were the smallest they had been since Turk could remember. He had taken a job at the $2.00 place window at Hialeah to tide things over, and had managed to get Henry a similar job at the $2.00 show window. But after three weeks of this Henry had had enough. He wanted to be the one to sit in a box with a pair of expensive field glasses in his hands and a fashionably dressed woman beside him. He wanted to be able to walk casually up to the $50.00 window and purchase a ticket on each race.

Henry had been looking over some travel literature that someone had left on an empty box seat. There were pictures of Arrowhead Springs and Lake Louise in the Canadian Rockies. Henry walked in to the small dingy hotel room that they were sharing, still looking at the folders. Turk eyed him silently over his track sheet. Henry sat down, hat on head, drinking in the beautiful vacation scenes, the swanky hotels, and the inviting sports. This was for him, he thought, this was his speed; that's where he should be, mingling with the sort of people that would appreciate being with Henry Mueller! Doing the sort of things that Henry Mueller should be doing! He decided. Finally, he spoke.

"Turk, I'm leaving. I'm fed up on touting at race tracks and selling tickets at windows. I'm tired of sleeping in flophouses and cheap hotels. I never should have tied up with you in the first place. You're small time, Turk. You always have been and you always will be. You might as well know it. I wanted to go for myself a long time ago, but I took pity on you—I was sorry for you because I didn't want you to think I was running out on you when you needed my help. You've put the crooked foot in every one of my plans to do something big just because it was a little risky. So what's the result? We've practically panhandled our way across the country living from hand to mouth. The only times we've made any money were when I made you go along with my ideas. I could have a lot of money in my pockets today if I hadn't listened to you. You've held me back long enough. I'm going to begin right now to make some money and enjoy myself. I'm getting out of here, Turk. I guess I'm a little too advanced for you. You're satisfied to place or show. I'm not. With me it's got to be win!"

Turk slowly lowered his racing form. "That's O. K., Henry, just be careful you don't get scratched!"

He watched Henry pack his bags. He was only hurt and disappointed that Henry had misunderstood his efforts to keep them out of trouble. He decided it would be useless to try and convince Henry that he had not wanted to hold him back, but only to save him from getting into a jam. It was too apparent that Henry had made up his mind and nothing would deter him.

Henry put his suitcase down and walked over to Turk. He put out his hand.

"I'm sorry, Gil—will you say goodbye?"

Turk rose from his chair. He took off the glasses that rested on his hawklike nose and extended a long bony hand. "Sure, Henry, and it's been swell knowing you. Good luck, and don't get scratched."

Henry bit his lower lip. "Thanks, you too."

He started for the door.

"Oh, just a second—"

"Yes?"

"I had a hot tip on a long shot today. He breezed in and paid 20 to 1. I made a C-note on him. You know our agreement, fifty-fifty. Here's your share."

Henry hesitated.

"Go ahead." Turk forced fifty dollars into his hand and Henry swallowed the lump in his throat. He had been a bastard and he knew it. Well, so what? What he had told Turk was the truth. Well, maybe he had been a bit blunt, but why be subtle with a guy like Turk? He was only a racetrack tout. Since when were you supposed to handle that sort of element with kid gloves? No, he wasn't sorry. Henry pocketed the fifty and the door closed behind him.

That night Turk ate his dinner in Pete's Hamburger Diner. His check came to twenty-eight cents. "Just under the wire," he said to the proprietor as he handed him three dimes. His two cents change was all the money Gil Turkel had in the world. "Oh, well," he sighed to himself, feeling quite alone, "tomorrow's another day!"

Before the season closed at Hialeah, Turk had over five hundred dollars in his pockets. The tide had turned and he now had time to wonder what had become of Henry. He headed north and west, inquiring as he went, but no one had heard of or seen Henry Mueller. There was considerable talk, however, of a Milton Henry who had left a trail of bad checks in his wake, of forging signatures, and obtaining money from women under false pretenses. When Turk reached the East Coast some six months later, he learned from a morning newspaper that his friend had been arrested and under the alias of Henry Milford was being held by the police on charges of forgery. That afternoon Turk was on the train headed for a town called Middleton to do everything he could to buy a defense for the man he had never ceased to call his friend.

Henry's trial cost Turk three hundred and fifty dollars and he had been ready to spend the rest when Henry's lawyer said he'd only be throwing the money down the drain. The last Turk had seen him, Henry was awaiting transference to Mohawk.

Henry put his arm around Turk. "You know something, Turk? You're one in a million. If I had stayed with you, I'd never be where I am. I was pig-headed, I guess. I remember very well what you told me that day I left. You said, 'Look out you don't get scratched.' Well, I did."

"I wasn't hoping you would, Henry, honest I wasn't. I just wanted you to be careful."

"I know that, Turk, and I've cost you a lot of money—I don't know when I'll be able to pay you back."

Turk prodded his friend with an affectionate jab. "What're you talking about—that wasn't my money, Henry, that was your money— that was your split of the take for the season. I was saving that for you anyway. I knew I'd run across you sooner or later!"

Henry couldn't check the tear that oozed out in spite of his efforts. "You're the goddamndest liar that ever walked, Gil Turkel! But I'll never forget you."

"And I'll never forget you, Henry."

The intrusion of the guard ended this last meeting, and Turk hastily walked out of the jail and headed toward the small hotel where he was staying. As he came to the intersection, a newsboy was loudly hawking the day's headlines. Turk walked directly past the newsstand as though he neither heard nor saw the shouting little urchin.

It was the first time in fifteen years that Gil Turkel had failed to buy the daily racing form.

The sudden slamming-on of the brakes as Turk sought to avoid a car darting out of a side road abruptly snapped Henry out of his reflective mood.

"Say, d'ya think you could stand a bite to eat?" Turk spoke hurriedly. "There's a place down the road here a ways."

"Boy, now you're talking!"

"Gotta fatten you up a little, you're thinner. But you ain't changed much, Henry, you're still a whore's dream."

Henry warmed to the flattery, the pats on the back.

"Well, here's the joint," Turk said as he slowed down. "It's the Tuckaway Inn. It's tucked away, all right. You can hardly see it."

Well hidden behind a grove of trees, the roadhouse was an attractive little place done in Old English style, with large shutters on the windows and a many gabled roof. In the courtyard was an open charcoal burner in which several halves of chickens slowly revolved on a spit over the hot coals. The aroma from the barbecue sauce filled the air. The prison suddenly seemed very far away.

"Smells good and it's a nice clean-looking joint, isn't it?" Henry grinned like a boy.

"Yeah, so far so good," Turk took in the place with a quick glance.

"There's a table over there by the window. Let's take it."

There were quite a few diners at the tables, all engaged in food and conversation. Henry and Turk sat down unnoticed.

There was a bar off to one side, where the habitués were lined up getting an early start. A group of teenagers were grouped around the record player waiting eagerly with a handful of nickels. On either side of the curved bar were a couple of slot machines hungrily swallowing up nickels and dimes from willing patrons. A woman in her late forties, dressed far too young for her years, giggled kittenishly every time she pulled down the lever. Her plump, bald swain stood there with a hand full of change and proudly put the coins in for her. Three nickels popped out as the machine hit a cherry combination, and she burst out with a scream of delight as if she had hit the jackpot. The procedure was repeated every time a coin dropped into the cup. Then she would reach over to the bar, take a sip of beer from her stein, and return to the machine with renewed vigor.

Henry was fascinated with all this. Here was his first contact with life as he had remembered it. He looked around him. To these people, drinking, eating, playing the juke box and the slot machines were everyday occurrences, normal and automatic, and to which they gave little or no thought. But to Henry, every move, every word, every action was of the greatest significance. He thought of himself with morbid self-pity as a man who had come back from the land of the living dead, restored to a civilization in the year of Our Lord, nineteen hundred and thirty-eight.

The waitress approached abruptly and placed two menus on the red plaid tablecloth.

"I'll have some of that barbecued chicken we saw coming in."

"Make it two," nodded Henry in agreement, closing the menu.

"Do you want the a la carte order, or do you want it on the lunch?" the waitress asked in the monotonous tone of perennial repetition.

"On the lunch," replied Turk. "Give me the works."

"Yessir."

Henry's gaze fell upon her legs as she departed for the kitchen.

"Like that?" Turk's eyebrows arched quizzically.

"Not bad." Henry took a sip of water. "I've seen better."

"So have I," agreed Turk. "Anyhow, after all this time you want something special, and I've got it for you when we get back to the city. A beautiful Spanish baby with great big black eyes and a skin like those face cream ads. In fact, that's her business—she's a beauty operator."

"Sounds interesting, Turk. Tell me more."

"Well, I met her through a girl I know that does the manicuring in this shop. Her name's Helen O'Connell."

"Who, the Spaniard?"

"No, that's my girlfriend's name. She's Irish, and brother, what I mean she's Irish. Swears like a trooper, but good-natured as hell. Give you the shirt off her back!"

Henry smiled. "And frequently does, I take it?"

"Well, she wasn't any pushover, believe me. She's been divorced and thinks a lot about her reputation. Says it's easy for a girl to get herself a bad name if she ain't careful. I went with her about five months before I connected. Of course, now I'm in solid."

They were interrupted again by the blonde waitress. She placed a small glass of tomato juice in front of each of the men, together with two salad bowls, and then departed. This time it was Turk who eyed her legs as she walked away.

"Hell, no," he said to Henry, shaking his head, "she couldn't hold a candle to Carlotta."

"Oh? Is that her name?" Henry raised the glass of tomato juice to his lips.

"Yeah. Carlotta Callahan! I forgot to tell you, she was married to an Irishman, too. Her real name is Cortez."

"From Cortez to Callahan! That's one for the book!"

"Well, anyhow," broke in Turk, "she didn't live with him very long, because he was a drunk. He was pretty well fixed, too. Advertising business. But he used to get himself soused seven days a week, and then come home and push her around. They were only married for a couple of years. He settled a nice hunk of dough on her. About ten grand, I think!"

Henry looked up sharply. "Really?"

"Yeah, she's got it socked away in the bank. She's very independent and likes to earn her own living. The dough is laid away for her kid's education."

Henry's face fell. "Oh? She's got a baby?"

"Yeah, he's about three years old now."

The waitress returned and brought with her the two orders of barbecued chicken and the rest of the trimmings.

Then as she walked away, Henry picked up. "So, what about Carlotta?"

Turk struggled with a chicken leg. "Oh, yeah, she's really a good looker, Henry. Tall, about five seven or eight, gorgeous figure, with a pair of knockers that look like they're gonna stab your eye out, and a set of the most beautiful white teeth you ever saw. Her skin is that real olive color like them Latins have, and she wears her hair in long braids across the top of her head."

"What makes you think I'd appeal to her? Sounds like she'd have plenty of men, the kind that could afford to spend money on her. Besides, I don't suppose any decent girl would be interested in an ex-convict." His tone was light, but Turk caught the bitterness.

He stopped chewing on a bone. "She wouldn't have to know, Henry. Tell her you just got in from out of town. You were away on a vacation."

Henry laughed. "Which, in effect, would be correct."

"Sure, nobody needs to know."

"And, my friend, what makes you so sure that she's going to turn over that lovely curvaceous body to me? Because of my irresistible charm, my handsome physique?"

Henry spoke as if jesting, but inwardly he was sure of himself. Those were the very attributes he felt he possessed.

"Well, I don't know," countered Turk. "You were never any slouch when it came to women. The two years I traveled with you before, as I remember it, you did pretty well for Henry Mueller. Boy, you had a line that was a little dandy!"

Henry's nostrils dilated as he smiled lecherously. "Not a line, Turk. Let us say, a subtle approach."

"Call it what you want. All I know is you got 'em!"

"And you think this one can be had?"

Turk wiped his chin. "Sure, I do. By the right kind of guy. You see, she's good friends with Helen and she tells her everything. She told her she was sick and tired of rich guys, because they think their money'll buy them anything. And she don't like racketeers because they're rough and tough and only think about one thing, and they either wanna pay for it or else they try to take it away from her. She says she can't stand men who are crude."

Henry smiled. "So Carlotta thinks most men are crude, eh? Well, I don't blame her. They are."

Turk agreed. "Sure, that's why she told Helen she'd like to meet a man who has something else on his mind besides jumping in bed with her. She says she figures all men are out for the same thing, but at least she'd like to meet one that can fast-talk her out of it."

"I see." Henry drew his tongue across his lips and moistened them in anticipation.

Turk winked slyly. "And you're the guy that can do it too!"

Henry's expression suddenly shifted.

"What's the matter, Henry?"

"I was just thinking," came the reply.

"About what?"

"About how I shouldn't be thinking of women. I should be thinking about more important things. About getting myself straightened out first. I've got a lot of straightening out to do, Turk. I've got to get myself organized, and find a place to live, and think of some way to make money."

"If that's what's bothering you, forget it. I've got a nice little place that's big enough for both of us. And money shouldn't bother you. We always managed before."

"Now look, Turk, that's out." Henry placed his knife and fork across the plate. "I owe you enough as it is. I'm not going to go on living off you." He was hoping Turk would insist.

"Hell, you know you don't owe me anything, and we're still partners, ain't we? What kind of a partnership would it be if we didn't split right down the middle? Of course you're going to stay with me. I wouldn't have it any other way."

Henry played with some bread crumbs on the table. "Gosh, Turk, that's awfully swell of you—you sure you have room?"

"Sure, I got room, and after we start making some real dough, we'll move to a larger place. Is it a deal?"

Henry smiled with satisfaction and relief. "It's a deal," he said quietly.

The waitress was back with a chant of "Apple pie, ice cream, jello and cheese."

"Apple pie for me," said Turk.

Henry looked disappointed. "No strawberry pie?" he asked.

"No, sir, just apple pie, ice cream, jello and cheese," she droned once more.

Henry took a deep breath. "Ice cream."

She started to leave. Turk called after her. "Oh, Miss, some more coffee, please!" She continued walking as though she hadn't heard. "Them hashers! You never know whether they hear you or not!"

"Usually they do," replied Henry, "but they're too spiteful to give you the satisfaction. They'd rather keep you guessing for a while, then they'll either bring you your order, or if this one happens to be a particularly ornery wench, she'll return without the coffee just for the sadistic pleasure of making you ask for it again. It's my personal but humble opinion that our little lady friend is an out-and-out bitch, because here she comes without your coffee!"

Turk looked up. "Sure enough!"

She placed the desserts in front of each of the men, and started to walk away. Turk spoke up. "I'd like some more coffee, Miss."

Her answer was curt and even a bit belligerent. "I heard you before, Mister." She continued walking without even turning around.

"How do you like that?" said Turk.

Henry chuckled. "See, I told you she was the bitch type!"

Turk was peeved. "We've been nice to her. I'm gonna tell her off when she comes back."

"Don't bother. You'll only be wasting your breath. She either had a spat with her boyfriend last night, or else she's going through her period. Ten to one it's that. Some women can be sadistic when they're menstruating. They'll take it out on the first person that's handy!"

Turk took a deep breath. "You sure know a lot about women,

Henry. I wish I knew as much."

"It's a gift, boy," Henry smiled, hitting his stride. "Look out, here's your coffee."

Turk moved his elbows from the table to make way for the hot coffee. "Thanks," he grinned.

She turned on her heel and walked away without acknowledging Turk's polite reply.

"Boy, is that a bitch for you," muttered Turk. "She could sour a guy's whole day. What the hell is the matter with her anyway."

"I told you before what I think is the matter with her. But I'll show you what we can do about it. All women are bitches, but they're all vain as hell. In fact, I'll say all women have two weaknesses: money and flattery. Give a woman enough money and enough flattery and you can accomplish almost anything. Here, I'll prove my point. Got about seventy-five cents in change?"

Turk searched his pocket. "Yeah, here's a half and a quarter."

"Thanks. Oh, Miss—"

The waitress came over. "Yes?"

"May I have the check?"

"Yessir, here it is. Two fifty-five."

"Thanks, dear. Your service was excellent. Here you are." Henry placed the seventy-five cents in her hand, and at the same time gave her fingers a slight squeeze.

"Oh, thank you, sir. Was everything all right? Can I get you something else?"

Henry smiled up at her and looked into her eyes. "No, thank you, dear, we've had plenty. Incidentally, what's your name?"

"Iris. Not that it's any of your business, though."

"Iris? That's a very pretty name. It means a very delicate and pale flower. Like your skin … delicate and pale." He ran his fingers gently over her arm. She blushed and her expression softened. "Oh, I don't think it's so unusual."

Henry followed through. "Oh, yes, it is, much smoother and prettier than most girls. Do you … uh … have a boyfriend?"

"Well, I did, but we broke up the other night."

"Oh, that's too bad. I'm sorry to hear it."

She pouted. "I'm not. I was, but I'm not now. Anyway, he was a dud. Never said anything interesting or exciting."

At this point Henry shifted into second. "Do you like interesting men?"

She fingered the tablecloth. "What girl doesn't?"

"And things that are exciting?"

"Well—that is, in a way. If they're not too exciting."

"You mean you don't like things that are too exciting?"

"No, I didn't say that. What I meant was that—that—"

"What you mean is that it all depends on whom you're with, isn't that it?"

She smiled shyly. "Yes, I suppose so."

Henry shifted into high. "Do you think *I* would be interesting?"

By this time her reticence began to fade. "Well, yes … I think you would be."

"Perhaps even a bit exciting?"

"A man isn't interesting unless he's exciting."

Henry smiled. "Come here, darling, I want to ask something. Excuse me, Turk."

She bent over and Henry whispered something in her ear.

She giggled, "Oh, you!" Henry whispered some more. Her expression turned serious: "Well, how about tomorrow night at nine?"

"Fine," said Henry.

"Oh, wait a minute, better make it Monday at nine. Yeah, Monday night at nine."

Henry winked. "It's a date!"

"Okay, goodbye." She winked back.

"Goodbye, dear."

Henry looked at Turk who was staring at him with eyes bulging. "Well, I'll be a sonofabitch," he said dumbfoundedly.

"You see," Henry crowed softly. "I just wanted to prove my point. A little money and a little flattery, and you can get almost any woman you want."

Turk still stared at him. "Well, I'll be a sonofabitch." He wasn't quite certain, though, why the waitress had postponed the date for the three additional days.

CHAPTER FOUR

Turk pulled up in front of the small hotel on West Eighty-third Street where he was staying.

"That's it," he said with a sigh of fatigue.

Henry looked up at the narrow twelve-story building. "Looks like a nice little place," he commented.

The two men walked into the hotel, entered the elevator and got off at the sixth floor. The corridor was narrow and the walls and ceiling were cracked and needed painting.

The door opened upon a typical hotel apartment, small and compact.

"Very nice, very nice," remarked Henry. "All the comforts of home. In-a-door bed and everything."

Turk's face brightened as if he were an agent squiring a prospective tenant. "Not only that, but look!" He pulled open a folding door and showed Henry the kitchenette. "See, here's where Helen cooks for me."

"Wonderful."

"And you see, this davenport opens up into a bed too. So you don't have to worry about there ain't enough room!" Turk began to open the davenport in demonstration.

"Don't bother." Henry took a deep breath. "Yes, everything is lovely. All I have to do now is get a job of some kind and pay for my share."

"Well, don't let it throw you, Henry. Your credit is O. K. with me."

Henry protested half-heartedly. "No, Turk, it's got to be on a fifty-fifty basis—as soon as I get going."

"Sure, Henry. But don't bother about it. You go ahead and get washed up. I've got to make a phone call."

In the bathroom Henry found the shaving cream and began applying it to his face. Funny, he thought, to be able to shave in a nice clean tile bathroom, bright electric light over a large mirror. Different from a prison cell. No bells or whistles to disturb his thoughts, no lights out, no marching in line to eat, no regimentation, he could come and go as he pleased, do as he pleased.

Turk appeared at the bathroom door, and his approach brought Henry back from his thoughts.

"Say, I think I've got something," he said jovially, "anyway, it sounds good."

"What?" inquired Henry.

"Two hot tips that a pal just gave me. He got them this afternoon by long distance and thought he'd pass them on to me. He says he's putting a hundred slugs on each horse. One's running in the fifth at Aqueduct tomorrow, and the other's in the third at Lincoln Fields."

"Think they're really good?" Henry asked as he began to dry the razor on the towel.

"Anybody else's, no. But this guy hasn't ever given me a bum steer yet. He knows all the jockeys and trainers. He told me to put a C-note on each horse to win."

"Are you going to?"

"Yeah, I'll take a flyer."

"Then here, take this ten and play it to win for me. It's the state's money, not mine, so if I lose it, I'm losing the taxpayer's money." Henry gave a slight sardonic laugh and handed Turk the ten-dollar bill that is each released prisoner's farewell gift from Mohawk.

"How do you want it? Five on each one?"

"What are the horses' names?"

"Fleetaway and Itinerary," Turk replied.

"Put the ten on Itinerary," said Henry as he applied some shave lotion to his cheek. "I don't know what my itinerary is going to be from now on, so I think I'll take a chance on him."

"Say, maybe that's a hunch," chuckled Turk. "I'll go along with you and put a hundred and fifty on Itinerary to win, and the other fifty on Fleetaway to place!"

Just then the telephone rang. Turk answered. Henry could hear a trickle of conversation but the running faucets drowned out most of Turk's voice. In less than a minute Turk reappeared at the bathroom door.

"That was Helen. Said she had been trying to get me before. I told her I had to go out of town for the day on business. She and Carlotta are having dinner together over at Helen's, and want me to come over and join them. I told her I had a handsome friend with me and she said to bring you along. Boy, that's what you call mental telegraphy!"

Henry was pleasantly surprised. "You mean I'm actually going to meet the beautiful Carlotta?"

"That you are, friend," said Turk jovially. "I'll make the introductions and from that point on, you're strictly on your own."

Henry was combing his hair. "How are you going to introduce me?"

"As Henry Mueller, an old business pal of mine just back from South America. Gimme the shaving soap."

"Say, that's very good. Henry Mueller, 'soldier of fortune' returning to the States after six years of wandering through the mountains of Chile and the jungles of Brazil!" Then as he leaned over and inspected his face closely in the mirror, "Hmph! That prison pallor hardly coincides with a man who just got back from a 10,000-mile tour of South America!"

"So what?" interjected Turk. "Everybody who travels don't come back with a sunburn! Now, get a move on, or we'll be late."

The clock in the lobby of the St. Francis Apartments showed six-forty-four when the two men walked in. In a couple of minutes they stood before the door of apartment 9D. Turk pushed the buzzer gently, and from inside came a cheery, "Coming!"

It was Helen who opened the door.

"Honey, this is my friend from out of town I told you about. Henry Mueller, this is Helen O'Connell."

"How do you do? Can I take your hat?"

"How do you do, Miss O'Connell. Thank you."

Henry felt comfortable immediately. He liked Helen's personality. She was about thirty and rather pretty in a beauty-parlorish sort of way. Her face was slightly rounded with a cute little turned-up Irish nose, and her complexion was faultless and satiny smooth, with the glow that comes from hours of diligently applied face creams. Her carefully coiffured hair had that shade of golden blond which comes from constant peroxide bleaching. She was about five feet five inches tall, and probably a little heavier than she should have been for her height, but not enough to detract from her appearance. Her full bosom was accentuated by the uplift brassiere that she wore, and as she walked back into the room, Henry noticed that her legs were neatly shaped and her ankles were trim.

"Come on in, boys, and make yourselves comfortable. Do you want to wash up?"

"No, thanks," replied Henry, "we already did."

"Yeah," laughed Turk, "all we want is food!"

"Well, dinner's all ready and waiting." Then she called into the next room. "Lottie, dear, come out of the kitchen and meet our guests."

Henry chose a comfortable-looking chair and sat down. When Carlotta entered the room, he rose to his feet.

"This is Mr. Henry Mueller, dear, a friend of Turk's. Henry, this is Carlotta Callahan, our Spanish colleen."

Henry nodded. "How do you do."

She extended her hand cordially. "Hello, Mr. Mueller."

Henry took her hand in his and clasped it warmly. "I've heard a great deal about you, Carlotta."

"Really? I'm flattered."

"On the contrary, you shouldn't be. Our friend Turk here is very bad at descriptions."

"Why? Did he tell you I was cross-eyed, and wore glasses, and had buck teeth and that when I walked down the street I scared little children?"

Henry was still holding her hand. "Not at all. He said you were lovely, which is about the grossest understatement that a man could make."

Carlotta's gaze fell slightly, and she quickly withdrew her hand.

"Thank you, Mr. Mueller, you're very generous."

"Well," continued Henry, "I've always looked upon compliments as a very insincere form of flattery. To tell a woman she is beautiful is a compliment and she loves to hear it, even if she knows it's probably far from the truth. But tell a woman she is captivating and bewitching, and you have told her, in essence, that she has all men at her feet!"

"The only man I've ever had at my feet was a chiropodist," she replied gayly, "but thank you anyhow, Mr. Mueller, for saying such nice things and accept my apologies for such a bad joke."

"I thought it was pretty good," chortled Turk. "Didn't you, Helen? Say, Carlotta's getting quicker on the uptake, ain't she?"

"For a foreigner she's doing all right," said Helen approvingly. "Pretty soon she'll be as good a Yankee as any of us."

"I hope so," came Carlotta's reply with an authentic Spanish toss of the head. "My ambition is to be as good a Yankee as Kate Smith, only not so big; as crazy as Gracie Allen, and as cute as Baby Snooks!"

"Good for you. Incidentally, you do have a very charming accent. How long have you been in this country?"

"Let me see—I came over the year of the World's Fair in Chicago— that was in 1933. That was the first thing I wanted to see. So, I've been here five years."

Henry sat down on the arm of the chair. "I think you've done very well for only five years."

"Did somebody say soup's on?" wistfully inquired Turk, looking very hungry and forlorn in a corner.

"Yes, I'm rather starved myself," Henry assented, lighting Carlotta's cigarette.

"Well, what are we waiting for? Come on." Helen snuffed out her cigarette in an ashtray, and led the way into the dinette.

Carlotta went to the buffet where a couple of bottles of liquor stood. "Who would like a drink first? Turk?"

"I can always stand a little pick-me-up."

"What will you have, Scotch or bourbon?"

"I'll take bourbon straight."

"Okay. Henry?"

"I'll have Scotch with a dash of lemon peel."

"A dash of lemon peel? How unusual."

"Yes, I know. That's the only way I like whiskey. The lemon peel gives it a little tang."

"That's the first time I've heard that, but then, I'm not much of an authority on drinks. Helen, one lemon please."

Helen headed for the kitchen. "One lemon coming up!" She returned a moment later and Carlotta fixed the drinks.

"Well," said Henry raising his glass, "here's to our charming hostesses."

"Thank you," replied Carlotta, "and here's to our handsome guests."

"Ha!" laughed Turk, "but you don't mean guests. You mean a certain guest. There ain't nothing handsome about this puss!"

"Oh, yes there is," cooed Helen as she patted his cheek. "I think my baby is bootiful."

"Thanks," simpered Turk. He pinched her buttock. "God, you bring out the beast in me!"

At the table Henry kept his eyes on Carlotta. He found her extremely attractive. Her face was oval shaped with high cheek bones, and her lips were very full and sensuous. Her teeth were large, but extremely white and straight. She had a very delicate neck and throat, and held her head high with a classic beauty. Her skin, not really olive as Turk had said, resembled the ivory of the pale Castillian type. Henry was particularly fascinated with her eyes, which were a greenish blue. They were large and had a tendency to slant slightly toward the upper corners, giving them an indefinite almond shape. He noticed her long and sweeping lashes had no artificial makeup. Her eyebrows were highly arched, giving her face a haughty, but exotic look. The nose was the kind magazine illustrators delight in using as a model, for it was arrow-straight with a faint suggestion of an upward tilt at the tip. When she talked, her nostrils dilated, and her eyes sparkled with animation. Her hair was as Turk had described it, coal black and very simply done up in braids across the top of her head, with a neat bun in the back.

The meal progressed with the conversation. Carlotta noticed that Henry did not take his eyes off her. She was puzzled, a little bewildered by Turk's strange companion. His manner was suave and he was obviously a man of culture, the exact opposite of unpolished Turk. A strange association, she thought—Turk, and this Henry Mueller. He was subtle and smooth—too smooth—gracious and very charming. He was good-looking, tall and a little thin, with very regular features, and a jutting, determined jaw. She liked the shape of his face, wide at the cheek line and narrowed down to an angle at the chin. What she didn't like, she thought, were his eyes and mouth. His eyes seemed shifty and cunning. His mouth was not warm or friendly. He knew how to affect its expression to suit the occasion; outwardly he could smile, and his lips would part in a delightful charm and gentility, but these attributes distinctly conveyed superficiality and falseness. Beneath this mask she felt him cold, calculating. No, Carlotta thought, she did not like his eyes and his mouth.

"I understand you have a little boy, Carlotta." It was Henry who spoke in an effort to direct the conversation away from himself.

"Yes," she answered enthusiastically, "he is a wonderful little boy."

"How old?"

"He is just four."

"Where is he? Home?"

"No, he is in Connecticut visiting his grandparents. His father takes him up there for the summer. They have a large beautiful home and a farm, and Terry loves to play with Sandy, the big Irish setter. Now, let's talk about you, Mr. Mueller. What do you do?"

Turk broke in hastily. "Oh, I forgot to tell you. Henry just got back from South America."

"Oh?" Carlotta seemed greatly surprised. "Well, you certainly have been keeping things from us, Mr. Mueller, and such interesting things. How long were you there?"

"About six years," Henry replied uncomfortably. Judas Priest! It just dawned on him! South America is definitely a Spanish-speaking continent, and Carlotta is Spanish. Damn Turk, he thought, for blurting that out. The stupid bastard. He never uses his head. Too late now, it's done—he'd have to go through with it. If only Carlotta doesn't ask too many questions.

"Gee, South America," sighed Helen. "That's where I've always wanted to go. Were you the lucky one!"

Henry folded his napkin. "Yes, it's quite a place," he said nonchalantly.

"Le gustó su viaje por Sud America?"

Henry blanched. "Hm?"

Carlotta smiled. "I said, *'Le gustó su viaje por Sud America?'*"

A cold chill shot up and down Henry's spine. He unfolded his napkin and his smile was nervous and forced. "I—I'm afraid I don't understand you, Carlotta."

Carlotta wrinkled her brow in amazement. "No? I am surprised. For a man who has traveled in South America for six years, you certainly should understand a simple thing like that. I asked you if you enjoyed your travels in South America, that is all."

"Oh."

"You mean you never understood or spoke one word of Spanish in all that time? To be in any country for six years and not learn some of the language seems almost an impossibility."

"Just one of those things, I guess. I always managed to be around places where they talked and understood English."

Henry did not look up to see Carlotta's reaction. He only knew that she did not believe him, and with good reason too. Of course she was right. Nobody could be that long in South America and not know Spanish or Portuguese. He felt like a fool, and Turk knew it as he watched Henry flounder helplessly trying to extricate himself.

"If I am not being too personal," continued Carlotta, "what took you there for so long?"

In the last couple of minutes, Henry had prepared himself for that question. "I went down to investigate some oil properties for the Gardner Oil Company. They were drilling a series of wells in Brazil, Argentina, and Chile. It took quite a while, naturally."

"Oh, how thrilling—how perfectly thrilling," came Carlotta's enthusiastic reply. "Please tell me more, I am fascinated!"

Was she kidding? Henry's brain was working feverishly. He wasn't quite sure now whether or not she was stringing him. He went on. "Well, it's a very interesting, but dangerous kind of work. You have all sorts of obstacles and hazards to contend with. Deadly jungles, malaria, tropical fever, dysentery, yellow fever, poisonous snakes, insects by the millions, and dampness—constant dampness. It rains every day in the jungles during the rainy season, and you soon become waterlogged, mentally as well as physically."

Helen was rumpling her napkin. She had an unhappy look on her face. "Maybe I don't want to go there now."

Carlotta chided her. "Don't be a silly goose. Mr. Mueller is talking about the jungles. The cities are beautiful, with big buildings, and street cars, and subways and modern hotels, and nightclubs, everything. I know, I have seen pictures of them."

Henry remembered a few pictures which he himself had seen in some magazines. "Of course, Helen. As a matter of fact, South American architecture is much more modern than ours. Some of their office buildings and apartment houses are really futuristic, with glass walls that absorb the sunshine for heat."

Turk forgot himself again. "Boy, I'll bet you can really get a tan down there!" Then he remembered. "I mean, if a guy spent all day at the beach—or something." His last statement fizzled out.

Carlotta seemed to be inspecting Henry's face rather closely. "It's quite evident you didn't take advantage of the South American sunshine, Mr. Mueller. In fact, I would say like the American Indian would, you are heap pale face!"

Turk and Helen laughed. Henry seethed inwardly, but managed an outward display of calm. He even smiled pleasantly. "I tried to keep out of the sun deliberately. Old Sol and I don't seem to agree."

Helen rose. "What do you say you boys go into the living room and Carlotta and I will clean off the table."

"Okay," said Turk as he pushed his chair back. "Come on, Henry."

Henry was glad of the break in conversation. He winked at Turk and gave a sigh of relief. Once in the living room away from the girls, he took out a handkerchief and mopped his brow. "Christ!" he muttered through his lips. "Was that a session!"

Turk made an effort to sympathize with him and at the same time protest his innocence. "Hell, Henry," he whispered, "I forgot about Carlotta being Spanish. I didn't know, I thought they speak South American down there!"

Henry hushed him as he caught sight of Carlotta entering the room. "She pushed me out and told me to entertain the guests, so here I am to bother you some more."

"We welcome such a bother, and hope for many such intrusions in the future, lovely princess!" Henry made a sweeping bow and gestured toward a chair.

"Oh, thank you, kind sir," laughed Carlotta gayly, as she curtsied and then sat down. "You know something, Mr. Mueller?"

"Please call me Henry."

"Henry.... You know something—"

"What?"

"I think you should have lived when they had knights and kings, and horses and armor. You would have fitted very well into those times. Who knows? You might have even been a king."

"A king?"

"Yes, I think that would have suited you nicely. But I'm not sure whether you would have been a good king or a tyrant."

"What makes you say that?"

"I don't know. I can't make up my mind. I think you have some of the qualities of both. There are certain people who are born to great destinies. Some become very powerful and influential. Their power turns their minds completely and they become drunk with it. Then they turn into tyrants and have only the desire to destroy. It is a pity, because some of them could have done a great deal of good for the world. They could have used their brilliant minds and their power for constructive purposes, instead of destructive things."

Henry sat fascinated. "You know, you amaze me, Carlotta. You're a very deep person."

"Not deep, just bitter sometimes."

"Why bitter? You've had a pretty good life, haven't you?"

"Have I? You see, when I speak of men having the good or bad qualities, the constructive ideals, or the evil thoughts of a tyrant who displays his power by destroying and making war on helpless people,

I refer to something that is very close and a part of me."

Henry stirred in his chair. He noted Carlotta's serious tone and wondered. "Really? Would you care to discuss it?"

"May I have a cigarette, please? Thank you."

Henry struck a match and after a long pause, during which Carlotta took several deep puffs, she spoke. "It is something I never talk about, but most of my family—father, mother, sister—were killed last year when Franco sent his bombers over to destroy Barcelona. Our whole house was smashed to a pile of bricks. They died in their beds as they slept!"

"I'm sorry to hear that, Carlotta," he said softly.

She continued. "I had two, big, handsome brothers. They were lined up against a wall and shot for being Loyalists. Because they wanted to live their lives in their own way, to work, and to vote, and be free, and because they refused to take orders from a dictator who wanted to rule the people for a personal and selfish power, they were shot down as you would shoot filthy mad dogs!"

There was little Henry could say. He did manage a somewhat futile and inadequate attempt to show his deep feeling over the story she had just told. "I can see now what you meant before about tyrants, Carlotta. I didn't have any idea it had struck so close to home."

She flicked the ashes in the tray. "That isn't all," she remarked coldly. "Now the other evil one, Mr. Mussolini, is taking it out on the poor Ethiopians, and I see in today's paper that Hitler is warning the Czechs!"

"Yes," replied Henry with a feeling of impending doom, "I think he is going to prove the worst of the lot. I just read a magazine article about him and he is definitely a paranoiac. He visualizes himself as a twentieth-century Napoleon."

Turk, who had sat rather stupefied and silent throughout the conversation, suddenly sat up bright and alert. "Say, that reminds me about a good horse to play tomorrow. There's a Napoleon running in the fourth at Bay Meadows."

Henry and Carlotta laughed. "You and your horses," she sighed.

Helen rejoined the group and soon a rummy game was in progress. It was eleven-thirty when Henry looked at his watch and decided it was time to be going.

"What's the hurry?" inquired Helen, "it's still early."

"You girls have to go to work in the morning, don't you?" replied Henry.

"Not I," said Carlotta as she totaled her score. "Tomorrow is my day off."

"What a coincidence! It's my day off too. Let's spend it together."

"Wonderful. We will go to the beach and you can get some tan on your face. One day at Coney Island and the sun will do more for you than six years in South America."

"Fine." Henry offered his hand and she took it. "Let's hope this is the beginning of a very long friendship," he said, looking into her eyes.

"I hope so." Carlotta withdrew her hand from his. She wasn't quite sure of herself. She wasn't quite sure she meant it. His strange personality had her wondering.

The evening ended, and Henry and Turk dropped Carlotta off in front of her apartment.

"Goodnight," Henry said at the entrance. "See you at ten tomorrow morning. Turk is going to let me use the car. He doesn't need it tomorrow."

"Goodnight, Henry. It's been nice meeting you."

He watched her as she walked into the building and disappeared. Then he returned to the car and they drove off. "She's lovely," Henry remarked to Turk.

"Yeah, she sure is," came the reply.

That night, as she lay in bed, Carlotta found herself thinking of Henry. There was something mysterious and foreboding about this new friendship. He had not come from South America, of that she was sure. Where had he come from? Who was he? What was his business? He was handsome, educated, suave. He was definitely an egoist, and very sure of himself. His manner was polite, but overconfident; his was the type of personality that one could easily admire or easily resent.

One thing was certain, Henry Mueller had a past that he meant to keep well buried.

CHAPTER FIVE

Henry stretched himself out on the warm sand and looked up into the sky. It was a perfect day with a bright, hot sun, and great fleecy white clouds drifting lazily across the expanse of blue.

"Isn't it simply a beautiful day?" asked Carlotta as she tied a silk bandanna around her hair.

"Perfect!" It was hard for Henry to believe that all this was taking place twenty-four hours after he had walked out of Mohawk. *God, it seemed years ago*. He looked at Carlotta. She was standing above him, her arms upraised, adjusting the red and yellow scarf into a turban. From her neck hung a small gold crucifix. She had on a two-piece white swim suit that adhered to her body as if it had been molded on her. Now he could see her form for what it really was. Her proportions were enough to thrill any man. And Henry noticed that that was exactly what was taking place. All eyes were on Carlotta, the hungry, wolfish eyes of the other men bathers and the jealous and admiring eyes of the women. He felt proud that she was with him and he basked not only in the sun, but also in the reflected glory of the lovely Carlotta.

She sat down beside him on the sand. "It's going to be a really hot day," she exclaimed. "You had better rub on some of this suntan oil, or you will burn like toast." She offered Henry the bottle of oil.

"I don't like the messy stuff," he protested. "You get all greasy."

"Just let me put some on your nose. You don't want that handsome nose to swell up and get all red so that you will look like a boozer!"

"A boozer? Say, you really know the language, don't you, slang and all!"

"Sure, I learn. You don't think I am like you. Six years in South America and you don't understand even the most simple sentence in Spanish. You know something, Mr. Mueller—"

"Henry."

"Henry. I think you tell a little white lie."

He made an effort to look innocent. "A white lie? About what?"

"Do you want me to play the child? Or do you want me to tell you what I really and truly think?"

Henry could only pretend that he was interested in her frankness. "Of course I want to know what you think. Do you have any reason to doubt me?"

"I would much prefer, Henry, that if this is going to be the beginning of a real friendship we start on a foundation of truth. I would like to feel that we are being sincere and open with one another. I would not care to feel that always I have in the back of my mind reasons to doubt you, or that you are hiding things."

Henry picked up a handful of sand and let it trickle slowly through his fingers. "And you think I'm hiding something?"

"Yes. It is not only that I do not believe you have just come from South America. That, I was not convinced of even for one minute—"

"No."

"You really didn't expect me to, did you?"

"Well—" He unconsciously bit his lower lip.

"Be truthful, Henry." She looked at him straightforwardly.

"No." He was uncomfortable, but her sincerity was disarming. "I rather thought you didn't."

"Please don't think I am trying to be the inquisitive busybody; it is just that I want to be your friend. Do you believe me, Henry?"

He smiled faintly. "Yes, I do."

"You see, I do not care where you come from, I think that is not important. So you may feel at ease with me. That is what I want you to be, at ease."

Henry gave himself a mental hypo. "What makes you think I'm not at ease?"

"You are an excellent actor with a very vivid imagination. You talk with the extreme air of confidence, but I am not so sure you even believe yourself."

Henry ran his tongue around the inside of his cheek. "What else?"

"I think you are conceited and that you have a superiority complex—shall I stop?"

Henry was now smirking. "No, go ahead, I'm enjoying this."

"… And I think you are utterly sure of yourself with women, and that you can be dangerous like the wolf."

He pursed his lips and gave a low whistle. "Say, little Red Riding Hood, aren't you afraid to be with me?"

"Not at all," Carlotta laughed; "you are a mystery man, but I do not even hesitate to tell you I like you. That I have admitted now, even against my better judgment."

Henry toyed with her avowal. "Do you think you'll have cause to regret it?"

"I hope not. So many people in this world turn out to be disappointing. I hope you will not be one of them. You see, I really am not a cynic. I have a great deal of faith in people, and I want you to help me keep that faith."

Henry took her hand.

"I'll try always to justify that faith, Carlotta," he said quietly.

"Thank you, Henry." She held his hand tightly.

Then, shaking her head impatiently as if to clear it of too much emotion, Carlotta rose. "Now, Mr. Henry Mueller, I race you into the water. Ten to one I can beat you!"

"What's the bet?" laughed Henry, jumping to his feet. "I'll bet you a kiss!"

"Nothing doing," she called as she ran for the water. "This is Coney Island. I like a little privacy like the Bronx Zoo!"

"O. K." shouted Henry as he ran after her, "if it's animals you like, here comes that wolf!" He caught up to her at the water's edge and tackled her ankles in a flying leap. They both went down just as a giant wave broke over the shore, completely submerging them both.

Carlotta's gay screams were drowned out by the roar of the surf.

When Henry walked into the apartment that evening, Turk greeted him with a broad grin. "Now you really look like you just came back from South America," he said examining Henry's fresh burn. "Boy, that's a little dandy. Does it hurt?"

"No," replied Henry taking off his shirt. "Lottie put some oil on for me."

Turk assumed a silly expression. "Oh? So it's Lottie now?"

"Yes, and stop looking like a goon."

"I'm not looking like a goon. I'm glad."

"Glad about what?"

"That you and Carlotta are getting along so well."

Henry examined his sunburned face in the mirror, "I think she's a wonderful girl, Turk. She's beautiful, she's intelligent, and she's got ten thousand dollars."

Turk's expression suddenly changed. "Henry, you wouldn't play a girl like Carlotta for her kid's money, would you?"

"Turk, my friend, you're too quick at jumping to conclusions. I didn't say anything about playing her for her money. I merely mentioned that along with her beauty and intelligence, she had a bank account, and I've always believed one should marry for love where there's money."

Turk's eyes narrowed. "Henry, I've always liked you. I ain't never had as much schooling and education as you had, and I know that when it comes to big words and deep subjects, you're ahead of everybody I ever met. People call you an intellectual. They call me a stupe. But there's one thing I got, and that's a conscience. Sure, I like to make money the easy way, same as a lot of other guys, but I wouldn't enjoy a penny of dough that was screwed out of somebody as fine as Carlotta and that kid of hers. A guy that would be cooking up a deal like that in the back of his mind is a low-down no-good son-of-a-bitchin' pimp!"

Henry swung around savagely. His eyes were blazing and his jaw protruded. He grabbed Turk by the shirt and tie and almost lifted him from the floor. Through clenched teeth he spat his venom. "You mind your own goddamned business, you hear?"

Turk's face grew purple as the tie formed a noose around his neck shutting off his breath. He began to choke. Henry released him and he fell gasping into a chair. Henry was breathing hard himself, and his heart pounded with the strokes of a sledge hammer. He ran his hand across his forehead, sat for a moment on the edge of the table, shuddering from emotional reaction. Then he went to the kitchenette and got a glass of water. He drank it in a solid gulp, and was about to put down the glass, when Turk's audible gasping struck his ears. He filled the glass again and walked over to Turk.

"Here. I'm sorry Turk. I … I lost my head."

Turk took the glass between his trembling fingers and sipped some of the water. "Thanks," he whispered.

Henry went to the bathroom and came back with a cold towel. He walked to the back of Turk's chair and placed the folded cloth across his forehead. "This'll help," he said awkwardly. Turk looked up and smiled.

"Turk, I didn't mean to do it."

"Hell, I asked for it."

Henry felt a little ashamed; it was not his nature to resort to violence. He fought his way out of nasty situations with cutting, cruel, vitriolic words; these had always been his weapons. Only fools and bullies used their fists. What had happened to his abhorrence of violence? Had prison life dulled his sensibilities, made him hardened and callous? Had he become like all the rest, cold and ruthless, a seasoned criminal who cared nothing about the feelings, or even the lives, of others? As these thoughts battled their way through Henry's mind, he looked again at Turk, this small, slight man with the thinning hair who didn't have the physical strength of a good strapping fourteen-year-old, and he felt like a heel.

Later, after Turk had fully regained his composure and emerged from the bathroom in shorts, he tried to show Henry that he had forgotten the incident. He was rubbing his scalp vigorously with a rough towel. "Nothing like an ice-cold shower to pep you up," he said with his usual gaiety. Henry was conscious of a distinct relief. He did not like to feel in the wrong.

As Henry started for the shower, Turk brightened with a sudden thought. "Oh, I almost forgot to tell you the good news."

"What good news?" queried Henry, unlacing his shoes.

"You know those two tips I got yesterday?"

"Yes?"

"Well, they both paid off!"

"Yeah?" When excited, Henry could lapse into the colloquial.

"Itinerary paid $9.40 and Fleetaway paid $6.80."

"Really? That's fine. I can use the money."

"On account of your hunch on Itinerary, I did all right. I put a hundred and a half on him, and it was a good thing I played Fleetaway to place. My pal was a little off on that one. Sometimes you've got to use your head on tips and play them to place or show, instead of on the nose."

"Yes, I know. I found that out a long time ago about tips, and not only tips on horses. Well, how did we do?"

"I already been down to the bookies and collected. I got $705.00 back on Itinerary and $170.00 on Fleetaway."

Henry whistled. "Say, not a bad day's work!"

Turk laughed. "Yep, I can remember when I was satisfied with a whole lot less!" He walked over to his trousers and withdrew a large roll of bills. "Here's your winnings on Itinerary," he said handing Henry several bills. "Forty-seven dollars."

"Thanks," Henry took the money and handed Turk back a bill. "Here's the ten I borrowed from you."

"You better keep it, you'll need it."

"No, thanks just the same. I'm going to look for a job tomorrow."

Turk stopped buttoning his shirt. "Honest? Gee, that's really swell, Henry. What kind of a job?"

"I don't know yet. Something I can fit in to. I'll look around."

Turk went over to the dresser, and picked up the bankroll. He peeled off ten twenty-dollar bills. "Say, Henry," he said, "would you let me stake you to some new clothes? After all, if you're after a job that prison drape don't look so hot."

Henry laughed. "Boy, you said it. I was thinking I'd have to get some new clothes somehow."

"Sure. Here, get something that looks a little like the stuff they're wearing this year. That Mohawk Special looks like something that was left over from the Chicago fire! Nobody would hire you in that."

"All right, Turk." Henry accepted the bills. "Thanks a million. But it's just a stake, remember," he added, "I'll pay you back as soon as I earn some money." Even as he said the words, Henry thought to himself, how many times have I said that before!

"It's just money," replied Turk good-naturedly. To Turk, these words had a very familiar ring too, but he didn't mind. Henry was his friend.

Henry spent the better part of the next day outfitting himself with the money Turk had given him. On the way home, he stopped at the beauty shop where Carlotta worked, and waited until closing time. As they walked out together, Carlotta hid her pleasure at this unexpected visit with a pretended rebuke. "I am not used to such bossiness, Mr. Mueller. You pop into the shop at five minutes to six and you say, 'Get into your street clothes, we are going to dinner!' No call on the phone to see whether or not I am going to be busy, or whether I have another engagement; no advance notice of any kind. Just poof! You pop in and take it for granted I am waiting for you!"

"You can still change your mind, you know. You don't have to have dinner with me," Henry said slyly, looking at her out of the corner of his eye.

Carlotta was enjoying this. "Tsk, tsk, tsk," she shook her head as she clicked her tongue, "you are getting more temperamental every day, Mr. Mueller."

Henry still feigned a hurt. "I shouldn't take you to dinner at all. I ought to let you starve until you speak more sweetly to me."

"All right—Henry, *darling*. Now, where are you going to take me to dinner?"

"What are you in the mood for?"

"Chow mein!"

Henry laughed. "Good enough. Then that's settled."

Half an hour later they were seated in a crowded, garish Chinese restaurant. After the waiter took their order, Henry looked around at the highly decorated interior, with its bizarre furnishings, and the Cantonese red motif of the walls and ceilings. "A very attractive place, but you know, this is strictly an American decorator's idea of a Chinese restaurant."

Carlotta pouted. "You make me feel sorry I brought you here."

"Not at all." Henry took her hand. "I think it's charming."

"I don't know how you can be charmed by anything."

"Why do you say that?"

"Because you are so aware of how everything works that nothing intrigues you."

Henry squeezed her hand. "You do," he said softly. "You intrigue me very much."

Carlotta looked at him searchingly.

"I wonder, Henry. I wonder if I really do?"

Henry felt his stride. "Darling—I've thought of nothing but you ever since we've met...."

"But we just met the other day. You don't even know me. Wait, I take that back. You probably do. You probably see right through and read my mind. You would not need more than a day or two to know any woman."

"Was that nice?"

Carlotta sipped some of her tea. "No, I suppose it wasn't. But I think it's true. I wish you didn't understand women so well. I do not think it is a good thing to see through people so completely. It spoils the romance."

"Lottie, darling, look at me. I think you're lovely, and that's all I want to know about you."

She started to speak, but Henry took the words away from her.

"You see, it doesn't take a man long to discover a few things about a woman. You are a very fine and wonderful person. Beautiful, yes, but something more—call it intuition if you want to, but I feel like an archeologist, digging into the catacombs of human minds, hoping to find somewhere that quality you have—the something that is the key to a door that has been barred to me all these years. The door is happiness!"

He looked up at Carlotta. She was staring at him, her eyes filled with mixed emotions.

"Oh, Henry." She held his hand more tightly. "Henry, my darling."

CHAPTER SIX

Several days later Henry telephoned Carlotta and told her it was very urgent that he see her immediately. They arranged to meet at her apartment. Henry appeared nervous and distraught.

"Henry! Is something the matter? You look upset!"

He threw his hat down on the davenport and sank down with a sigh.

"Henry, darling, what's the matter? What's bothering you?" Carlotta sat down beside him.

Henry tapped his fist into the palm of his other hand a couple of times. "Oh Carlotta, I should never have come to you," he said in an anguished tone.

"Why not? Why shouldn't you come to me? I am your friend, Henry."

"Could we ever be more than that, Lottie? I want to be more than just your friend. You must understand that my feelings for you go a lot deeper than that, my darling."

Carlotta ran her fingers through his hair. "I was hoping to hear you say that, Henry, *mi amor*. My feelings for you are already deep as a love should be."

Henry looked up, eyes glassy. "You—love me?"

"I suppose if I were timid and shy like a little girl, I would say nothing until the man has made the first declaration. But I am not a little girl, Henry, I am a grown woman who knows that it is futile to hide the love and pretend indifference. Life is too short. Yes, Henry, I do love you."

Henry took Carlotta in his arms. "My darling," he said softly, "my dearest darling. I love you, too; madly, passionately, and with all my soul." She turned and looked up into his eyes, awaited with a tense passion this first kiss. Henry pressed her closer. Her lips parted slightly as his met hers, and the embrace was long and ecstatic. When they separated a full minute later to catch their breaths, Carlotta's eyes fluttered open and she whispered, "I love you, I love you, my darling. Kiss me again and again, *mi amorsito lindo*."

Carlotta was the first to break the silence. "Now, Henry darling, you must tell me what it is that is bothering you."

Henry took a letter from his inside pocket and handed it to her. "Read this," he said with a tremor in his voice. She unfolded the letter slowly, and began to read aloud:

"My dear brother Henry:

"I know this will not be pleasant news to hear, but there is no sense in pretending further that things are all right. We've had so many troubles, and now this. Henry, we're up against it. First Fred's accident, and hospital bills, then Pa laid up with arthritis. He still hasn't been able to go back to work, so there's been no money coming in since last December. Now, Ma's eyesight is going. Henry, it's pathetic! She practically has to feel her way around the house. She doesn't even go outside anymore and she can only get as far as the porch. Doctor Bauer says that there is a specialist in San Francisco by the name of Phillips who could cure her by a new type of operation, and he says it's her only chance. If nothing is done, it is only a matter of another six months before she's completely blind.

"It'll take at least $1,500, and we've scraped together $500 but we just can't get any more. Henry, we know that if there is the slightest possibility of your raising the money, you will not fail us. Remember, this is Ma's only chance to keep from going blind. We've got to do this for her, Henry.

"Pa and Fred send their best, and I'm sure if Ma knew I was writing, which she doesn't, she would want me to send you her love. The children are well and we all hope you are. Please don't fail us. Let me hear from you immediately.

Your loving sister
Peg"

Carlotta folded the letter and looked at Henry. There were tears in her eyes. "Oh, Henry, I am so terribly sorry. Now, I know why you are so upset." She took his hand in hers. "I feel so bad inside myself for your dear mother, almost as if she were my own. How long has she had this trouble?"

Henry glanced at the carpet. He avoided her eyes. "It started about five years ago. But I didn't realize that it had become so bad. You see, I haven't been home for about ten years!"

Carlotta remonstrated. "You haven't been a very good son, have you?"

"No, I guess I haven't been what you would call devoted, but the fact remains that I can't let them down now."

Carlotta moved closer toward him. "Oh, no, *mi amor*. Oh, never."

Henry paced his words, timed his drama. "There's only one hitch in the whole thing. I haven't any money to send to them!"

Carlotta leaned back on the davenport. "Oh!"

Henry buried his face in his hands. It was easier that way. He would have to face her later, but at least for the time being he wouldn't have to run the gantlet of her penetrating, searching eyes. Carlotta's eyes bothered Henry more than anything else. If only they weren't so trusting. He slowly raised his head. "Now you know, darling."

Carlotta was aghast. "You mean you have nothing at all to send them?"

"Not a cent. I'm completely broke!"

"But the oil company? Are you not earning any money with them?"

"I quit."

"Why?"

"It just wasn't the right job for me."

"Oh." She looked at him, puzzled.

"I'm looking for a new job right now."

"Henry, darling, look at me. I am completely at a loss with you. Things have happened between us so quickly, I have not had the time to think about us from the intelligent point of view. We meet, we fall in love, we do not take time to rationalize. You see, I know nothing about you, where you come from, what you do, where you are going— nothing. I take for granted you are a worldly man. You tell me you travel all over South America for a big oil firm. If I should disbelieve you, I say to myself, Carlotta, you are not fair, you know nothing but what he tells you, and if you have faith, you must take people at their word. So you see, Henry, dear, I do not want to doubt what you tell me. I want to believe in you."

Henry bit his lower lip. "I know you do, Lottie."

She continued. "Now you tell me you do not work anymore for this company, that you are broke. I am bewildered. If you have worked all this time for a company, surely you must have saved something?"

This was not the time for explanation. Henry buried his face again and gave a slight shudder. "I've made money and enjoyed myself … now, I'll have to let my mother down. I haven't saved a cent, I tell you."

Carlotta thought for a moment. "Henry, have you mentioned this to Turk?"

"No, I haven't for a very good reason." He paused for dramatic emphasis, then spoke as if the words were almost too painful to utter. "You see, I—I owe Turk a lot as it is."

Carlotta answered very quietly, almost in a half-whisper. "I see—"

"I'm in a horrible spot, Carlotta," Henry said in an anguished tone. "I don't know what to do and I haven't the heart to see this happen to my mother when I could save her with only a thousand dollars!" Henry turned away, a mask of tragedy. For a full minute he heard nothing but Carlotta's gentle breathing. Then the silence was broken.

"Henry, *mi amor*, look at me. I think I can get you some of the thousand dollars to send to your mother!"

Henry looked up. "What did you say?"

"I said I think I can get you some of the thousand dollars to send to your mother."

He faked a bewildered expression with the deftness of a skilled actor. "You?"

"Yes," Carlotta replied softly. "I have some money laid away. It is for my son's future, but at the moment, your mother's sight is more important. I could not live with myself if I thought that because of my selfishness I allowed your dear mother to suffer the loss of her eyes. No, I could not do that."

"But, Lottie, this isn't your responsibility, it's mine." He tried to make the protest as genuine as possible.

"No, my sweet," she answered with a smile. "That would be a poor kind of love, would it not, if we were to shirk each other's responsibilities? I cannot love that way."

Damn it, he thought, if only she would stop looking at him with those eyes. They were like fire and seared right into the brain. "Lottie, I—I don't know what to say, this is all so unexpected—I only came over here to talk with you because I didn't know whom else to come to."

Again her soft fingers combed their way through his hair. "I'm glad you did, Henry. I want you to always feel that you can come to me with anything."

"Thanks, Lottie."

"Come over tomorrow night. I will give you what help I can."

"Darling! I'll pay it back just as soon as I can, I swear." Once more, briefly, Henry Mueller felt like the heel he knew he was.

In the weeks that followed, Henry lived a carefree and easy life. The job that he always had "lined up" never quite seemed to materialize. Turk was baffled by Henry's affluence, which seemed to increase as the days passed. They spent a great deal of time together at the track and their luck was the best it had even been, but Henry spent money freely and soon his betting and his gambling at poker had taken its toll. When he got down to his last hundred dollars, he made up his mind that he would have to make the drastic move that he had thus far avoided. He and Carlotta were dining together in a quiet little Bohemian restaurant when he reached across the table and took her hand.

"Darling," he said softly, "I'd like to ask you something that's been on my mind for weeks."

"Yes?" She looked exceptionally beautiful tonight and Henry felt he could be doing a lot worse.

"Do you think you could manage to put up with me for the rest of your life?"

Carlotta looked up sharply from her plate and dropped her knife and fork. "Mr. Mueller, is this a proposal? A real honest-to-goodness proposal?"

"Yes, darling." Henry replied condescendingly, as though this was the biggest sacrifice that he could possibly make. Carlotta was too elated to be conscious of anything but the joy that the question aroused.

"Henry, you are serious? You mean a real wedding with a priest and—" she caught herself.

The martyr spoke again. "Yes, my sweet, a real wedding to be performed by anyone you want!"

Carlotta jumped up and circled the table. "Darling, kiss me, I don't care if we are in a restaurant or not. I am so happy. Kiss me!"

They were in a rather obscure booth, so Henry didn't mind. She sat down beside him and he kissed her fervently. He always enjoyed kissing Carlotta; she was responsive and lovely to embrace. Funny, how she had managed all these weeks to keep from giving herself to him. It had been a shock to his ego that she had been able to restrain herself, but Carlotta was different. It wasn't that Henry had not tried, discreetly, but he found that Carlotta had will power along with her passion. Her restraint was the result of experience with men. She had found it no easy task to send Henry home night after night, and then cry herself to sleep in an agony of desire, but she felt that her submission would be the beginning of the end. She did not realize that Henry's interest in any woman had long since failed to be influenced by her virtues. All right, he would marry Carlotta; she had money in the bank. It was a means to an end. He would treat this as a pleasant episode, an inviting wayside inn, on the road that led to the greatness which Henry Mueller felt sure lay ahead.

"Tell me, darling," Carlotta asked slightly bewildered, "how you come so suddenly to ask me to marry? Not one word of warning; just five minutes ago we talk about the movie we saw the other night, and then, boom! You propose to me!"

Henry tried to sound modest. "That's the way I do things, I guess, on the spur of the moment. I had been thinking about it, but I guess I was afraid to pop the question."

Carlotta laughed. "Afraid I would accept, no?"

Henry laughed too. "Don't be silly!"

She looked with burning anticipation into his eyes. "Oh, *mi amorsito lindo, yo te amo, yo te amo!*"

"What does that mean?" Henry murmured as he held her hand.

"That means, you are my beautiful love, and I love you, I love you!"

He kissed the palm of her hand and then the tips of her fingers. "And I love you too, my dearest." Henry wasn't lying. He told himself that this was real, if temporary. Why not? He was capable of loving the same as anyone else.

Carlotta searched his eyes. "Do you love me very, very much?" she asked fervently.

Henry paused, employing his histrionic ability to add weight to his reply. Then he answered softly, "Yes, my darling, very much."

"—and will you always say that to me—always?"

There was a fraction of a pause as Henry took her other hand and caressed the palm with his lips. Then he drew her close to him and kissed her tenderly, then unrestrainedly. They were not aware that the waiter had appeared with their steaks.

"Who gets the medium rare?"

They sprang apart and Carlotta's face flushed. "I do," she said, half-dazed, half-embarrassed.

The waiter smiled. "Too bad you don't like your steaks well done!"

"Why?" Henry asked, wiping the smudge of lipstick from his face.

"Then I would come five minutes later and you wouldn't have any interruption!"

"It's all right, who can eat now anyway?" said Carlotta joyously.

"Waiter, congratulate us, we have just decided to get married!"

The waiter beamed. "No foolin'? Well, congratulations to you both."

They both thanked him. He stood there with a silly grin on his face. "You mean it just happened—you didn't know about this before?"

"No," cried Carlotta, "he just proposed to me between the soup and the steak!"

Henry and Carlotta were married in a quiet little ceremony in Nyack. Turk had driven them there in his car and he and Helen were the witnesses.

On the way back, Henry took the wheel and Carlotta sat beside him. Turk and Helen fell asleep in the back seat, and Carlotta sat quiet and pensive, her arm under Henry's. No word was uttered for perhaps fifteen or twenty miles. Then Henry, who also had been deep in thought, turned and patted her hand.

"What're you so quiet about, dear?"

"I was just thinking," replied Carlotta. "Thinking how happy I am, and how much I want us both always to be happy." She turned and looked at her husband. "We will be happy, won't we, Henry *mi amor?*"

Henry took her hand and kissed her fingers. "Of course we will, my darling. Why shouldn't we be?"

"I don't know any reason, Henry, only I was so unhappy before, that I want this to be the perfect heaven. I want to be a good wife and a good mother."

A good mother! Henry had almost forgotten about Carlotta's son. He still had not seen her boy.

"When is Terry coming home?" he asked.

"He will be back in one week and I am so glad. I have missed Terry so, but the farm is good for him. He will come home fat and brown like the nut."

"We haven't met yet. Do you think he'll like his new father?"

"Oh, my darling, he will love you, as I do."

Henry wasn't too sure that he would be able to return the affection. He had never been around children much and this new situation would be a test of his capabilities as a parent.

There was silence for a few minutes and then Carlotta had a new thought. "Oh, Henry, the first thing we must do when we get back to the city is send your folks a telegram. We must let them know. I'm sure it will make them very happy."

Henry kept his eyes straight ahead on the road. "Yes, of course, dear. I'll take care of it just as soon as we get back."

"By the way, how is your mother getting along?"

"Oh, fine! I meant to tell you, dear. I received a letter the other day. The operation was successful and she's doing marvelously. Thanks to you!"

This was pretty weak but Carlotta was too happy to notice it. "No thanks to me. Thanks to God," she said reverently.

There she goes again, Henry thought to himself. Always getting spiritual. If only she weren't so damn religious and idealistic. Henry's religion had become the works of the philosophers, and his house of worship was his brain. If she wanted to be pious and devout, that was up to her, just so long as she didn't try to inflict her way of life on him.

Carlotta smiled. "And darling!"

"Yes?"

"We will have to look for a little larger place now. Terry will be home next week and we must have at least three rooms. We cannot get along without a bedroom now."

"That's right. Well, you begin to look for a place tomorrow, and anything you find will be all right with me. In the meantime I'll drive over to Turk's place now and get my things, and take them over to your apartment. Is that all right?"

"Of course, dear." It sounded funny to Carlotta to be agreeing to something like that. Her new husband moving into her apartment to spend their honeymoon. It suddenly struck her as being terribly unromantic. Something as exciting as this should have more fitting surroundings. It took the edge off the occasion. This was something special—after all, a girl doesn't get married every day. She was at least entitled to spend her wedding night in an atmosphere of love and romance.

"Darling—" This time her voice was petulant.

"Yes?"

"Would you mind terribly much if we didn't go back to my place tonight?"

"Why?"

"Please don't think I'm being a silly child, but I don't want to spend my wedding night at home in that little apartment. It's too ordinary for this beautiful occasion. I would like to go some place nice. Would you mind too much?"

Henry put his arm around her. "No, sweetheart, I don't mind. I think it's a marvelous idea. I should have thought of that myself."

"And you don't think I'm being silly?"

He leaned over and kissed her cheek. "You're being romantic and I love you for it. Where do you want to go?"

"Any nice place you want to take me to."

Henry thought for a moment. "How about the St. Regis for about three days?"

Carlotta brightened. "Oh, my darling, that would be magnificent!" Then her expression changed. "But wouldn't it be terribly expensive?"

"Not so much—and we can see a few shows, and take in some of the nightclubs, and have ourselves a real honeymoon. How does that strike you?"

"Oh, Henry, *mi amor*, that would be heavenly! Three glorious days of a honeymoon that I did not even expect. Oh, I am so thrilled! But darling—"

"Yes?"

"Are you sure we can afford it?"

"Why not? You've got your checkbook with you, haven't you?"

CHAPTER SEVEN

In the following weeks Henry made no visible attempt to seek employment, and Carlotta found herself playing the role of wife and provider. The irons that he continually had in the fire never quite seemed to materialize. Always something new and better was in the offing—the kind of position that required a definite type of handling and which wasn't to be had for the mere snap of a finger. These were the things which Carlotta heard week after week. In the meantime, Henry spent money faster than Carlotta earned it. More than once she was forced to draw money from her son's bank account.

During this time Henry and Turk were at the bookies or the track almost every day. Turk had his own ideas about the source of Henry's income, but he knew that was no longer his affair. He had learned that it was unhealthy to mix in Henry's private affairs, and if Carlotta had married a man of Henry's nature she would have to make the best of it. It wasn't that Turk didn't feel sorry for her, but he knew that Henry was not a man to be crossed or denied. He only hoped that the marriage would turn out all right and that Carlotta would be able to handle her own financial affairs.

Carlotta was torn between her love for Henry and her concern for her son's future. At the rate Henry was eating up the money that was laid aside for Terry's future and his schooling, it wouldn't last two years. She became aware that the moment this money was no longer forthcoming, there would be an upheaval in her home. It was not pleasant to be faced with the fact that Henry's love for her was not so deep as she had thought.

Each time she had made up her mind that he would no longer play upon her emotions, that she was going to say no, that she was going to put her foot down, Henry would invariably wind up with whatever it was he wanted. She found herself powerless before him, but she knew that it was not a healthy state. She was terribly in love with a man she could not understand. She was not a spiritual part of his life. Henry had never taken her completely into his confidence. His past was still as much of a question mark to her as it had ever been. She knew that there were things in Henry's life that would forever remain a mystery. She could not claim any of his past, but she could not even be sure of his future. She could not even be sure of his love. Carlotta was frightened, bewildered and unhappy. The disappointments, heartaches and frustrations which she had prayed would be absent from this second marriage were all too present. Then there was also Terry.

Terry, despite all efforts by his mother and a few unenthusiastic attempts by Henry to win him over, remained adamant. His resentment toward the man who was an intruder in his small world increased with each day. He refused to call Henry "daddy," "uncle," or even "Henry;" he merely referred to him as "that bad man." This added to Carlotta's already unhappy frame of mind. A love based upon her ability to keep Henry supplied with money was no love.

It took Carlotta six months to realize the situation was hopeless. Her pride smarted under the knowledge that she had been taken, that Henry had married her as a means of temporary support. She now knew that the moment she stopped giving him money, this so-called love, this beautiful cloak of affection and devotion which Henry wore so well, would turn to sackcloth and ashes. There was no sense in deluding herself further. She would tell Henry that he had to earn his own keep, that she was through supporting him while he took life easy and gambled away Terry's bank account. If he really loved her, he would stop being a parasite and go out and earn a living—any kind of a living, just so long as he did something that was honest and worked for his money like other men. If he rebelled at her decision, then she might as well face the truth. She steeled herself against the disarming gestures at which she knew Henry was so expert. This time there would be no faltering, no bargaining. The decision would be irrevocable.

Henry came home that evening for dinner. The conversation was of routine things. Henry noticed that his wife was a bit quieter than usual, but attached no special significance to her behavior. She cleared away the table, did the dishes, and put Terry to bed. When she came back into the living room, Henry's understanding of his wife's psychology caused him to be particularly attentive. He sat down beside her on the davenport and caressed her tenderly. Whatever it was that was upsetting her, the magic of his words and the healing power of his kisses would soon take care of the disturbance. Henry did not suspect the import of the situation or the reserve of strength that Carlotta had built up for this moment.

"Henry …" she spoke softly, with a coolness and calm that gave full indication that this time she was in complete mastery of her emotions. "Henry, I want to talk to you very seriously."

"Yes?" Henry sensed the impending challenge of her words.

"I don't know whether or not you realize it, but in the past six months I have given you almost four thousand dollars of Terry's money. Money that his father gave me to put aside for his education. I have told you that this money is not rightfully mine, that each time I draw out from this account it is like draining blood from my body, but never once have you shown any indication that it bothered you or made any difference to you at all."

Henry floundered about: "Well, I—I—"

She interrupted his futile attempt to speak. "I have waited patiently all this time, Henry, for you to make some effort to locate yourself and earn a decent and honest living so that I could be proud of my husband. I wouldn't care what it was, or even if you only made twenty-five dollars a week. The amount is not important. I have not been a wife who would make demands, or expect a big income from my husband. I want only that he should be a man and not a parasite!"

Henry's face flushed. "Is that what you think I am?"

There was a pause while she took a deep breath. "I am afraid I have no alternative but to think that. You have been living off me since we got married. I even paid for the honeymoon. You have not contributed one cent to the upkeep of this house. I have paid the rent, paid for the food we eat and the clothes we wear. The forty dollars a week salary I earn always was enough for Terry and me, but to support a husband too on that, especially a husband whose time is spent gambling, is a human impossibility. I cannot sit by and watch my son's future being slowly taken from him. He is entitled to live and be taken care of. He is too young to look out for himself, so I, his mother, must look out for him."

Henry was twirling his key chain. "So, what're you getting at?"

"Henry, darling, I love you. But can't you see, my darling, I want to respect my husband too? I want to look up to him and admire him, but before a woman can respect her husband, he must have his own self-respect."

This was new to Henry. His wife had never before spoken so bluntly as this. He was confused and thrown off balance by this sudden barrage of truths. "You're certainly letting me have it with both barrels tonight, aren't you?" he began in a weak defense.

"No, Henry, my dear. It is not my way or my nature to be domineering or to be nagging. I merely want to find out for my own happiness whether you really love me or whether I am just a convenience to you."

"Whatever gave you that idea?"

"It is something I must prove to myself."

"How do you intend proving my love to yourself?"

"By shutting off my bank accounts to you, and asking you to support me and yourself from now on!"

"Oh?" Henry smiled faintly. "So that's what you intend doing, eh?"

"Yes, Henry, I must. Beginning tonight, you get no more money from me. I want to see if I am married to a man who has decency and self-respect, besides conceit. I want to see whether I am married to a man who has ideals and a backbone, besides a beautiful vocabulary and a brilliant mind. I want to see if under all the education that my husband takes pride in, he has anything to back it up. In other words, I want to see if my husband has any good old-fashioned American guts!"

Henry jumped from the davenport and wheeled around. "That's enough," he shouted at her angrily. "Who the hell do you think you are, a female priest? I'll live my life the way I goddamn want to!"

Carlotta was seeing the results of her test all too soon. She now could stand her ground with nothing to lose, and this realization gave her the strength and the determination she needed. She spoke with quiet conviction, and her words were measured. "Yes, Henry, you may live your life any way you want to, but no longer off me!"

Even as the words fell upon his ear, Henry knew that they were released with the full impact of one who delivers a knockout blow. In defiance he snarled, "Okay! Then you can take your damned money and stick it!" And putting on his hat and coat, he walked out without another word.

Carlotta cried bitterly when Henry left. Henry did not love her, perhaps had never loved her, and she had been the victim of a marital swindle. The money that he had taken from her was unimportant. It could be replaced by hard work and systematic saving. But the fact that Henry had taken her love and used it hurt her cruelly.

Terry came out of the bedroom, sleepy-eyed and bewildered. He tugged at her dress as she lay on the davenport sobbing. "Mommy," he called, looking confused and rubbing his eyes, "what's the matter

Mommy, did the bad man make you cry?"

Carlotta sat up still shaking with grief and clasped her son to her breast. "Yes, Terry, he did!" She continued to weep. It was the first time that Carlotta had failed to reprimand her son for referring to Henry as "the bad man."

Henry walked through the deep snow toward Turk's hotel feeling depressed and very much displeased with himself. He felt remorse, as he had when he had faked the letter about his mother's eyesight. He would get over this state of mind, however; it never bothered him before for more than a few hours. Fortunately, he had a way of dismissing unpleasant thoughts. Was it a lack of conscience? He wasn't sure. He only knew that whatever he did was for the benefit, the welfare, and the furtherance of Henry Mueller. Anything to the contrary was unimportant and of little or no significance. Maybe the way he had existed, his forms of livelihood, the money he had taken from Carlotta and Terry, were cheap and petty, but they were just a means to an end.

Carlotta had said that he had no guts. The scene in Warden Riley's office flashed before him as he walked through the quiet night. Henry turned the phrase over in his mind. What was guts? Sweating all week long in a steel mill or stoking a red-hot furnace in the clammy hold of some ship? Any moron could be taught to do that kind of work.

Just because he couldn't stand any kind of work that was dull, stupid, and monotonous, did that mean he did not have guts? If that were the case, then he preferred being the way he was. He had a mind that would more than make up for any other deficiency. He trudged along in the heavy snow feeling decidedly less remorseful.

Turk was surprised to see that his unexpected caller was Henry. "Boy, are you full of snow," he remarked as Henry stamped his feet and brushed the big flakes from his hat and coat. "Come on in." Henry entered the apartment and after removing his coat, sat down with a deep sigh in a chair near the radiator. Turk sensed that something was wrong.

"What brings you out on a night like this?"

"Oh, I've got a little something on my mind," Henry answered him.

"Anything important?"

"Rather."

Turk looked apprehensive. "Not you and—Carlotta?"

Henry crossed his fingers over the back of his hands, and took a long breath. "Yes, that's exactly what it is. We're going to separate."

Turk threw down the paper he had been reading. "No!"

"Yes, Turk, we're all washed up. At least I am. Tomorrow I'll go back and get my clothes."

Turk looked nonplussed. "Why, Henry? Do you want to tell me?"

Henry evaded the real issue. "Oh, it's just one of those things. I never should have married, that's all."

"But I thought you and Carlotta were getting along swell. In fact me and Helen was saying just the other day that you and Lottie were like a couple of turtle-doves. You were always kissing her and making love—I never thought there was anything wrong in a million years."

Henry rubbed his hands together. "Well, we won't go into the pros and cons of that." Then he changed the subject. "What's new?"

"I'm thinking of pulling up stakes in this town for a while."

Henry's face fell. "Oh? When did you decide this?"

"I've been thinking about it for a few days now. There's a deal on in Chicago. I've got a chance to be cut in something that looks pretty good, and it's right up my alley. Sam Winters wants me to manage a couple of his gambling houses in Chicago. A hundred slugs and a percentage of the take."

"When are you leaving for Chicago?" Henry asked.

"I think I'll leave about Sunday," came the reply.

Henry got up and strode over to the window. After looking out for a moment, he turned around and faced Turk. "How would you like company?"

"Are you kiddin'?"

Henry was smiling. "No, I'm not kidding. I'd like to get out of here too."

"But, Henry, can you just pick up and leave your wife like that?"

"Why not? What's going to prevent me? So I'll just leave, and she can divorce me on any grounds she sees fit."

"Ain't that kind of cold-blooded, Henry? Carlotta is too swell a kid to be treated like that."

Henry walked over to where Turk was standing. He put one hand on his friend's shoulder. "Look, Turk," his voice was cold and serious, "my life is my own to do as I want with it. I married Carlotta, sure, but so have a lot of other men married women, and when the time came, they left. Marriage is a win-or-lose proposition, and they don't give any guarantees with the license. I'm not cut out for marriage any more than you are. I've known it for a long time. All my life I've come and gone as I pleased—no questions asked. I tried, but I can't quite make the grade. Marriage is too confining, it entails too much responsibility and too many personal sacrifices that I don't feel like making. It's a proposition that requires an attitude of complete self-denial that I don't feel prepared to make. I'm a pretty selfish person, Turk. It's too bad, but that's the way I am. I loved Carlotta when I married her, but—"

"But you loved her dough more, ain't that right?"

Henry's face flushed as it always did when he was taken by surprise. Turk went on. "I'm sorry, Henry, I couldn't help throwing that at you. The last time I said something like that, you got mad and I almost wound up a corpse. I don't think you'll get sore at me again, will you?"

Henry sat down on the davenport. "No," he sighed, "you seem to have my number pretty well. I guess there's no sense in trying to fool somebody who knows me as well as you do."

Turk lit a cigarette. "Sure, I know you, Henry, and it's a funny thing—as well as I know you, that's how completely fogged I can be at times."

"Fogged? In what way?"

"By the way I keep sticking to you in spite of the fact that you've been lousy with me. I don't know of anybody that you've actually done any good for. You've only used people for what you can get out of them. And then when you can't get any more from them, you throw them over. I'm pretty sure that if you were to tell the truth about your marriage, that's the reason you're leaving Carlotta. I know you've been living off her ever since you got married, but it's none of my business. I only hated like hell to see the girl get such a raw deal. I don't think she deserved it."

This was the first time Turk had ever gone so far with Henry. He was leaving the city anyway, and if their friendship was to end because of a few truths, that would be all right with him. To his surprise, Henry was docile and not the least bit antagonistic.

"You're right, Turk. She is a swell kid and it's just as well I'm leaving her. She does deserve a better break. I'd only ruin her life."

"And me. Look at what I've taken from you in the years that I've known you. That's the thing that's got me up a tree. There were times when I felt like telling you to go to hell. But it's a funny thing about life and people—you'll take a lot of guff from some, and others you wouldn't waste five minutes of your time on them if you thought they was louses."

Henry stretched himself out comfortably on the sofa. "Do you think I'm a louse?" He wasn't too disturbed by the question or the possibility of its answer.

"I don't know—I've felt like saying yes, plenty of times."

"It would have surprised me more if you'd said no."

"Well, whether I thought so or not, I know it wouldn't bother you too much. You've got a way of brushing off what other people say about you pretty well. I never seen you really get down over anything in the whole time I've known you. Sometimes I wonder myself if that's not a good way to get along. Nobody can hurt you, but a guy who can live that way has to be born hard. Me—I couldn't. It would bother the hell out of me. Are you a good sleeper?"

Henry clasped his hands behind his head. "Excellent."

"That's the thing that gets me. If I did some of the things that you did, I couldn't sleep nights."

"Oh, I don't think it's quite that bad. I've never murdered anybody."

"No, not yet," said Turk dryly. "But I'm not sure you'd let that stand in your way if you wanted something bad enough."

Henry's smile gave way to a more cold seriousness. "I don't know. I never thought about it."

Turk put his cigarette out in the ashtray. "Well, anyway, I've stuck to you through the years. Why, I don't know. I found out years ago you're no good for nobody, and still I stick to you. I suppose it's some kind of power you have over people."

Henry rose from the davenport and walked over to him. "Turk, you're a swell guy, and if I've ever hurt you, I'm sorry. Let's shake hands on our friendship."

Turk took his hand. "You win again, Henry."

There was a faint smile on Henry's face. "You're the tops, Turk. Do you still want company on the train, or would I be imposing?"

"You know better than to ask a question like that."

"Then it's a deal? We'll be together as we used to be?"

Turk returned the smile. "Sure, it's a deal."

Henry took a deep breath of satisfaction. "I think I'm going to like Chicago!"

CHAPTER EIGHT

The cab pulled up in front of a hotel once widely advertised as the tallest in the world. As Henry stepped out, he gazed upward. "Almost like one of our native buildings, eh?"

Turk squinted skyward. "Yeah, pretty big at that." He paid the driver, and they entered the hotel.

"Front, boy," called the commanding voice of the room clerk as the desk bell sounded. "Room 2210 for these gentlemen."

They were whisked upward in a high-speed elevator and shown to a double room.

"Not bad," commented Henry as he looked about.

"I've seen 'em and slept in 'em a whole lot worse," laughed Turk.

"I'm going to wash up and then take a stroll," said Henry, walking into the bathroom. "I haven't been in Chicago in about ten years. I want to see if the town has changed any."

"The pleasure's all yours," yawned Turk, "I'm gonna sleep."

By the time Henry left the room, the only sound beside the click of the closing door was the rhythm of Turk's deep snores. Henry walked out of the lobby and found himself on Madison Street. He headed east and, in a few minutes of idle rambling, came to the intersection of State and Madison Streets. He paused just long enough to cross with the policeman's whistle for the east-west traffic, and continued until he came to Michigan Avenue. The boulevard was alive with scurrying traffic, endless streams of cars and buses jammed the broad thoroughfare, and taxis were everywhere. At the corner, Henry hesitated for a moment trying to decide whether to walk north or south. North seemed more intriguing, and he threw back his shoulders and set out along Chicago's famous boulevard.

He enjoyed his walk thoroughly and estimated he had covered a full mile and a half in his journey along Chicago's Near North Side. He had better start back; that would give him a round trip of three miles, a good day's exercise for anybody, and then he could rest up for an hour or so before dinner.

But first he would find a washroom. Where would a likely place be? He glanced around. Across the street was the swanky Blake Hotel. He crossed the boulevard with the green light and walked southward to the side street entrance of the hotel. The uniformed doorman pulled open the door with a smile as Henry approached.

"Good afternoon, doctor," he said in cheery greeting.

"Good afternoon," Henry replied, a little puzzled. He walked up the short flight of stairs to the lobby and looked about for a bell boy. The only one to be seen at the moment was heading for the elevators with two suitcases, followed by an elderly woman. There was no one else available, so Henry approached the desk. The clerk smiled pleasantly. "Good afternoon, doctor, you're a little early today. Would you like your k—" suddenly the clerk's expression changed to bewilderment. "Oh, excuse me, sir, I thought you were Dr. Bartok! Why, I've never seen anything like it! Are you his twin brother?"

Henry smiled pleasantly at this mistaken identity. "No, I'm afraid not. In fact I'm not even acquainted with the gentleman."

"Now I can tell very easily," laughed the clerk. "Dr. Bartok speaks with a foreign accent."

Henry nodded. "Oh, I see."

The still blinking clerk went on. "Not only that, but he has a large scar on his right cheek. Or is it his left? I'm not sure which cheek it's on, but anyway if it weren't for the scar and the foreign accent, he could easily be you! The resemblance is the most remarkable thing I ever saw."

Henry treated the matter indifferently. "Well, I suppose those things happen. I've heard of people having doubles, but I didn't know I had one." Then, dismissing the subject, "By the way, can you tell me where the men's room is?"

"Yes, sir. Down those stairs and you'll find it in the arcade."

Henry thanked him and walked toward the stairway. He smiled satisfaction. He must have a professional air. Being addressed as "doctor" touched off a spark and made him think about what might have been. Too late now. He pushed open one of the swinging doors marked "Men."

The colored porter was sitting in a corner, his head dropped in peaceful siesta. At Henry's entrance, he was on his feet in a flash, his great expanse of white teeth dazzling against his coal black skin. "Aftuhnoon, doctuh, aftuhnoon." His broad smile was exceeded by his obsequious bows.

"Hello," Henry answered as he returned the smile. Another one!

Here was the third to mistake him for the doctor. Just for the fun of it, he would adopt a bit of a foreign accent and see how far he could go without the porter's detecting the difference. He continued on through the second set of swinging doors and in a few moments reappeared.

The still smiling porter was awaiting him, standing by a half-filled basin of clean water with a fresh towel draped across his arm.

"Yessuh, heah you are, doctuh; how you today, doctuh?"

"Fine, thank you, George, how are you?" Henry's attempt at a foreign accent seemed amusing to his own ears.

"Ah'm fine, doctuh, only mah name's Bill. George is the night man." He handed Henry the towel for his dripping hands. "Kinda unusual to see you 'round heah this time o' day, doctuh."

"Yes, it is a bit unusual. But then, so are a lot of things, is that not so?" Henry smirked at his own skill in adopting a continental dialect.

"Right you are, doctuh, right you are!" The porter broke into a hearty laugh, as his giant whisk broom fell with vigorous strokes against Henry's coat.

"Here you are, Bill." Henry proffered a quarter.

"Thank you, doctuh, thank you. Aftuhnoon, doctuh."

"Goodbye."

Henry walked out into the avenue and started southward to his hotel. With each block his amusement over the incident grew. By the time he had reached Randolph and Michigan, where stands the block-long Chicago Public Library, his amusement had given way to curiosity. Who was Dr. Bartok? What kind of a doctor was he? What did he specialize in? Where was his office located? What kind of a clientele did he have? What was his background? Was he married or single? What was his nationality? The questions tripped over one another as they raced through Henry's brain. Could some of them be answered? Maybe they could; he walked up the steps of the big library and made his way to the information desk.

"Excuse me, do you have a directory listing the licensed physicians and surgeons, and something of their histories?"

"Yes, we do," replied the young woman. "That is, we have one listing those who are members of the American Medical Association, and another called *Who's Who in Medicine*."

"That's fine. May I see it, please?"

Henry was directed to the reference section of the library and soon a large book was being handed down to him from one of the upper shelves. He carried it to a wide table and opened it. The pages slithered by as his fingers hastily shuffled through them. Barker, Barlow, Barlund, Bart, Barten, Bartok, Viktor Emil—specializing in neuropsychiatry; born August 10, 1897, Prague, Czechoslovakia; son of Anna Drachas and Edouard Bartok, Slovak Minister to Rumania, 1904-1910. Graduate of University of Prague; assoc. prof. of neurology, Univ. of Vienna; Ass't. Chief, Polyclinic Hosp., Vienna; Prof. Experimental and Applied Neurology, Univ. of Leipzig; Chief of Staff, The Copenhagen Institute of Mental Diseases; came to United States in 1933, was professor of Neurology at University of Fort Dearborn, 1934-1937; Mem. of Lecture staff, University of Fort Dearborn, also honorary prof. of Neurology. Went into private practice in February 1927. Awarded Nobel Prize in 1936 for discovery of treatment for schizophrenia by insulin shock. Author of three textbooks on *Neuropsychiatric Diseases and Their Treatment*; author of *Modern Psychiatry through Psychoanalysis*; *The Neuroses of the Twentieth Century*, and *Man and the Mind*. Bachelor. Mem. A.A.A.S.; A.M.A.; Amer. Neurol. Ass'n.; Amer. Physiol. Soc., Amer. Therapeutic Soc.; Mem. Neuropsychiatric Ass'n.; Mem. The Athletic Club, Columbus Yacht Club, Townhouse Club, Bridle and Cycle Club, Forest Hills Country Club. Residence, Blake Hotel. Office, 34 No. Michigan Ave., Chicago, Ill. By appointment only.

Henry slowly closed the book, but only after he had reread the page several times. So that was the history of Dr. Bartok! Now he knew who this man was whom he so closely resembled. No less a personality than a specialist in mental diseases, and what a background! Professor of neurology at three universities and a Nobel Prize winner! Henry sat there for a few minutes in a state of complete abstraction. He suddenly opened the book and read the page again. Member of five clubs! He must be wealthy and pretty much of a socialite to belong to that many clubs. Then his choice of residence, the Blake Hotel— one of Chicago's finest and most expensive. His practice must be large, and above all, of the caliber that could afford to pay the rates that a top specialist in the psychiatric field would charge. Henry took a pencil and a piece of paper from his pocket and copied the page down. He returned the book to the shelf and left.

As he walked slowly back to his hotel, Henry could think of nothing except the irony of the fact that this man should be a specialist in psychiatry—the subject that had always fascinated him. The trick that nature had played in fashioning two persons so much alike, even to their intellectual interests, amazed him. Before he could be thoroughly convinced of the identical likeness of Dr. Bartok and himself, he would have to have further proof. Either the proof of his own eyes, or someone who knew him, but who had never seen Dr. Bartok. That person would be Turk. Turk was the only one in Chicago who knew Henry well enough to be able to make a convincing comparison. If Turk said they looked alike, that would satisfy Henry. And what if Turk said he and Dr. Bartok looked as much alike as two peas in a pod? Then what? What would be accomplished or gained? Henry decided he wouldn't think about that now. He bought a paper at the corner newsstand and made for his hotel. He was glad it was near dinner time. He felt hungry after his long walk.

It wasn't until Turk and he had finished dinner that Henry told his friend about the strange incident. Turk showed little interest over the tale of Henry's mistaken identity, and sought to dismiss the subject with a shrug of the shoulders.

"So what?" he frowned. "So you was mistaken for a doctor! I was mistaken for Ned Sparks once. That don't make me a movie star. So because you was mistaken for a doctor, that don't mean you can go around with a little black bag and examine people!"

Henry smiled faintly. "No, but it might mean I could possibly resume the study of an old favorite of mine, psychoanalysis."

Turk looked at him with a quizzical expression. "What're you talking about?"

"Read this," replied Henry, as he handed him the copy of Dr. Bartok's history. Turk took quite a few minutes to digest the thumbnail sketch of the neurologist's career. Then he uttered a long "Hmmmm," as he settled back in his chair. "This boy's really got it on the ball, ain't he? Where'd you get the dope?"

"From the reference department of the Public Library."

"So this guy's a famous psychiatrist?"

"Famous and wealthy, if I'm not mistaken."

"How can you tell?"

"Look at the clubs he belongs to. One of them's a yacht club, which means he owns a boat. You don't own boats on peanuts. He lives at the Blake, one of the best hotels. It all adds up, to my way of thinking, that Dr. Bartok, the eminent psychiatrist, is definitely in the upper brackets. And besides, if the directory is up to date, he's a bachelor."

Turk leaned forward. "Okay. I follow you so far. Three people in the Blake took you for this Dr. Bartok, who is a famous psychiatrist, and according to your way of thinking, he's up in the bucks. So what has that got to do with you, and where do you fit into the picture?"

Henry took a pencil from his pocket and began to draw meaningless lines on the tablecloth. "Turk," he said casually, "did you ever try to fit the pieces of a giant jigsaw puzzle together? If you have, you know it sometimes takes a long time and a lot of patience."

Turk lit a cigarette. "And you're going to try to make a jigsaw puzzle out of this?"

"No, not exactly. You asked me where do I fit into this picture? That's what I'm going to try to find out. But first of all, I've got to get a few things settled in my mind. Number one: do I resemble Dr. Bartok as much as these people thought? That's where you come in."

"Me?"

"Yeah. I want you to do me a favor. Tomorrow I want you to go up and see this Dr. Bartok and get a look at him."

Turk's face showed evidence of his lack of enthusiasm over the idea. Then grudgingly he spoke. "What kind of an excuse can I give for coming up?"

"Very simple. Just tell the girl at the desk you're waiting for a friend who is supposed to meet you up there. Tell her this friend is to be a new patient."

"Yeah? Then what?"

Henry emphasized his instructions with the point of his pencil: "Then you just sit there and take in everything that you can. Time your visit so that you get there about eleven-thirty. Doctors are bound to go to lunch somewhere between twelve and two."

Turk looked unhappy. "Suppose this guy don't eat lunch?"

"Then we'll talk about it some other time. Anyhow, the visit won't be for nothing, because you'll be able to tell me a lot about his office, and the type of people he caters to."

"And when you know that, where are you?" asked Turk casually as he blew out a cloud of blue smoke and glanced up.

Henry smiled. "Who knows? Maybe I'll be in a better position to fit some of the pieces of the jigsaw puzzle together." He spied the waiter. "Check, please."

That evening Henry's thoughts were a jumble of speculations and schemes.

The operator phoned the room at nine the next morning, and he and Turk had breakfast in the hotel coffee shop. After they had finished eating, they settled down for an hour until the selected time for Turk's mission to Dr. Bartok's office. "By the way," continued Turk, "when I speak to Sam about his proposition, should I ask him about a place for you? After all, you're going to need a job. Whatever you've got with you ain't going to last forever."

"Yes, I know, Turk, and it's swell of you, but let's wait until I've had an opportunity to look at a couple of other things. If these certain other things don't materialize, I'll be more than appreciative if you talk with Sam about me."

"Any time at all, Henry. Just say the word."

"Thanks." Henry slid further down in the comfortable chair and soon his eyes closed in a welcome nap. It seemed only five minutes before he was jarred out of his deep slumber by Turk's hand on his shoulder.

"Sorry to wake you, Henry, you looked so peaceful, but I just wanted to let you know it's time for me to go up to this doctor's office. What's the address again, 34 North Michigan?"

"That's right," Henry answered sleepily. "And don't forget what I told you. I'll be right here waiting for you."

"Okay. See you later." Turk picked up his hat and coat from one of the nearby chairs and left.

Now that Turk had actually departed on this strange mission, Henry found it difficult to relax. He tried to doze again but he was now in no mood for sleep. Within an hour he had been in and out of four different chairs. He walked over to the newsstand, and bought a magazine. He skimmed through the pages, hardly noticing the contents, and then threw the magazine down on a chair. He got up, walked around the lobby, and then came back. With the idea that a little fresh air would feel good, he got his hat and coat from his room and went outside. On Madison Street, he found the lunch hour had brought out droves of workers who pushed and jostled him. It was a poor time for a walk, and he returned to the lobby. For a while he sat with his hat and coat on, and then became overheated. He took off the heavy ulster, and threw it on a chair. This time he found a newspaper on the davenport and occupied himself for the next half hour with the news. When he glanced at his watch, Henry discovered that the time was only one-fifteen. It was two hours since Turk had left. Two hours—more difficult to kill than any that he could remember since he was at Mohawk. When he caught sight of Turk entering the lobby a half-hour later, his heart began to palpitate. As Turk approached, he noticed that there was a look of serious concern written on his face. Turk did not smile or greet him. He said, "Let's go upstairs and talk!"

By the time they entered the room, Henry was near the bursting point. As the lock in the door clicked, he exclaimed in a voice that clearly indicated his high pitch of excitement. "Well, for Christ's sake, talk, will you?"

Turk walked over to one of the chairs and sat down with his hat and coat still on. He looked at Henry with a dazed blank expression. "If I hadn't seen it with my own eyes, I'd of said it ain't possible—it couldn't happen, except in a movie!"

Henry grabbed a chair and pulled it up close to Turk. "You mean—"

Turk interrupted and spoke in a slow methodical voice that was devoid of all trace of emotion or excitement. "I mean this guy Bartok is you—*from head to foot. Same face, same build, same height, same hair, everything.* I've never seen anything like it. Are you sure you ain't got a twin brother?"

"Of course not. So I could really pass for him, huh?"

Turk took a long breath. "Pass for him? I'll bet if you changed your voice, and talked in that foreign brogue he uses, you could come back from lunch and be him!"

Henry leaned back in his chair, and a faintly saturnine smile crept across his face. "Really?" He tilted the chair backward and clasped his hands behind his head. "That's peculiar—"

Turk shook his finger in a gesture of warning. "Look, Henry, I don't know what's in back of that scheming mind of yours, but it sounds to me like what you're cooking up don't smell very kosher. I only went up there to get a gander at this guy because you were all hot and bothered about it. You got me to wondering, so I went up there strictly to satisfy my curiosity, that's all."

Henry answered him softly and with a distinct attempt at being placative. "All right, Turk, all right. I was just inquisitive, that's all. Don't go jumping at conclusions. You can't blame a person for getting a little excited. After all, it isn't every day that you find you have a double walking around. Particularly, when it turns out to be such a perfect double—almost."

Turk finally removed his coat and hat. His suspicions of Henry seemed allayed for the moment. "Yeah, almost is right. If it wasn't for that foreign accent, it would be perfect."

"I wasn't thinking of only that. Tell me, Turk, hasn't Dr. Bartok got a scar on one of his cheeks?"

There was a slight pause while Turk wrinkled his brow in thought. "I don't know, Henry, I didn't notice. He was in a hurry when he walked out."

"I'm pretty sure there is, but anyhow tell me something else. What kind of an office has he and what sort of people were in the reception room?"

"Well, from what I could see he's got a pretty rich bunch of people on his books. His office is very modern, and all in mahogany. That's what the girl said it was. I did what you told me to. I said I was waiting for a man who was to be a new patient. She wanted to know who recommended him and so forth. Then she said she wasn't even sure Dr. Bartok would be able to fit him in. She said he had pretty near a full schedule now. It seems that he gives each patient one hour. That means he don't see more than about eight people a day."

Henry was scratching his chin. "That's right, unless he has hours in the evening."

"The girl said he don't work nights," replied Turk as he twirled his hat around in his hands. "I only saw three patients the whole time I was there. One was a man and two were women. Both the women were dressed very expensive and wore a lot of diamonds, and the man looked like he could be a banker."

"That's very interesting," said Henry, as he walked over and sat on the edge of the bed. "So far, my guesses all seem to be correct. Now, I'll make one more. I'll venture to say that Dr. Bartok doesn't get less than fifty dollars a visit."

Turk whistled. "Fifty dollars a visit? That would be four hundred dollars a day. That's twenty-four hundred bucks a week!"

"Correct." Henry smiled. "And even if he got only twenty-five dollars a visit that would still be twelve hundred a week! The chances are he wouldn't be bothered for twenty-five dollars. He's too big a man. Ordinary psychiatrists charge up to twenty-five a visit."

Turk still blinked in amazement. "Jeez, that means this Bartok knocks off about a hundred grand a year!"

"At least. The chances are he makes closer to a hundred and fifty thousand a year."

"That ain't hay," exclaimed Turk. "Judas Priest, I didn't know doctors could make that kind of dough."

"Very few do," replied Henry. "A few top specialists can make that kind of money. The funny part of it is, Dr. Bartok makes that kind of money for doing nothing but psychoanalyzing people. In other words, talking to them. Drawing them out—asking them about their early childhood, and about their parents, and their home life. Some psychiatrists specialize in dream analysis. I don't know whether Dr. Bartok does or not."

"What's that?" inquired Turk with decided interest.

"That's a method used to psychoanalyze certain type of neuroses, by the interpretation of the patient's subconscious mind, which expresses itself in the form of dreams. Through the interpretation of these dreams, the doctor tries to discover what caused the neurosis, and how to cure it." It amused Henry to see how far Turk was out of his depth.

"Gee, you certainly know a lot about it."

"For years it was a hobby of mine. I read every book I could get my hands on—and six years gave me plenty of time! I was always fascinated with how the human mind works, and why some people develop distinct psychoneurotic tendencies that throw their lives completely out of kilter. I think almost every person alive has one or more deficiencies in their makeup, but they only become patients of a neurologist when they allow those deficiencies to take over their mind and enslave it. Most neuroses are directly or indirectly traceable to fear and frustration. Frustration is almost as bad as fear. People want to express themselves in some way and if they can't, the desire to accumulates day by day and grows and expands, until the individual finds it impossible to stand up under the mental pressure and then something gives way."

"Jeez, I'll bet you know as much as them quacks do!" Turk exclaimed, "with all that studyin' you wouldn't have no trouble getting people to pay you twenty-five dollars a visit!"

Henry laughed. "Oh, no? There's a little matter of a doctor's license which I don't possess. That, and an office, and a reputation. But there's somebody who does have all those things, and the practice already built to go with it. Namely, one Dr. Viktor Bartok."

Turk, picking his teeth with a toothpick he had found in his vest pocket, interposed, "—Who looks enough like Henry Mueller to be his twin brother!"

"Let's think about it the other way around. Henry Mueller, who looks enough like Dr. Bartok to be the eminent psychiatrist himself!"

Turk eyed him suspiciously. "That's a pretty tall order, ain't it?"

Henry pursed his lips. "Oh, I don't know. All depends on how you look at it. Nothing ventured, nothing gained, and a hundred thousand a year is a pretty sweet income."

"Yeah, especially for just sitting and talking to a lot of rich people who ain't got nothing else to do with their money."

"I couldn't think of a pleasanter and more fascinating way of making money." Henry walked over to the dresser, picked up a comb and ran it carefully through his thick wavy hair. "And I wouldn't mind living at the Blake, swimming at the Athletic Club, or yachting in Lake Michigan."

"For a guy who's only about six months out of Mohawk, that's pretty big talk."

Henry turned around and faced his companion. "Turk, there's an old saying: 'Think small, be small.'"

"You're pretty sure of yourself, ain't you?"

"I'd much prefer to think of myself as a man who possesses a great deal of self-confidence. It's a very important attribute. When a man loses confidence in himself, he's really on the downgrade. I very much like the idea, Turk, of showing others how to acquire that confidence, and teach them how to go about banishing their fears and frustrations."

"What do you expect this guy Bartok to do? Just turn over his practice to you? Make you a present of his office?"

"No, not exactly. Something as imposing as that can't be had for the mere snap of a finger. Stepping into Dr. Bartok's shoes is going to be no easy matter."

"Stepping into Dr. Bartok's shoes?" Turk sank slowly into a chair. "Are you out of your mind?"

"Not at all."

"You're kidding."

"What makes you think I'm kidding?"

"You'd have to be. What you're cooking up in your mind is crazy. It's going to get you scratched again."

"Oh, I don't know. Sometimes the only difference between crazy and real is energy, courage, and vision. Twice in my life I was told I didn't have any guts. I'm going to prove to myself that I have. Because what I'm contemplating requires courage of the greatest kind."

"Henry! Cut the jokes. What you're talking about is *murder!*"

Henry assumed a pained expression. "Please, Turk, don't use the word murder. It's so unpleasant. Let's just say a sort of 'disappearance' of a certain individual."

"Dr. Bartok."

"No, not at all. Dr. Bartok doesn't disappear. Henry Mueller disappears. Of course, if you want to be technical about it, I suppose you could say the real Dr. Bartok fades out of the picture, and another person carries on where the original Dr. Bartok left off. But as far as the world is concerned, the only person who actually disappears is Henry Mueller. Only one other man besides myself will know the truth—Gil Turkel."

"And how do you know I won't blow the whistle for the cops?"

Henry smiled broadly, but there was cruelty written in the smile. "You won't. For one thing, Gil Turkel is my pal, and pals don't double-cross—not real pals. For another thing, this is much too risky a proposition for anything to go wrong. In fact, since we're pals, I'll cut you in on a fifty-fifty take. That ought to make everything—shall we say, even-Stephen?"

Turk rose from the chair, and began putting on his hat and coat. "No, thanks. You can deal me out. Whatever you do about this crazy scheme, you're strictly on your own. I don't want no part of it. As far as you ever having to worry about my spilling my mouth, forget it. It ain't in me to pull a double-cross on a friend and blackmail ain't my business." He started for the door. "See you later. I'm going out and get some fresh air. I need it."

Henry watched him as he closed the door behind him. He took a fifty-cent piece from his pocket and flipped it in the air.

CHAPTER NINE

The following day Turk met Sam Winters. They had a two-hour conference, and it turned out better than Turk had hoped. One hundred dollars a week guaranteed, and five percent of the profits. He would divide his time between Winters' two North Side houses and see that everything ran smoothly. Turk didn't have to worry about raids, or getting into trouble with the police. Sam Winters was a well-known gambler with a wealthy patronage and knew enough politicians to get police protection.

Turk returned to the hotel to tell Henry about the deal, and that he was going to take a room in one of the furnished apartment hotels on the North Side in order to be near his houses. Much to his surprise, when he entered, he found Henry packing his suitcase.

"Going somewhere?" inquired Turk.

"Yes, I'm checking out." Henry closed the lid and snapped it shut. "I think it's better this way. There's a few things we don't see eye to eye on."

"You're damn right. When it comes to fooling around with killing, I draw the line. As far as doing time behind the bars, I'm still batting zero, and that's the way I want it."

Henry slid the suitcase off the bed and set it down on the floor. "Sure, Turk, that's all right with me. You go your way and I'll go mine. You told me that night in your room back in New York that you often felt like telling me off anyway. So it's a deal. No hard feelings. Incidentally, how did you make out with Winters?"

Turk sat down on the bed. "I go to work for him starting tomorrow night. He's a right guy to deal with, too."

"Did you get your five percent take?"

"He gave me everything I asked for."

"Wonderful. You should be able to make at least fifteen thousand a year."

"Yeah. That's what I figure. I'm going to have to move to be near the places."

"Oh? Then it's just as well I'm leaving."

"It's too bad we can't live together like we always did."

"No, it's just as well we don't. My plans are indefinite and if they should follow certain trends, I'm sure you wouldn't want to be involved."

"You're right, Henry, not if you're going to carry out this crazy idea about that quack. I still say it's crazy."

"We won't talk about it. Nobody's going to make up my mind for me. But you must know me well enough by now to know that once I get my plans made, I don't allow anything to stop me." There was grimness in Henry's voice.

Turk was taking off his overcoat. "Yeah, I know, Henry. That's what scares me. I'd hate to see you get into trouble again."

"Don't worry. This time I'll be careful." Henry threw his coat over his arm. "Well, goodbye, Turk. I'll be seeing you around."

Henry found a cheap room on Superior Street, a few blocks away from the Blake Hotel. He rented it under the name of Henry Milton and paid the landlady a month's rent in advance. He chose an obscure room in the back of the building, not because he liked it but because he felt that the less conspicuous he was, the better it would be.

Living in a back room, small and dingy, with cheap furniture and a hard bed, would only be temporary. Soothing thoughts of luxury and wealth, of cabin cruisers and country clubs, of clothes and cars, and of fawning socialites, lulled Henry to sleep in his new and distasteful surroundings.

The following days were spent in "casing" Dr. Bartok. Within a week, Henry had a notebook with a day-by-day record of Dr. Bartok's activities as complete in detail as one accumulated by an F.B.I. operative. Every move, every action was registered and cataloged. Each morning at eight o'clock Henry was inconspicuously strolling about in front of the Palmolive Building across the street from the Blake. He found that in good weather Dr. Bartok walked to his office, in bad weather he took a taxi or used the bus. When he did walk to the office, Henry trailed him half a block or so behind. He discovered little mannerisms and habits that he did not like. Dr. Bartok was a chain smoker; he apparently smoked an average of two packs of strong Turkish cigarettes a day. This was a real source of concern to Henry, since he had always detested the tobacco habit. Now, he would have to force himself to become a smoker. It was unpleasant, but a necessary evil.

When Bartok left his office each evening around six-thirty, Henry was a pedestrian engaged in window shopping. By now he had grown a small moustache and wore a pair of dark glasses. The shabby appearance of his clothes, the sharply pulled down snap brim on his felt hat, along with the other newly acquired props, hid his resemblance to the psychiatrist.

Among other things, Henry discovered that the doctor owned a Cadillac sedan which he seldom used except in the evenings when he had some social engagement. The car was kept in the North-Lake Garage, the name of which was plainly printed on the motorcycle which the hiker usually attached to the rear bumper, for use on the return trip to the garage.

On many evenings, Henry trailed Dr. Bartok to the 1220 North Lake Shore Drive Apartments, which was just a few blocks from the Blake. He wondered with whom the doctor spent so much time in this building, and waited hours in an effort to learn the identity of this person whom he had never seen leaving or entering with Bartok. If it was a woman, why was Bartok so secretive? If it was a private patient to whom he was administering a home treatment, which was unlikely, why wasn't he down in an hour, the maximum time usually given by a psychiatrist? Henry was convinced, as he paced up and down at the far end of the block, that these were social visits, spent with a woman.

The important thing to Henry, as the days went by, was how to go about plotting the disappearance of his quarry. The doctor's habits and private life were a primary consideration. Before Henry could form any plans to dispose of Bartok, it was necessary to know as much about his personal life as possible. This was a thousand times more complex than just planning the potential killing of an individual. In addition to disposing of Dr. Bartok's body so that it would never be discovered, Henry had to know in minute detail the part he was to play. In short, not only did this venture require the perfect murder, but also the perfect masquerade. The slightest wrong move, the smallest slip in his plans, and he not only would go back to jail, but to the electric chair. Henry was determined that this would never happen.

It was almost the end of March when Henry began seriously to plot the murder of Dr. Bartok. His notebook was now filled with every move, action and habit of the man he had been trailing and studying for a month. Each day had been recorded and indexed. By a series of telephone calls, he had managed to learn the name and something of the background of Evelyn Hahn, the doctor's secretary. On several occasions he had even spoken to Dr. Bartok himself on the telephone, on the pretext of being a prospective patient. In this way he had been able to study the doctor's voice, accent, and inflections.

After half a dozen or more methods of doing away with Dr. Bartok had been decided upon and discarded, Henry came to his final and definite decision. The actual killing would have to take place in Dr. Bartok's own car for a quick and safe getaway. It must be done speedily and silently, and would have to be bloodless. Having possession of the car, Henry would then be in a position to drive to a previously selected point somewhere along the Desplaines River, and with rope and iron weights, dump the body into the stream. All this would have to be done on an especially dark night and on a night other than the night of the murder. Then it would be comparatively easy to strip the clothes from the body and make a complete switch in wearing apparel. Once this was accomplished, he could return to the city in the doctor's clothes and car. From that moment on, he would be Dr. Viktor Bartok.

But how was he to go about getting access to Dr. Bartok's car while the doctor himself was in it? Then too, Dr. Bartok had a large crescent-shaped scar on his cheek which extended to the corner of his mouth. The foreign accent could easily be copied. The scar would be an entirely different matter. Flesh scars cannot be faked. The only way a flesh scar could be duplicated would be—Henry shuddered. For the present he would concentrate on the more important issue of determining how, when, and where to acquire the doctor's car. That would be the answer to only half of the puzzle, but once accomplished, Henry knew the other pieces would fall into place.

Several days later while Henry was loitering across the street from the Blake, the doctor's car pulled up to the curb with the North-Lake Garage motorcycle attached to the rear bumper. A moment later Bartok appeared. He exchanged greetings with the hiker and drove off. Suddenly everything became crystal-clear in Henry's mind. Of course! That was the solution! If he could get a job with the North-Lake Garage as a hiker, he would have access to the doctor's car. Sooner or later, Bartok would be bound to drive up to the garage late at night to pick up one of the men and be driven home. That hiker must be Henry Mueller. He tingled all over with excitement as the possibilities of this new thought pyramided in his brain. All he had to do was acquire a job with the North-Lake Garage and then get on the night shift!

Henry lost no time in applying to the North-Lake Garage for a job as hiker. They were all filled up at the present, he was told, but there might be an opening soon. He left his name and phone number and went back home.

That night Henry sat down with a map of Chicago before him to plot the course he would pursue following the murder of Dr. Bartok. He knew that sooner or later he would be employed by the garage. There is usually a fast turnover with garage hands. He was in no hurry. In the meantime, he would plan everything so that there would be the fewest possible difficulties. For one thing, it was now time to give serious consideration to the scar on Dr. Bartok's cheek.

Henry had never seen the doctor's face closely, but he had purchased copies of most of Dr. Bartok's works on psychiatry in which he found pictures of his intended victim. The scar was plainly discernible on the left cheek, and Henry carefully measured the size and area on his own face. According to his calculations, the scar was about one-quarter inch wide by two and three-quarter inches in length, and at the time of injury was perhaps a quarter of an inch deep. It was definitely crescent-shaped, with the top of the crescent even in line with the middle of the ear, and the bottom touching the corner of the mouth. Possibly it was the result of a sword or saber gash received in a fraternal duel, for facial scars were considered a mark of heroism and distinction in some European universities and the owners bore them with pride. It seemed logical to believe that this was how Dr. Bartok had acquired his. This would be no simple matter, Henry thought, carving a strip of flesh out of his face the dimensions of Bartok's scar. It would have to be at least an eighth of an inch deep and a wound of that depth would require stitching. There was a hospital a few blocks away; he could run over there and have the stitches put in by any of the staff men, and say that he had been in an auto accident, that his face had been cut by flying glass from the windshield. But the possibility that someone at the nearby hospital would know Dr. Bartok and recognize the similarity was too great. Not only that, but the attending physician might ask too many questions and he would feel safer if there were no hospital records. No, that was risky; that would be leaving himself open for too many opportunities for investigation. He must do it all himself. After all, he had had two years of medical school. It wouldn't be too difficult; just a simple superficial incision that would require a few stitches. He tried to bolster his courage. He knew that it sounded a lot simpler than it was going to be. It takes a hell of a lot of guts to perform something like that on oneself, Henry concluded with a certain satisfaction. Very few so-called brave guys would be willing to stand in front of a mirror and lay open the side of their cheek, deliberately carve out a strip of human flesh dripping with precious blood, and then stand there and carefully insert the needle through the skin, back and forth until the wound was closed. If that didn't require guts, Henry told himself, then nothing did.

That afternoon he went to a surgical supply house and returned with a small scalpel, hemostat, needles, suture, hypodermic syringe with anesthetic, scissors, cotton, bandages, adhesive tape, rubber gloves, sterilizing agents, grain alcohol, and smelling salts—just in case. For a minor operation it seemed like a lot of instruments and precautionary measures, but he was taking no chances.

Henry had had nothing but a cup of coffee all day, so he thought maybe the peculiar feeling in his stomach was hunger pangs. Maybe he should get some food inside to give himself strength for the task. He went to a good restaurant and had a steak. Before he had finished, he was nauseated. He knew now that the peculiar sensation he had experienced earlier was not a hunger pang. He left the restaurant in a hurry and reached his room in time to vomit everything he had eaten. He lay down on the bed, quivering all over. So, he thought to himself, the thing had really gotten him down. He was really weaker physically than he had imagined. He couldn't take it! In a few minutes he was soaking wet with cold perspiration. He got up and went over to the window and raised it all the way. He pulled up a chair and sat down, taking deep breaths of the cool, fresh air. He shouldn't have tried to eat; he would know better the next time. Anyhow, everything was off for tonight. He was now in no condition to undergo or even attempt the operation.

The next morning Henry had a very light breakfast of orange juice, toast, and coffee; he ate nothing the rest of the day. When evening came, he fortified himself for the ordeal with several shots of whiskey which he ordinarily never touched. Then he went to his room, boiled all the instruments, cleansed and scrubbed himself, spread the instruments out on a clean towel, and after rinsing his hands with alcohol, shook some sterile powder into the rubber gloves and pulled them on. He reshaved his left cheek to eliminate any stubble, sterilized the skin with alcohol, and filled up the hypodermic syringe with anesthetic. He then chose a likely spot on his cheek to insert the needle. He winced as the sharp prick found its way into the flesh. Slowly he pushed the plunger down and emptied the contents.

He felt the novocaine taking effect, and the entire left side of his face slowly began to numb. Ten minutes later Henry decided he was ready for the knife. He pinched his face all over for a test and felt absolutely nothing. He knew he would feel no pain when the knife cut deeply into the skin, but nonetheless tiny beads of perspiration stood out on his forehead as he picked up the scalpel. He had always been deathly afraid of a knife. The picture of Dr. Bartok lay before him in the open book. He measured once more the area to be opened … from a half-inch below the cheek bone to the corner of the mouth. Steadying his hand, he sank the razor edge of the scalpel a quarter of an inch below the surface of the skin. The glistening instrument in his fingers parted the flesh as if by magic. Steady, steady, he told himself … cut evenly—deeply—begin to curve toward the mouth—now start rounding here—cotton to catch the blood—continue cutting—now only a half inch to go—steady—steady.

Minutes later Henry examined the neat patch on his left cheek. He gave the adhesive a last pressure with his fingers and stepped back from the mirror, complimenting himself on his skill in doing such a neat job of cutting and stitching. His medical training had certainly helped him here. This was an incident in his life he would not soon forget. Guts? He wished Warden Riley could have watched him. He pulled off the rubber gloves, washed the instruments and put them away, then decided it was time to lie down and rest. He felt a little quaky. It next occurred to him that the anesthetic would soon be wearing off and he had better take a few aspirins to combat the pain that his cheek would soon be giving him. He had no opiates to give himself, so the aspirins would have to suffice.

Henry's head sank into the soft pillow on his bed. To sleep, to dream about pleasures yet to come, about a life filled with adventures yet to be lived! Only one more obstacle to overcome—to eliminate the man whose existence was the only barrier between him and the starring role he was to play. But all in due time! The first act was now ended—there would be only a short intermission before the second act of this strange drama would soon be unfolding.

The heavy slumber into which he had fallen saved Henry from consciousness of the excruciating pain that came with the wearing off of the anesthesia.

In the ensuing days, Henry did little except to keep tab on Dr. Bartok to discover whether there were any phases of his life that he had not uncovered. He took care to approach no closer than a half a block to the doctor. But the unexpected occurred. On one occasion while Henry was outside the 34 North Michigan Building, Dr. Bartok, who had a few moments earlier entered the building, suddenly reappeared. Henry, who had been facing in the opposite direction, unconsciously turned toward the revolving doors as Dr. Bartok emerged. They almost collided.

As he came face to face with Dr. Bartok, Henry's amazement at unexpectedly bumping into him gave way to a horror that almost stopped his heart. He felt his blood run cold and a terrifying feeling of panic overtook him as he saw the scar on the doctor's face. It was on the *right* cheek! Good God! Had he been misled by the photograph? As Dr. Bartok entered a cab standing at the curb and drove off, Henry came to the full realization of his error. His stomach quivered, and he swayed against the building as though he would collapse. His heart, which a second before had literally stood still, was now racing frantically.

How could he have been taken in? There was only one answer. The photograph of Dr. Bartok in all the books Henry had seen showed the scar on his left cheek, because the negative had been reversed by the engraver when the plates were made up. That was the only possible explanation. So, after all his careful schemes and plans, after all the tracing, following, shadowing, recording every move, every action, every habit of Dr. Bartok, he had been tricked by a photograph! There was no retracing his steps now, no way to correct the error. He felt the patch on his face; winced to think of the scar that he would carry with him the rest of his days, and now it was all for nothing! His ambitions, his dreams of becoming someone of prominence, of wealth—everything had suddenly been knocked into a cocked hat!

Henry walked to his room, threw himself down on the bed, and sank his teeth into his lower lip to keep from crying out in anguish. It wasn't an easy matter to forego a setup that was as made to order as this was. He had been defeated in his most pretentious ambition. He had started out to outsmart life, and now life had outsmarted him. He had been thoroughly and decisively beaten, and it was no easy thing for Henry Mueller to admit defeat.

On the following Tuesday, after Henry had finally made up his mind to discard his grandiose scheme, the landlady knocked on his door to tell him there was a telephone call. He went downstairs to take it, certain that it was the North-Lake Garage people as they were the only ones to whom he had given his phone number. He was right in his assumption; it was the manager of the garage, Mr. Johnson. A job was open now. Did he want to take it? He told Johnson he would call back in an hour to let him know. He had been figuring on leaving town and wasn't sure whether or not to accept. Yes, he would definitely let Mr. Johnson know in one hour.

Henry walked back up to his room and the whole problem of Dr. Bartok was again on the fire. Would people remember Bartok's scar was on the right cheek? They wouldn't be sure. Even at this moment Henry couldn't be certain whether the mole on Turk's face was on the right or left side, and he had been close to Turk for a long time. He was almost sure it was the right side, but he wouldn't bet on it. If he stepped into Bartok's shoes—people would be confused—but they couldn't be certain. Should he accept the job and take a chance on getting by with the scar on the wrong cheek? Killing and disposing of Dr. Bartok did not bother him in the least. He had worked out that part of his scheme in perfect detail by diagram and map. The scar was the only hitch. Somehow, he felt he would be able to combat any situation which might arise. His alert brain had always served him in the past; why should it desert him in the future? He was confident it wouldn't. Yes, he would still be able to realize his ambitions, which a few days before had seemed to slip out of his grasp forever. Yes, he would take the job.

Henry's first day working for the North-Lake Garage was spent in familiarizing himself with the customers' names and their cars. He was also shown how to do a greasing job, and then was told to sweep out the lower half of the two-story garage. He was asked if he would mind being shifted to working nights instead of days, as there was more need of help at nights. Henry adroitly showed reluctance in working the night shift but agreed because he needed the money.

In his first three weeks at the garage, he did not get a glimpse of Dr. Bartok. On the few occasions that Bartok used his car, Henry was picking up someone else's and one of the other men drove the doctor home. This was all right with Henry. He wasn't ready for the killing; there were a few small details to be cleared up before the jigsaw puzzle would be ready to complete.

The rainy month of April passed, and the bright warm sun of May bathed Chicago in a welcome spring. Henry slept in the mornings, getting up at two or three in the afternoon. He would spend the rest of the day strolling about Lincoln Park, at the Zoo, or the Chicago Historical Society, or sometimes he would sit near the lagoon. He usually had a copy of one of Dr. Bartok's books with him which he was careful to allow no one to see. He had read most of the psychiatrist's works in the past month; he wanted to absorb as much of the man's theories on psychiatry and psychoanalysis as possible, so that he would have a working idea of his victim's methods. He read aloud to himself in the foreign accent to accustom himself to the dialect.

Although the incision on his face had healed and the stitches had long since been removed, Henry continued to wear an adhesive patch over his cheek. Underneath it was a red scar the exact size and shape of Dr. Bartok's, except that it was on the wrong cheek. To fellow workers who questioned him about the patch, he explained that he had been thrown against the windshield and cut his face while driving with a friend on the road to Milwaukee. It was an acceptable story and no one doubted him. Certainly no one could see any resemblance between this moustachioed, shabby roustabout and the suave, polished, immaculate Dr. Bartok.

With the advent of warm weather, Dr. Bartok had resumed his favorite sport of golf, and on weekends he would drive out to his country club, returning late on Sunday nights. Henry soon learned this and made his final plans. He secured a twenty-foot coil of stout rope, and several heavy pieces of iron and steel to be used as weights. These were thrown casually in an unused corner of the garage, where they would lie until Dr. Bartok called for his car on the fatal morning. Henry would see to it that the rope and the weights were put into the trunk of the car the previous night. He must have them with him when he drove the doctor home on Sunday night, and this he had made up his mind he was going to do. He would make sure that when Bartok's Cadillac drove up to the garage on Sunday night, he and no one else would be on hand to drive the doctor home—the wet, marshy home that Henry had planned for him.

A week later, on Friday night, Henry put the rope and the weights in the trunk of Bartok's car, returned to his room at the end of his shift on Saturday morning, and went to bed. He hoped Dr. Bartok would not discover the things in the rear compartment, but if by chance he should, it would make no difference. Bartok would probably mention when he was being driven home that by mistake someone had put several things in his trunk, and ask to have them removed. That would not interfere in the least with Henry's plans. And even if his victim did not use his car this Saturday to spend the weekend at his country club, there would be other opportunities.

At one o'clock on Saturday afternoon, Dr. Bartok called for his car, and from the manner in which he was dressed—slacks, sweater and sport jacket—it was quite apparent that he was headed for his country club. Henry would have been relieved, but at that moment he was deep in slumber in his room. The car was delivered to Bartok, and he headed north on Lake Shore Drive—his destination being the Crest Hills Country Club.

At eleven forty-five on Sunday night Henry was busy checking the tires on another patron's car when the sharp blast of a horn announced that a car had pulled up in front of the garage. He had purposely busied himself checking tires and batteries, so that he could tell one of the other men to take the call when other customers had driven up. Twice before, during the last hour, he had looked up from his work with bated breath at the sound of a horn outside the entrance, only to find it was the wrong car. This time it took only a fraction of a second for Henry to recognize the green Cadillac car standing at the curb as Dr. Bartok's. It was perfect timing; the other two men were out on pickups. He walked quickly to the car, opened the rear door and seated himself in the back.

"Good evening." Bartok greeted Henry pleasantly as he entered.

"Good evening, sir," came the polite reply.

The car sped away from the curb and headed north on Clark Street. "You're new, aren't you? I don't believe I have ever seen you before."

"Oh, I've been here for a few weeks," Henry answered casually, "I suppose I've always been out on pickups when you drove up."

"Yes, I suppose that is it. I don't use my car much anyway, so I am not too familiar with the men."

The car turned east on Schiller Street. Henry drew a long silk scarf from his pocket and twisted it to form a cord. As Bartok pulled to a stop at Dearborn Street, Henry moved like a panther, threw the corded scarf around the other man's neck and pulled the twisted ends with all his strength. Then he grabbed a small piece of iron pipe about six inches long and pushed it through one of the twists in the scarf, forming a deadly garrote. With each revolution the doctor's struggles became fainter. In less than two minutes, Bartok's head slumped forward. Henry quickly leaped to the front seat, pushed the limp form of Dr. Bartok to one side, and took the wheel. He stepped on the gas, circled the block, and pulled into a dark alley off Clark Street. There he shut off the lights and once more applied the noose to the doctor's neck, just to be on the safe side. He turned the death weapon with all his strength, as a plumber would turn the handle on a threading machine.

When Henry had reached the point where he could no longer turn the handle, he held the pipe steady for a good three minutes in his quivering hands. The perspiration streamed down his face and he breathed as heavily as if he had been running for blocks. This was the climax of what he had planned for weeks, yet he was surprised at his own calm. It wasn't too bad killing a man this way; he didn't feel nauseated as he had the first time he had tried to carve the scar on his face. It was dark in the alley and he couldn't see Bartok's startled bulging eyes, the purplish face distorted with pain, the bared teeth gnashed together in a rictus which had practically severed the extended tongue and left a portion of it dangling loosely by a few strands of flesh, nor the cords in the neck that stood out grotesquely like a chicken's distended gizzard. And it was well that he did not.

Now he must work fast. He must get back to the garage so that his absence would not seem unusually prolonged. He dragged the doctor out of the car, opened the trunk, trussed up the body as well as he could with the rope, lifted the doubled-up lifeless form into the rear compartment and slammed the lid shut. Tomorrow night he would complete the job. At least for now, he would have to go back to the garage as Henry Milton. Just twenty-four hours more and he would become Dr. Viktor Emil Bartok, neuropsychiatrist. He turned the key in the trunk and locked it securely. Then getting into the car, he switched on the lights and started the motor. As he shifted into first, Henry noticed the time on the dash clock. The whole affair had taken only nine minutes, not much more than it would have normally taken to drive the doctor home and return. Henry's nerves tingled with the stimulus of triumphant satisfaction. Everything had gone as smoothly as clockwork. Tomorrow he would get rid of the body and begin his newest and greatest adventure. He pulled into the garage and parked the car, leaving the keys in the ignition, but carefully removing the trunk key. In the morning he would tell the manager that he was leaving, that he had been offered a better job somewhere else. His check could be mailed to the Superior Street address; he would never call for it.

Returning to his room at the end of the shift, Henry removed his dirty working clothes and pulled off the patch on his face. Then he shaved off his moustache and applied a cosmetic pancake base to the scar, which dispersed its redness and made it look like an old wound. He put on his good clothes and packed his bags. The great impersonation was about to begin. He took a last look at himself in the mirror. Yes, there was no question about it—he was a dead ringer for Bartok now, except for the scar. He must convince any doubters that they were mistaken, that the scar had always been on the left cheek. And he must never forget to speak with the doctor's foreign accent. He must keep his wits about him at all times. From now on he would be treading on dangerous ground—the penalty for laxity was death.

Henry closed the door behind him, leaving the hated, dingy room forever. No one in the house saw him leave. He walked to Michigan Avenue and blithely hailed a cab.

"The Blake, please."

As the cab headed north on the drive, Henry began to adjust himself to the actuality of his daring adventure. Unpredictable as the future was, one thing was certain. He would have access to money and all the wonderful things it brought; that was sufficient compensation in itself. And as the Blake came into sight, Henry knew that the third and final act of his carefully staged drama was about to unfold.

CHAPTER TEN

"Good morning, Dr. Bartok," came the cheery voice of the doorman as Henry stepped out of the cab. "Been out of town?"

"Yes, for a few days. Send these things up to my room, will you?"

"You bet, doctor. Take care of them right away."

Henry walked up the stairs to the lobby, and went straight to the desk.

"Good morning, doctor." This was not the same room clerk that he had seen the other time.

"May I have my key," Henry said casually.

"Of course, doctor—and here's some mail for you."

"Thank you." Henry started for the elevators. Again he was greeted by the elevator boy as "doctor." It was working like a charm. If only everything ran this smoothly. He glanced at the key in his hand. Room 824. Without further conversation, he was taken to the eighth floor.

Turning the key in the lock, Henry opened the door and found himself in an exquisitely styled apartment. It was a three-room suite with a large living room, bedroom, and kitchen. In the center of the floor was a soft and luxurious blue-green throw rug. The living room from rugs to ceiling was tropical in atmosphere, with sea-green lamps and shades shaped like Chinese coolie hats. The bamboo-framed pictures on the wall displayed large tropical birds. Above the Chinese-red davenport, and blending perfectly with it, hung a brilliantly executed study of race horses grazing in the pasture, hand painted on linen. In one corner stood a bleached mahogany combination radio and phonograph, with two large cabinets nearby crammed with symphony recordings. Obviously Dr. Bartok had been a lover of the classics and an esthete to boot.

The boy brought up the bags and left. Henry walked about the apartment, visually drinking in the delight of his new home. At one side of the living room was a door that seemed to lead to a closet. Henry opened it to put his things in, and a light automatically switched on, disclosing a mirrored bar stocked with every type of liquor. Rows of imported whiskeys, wines, and liquors lined the shelves. He blinked his eyes at the stock and wished he had cultivated more of a taste for liquor. He had to learn to smoke—Dr. Bartok had been a heavy cigarette smoker and he might as well cultivate a taste for alcohol, too. The characterization must have no flaw, no matter how slight.

He closed the door of the bar, continued his inspection of the apartment. On the table near the window stood a double-framed picture of an attractive woman and a little girl about twelve years old, doubtless some relative. On the mantel were other pictures of an elderly man and a woman, probably Dr. Bartok's mother and father. Henry walked into the bedroom. On the writing desk was an autographed picture of the same attractive woman. He picked it up and read the words: "To my darling brother Viktor with all my love, Meta." So that was Bartok's sister and the little girl was evidently her daughter. Where were they and where did they live? Dr. Bartok had only been in this country a little over six years; perhaps his sister was still in Europe. On the other hand, the writing was in English; perhaps she was in the United States, perhaps even in Chicago! Henry put down the picture and walked to the bedroom closet. There were at least a dozen handsome business suits hanging on the rack, and there was no doubt that they would fit him. He pulled a gray-blue worsted off one of the hangers and slipped it on. It fitted perfectly. Henry looked at himself in the mirror. He nodded his head and saluted the new Dr. Bartok.

Suddenly it dawned on him that this was Monday morning—Dr. Bartok would ordinarily be leaving for his office at this time. Henry glanced at the electric clock on the desk. It was eight twenty. What should he do? He couldn't simply stay away; it would arouse too much suspicion at the office. Yet Henry knew that he was in no position to begin treatment of Bartok's patients. He would need at least a month to go over all the case histories in the files and acquaint himself with the patients and their cases. Then he would have to study the psychological factors involved, the form of psychoanalysis and treatment that Bartok had been using. Henry fully realized what he had let himself in for; it was going to be a super-human feat to continue with the treatment of perhaps a hundred patients who were being individually studied and psychoanalyzed. It wasn't as if he were starting from scratch with a brand-new clientele; that would be much easier, since then he would have only to follow his own form of treatment. This was certain to be far more exacting, and unquestionably far more perilous. Nor had he forgotten the important factor in tracing any criminal. He might look like Bartok, act like Bartok—even seem to be the great psychiatrist himself—but should anyone denounce him, his fingerprints would furnish the damning evidence of his guilt. Yes, the jigsaw puzzle was practically complete. Nothing must be spoiled by carelessness or lack of preparation. When he resumed Dr. Bartok's practice, everything must dovetail like a perfectly gauged machine.

Henry went to the writing desk and searched the drawers. He found innumerable letters, as well as a big pack of cancelled checks. This was important, as he would need a copy of Bartok's signature to forge. To his pleasant surprise, the doctor's signature was plain and would not be difficult to duplicate, though the chirography was European in style. For the time being, he would concentrate only upon the signature and try to copy the general handwriting later. His search for the doctor's bank books was fruitless; he concluded that they were at the office. The check stubs, over a year old, showed a balance of $2,678.75 in the American National Bank, but Henry was sure there were larger current accounts. In the meantime, he had better start practicing the signature, because writing checks would be one of the first things he would have to do perfectly.

For the next half-hour Henry busied himself with pen and ink, and at ten minutes to nine he had an almost exact copy of Bartok's signature on a piece of paper which he had written without having to look at the original. He compared the two carefully and was at last satisfied with the forgery. At nine sharp he phoned the office and spoke his first words as Dr. Bartok to his secretary, Miss Hahn.

"Hello, this is Dr. Bartok."

"Oh, good morning, doctor. Something wrong? You're usually here by this time."

"Yes, I know. I'm still at the hotel. I do not feel very well. I will be down later. In the meantime, will you please cancel all my appointments for the next thirty days?"

A bewildered voice came back over the phone. "For the next thirty days?"

"Yes, I am going to take a much-needed rest. I—I had a slight heart attack over the weekend."

"Oh, Viktor! I had no idea—"

He interrupted her quickly. "Yes, I know, I have more or less kept it to myself." He wondered about the "Viktor."

"Oh doctor, I'm so sorry—how're you feeling now?"

"I'm feeling all right at the moment, but I do not think I should go back to work for at least a month."

"Of course not. Shall I send Dr. Sawyer over to see you?"

"No, that won't be necessary. I'll be down to the office later in the day. All I need is a long rest."

"I know, doctor. You've been working pretty hard."

"I'll see you later, Miss Hahn. Don't forget to notify all the patients and tell them I will be back July 1st and you can start making appointments for that date."

"All right, doctor."

"Goodbye, Miss Hahn, see you later."

"Yes, goodbye, doctor."

Henry put the phone down and smiled to himself. He thought the accent sounded very good. After all, he had had to trust to his memory; he had only heard Dr. Bartok speak on three or four occasions. He felt he had done fairly well, and Miss Hahn didn't seem to have the slightest doubt that it was really Dr. Bartok. She even called him Viktor. Yes, he was doing all right. The smile suddenly gave way to a yawn. He was beginning to feel sleepy. This had been his bedtime while on the night shift at the garage. He walked over to the bed and was about to throw himself down on its inviting satin spread, but suddenly thought better of it. If he was to convince his new secretary that he had suffered a heart attack and was badly in need of a rest, the less refreshed he looked the better.

Henry called room service, had breakfast sent up, and spent the rest of the morning going over his final plans to dispose of the body in the trunk of the car. He would not feel at ease until all traces of the man whose identity he had usurped were swallowed up by the swirling waters of the Desplaines River. Tonight he would empty the pockets of the dead man and remove the keys, billfold, identification card, papers and other articles of importance.

Satisfied with his plans, Henry strode over to the record cabinet and pulled out an album of Tchaikovsky—his favorite composer. As the exciting strains of the Fourth Symphony filled the room, Henry sat in a comfortable easy chair, feeling smug and serene in his new surroundings. He took a cigarette, lit it, drew the smoke in, but quickly blew it out again. There was plenty of time to learn to inhale. Relaxing in a soft, down-filled chair, listening to beautiful music in a smartly furnished apartment, being master of all he surveyed, was extremely satisfying to his well-being. Only one element was lacking—a gorgeously gowned and seductively formed woman to enhance the scene. Had Bartok had a secret love life? Was he interested in women? From all indications, it appeared that the doctor was too busy to find time for a sex life except perhaps for those puzzling visits to the 1220 Lake Shore Drive Apartments. The symphony ended and his brief excursion into the world of blue smoke and day dreams came to a sudden halt. Crushing out his cigarette, he decided it was time to make an appearance at the office. He walked over to the closet to select a suit.

At two-thirty in the afternoon Henry stepped out of the elevator on the sixteenth floor of the 34 North Michigan Building and walked down the corridor to room 1612. On the frosted door glass was the name Viktor E. Bartok, M. D. Henry hesitated for a second, took a deep breath and opened the door. As he walked in, he saw the secretary seated at the desk and talking to a fashionably dressed woman. Henry's heart began to palpitate. The first crucial test was at hand.

"Oh, here's Dr. Bartok now," said Miss Hahn with a sigh of relief.

The woman turned around and with an anxious look on her face addressed Henry. "Hello, doctor, I'm so glad to see you."

Henry's reply was, "Thank you."

The secretary looked a bit distraught. "Hello, doctor. Sorry to bother you, but Mrs. Garfield is rather upset about her cancellation. I tried to explain to her that you've been ill."

The patient, fortyish, well fed, and decked in furs and jewels, spoke in a soft and sympathetic tone. "Oh, doctor, I'm so sorry to hear you're not feeling well. Yes, I can see now, your eyes are red and you do look as though you need a rest." It was plain that his unexpected appearance had embarrassed her.

Henry forced a smile and said again, "Thank you."

"It was very selfish of me to get upset just because of a cancellation, wasn't it? Please forgive me, doctor!"

He decided to be generous and unctuous. "It is I who should ask for forgiveness, my dear Mrs. Garfield." Henry took her gloved hand in his, and patted the fingers. "You do understand, don't you? I'll be able to take care of you so much better when I come back."

"Of course, doctor!" She beamed with flattered satisfaction.

"Now, Miss Hahn will arrange for your appointment, Mrs. Garfield," he said as he walked through the reception room and to the door marked "Private."

She called out to add solicitude. "Goodbye, doctor, and have a good rest." As he entered Dr. Bartok's private office he turned to give her a patronizing smile and a last "Thank you."

Once inside, he exhaled heavily and sank into the comfortable leather chair behind the desk. Henry glanced about the room. The first thing to catch his eye was a series of framed documents on the wall, including an honorary certificate from the University of Vienna, Bartok's citizenship papers, the Nobel award, and membership certificates in various neurological and psychiatric societies. One in particular aroused his attention and he walked over to examine it closely. It read: "From the President of the United States of America, to all who shall see these presents, greetings:

Know ye that reposing special trust and confidence in the patriotism, valor, fidelity and abilities of Viktor Emil Bartok, I do appoint him Captain, Medical Corps, of the Army of the United States...."

So, the same year Bartok had become a citizen, he had applied for a reserve commission. He certainly hadn't lost any time in showing his patriotism! Henry smiled acknowledgment of this unexpected inheritance, saluted the framed document, walked back to the desk chair, and sat down. Leisurely he surveyed the office in minute detail. Next to the desk was a large upholstered living room chair, modern in design. Across the large and brightly colored office was a beige and brown settee and another smartly styled easy chair in lime green. In either corner of the room were bleached mahogany plant stands with live Chinese water lilies on them. The carpeting was chartreuse. Air conditioners kept the temperature at a pleasant seventy degrees. The place had more the atmosphere of a luxurious sitting room than a doctor's office. Ashtrays and cigarettes were placed conveniently. The pastel, muted decor was suggestive of complete relaxation. Dr. Bartok had evidently been fully aware of the importance of surroundings in aiding the patient to unburden himself. Nothing anywhere had the slightest indication of a professional office, and Henry apostrophized Dr. Bartok's display of showmanship.

Opening the desk drawer, he found a checkbook with the office expenditures on the stubs, showing a bank balance of $4,812.16. This was what he had been looking for. Rent, electric light, telephone company; Miss Evelyn Hahn, $45. Now he knew how much to pay her. Henry wrote out a check for $180, and he signed it Viktor Emil Bartok. Then he compared it with one of the cancelled checks he had brought with him. It was damned near perfect; and it should be, Henry thought, I've forged enough of them.

There was a knock on the door, and at Henry's "Yes," Miss Hahn entered. She was an attractive, smart-looking woman about twenty-five years old, of medium height. Her brown hair was worn in a carefully groomed pageboy style. Her only makeup was lipstick. She wore a plain, brown, tailored suit with an expensive lace handkerchief in the left breast pocket. Her fingernails were well manicured but devoid of any color. It was apparent that she was a person who strove for naturalness and dignity necessary to her position.

As she walked in, Miss Hahn removed the light plastic-framed glasses she wore and spoke in a voice that showed the anxiety she felt over the doctor's sudden illness. "Are you feeling all right, doctor? I've been worried."

Henry feigned a weariness and made an effort to breathe with difficulty. "Thank you, Miss Hahn, it's very kind of you to be concerned!"

"Why shouldn't I be, doctor? After all, I've been with you ever since you opened up these offices. You must know that I'm concerned in everything you do."

"Yes, Miss Hahn. I know, and I'm deeply appreciative." Henry wondered over the seriousness of her tone. Had Bartok been aware of this interest or had she kept it hidden under a cloak of reserve and efficiency? He sensed that the look in her eyes was more than solicitude. She certainly was a type of woman that a man could find very desirable. A multitude of possibilities flashed through Henry's mind. He must find out quickly which the correct one was, but for the time being he could not take a chance on overstepping himself.

Miss Hahn broke the momentary silence.

"I—I certainly had a devil of a time this morning with the patients. They all wanted a detailed explanation of the sudden cancellations. Mrs. Garfield was the worst. She was raising particular hell just before you came in, but you calmed her down in short order. She was all smiles when she left. A couple of words from you accomplished more than I did in fifteen minutes."

"I think you did very nobly, Miss Hahn. Now I will tell you what I want you to do. First of all, here is a check for four weeks' salary in advance. Take a vacation—I'm sure you can stand one."

"Oh … thank you, doctor." He did not notice that her face fell.

"Did you notify all the patients that I will not be able to see them until after July 1st?"

"Yes, I did doctor. The first Monday in July is the 3rd. I made appointments for then."

"Good. Now, I will give you another check to cash for me, and then I want you to go to the railroad ticket office and get me a ticket for some pleasant place where I can rest. Where do you suggest?"

"How about Colorado Springs? It's awfully nice down there. I don't think you've ever been there. Remember we talked about it the last time, or have you … forgotten?"

"Er—yes. That's right. Fine. Then you buy me a ticket for Colorado Springs and wire the hotel down there for reservations. What's the name of the hotel?"

"The one I'd suggest is the Biltmore. Do you think you should go away so far … alone?"

"Alone? Of course. I'll be all right. Let's see, today is Monday. Tell them I will arrive on Thursday. That will give me time to clean up a few matters."

"Yes, doctor. You're sure you'll be all right? This isn't serious?"

"No, Miss Hahn, I'll be as good as new when I get back. You see, this is not the first attack I've had."

"You never told me that your heart had bothered you before. You always said you were as healthy as a bull."

"I know. We sometimes like to overestimate our stamina. I think maybe this golf is too strenuous. It was on the golf course that I fainted."

"Oh, heavens!"

"Oh, I was all right after I rested up in the clubhouse."

"You mustn't do any golfing at Colorado Springs," warned the secretary in an affectionate tone. "Please, Viktor, darling, for my sake?"

He looked up into her eyes. Well, so that was how it was! Viktor, darling! No secretary would use such endearing terms to her employer unless there had been an unprofessional relationship. He wondered how far they had gone. This was taking on new dimensions and Henry was enjoying the situation. He answered her tenderly and disarmingly. "I promise, my dear."

He wrote out another check for two hundred dollars and handed it to her. "Here you are. Now get me a reservation to Colorado Springs for Wednesday. I don't know the railroad. You will find it for me, yes?"

"Of course, doctor. Do you want a roomette or a compar—" She stopped abruptly. Henry looked up sharply. She was staring at the left side of his face.

"Something wrong?" Henry asked, apprehensively.

"Your face—the scar—am I crazy or has that always been on your left cheek?"

He smiled. "Not unless it moved over night. Why?"

"That's the funniest thing. I've worked for you almost two years now, and I could have sworn that scar was always on the right side of your face!"

Henry bit his lower lip. "Would you swear to it now?"

"Of course not, now that I'm looking right at you."

"Our imagination sometimes plays tricks upon us."

She still looked puzzled. "It certainly does. It seems every time I came into your office, the light from the window used to fall on the right side of your face, showing up that scar very plainly. Now the light is hitting your right cheek and nothing is there. It's perfectly smooth."

"Miss Hahn! I think you are as badly in need of a vacation as I am."

Her bewildered expression changed to a laugh. "Yes, I guess you're right. Either that, or I'm badly in need of a psychiatrist myself."

"There are two ways I could take that. Professionally or otherwise?"

"What do you think? After all, you're the doctor."

"I'm quite sure it isn't professionally."

She took a deep breath and her nostrils dilated as she exhaled. "I'm quite sure you're right." She turned and started for the door. "I'll take care of this right away," she added as she hurried from the room.

Henry sat for a long moment pondering this unexpected office intrigue. He must handle her very carefully. What role in Bartok's private life had she played? Should he replace her with a new secretary? He could have no legitimate reason to offer her; after all, she had been with Bartok since the beginning. As much as Henry feared her, her knowledge of the office and the patients would be far too valuable to him. No, she was necessary to his new life. He would await further developments and rest his confidence on his own ability to master the unexpected. Indeed, he welcomed the unforeseen tests of his new life as a stimulating challenge.

That night Henry called the North-Lake Garage and the car was delivered to him. This was the part of the plan that he disliked the most. As he passed the city's north side limits and headed for the highway, he felt sick and ill at ease. He glanced at the dash clock. It was two-fifteen in the morning. The highway was deserted, and Henry had a strange feeling of being alone, of driving to a weird funeral, and officiating at a ghastly burial. He drove for another half-hour before he came to the side road shown on the map beside him. Turning off the cement highway, he followed the winding gravel road that led through the county's forest preserve. Soon groves of trees and thick foliage enveloped the lone vehicle and shut off from view the few stars that blinked in the clouded sky. The road curved and twisted, and Henry slowed down to a scant ten miles per hour, as he threaded his way along the pitch-black path that led to the Desplaines River.

Soon, through the misty beam of the headlights, he could make out the shimmering of water. He stopped the car and got out. The sound of a swiftly moving stream told him that his destination had been reached. He opened the trunk of the car and pulled out the dead body. Then he dragged the lifeless form of the doctor into a clump of bushes, loosened the rope, emptied the pockets of all their contents, and transferred them to his own. Next he ripped the labels out of the clothes, took off the shoes because of their identifying trademark, and threw them back into the trunk.

He took the doctor's wrist watch and a diamond solitaire ring from his finger, and then unwound the garrote from the doctor's neck. The moon threw a pale eerie light on the distorted face of his victim, and Henry chilled at the revelation. His only desire was to get this over and done with as quickly as possible, and drive away. He began to work feverishly. He took a roll of adhesive tape from his pocket and placed strips of it across the doctor's face, until hardly any portion of the flesh was visible. Then he did the same to the fingers. If the body were ever discovered and the adhesive removed, the soft rotting flesh would cling to the tape, and the face and fingers that had once belonged to Dr. Viktor Bartok would peel off in strips, forever concealing the identity of the decayed corpse. The only other means of identification would be the dental work. Henry knew this was a reasonably remote possibility as Bartok had lived all but six years of his life in Europe, and the probabilities of checking up on foreign dentistry, especially with a person who had lived in several different countries, were slight.

When he had finished, he again tied up the body with the stout rope, this time adding the iron weights. Then he attempted to lift his victim back into the car, to be driven to the point of disposal, but found that the iron weights made the task impossible. Henry thought fast. His car was parked on the edge of the road, and although it was unlikely that anyone would be coming along this lonely path, at this time of night, he could not afford to take a chance. There was only one thing to do. If he could not lift the body, he would drag it. He took one end of the rope and pulled the crumpled figure to the back of the car and tied it to the rear bumper. Then he took a hasty last look in the bushes where he had been working to see that nothing had been left behind, and jumped into the car. In a moment he was under way, towing after him his macabre cargo.

Henry made his way slowly toward the bridge spanning the stream that he had marked on his map. According to his calculations, it should be within a quarter of a mile of the spot he had just left. From there the road turned and ran parallel with the river to a point where it again turned and crossed the stream. The middle of that bridge was his destination. He drove on at a slackened pace, his eyes glued to the rearview mirror with apprehension, lest a pair of headlights appear from behind, and fall upon the unbelievable sight that would be revealed in their beam.

Suddenly from out of the blackness ahead of him, a light loomed against the horizon. Henry's heart began to pound. Closer and brighter came the gleam. And then from the distance, he could make out the moving headlights of an automobile weaving toward him on the winding road. Henry was almost blinded by the brilliance of the powerful headlamps, and he pulled over to the side of the road and slowed down to a crawl. On and on came the lights until they were almost on top of him. Henry's clammy hands went colder and he could feel the throbbing of his racing heart pulsating against his temples, his neck, and the roof of his dry mouth. God! If he were caught now, it would be as red-handed as anyone in the history of crime. The evidence was right with him, tied to his car.

As the car approached, the driver slowed down and Henry could hear the tires grinding to a stop on the loose gravel.

"Hey, Mister!" The voice came sharply through the lowered window. He pulled alongside Henry's barely moving car, and in the pitch blackness, he could not know that his action turned Henry's face a ghostly white. The big Cadillac halted as Henry, in a lightning decision, concluded he would arouse less suspicion by being friendly. As the two cars drew abreast, Henry saw that his interlocutor was a teenaged youngster with a girl snuggled up closely beside him.

"We're kinda lost. Can you tell me how to get back to the highway?"

It was apparent they had been out for a bit of "necking" and had forgotten the hour. Both looked tired and considerably frightened as if they contemplated stringent disciplining from their parents.

"Straight ahead, sonny." Henry could afford to be courteous. "It's about a mile down."

"Thanks, Mister." The car sped on, its occupants too engrossed in each other to be aware of what lay in the inky darkness on the road behind them.

Henry wiped his brow with the back of his hand and drove on. In a few minutes, the road turned and he found himself at last approaching the wooden span. He stopped the car in the center of the bridge and got out. The only sounds were the rippling of the stream below and the buzzing of myriad insects swarming in the warm spring night. He quickly glanced in both directions. Nothing was to be seen anywhere. A moment later, the stillness of the quiet forest was broken by a thunderous crash as a human body with its burden of heavy iron weights splashed the swirling waters down to its final resting place.

Henry returned to the car. From this moment on, he was Dr. Viktor Emil Bartok, eminent psychiatrist, Nobel Prize winner. As the automobile circled back toward the city, his thoughts drifted toward his new life. His hand found its way into his coat pocket, and to the diamond ring that had once been worn on another hand. Now it would grace a new finger. He slipped it on. It was a little tight, but not uncomfortably so. Then from out of the other coat pocket he took a pack of the doctor's favorite cigarettes. They were among the articles that Henry had taken from the body. He put one between his lips, pressed the dash lighter, and a few seconds later, he was drawing in deep puffs. He rolled the window completely down. The tension of the hour just past gradually faded as the cool, sweet-smelling air of the freshly plowed fields caught his nostrils.

CHAPTER ELEVEN

Henry awakened at eleven the next morning in his newly acquired suite after a restful and much needed sleep. He had fallen into bed at four-thirty A.M., completely exhausted from his ordeal. He had gone almost forty-eight hours without rest, save a two-hour nap the day before when he returned from the office. He showered and shaved and then called room service to send up orange juice, a cereal, ham and eggs, and toast and coffee. As the waiter lifted the napkin and uncovered the tray, Henry rubbed his hands together and prepared himself for the heartiest meal he had had for quite a while.

"*Oui, monsieur*, everything is steaming hot. It looks appetizing, *non?*"

"Just ham and eggs, but to me it is the most beautiful food in all America," laughed Henry. "Right now, *garçon*, I have the appetite of a gourmand!"

"*Bien, monsieur*, I hope you have a most delightful meal."

"Thank you. Here you are."

"*Oh, merci beaucoup, monsieur. Monsieur le docteur, n'est-ce pas?*"

Henry called upon his high-school French. "*Oui, c'est vrai. Je suis un docteur.*"

"*Vous êtes francais?*"

"*Non.*" Henry hesitated for a second. "*Je suis un Czech.*"

The little Frenchman opened his eyes wide and fingered his carefully waxed moustache. "Oh, you are a Czech! I have been there. It is a most beautiful country. Prague?"

"Er—yes."

Henry was wary of even this conversational gambit.

"Yes, a most beautiful country," sighed the waiter again. Then, to Henry's relief, he started for the door. "Thank you, doctor. A pleasant good morning to you, sir."

With the horrors of the night before completely eradicated from his mind, Henry placed a Rachmaninoff concerto on the phonograph. Dressed in Bartok's black satin lounging pajamas, he felt little like Henry Mueller, ex-convict 147963. That was all a million miles away.

Eventually, the articles that Henry had taken from the pockets of his dead predecessor caught his eye where he had placed them on a table the night before. He strode over and examined them. The billfold, with the identification cards inside, contained one hundred and sixty dollars in cash. The key chain had nine keys attached, one of which seemed to be a vault key. Where was the vault located? The key had only a number stamped on it, D43962. No other identifying marks were visible. Then there was a savings account bank book, also from the American National Bank. The balance was … $58,475.42! Henry smiled to himself. That was the most important article of all. Chances were, the vault was in the same bank. No doubt there were stocks and securities in the vault which would prove to be a nice little nest egg! He pursed his lips with satisfaction as he slipped the book into the cover. There were other incidental items—loose change, cigarette lighter, fountain pen and pencil, a wrist watch with which he promptly replaced his own. Henry's eyes suddenly fell upon an opened letter taken from the dead man's coat pocket. It was postmarked Pasadena, Calif., May 22nd. That was only a week ago. On the back was the name Mrs. Meta Dvorak, and a street address. He took out the letter and read it.

"Dear Viktor:
"It has been sometime since we have heard from you. No doubt you have been very busy as you usually are. We were hoping you might come out to California for a vacation which you certainly should take at the first opportunity. It is so lovely here and the weather has been ideal. You would love it out here. Always you write that someday you will pay us a visit, and here you have been in this country six years and still we haven't seen you.
"Kristina thinks next year she might apply for enrollment in one of the classes of the Art Institute in Chicago. And she insists that she wants to make a career of her art work, and that the Art Institute has one of the finest schools in the country. So, if she decides that she wants to go there, you will no doubt be seeing your little niece whom you haven't seen since she was a baby. She adores you and never stops talking about her famous uncle.
"Take care of yourself, Viktor, and don't work too hard. Kristina and I want to thank you for the lovely gifts you sent to us, and we both send our love. If you can find time to write, we'd be so happy to hear from you. Regards,

"Your loving sister,
Meta."

After reading the letter, Henry's emotions were mixed. He now knew that Bartok's sister resided in California, but he did not like the news of her young daughter's possibly coming to art school in Chicago. Not that he had any reason to be afraid that a school girl would become suspicious, but he had no desire to meet a member of Bartok's family. Besides, he detested young people with their endless chatter and questions. But it was time enough to cross his bridges when he came to them.

That afternoon, Henry went down to his office. Miss Hahn greeted him as he entered.

"Hello, doctor, I'm glad to see you looking better today."

"Yes, thank you, I rested very well last night. Were there any important calls?"

"Several patients called to inquire about your health, and two new patients. I gave them appointments for some time in July."

"Good."

"And, oh yes, Dr. Felix Marantz called."

"Dr. Felix Marantz?"

"Yes, he says he's an old colleague of yours from. Vienna."

"Oh, yes, yes. University of Vienna." Henry took a guess. He knew Bartok had taught there. "What did he have to say?"

"He said he was going to be in town only until tomorrow night and wanted to see you very badly."

"Did you tell him I had been ill?"

"Yes, I did, doctor. In fact, when I told him that, he seemed more anxious than ever to see you."

"Didn't you tell him I was going out of town?"

"Yes, I did. I told him you were going away for a month's rest."

"And?"

"Well, he seemed determined to see you. Of course, since you're such old friends, I thought you might be anxious to see him yourself."

"Oh, certainly, certainly, I should be more than happy to see him under ordinary circumstances. It was only that I have such a short time before going away, I wanted to utilize every minute cleaning up important matters."

"Yes, I understand, doctor."

"I'm glad you told him I wouldn't be able to see him."

"But I didn't, doctor. He was so insistent, I told him you'd be in for a couple of hours this afternoon, so he said he'd be here at four o'clock."

"Oh." Henry's face fell. It was three o'clock now. He couldn't deliberately run away. That would be too obvious and too discourteous. He'd have to get used to these unexpected things.

"All right, Miss Hahn, thank you."

"Oh, by the way, doctor, here are your train tickets. I got you a compartment on the Zephyr, leaving from the Union Station at six-fifteen tomorrow evening. I also wired the Biltmore you were coming."

"Oh, fine, thank you. You are very efficient, Miss Hahn. I don't know what I would do without you."

She smiled. "Thank you, doctor. You mean as a secretary, of course?" Her tone was the least bit caustic.

Henry was confused. It was apparent that she did not relish the implication she was merely an efficient secretary. She evidently had been given reason by Bartok to feel that she was much more in his life. Was his own attitude toward her too formal and reserved? Was that what made her feel that there had been a sudden change in the sentiments of her employer? Henry didn't know how much reserve or fondness he should manifest for this attractive young woman who was to be an everyday part of his future life.

"As a secretary and a woman," Henry answered discreetly. He was not aware that as he closed the door Miss Hahn had opened her purse and taken out a dainty lace handkerchief to wipe her tear-filled eyes. He was far too occupied with his own thoughts to be disturbed over the reactions of his secretary. A multitude of questions were flashing through his brain. Who was this Dr. Marantz? How well acquainted was he with Bartok? Had they seen each other in recent years? Was he also a professor at Vienna University or was that just a bad guess? Would Marantz be suspicious of anything wrong or out of the ordinary, and would he try to trip him up? How would he be able to discuss old times with someone he had never seen before? He would let Marantz do most of the talking.

Henry tried to be calm by going over the card file of active cases in the office. He was going to take the card file with him to Colorado Springs to acquaint himself with the patients and their disorders. Fortunately, Dr. Bartok had kept an up-to-date record of his treatments and the patient's progress. There were numerous terms and references that Henry could not altogether understand or decipher, such as: *3/14 Ph. Sig. or Cop. No. 274 Schiz. and Leip. Gerhardt's P. 263 Cycl. Flegtmeyer, Reg. 1928*. They were evidently reference symbols and corresponded with other cases either in textbooks or in the files of the institutions where he had practiced. He decided he would not worry about it. For the most part the cards were typewritten and the information plainly summed up. He took a card from the file at random:

Traynor, Albert G. 39   Adv. Exec V.P. & Treas.
1426 Greenleaf—Cam. 4071   Wallis, Traynor Adv. Co.
Evanston, Ill.   400 N. Michigan
                                          Gre. 4300

Rec. Dr. Howard Keeler
1st Diag. 5/28/38   Sal. $40,000 per annum.
Bor. May 2, 1899 (F. James Frederick Traynor, dec. Aug. 27, 1928
Mar: June 19, 1923 (M. Martha Simmons, still liv.) to Edna Carter
Child: Howard 11   2 sis. (1 mar.-1 div.) (all liv.)
    Joyce 8   1 bro. (Bachelor)
Ed: Grammar   Pers. Hab.: Alcohol—excess
   High   Cigarettes —   "
   Princeton Univ.   Gambling—mod.
                                          Hobbies: Golf
                                              Sailing
                                              Ant. fire-arms
Symp.: Severe headaches, worry,   Sex life: Wife—passive—
   Moodiness, Melancholia,   frigid
   Habitual Drunkenness,   He—intense
   Suicide Complex   Mistress-5 yrs.

Diag: Warm personality, charming, intelligent businessman, no longer loves wife. Would like to divorce her but has no grounds and realizes if he did, he would lose children. Complains of no understanding from wife, no tolerance, unsympathetic and displays no affection toward him. Detests wife's friends, bored on social functions. Loves to be with mistress who has full knowledge of his desires, and completely understands his temperament, appreciates his sense of humor. Wife frustrates his natural desire to be gay and continually censures his actions as not being reserved and dignified. He on the other hand abhors reserve and dignity, likes to tell dirty stories and swear. Wife inhibits him at every turn. Loves his children, hates his wife, has begged her to try to effect more understanding and tolerance, would be willing to continue marriage on that basis.

Henry turned the card over. It read:

6/3/38   Lengthy discussion on personal habits
      (normal except liquor.)
6/6/38   Lengthy discussion on sexual habits
      (only satisfaction with mistress. Advised continuance.)
6/8/38   Lengthy discussion on early childhood
      (Pampered— spoiled by mother.)

6/11/38 Lengthy discussion on early homelife (normal)
6/13/38 Lengthy discussion on 1st five years of marriage
　　　　　(complete understanding tho sexually incompatible)

Began treatment by Psychoanalysis:
6/18/38 (Restrained)
6/20/38 (Restrained)
6/22/38 (Slightly Restrained)
6/24/38 (Loosened up)
6/25/38 (Talkative)
6/27/38 (Responsive)

Began treatment by Psychiatric Counsel:
6/30/38 (Receptive)
7/2/38　 (Very Receptive)
7/3/38　 (Very Receptive)
7/5/38　 (Slightly Restrained)
7/6/38　 (Receptive)
7/9/38　 (Good humor)

Returned to treatment by Psychoanalysis:
7/11/38 (Definite Improvement)
7/13/38 (Definite Improvement)
7/14/38 (Definite Improvement)
7/15/38 (Definite Improvement)

The records of visits and the degrees of improvement continued on another card attached, but Henry did not study the case further except to note that Mr. Traynor was still a patient after undergoing treatment for a year. He would no doubt be meeting the advertising executive in the near future. Henry did not know the exact form of psychoanalysis that Bartok had been using, but obviously Traynor's case was one requiring patience. It was necessary to instill self-confidence in him, to urge him to rise above the pettiness of his wife, and to advise him to retain his mistress and the love and affection that she offered. She provided a good balance for his whole mental structure. Naturally, Henry reasoned, divorce would be the easiest solution, but, since Traynor's wife refused to give him one, and since he did not want to part with his children, the only alternative was to acquire a good mental balance which would survive domestic strife. Bartok, in his evident counsel to continue an extramarital relationship, must have realized that his patient's health was his first obligation. This was not only good medicine but good logic.

Henry's musings over the interesting case before him were suddenly interrupted by the sound of the telephone buzzer. It was Miss Hahn informing him that Dr. Marantz had arrived. Henry glanced at the desk clock. It was exactly four o'clock. Apparently punctuality was one of Marantz's traits.

"Of course, send him right in," Henry answered with forced enthusiasm. He squared his shoulders for the ordeal which was to follow.

"Felix, how are you? It's so good of you to come." Henry extended a warm hand as he stood up and greeted this stranger.

"Viktor, Viktor, I am so happy to see you." They shook hands vigorously and after closing the office door, Henry pulled up a large easy chair.

"Sit down, Felix, and make yourself comfortable."

"Thank you. I expected to see a sick man. You look healthy to me!"

Henry took a quick inventory of his visitor as he sat down beside him. He had noticed immediately that Marantz spoke with a thick foreign accent. He was either German or Austrian by birth, and was stocky for his height, which was not over five-feet-five. He wore glasses with extremely thick lenses and was totally bald save for a straggly fringe around the lower half of his squarish head. He had large ears and a small pug nose with a prominent wart on it. His hands were short and thick with stubby fingers, and his legs were chunky and bowed. His entire appearance struck Henry as being almost gnomish. When he spoke, his face wrinkled and his beady eyes sparkled.

"How have you been, Felix? Tell me about yourself."

"There is not much to tell, Viktor. I am naturally happy to be in this country. I can thank Mr. Hitler for that!"

This last statement confirmed his suspicion that Marantz was Jewish. "Yes, it is unfortunate that he has so much power," Henry said, lighting a cigarette. "I would offer you one, Felix, but I know you don't use them."

"That is right. You have a remarkable memory, Viktor." He was unaware that Henry had caught sight of a pipe protruding from his breast pocket. "I smoke only my old briar. It has traveled many places with me and has been a wonderful companion." He withdrew the pipe and filled it from a well-worn leather pouch. "Ja," he went on reflectively, "Hitler has done much to upset the equilibrium of Europe. Vienna is no longer the Vienna we knew. It is full of gangster soldiers marching up and down shouting 'Sieg Heil' and making everyone give the Nazi salute."

Henry leaned over as he struck a match and lit Marantz's pipe.

"Did the Nazis harm you in any way?" he asked.

"No. Fortunately, I was able to get out of Vienna before they could make trouble for me. Some of our colleagues were not so fortunate. Remember Professor Sackheim—Rudolph Sackheim?"

"Er—yes."

"The last I heard of him he was in a concentration camp at Dachau."

"What happened?"

"Well, of course, all Jews on the faculty at the University were thrown out. I did not wait for that. I could see the handwriting on the wall. But Sackheim, who is such an idealist, stuck to the finish. I understand he was dragged bodily from the classroom. Then to make matters worse, he berated Hitler and the whole Nazi party. This he should not have done. He could have been shot."

"From what I've read about Dachau," replied Henry dryly, "it probably would have been just as well."

"Ja, Ja." Marantz continued to puff away, and the smoke was thick and acrid. "Dr. Goldschmidt—you remember him—?"

"Of course."

"He fled to Slovakia thinking he would be safe. Now Hitler has that too. Poor Goldschmidt! And he with four children and a sick wife!"

"Tell me—you just arrived in the United States?"

"A month ago."

"Then where have you been all this time? You must have left Austria over a year ago?"

"That is right. Germany declared the Anschluss in March, 1938. I left in February. Through a little politics and a little *schmeering*, I was able to get a visa to Portugal. I was in Lisbon for almost a year before I could get a visa for America. The quotas are small and one must wait and wait. Finally, I was given my passport and told to be ready in March."

"How about your family?"

"Oh, they are with me. They are now at the hotel. You see, I am on my way to Lowell, Iowa."

"To Midwestern University?"

"Ja, I am extremely fortunate. I am to teach there."

"How wonderful! Congratulations."

"Thank you."

"How did you manage the connection so soon?"

"Through Professor Branstedt. You must have met him when you were at Leipzig—"

"Oh, yes, he's the one who—er—"

"—made such tremendous strides in osteomyelitis."

"Oh, yes, yes, of course! I know him quite well." Henry was delighted with the way Marantz unsuspectingly followed up his leading questions.

"Well, Branstedt and I were always very close. He came to this country in 1933 and has been at Midwestern ever since. When I arrived in New York I got in touch with him. He wrote me that he had discussed me with the board and that they could use my services in the medical school there. That is, as they say in American slang, a real break!"

"Indeed, yes," laughed Henry. He still did not know what Marantz taught or what his specialty was.

"Now, about you. I see you have done very well in Chicago. You were at the University for two years, weren't you?"

"Yes, then I decided to go in for private practice."

"And a very excellent decision from the looks of your office. You have quite a reputation, Viktor, in the psychiatric field."

"Thank you, I am flattered."

Marantz relit his pipe, which had gone out.

"*Nein*, no need to be modest, Viktor. After all, a man is not awarded the Nobel Prize for nothing."

"That was very unexpected and sometimes I feel that it was unwarranted. I'm sure there were others who made greater contributions to medical science."

"If there were, I'm sure the Nobel Committee would have chosen someone else instead of you. Let us not underestimate our value. If I was not a good gynecologist and obstetrician, I would not be asked to teach at Midwestern."

"Very true, Felix, very true." A placid smile came over Henry's face. Marantz himself would supply him with the background material he needed to handle this interview successfully.

"Yes, my dear Dr. Marantz," he resumed, "I always said if I ever got married, I would want you to deliver my baby. In your hands, I would have enough confidence to have you work in the dark."

"Please, please," chuckled the professor, "I am a doctor, not a magician. Anyway, I'm convinced you are a confirmed bachelor. Now, to change the subject, what is this with you being sick, and closing up your office?"

Henry had anticipated this question. "Yes, Felix, I'm going away tomorrow for a month's rest."

"What is the matter? I told you before you looked wonderful."

"Thank you, but you as a doctor know outward appearances can be very deceiving."

"Of course, we know that only too well. So tell me, Viktor, what is so seriously wrong that you suddenly decided to cancel all work for a whole month?"

"I—I had an angina seizure over the weekend."

Marantz looked disturbed. "So? That is not good. When did you first become aware of this?"

Henry's hesitation had the effect of conveying an impression of reticence.

"Well, I—let me see—I think it was about a year ago that I had the first attack."

"So." He emptied the ashes from his pipe into the stand nearby. "Did you have a cardiograph taken?"

"Not lately. About a year ago."

"What did it show?"

"It—er—the diagnosis showed an enlargement and faulty muscles." He hoped that was essentially correct. It evidently was, as Marantz did not look perplexed.

"Um hm. And what are you taking when you have these attacks?"

"Uh—nothing."

"Nothing? That is strange. Not even any amyl nitrate and nitroglycerin?"

"Oh, that, of course. I thought you meant what am I taking between the attacks." Henry was beginning to perspire.

"I know one thing you shouldn't be doing and that is smoking. That is very bad. And your secretary tells me you have been golfing. That is also not good."

"Now stop fussing over me like an old hen," laughed Henry as he rose from his chair. "You always were an alarmist, if I remember correctly."

"Not an alarmist, Viktor, a precautionist."

"Excuse me a moment." He walked to the door and opened it. "Miss Hahn!"

"Yes."

"You may go. There is no need for you to stay until six."

"Oh. All right, doctor. Thank you. Uh, may I see you for a moment, doctor?"

"Yes, of course. Excuse me, Felix." He walked into the outer office. "Yes?" He regarded Miss Hahn levelly.

"I just thought I'd like to say goodbye. After all, we won't be seeing each other for a month."

"Yes, yes, that is right. Forgive me for not thinking about that myself, but I have been rather upset with one thing and another—"

"Don't apologize, Viktor, I realize you haven't been yourself, but I'm terribly, terribly confused. I—I had begun to believe that things between us had reached the stage where I could indulge in future planning, but I guess that's all been wishful thinking—"

Henry looked at his secretary. Her eyes were glistening. It was apparent that she was terribly bewildered and unhappy. But he was more confused than she. How could he know that Bartok had openly vowed his love, that he had planned a vacation with her, had told her they would never be parted? He couldn't. Nor could he know that his request that she arrange accommodations for this vacation without her had struck her like lightning striking a tree. He groped for something to say, something to ease her troubled mind.

"Evelyn, I—I don't know what to say—" for once, Henry was lost for words.

"Don't, please, Viktor, don't say anything. You don't have to offer any explanations to me." He stood there awkwardly and helplessly, as a tear slid down her cheek. Then she caught up her hat and purse, turned and extended her hand.

"Goodbye, Viktor, take care of yourself—and if you can find a moment, drop me a card."

They shook hands, and she darted from the office. He slowly walked into the office. "Forgive me, Felix, for this interruption."

"Ja, of course."

"I was just saying goodbye to my secretary."

"She looks like a fine person to me. She is extremely charming and attractive. How long have you had her?"

"Ever since I opened up here."

"Oh? Then she should be very valuable to you."

"Yes, she is. She's a very rare combination of efficient secretary and feminine fascination. I'm finding her more interesting each day."

"Really? Maybe my confirmed bachelor friend is not so confirmed, eh?" Marantz chuckled heartily, his rotund little belly quivered. "Ja, ja, I think maybe it would be a very good thing, There are many advantages to marriage, particularly so as you grow older. Life can be very dull and lonely when you are constantly by yourself."

Henry sat down behind his desk. "Yes, I am inclined to agree with you, Felix, but so far, my life has been anything but dull and lonely. There have been so many things to occupy my time that I never find occasion to be bored."

"Ja, that I can understand very readily, but remember there is an old axiom: all work and no play—"

Henry interrupted with a laugh. "Ah, do not worry about that—I am human as well as a doctor!"

"That is better," Marantz nodded his head approvingly. "You know a woman can be a great incentive to a man. Ach, here I am being philosophic with you—trying to tell you about human psychologies, and you are perhaps one of the world's most gifted psychologists."

"Thank you, but you know sometimes human frailties are the most pronounced in those who seek to find them in others."

"Ja, ja, that is unfortunately true," sighed Marantz. "Viktor, I think you have coined a new quotation. I like that—did you ever use that phrase before?"

"I—I don't think so. It just came out, that is all."

"Human frailties are sometimes the most pronounced in those who seek to find them in others. Ja, I must remember that." He paused, looked at Henry. "Viktor—"

"Yes?"

"I have always prided myself on an excellent capacity for remembering things. In fact, I have been told by some of my friends and colleagues that I have a photographic mind."

"Yes?" Henry knew what Marantz was leading up to. He had felt him staring at the left side of his face.

"Am I wrong, or was that saber wound always on your left cheek?" Henry began to bite his lower lip.

"I'm afraid so," he laughed casually. "I've never known a scar to get tired staying on one place, and decide to move to a more comfortable spot."

"*Ach, nein,* now you are making jokes. I am serious."

"Felix! You're not really! You couldn't be."

"But I am. It has been bothering me for the last ten minutes, ever since I became aware of it on the left side of your face. You see, I remember very distinctly a conversation you and I had one time. We were discussing this scar and how you happened to acquire it. You described your duel with a member of one of the other fraternities, and you pointed out the fact that he was left-handed and always had a tendency to strike at your right. You said it was during a thrust to the face that you tried to parry, but you were not quick enough and that you caught the saber full on the right cheek."

"Left cheek!"

"Right cheek, Viktor, right cheek!"

"Where is it now?"

"On your left, of course, but it wasn't there the last time!"

"Felix, how many *schnapps* did you have today?"

"About half a dozen—but that has nothing to do with it!"

"You are stubborn, Felix, as you always have been."

"It is not I who am stubborn, it is you. I remember very distinctly that you told me that he struck your right cheek."

Henry saw that he was accomplishing nothing, so he tried humoring his visitor. "All right, if I give in and say you were right, does that make matters any better? The scar is still on the left cheek, and all the arguments in the world cannot change that! True?"

"Ja, that is so, but how did it get there, that is what is puzzling me."

"I have the solution."

"What?"

"Maybe I am not Viktor Bartok," said Henry boldly. "Maybe I am someone else masquerading as Viktor Bartok!"

"Ach, Viktor, please, no more nonsense. You always were so serious about everything; now, since you have been in this country, you have adopted this silly American humor of—kidding, they call it? And my vocabulary of American slang is not so bad either, eh? Even if I spent six years studying Oxford English."

"I should say not! Where did you learn slang?" Henry was eager to avoid any further risky conversational topics.

"We lived for a month in New York with my wife's sister. They have a home in the Bronx and two boys fourteen and sixteen. I heard enough slang in four weeks to last me the rest of my life!"

"I can imagine."

"Well, Viktor, I have taken up enough of your time today." He took his hat from the desk. "After all, you are leaving town. Tomorrow, is it?"

"Yes, tomorrow night. I do have quite a few matters to clean up before I go."

"Where are you going for your rest?"

"Colorado Springs."

"So, Viktor, my friend, take care of yourself and have a good rest." Henry grasped his short chunky hand affectionately. "Just to be on the safe side, don't you think you should have a thorough check-up by a good heart man before you go away?"

"Yes, Felix, I'm going to do that tomorrow. Now don't you worry about me."

"All right. Goodbye, Viktor. After I'm settled at the university I will write and let you know how things are."

"Yes, by all means do, Felix, I shall be anxious to know how you're getting along."

"Ja, and I will also be anxious to know about you. Do not forget to take your amyl nitrate and nitroglycerin with you."

"I won't."

"—and do not play golf, and stay away from cigarettes!"

"Yes, yes, now stop making this a professional call. This was supposed to be a social visit."

"All right, I say no more."

"I'll walk you to the door. Don't forget to say hello to your wife and sons—"

"Sons? You mean daughters!"

"Oh, yes, of course, I was thinking of the two boys—your nephews—" Henry flushed at his *faux pas*. He had tired from the strain of this long session, but happily Marantz paid little attention to the error. Henry opened the entrance door.

"So, Viktor, once more, goodbye. It was nice seeing you again."

"Goodbye, Felix, it was a great pleasure to be with you. Don't forget to let me hear from you. I'll be back July 1st."

"Ja. Good luck."

"To you too." He watched the squatty figure of the doctor disappear around the corridor, then turning, he walked back into the reception room and locked the door. Once in his private office, he literally fell into the chair. He had come through this long and trying session with more success than he had dared anticipate. Marantz had noticed the scar, but he felt sure that he had convinced him, just as he had Miss Hahn, that it was imagination. Henry couldn't help gloating over the way he had led Dr. Marantz to disclose the information about himself that had enabled him to carry on a conversation. And he was quite proud that he had correctly guessed the origin of the scar.

He returned the card he had been studying before the visit to the "T" index, and prepared to take the file of active cases with him. Then he rummaged through all the drawers in the desk and the large steel file cabinet, and withdrew whatever papers looked of interest and importance. These he hastily stuffed into an empty briefcase, and left the office. He had just closed the door to the private office when he was startled by the ringing of the telephone. He lifted the phone on Miss Hahn's desk apprehensively.

"Hello."

"Hello, darling," The voice was feminine and alluring. "How are you?"

"Uh, I'm—I'm all right—now, thank you." He was taken aback, but quickly recovered. "How are you?"

"I'm all right, but what's the matter with you? Your secretary told me you were ill and that you were going away for a rest. It's very fine that I have to learn those things from a secretary. I'm not used to that kind of treatment, Viktor. You've always been very considerate of my feelings, darling, and here you haven't even phoned me!"

"Yes, I know—dear—forgive me." Henry ran his fingers through his hair. Who in Christ's world was this? He thought fast. It must be another love of Bartok's who had spoken to Miss Hahn earlier in the day. They were probably love rivals unbeknownst to each other. He decided to play along. "You do forgive me, don't you, dear?"

"I suppose. You always have such disarming ways of getting one to overlook your shortcomings. I sometimes wish you didn't have such continental mannerisms. That's my weakness and was my downfall with you."

"Downfall?" This sounded rather interesting.

"Well, if you want to call it that."

"But I didn't call it that. You did."

"Yes, I know, that was just another way of saying my—rebirth!"

"Ah, that sounds a great deal more flattering."

"Flattering? Since when do you like flattery? You always told me that you couldn't stand it, that you detested flattery."

Henry gathered that the compliments and cajolery that were so necessary to the bolstering of his own constantly fluctuating ego had not been welcome to Dr. Viktor Bartok. His had evidently been a modest personality; yet Henry couldn't resist the opportunity to play the lover.

"Of course I detest flattery, except when it comes from you!"

"Viktor! You have never said such beautiful things to me! I forgive you a thousand times! I love you, I love you!"

"Thank you, my darling." He was intrigued with her voice. It was cultured and soft and distinctively enchanting. He wondered what she looked like.

"Now tell me about this nonsense of your becoming ill. Didn't you play golf at the club over the weekend?"

"Yes, I did, dear. It was on the golf course that I took ill."

"Oh, you poor dear! What did you have, a tummy ache?"

"No, it was something a bit more serious. Serious enough to take me away from Chicago for a month."

"A month?" The change in her tone showed that she recognized the implications of his statement. "Oh, Viktor, darling—tell me please, what happened?"

"I … I … had … it's my heart."

"Oh, God, no ! Viktor … you never told me!"

"I know. I never wanted to worry you."

"Oh, darling, how could you keep that from me? And here I was scolding you before for neglecting me. I'm so sorry … it is I who should be scolded."

"No, my dear, there is no need to reproach yourself. After all, you didn't know anything about it."

"How are you feeling now, my darling?"

"Very much better, thank you."

"When are you going away?"

"I leave tomorrow evening at 6:15."

"Where are you going?"

"To Colorado Springs."

"Viktor, I must see you before you leave."

"But, my dear, I—I … don't … think it … will be possible … I have so many things to … clear up before I go …"

"Viktor, I won't take no for an answer.… Is business more important than I am?"

"Of course not, it's just that my time is so limited.…"

"Darling.…" her voice had a ring of determination, "I said I won't take no for an answer. You have to take time to eat dinner, don't you?"

"Yes, I suppose.…"

"Then what's the difference whether you eat alone, or eat with me? It'll still take the same amount of time, and I'll be able to be with you before you go. After all, you're going for a whole month. That's a long time. I'll be worried and lonesome. Please, Viktor, darling.… Yes?"

Henry's curiosity got the best of his better judgment.

"Well … all right … where?"

"Are you going home now?"

"Yes."

"Well, suppose I save you time and energy by meeting you in the lobby of the Blake. Then we can eat in the dining room there. Is that all right, dear?"

"Oh yes, and darling.…"

"Yes?"

"Stop in the Blake florist first and buy an orchid. Compliments of Dr. Viktor Bartok!"

"Thank you, my sweet—that was very thoughtful of you."

"Not at all. When I see a beautiful lady with a beautiful orchid, I'll know it's only one person.…"

"Viktor! You leave me speechless—you have never been so gallant!"

"Maybe in the last few days I've had time to think about a good many things that I never thought about before. Sometimes we allow ourselves to become unappreciative. Is that not right, my dear?"

"Yes, Viktor. I've waited so long to hear you say things like that. The sound of your voice is so thrilling tonight. I can't wait to see you. What time, my darling?"

"It's six-ten now. Say about eight?"

"That'll be perfect. In the lobby."

"Yes. Don't forget the orchid."

"I won't. Goodbye, Viktor."

"Goodbye … dear."

So, he thought, that was how it was! Another *affaire d'amour* in the supposedly quiet and decorous life of Dr. Viktor Bartok. He was doing all right for a dignified physician. Two romances running at the same time. Quite a Don Juan in his own modest little way! Henry was intrigued by the turn of events. There had been nothing staid about Dr. Bartok. He had been a man of great medical knowledge, but he had been also a man of human instincts and human requirements. He must have had a wonderful personality, an abundance of charm and *savoir-faire*. Only all these liaisons of the doctor's, interesting though they promised to be, weren't going to make his own masquerade any easy role. He had come a long way: too far to have the props kicked from under him by any woman. He had made a dinner engagement with a lady and he had no idea of her identity, her looks, or her status. All he knew was that she would wear an orchid. He hoped that not many women would be wearing orchids in the Blake lobby tonight.

CHAPTER TWELVE

"Lobby floor!" announced the elevator boy. Henry stepped from the car, walked to the desk and told the clerk he would be in the dining room for calls.

He walked across toward the west lobby and glanced at his watch. It was five minutes of eight. He saw a number of women but all without an orchid. Seating himself by the fountain, he faced the main lobby so that his unknown caller would be sure to see him sitting there. Even if he did not know her, she would recognize him. There shouldn't be too much difficulty. She would smile as she approached and say, "Hello, darling" or "Hello, Viktor, dear," thus identifying herself. Anyhow, she would be wearing the corsage, and that, plus the greeting, would surely identify her.

Some ten minutes later, at eight-five, Henry caught sight of a woman, fashionably dressed, crossing the lobby. She was wearing a large orchid on her left shoulder, but good God, she was easily a size 40! She spoke to the clerk and then walked toward the elevators. He muttered a prayer of thanksgiving. A few minutes later, two other women wearing orchids walked up the steps of the lobby. They were followed a moment later by two men dressed in evening clothes. It was apparent that some kind of an affair was taking place tonight. He called one of the nearby bellboys. "Something going on this evening?" he inquired.

"Yes, sir. There's a wedding reception in the ballroom."

"Oh … thank you." No sooner had he spoken than an unescorted woman came toward him. She was dressed in a smart dinner gown, and from her shoulder sprouted the largest orchid he had ever seen. She was staring right at him, grinning the biggest grin that a mouth could accommodate. Her face was long and horsey looking, ending in a lantern jaw. To this was added a mop of bleached blonde curls that hung about her scrawny neck, and only emphasized her age, an easy forty-five. She was making straight for his chair! Henry's heart began to sink and he found himself sliding down into the seat. As she came closer he saw that, on top of everything else, she had a squint. Then she spoke.

"Hello, darling, did I keep you waiting?"

Henry closed his eyes.

"Only a few minutes," came the answer behind him.

His eyes flashed open. She wasn't standing in front of him. There she was, being greeted by her escort, who was fat and bald and who stood a half-head shorter than she. Henry had not been aware that the chair back of him was occupied. He mopped his brow.

The guests attending the wedding reception began to arrive in droves, and Henry soon discovered to his dismay that the lobby was beginning to fill with orchid-bearing women. "Just my luck," mumbled Henry to himself, "Tonight, of all nights, there would have to be a wedding reception, and the place is lousy with orchids!"

He began to wonder what had become of his caller and he lowered his head to look at his wristwatch. A pair of hands suddenly slipped over his eyes, shutting off everything.

"Guess who?" The voice was the same soft, alluring one that he had heard on the telephone.

"I … I can't guess …" His fingers found their way to her wrists. They were small and delicate. He ran them up her arms. They felt smooth, satiny, and pliable, as feminine flesh should feel.

"You are in my power," she whispered in his ear, "and I won't let you go until you guess who it is."

"Is it the Old Witch of Inverness?"

"No! Guess again."

"Is it the Sorceress of Cyclops?"

"No. Guess again."

"Then it must be Isolde the Beautiful, come to life and more lovely than ever!"

"Viktor, darling, I never knew you could say such wonderful things." She withdrew her hands from his eyes and stepped in front of the chair. Henry rose.

"Thank heavens," he said.

"Thank heavens for what?"

"For a great many things."

"For instance?"

"You."

"Me?"

"Yes."

"Why should you thank heavens for me?"

"For being as lovely as you are."

"How sweet of you, Viktor!"

"And also because you're not wearing an orchid."

"No, the florist was sold out, so I bought gardenias instead. I hope you're not disappointed."

"On the contrary. I was never more happy to see a gardenia in my life! As you probably notice, every other woman here is wearing an orchid this evening. I shall most likely see orchids in my sleep tonight!"

She laughed gaily and put her arm under his as they walked toward the dining room.

"I didn't expect you to sneak up behind me that way. I was watching the main entrance."

"Ah, always expect me to do the unexpected! I came in the Oak Street entrance. I'm sorry to be late, dear, but I couldn't get a cab, so I walked. Anyhow, it would be a shame to take a cab from my building to the Blake. Walking is so good for the hips, darling. I should walk a few miles instead of a few blocks."

A few blocks! That meant she lived nearby. The Blake was ten-hundred north. He used to trail Dr. Bartok two or three nights a week to the 1220 Lake Shore Drive Apartments. That was exactly two blocks away! Bartok had been secretive about those visits. He had always entered alone, and left alone. Henry felt sure that before the evening was over, he would learn not only the identity of his charming guest, but the identity of Bartok's friend at 1220 Lake Shore Drive. And hers would be a delightful identity to learn!

"Good evening. Table for two?" It was the headwaiter who greeted them at the entrance to the dining room.

"Yes, please."

"Yes, sir. This way, sir, madame." He escorted them to a cozy little table in a secluded corner. "How is this, doctor?"

"Fine, thank you."

"I'll see that you get served immediately." He seated them, handed each a menu, and went off in search of the waiter.

Henry now had an opportunity to study the woman who sat opposite him. She was wearing a beautiful fur jacket, which, at that moment, she was attempting to remove.

"May I help you, dear?" He started to rise.

"No, no, please don't bother, Viktor, I'm just going to slide it off my shoulders."

"It's very beautiful."

"Thank you, darling, but you've seen it a dozen times."

"I know, but I like it better each time I see it. What kind of fur do you call that?"

"Viktor, I thought you had a faultless memory. It's Russian sable, darling."

"Oh, yes, that's right. You must forgive me, my dear, I'm afraid my memory is slipping."

"As long as you always remember to say the beautiful things you said to me on the phone, I don't really care whether your memory is slipping or not!"

Henry laughed. "Very well said, my dear." He looked squarely into her eyes. They were large and hazel-colored, speckled with green, and the lashes were long. Her face was oval-shaped and fine-boned, her hair a lovely shade of chestnut-brown, carefully groomed in a high coiffure. She was dressed smartly but simply in a black dinner dress, the low neckline displaying a full and handsome bosom. It was there that Henry's gaze fell and rested until her voice brought his eyes back to hers.

"You don't look as though you've been ill, Viktor. You're a little pale, it's true. You had a beautiful tan from golfing the last time I saw you. You certainly lost it in a hurry."

"Yes, I did. I will get it back in Colorado Springs."

"Do you have a cigarette, dear? I'm all out."

"Yes, of course." He felt his pocket. "No, I'm afraid not. I guess I left them up in my room. Oh, here comes the waiter."

"Good evening, madame, good evening, sir—oh, *bon soir, monsieur—*" It was the little French waiter who had brought up his breakfast. "I did not recognize you at first. *Comment allez-vous, ce soir?*"

"*Je suis très bien, et vous?*"

"*Merci, bien. Très bien.* What can I get you? A nice cocktail? Manhattan? Bacardi? Martini?"

"Yes, I think that would go very well. Darling?"

"I'll have a dry Martini. Extra dry, please."

"*Oui*, madame."

"I'll have some Black Label with a dash of lemon peel. And some cigarettes, please," Henry ordered.

"Yes, sir. Any particular brand, sir?"

"Bring me a package of Melachrinos. And what kind do you care for, dear?"

"Viktor, shame on you. Your memory is atrocious this evening. Philip Morris, waiter."

"Yes, madame. Thank you." He pranced away hurriedly.

"You surprised me, dear. I've never heard you speak French before. I didn't even know you knew the language."

"Oh, I know a little—just enough to get by with a greeting. After all, one does not stay in Paris very long without picking up something of the language."

"Every day I'm learning more about you. Here we've known each other almost two years and you have never told me you were in Paris. Were you there long?"

"No, I would say perhaps six weeks. I was on a vacation."

"Did you like Paris?"

"Very much. It is colorful and gay, and completely uninhibited."

"And so are the women, I understand."

"Yes—I suppose that could be said."

"Did you find the French girls pretty and captivating?"

"Yes, but invariably a pretty girl over there has an ugly smile, because her teeth are uneven and dark." He read that once in a magazine on "Foreign Beauty vs. American Beauty." Henry began to quote from the article. "You see—dear," (he wished to Christ he knew her name, so he wouldn't have to keep repeating "dear" or "darling" all evening) "foreign women cannot compete with American women when it comes to beauty, because, as babies, they are not given orange juice nor the quantity of milk and other foods containing calcium that are so necessary to good strong white teeth such as our—I mean your American women have."

"Oh, I see."

He certainly was grateful for his elementary subjects at pre-med school.

"You see, you are lovely and captivating because among other things you have beautiful teeth."

"Thanks to orange juice—"

"Yes."

"And milk."

"Yes."

"Well, I don't know. I guess I must have played somebody a dirty trick somewhere—"

"What do you mean?"

"I hate orange juice—always have and my mother never could get me to drink milk even when I was a baby!"

"Then that makes you the exception to the rule, I guess. What did you drink as a child?"

"Dry Martinis, I suppose!" They both laughed.

The string ensemble began to play dinner music. The cocktail came, and they ordered dinner, which they ate leisurely while listening to the music and to each other's conversation. Henry found his companion delightfully refreshing. She had a scintillating mind and a sharp sense of humor. It was apparent that her background was that of the upper strata and that she moved in the atmosphere of Chicago's four hundred. He was still unsure of the extent of Bartok's interest, although there was little question in his mind of her being the doctor's inamorata. She was certainly desirable, and Henry admired Bartok's taste in women. He would have no time for lovemaking now, but it was interesting to anticipate what might take place upon his return to Chicago. So far, there was no hint that she had the slightest reason to doubt the identity of her escort. Would she be able to detect the impersonation under more intimate circumstances? Would there be differences in words—actions—caresses—techniques? Henry knew that when it came to making love, a woman can be extremely sensitive to the slightest inconsistency of her lover. There would be ample time to think about that in the days to come. One thing puzzled him. Which of the two women was Bartok's real love? Or was it neither one? They were very different. Evelyn Hahn was perhaps twenty-five or twenty-six years old, intelligent, but unsophisticated. She was not beautiful but had warmth and complete sincerity. This woman who sat opposite him was at least thirty or thirty-two years old, and was decidedly worldly, a complete sophisticate, cultured and polished as well as intellectual. Besides being devastatingly beautiful, she had dignity and poise; but although she sparkled with personality, Henry was not sure of her sincerity. She too, he thought, was egotistical, dependent upon the reactions and impressions of those surrounding her.

Yet, Henry reasoned, she was not a phony. Her educational background was Smith or Vassar. Either she or her family had money. She spoke as one who has traveled extensively. Why wasn't she married? A woman of her beauty and charms would be attractive to any man. Why was she content to be just Bartok's mistress? Of course, that was still just conjecture, but a pretty sure one. It might be that she was willing to forego all offers to be a part-time love of Bartok's. If that were so, the psychiatrist must have had an overwhelming attraction for her.

"What are you thinking, dear?" It was she who spoke and terminated his speculations.

"About you, my darling, and how much I'm going to miss you when I leave."

"Don't say that too often, Viktor dear, I'm liable to use it as a good excuse to go along with you!"

Quickly he intervened. "Thank you, my sweet, that would be delightful, but this time I go alone. A change of atmosphere, a change of environment—even people—is necessary for everyone once in a while. Then one comes back refreshed and revitalized." Slyly, gauging her reaction, he added: "I will return more ardent than ever before—"

"Any more ardent than you've been, darling, and I'll have to sneak some saltpeter in your food when you're not looking!"

Henry's eyes popped. From now on, he would know how to direct his conversation and his aims. When opportune, he would pick up Dr. Bartok's romance where Bartok had left off. Then, with this lovely and alluring woman, his only concern would be whether or not he was able to do justice to his predecessor.

The waiter was back. "Pardon, *monsieur*. You are ready for coffee and dessert?"

"Yes. What do you suggest?"

"Naturally French pastry, *monsieur*. It is *par excellence!*"

"All right with you, dear?"

"I suppose. I'll have to go to Elizabeth Arden's tomorrow and have it pounded off, but for tonight it's French pastry."

"You're a Spartan, dear. I like to see a woman have the courage of her convictions. Two, waiter, and coffee."

"Very good, sir." He scampered away in the funny quick little steps that made him appear a musical comedy version of a French waiter.

"He's cute," she said, "what's his name?"

"I'm not sure. Probably Pierre. It usually is. He's very efficient, and very sociable. Sometimes he brings up my breakfast."

"Oh? Since when have you started eating breakfast?"

"Hm?"

"I said since when have you started eating breakfast? You never have before."

"Since … I … started getting hungry."

"Well, you certainly have become a changed man since last week!"

"Er … yes. My appetite has been slowly returning. I actually like to eat now in the morning."

"Viktor, for a sick man you certainly don't possess any of the symptoms. You did justice to your dinner tonight, and now you tell me you've gone back to eating breakfast! On top of that, you don't act sick, and you don't look sick. You know what I think?"

"No, what?" Henry began to bite his lip.

"I think you're a big fake!"

His mouth went dry. "Fake?"

"Yes, I think you've cooked up this whole idea of a heart attack just to get out of town."

He felt his blood run cold. "That's a bit ludicrous. Why do you say that?"

"Because I think you want to get out of town and leave me so that you can meet your other women!"

"Oh, so that's it!" He quivered with relief after the first blow of her innuendo. "Darling, how could you think such a thing? You may dismiss your fears. I'm really going away for my health. The attack was not severe enough to interrupt my normal activities, but I am taking no chances. I must rest up. And as far as another woman is concerned, if there were such a thing as a male chastity belt, I would wear one just to prove my constancy."

"Darling, forgive me. Any man that would do that for a woman is either very much in love or very much incapacitated!"

Henry laughed heartily. "My dear, you're precious. You have a quick wit and a fine sense of humor."

"Thank you, my darling. I'd much rather hear you say that than anything else. That's far more important than being beautiful or charming. I think a good sense of humor can fortify a woman for that tiresome necessity, old age—so that when it comes, one can accept it with a smile and grace—the way an old friend should be greeted and welcomed."

"Well, you're quite a philosopher in your own right, aren't you? And a very beautiful philosophy you've just expressed. So you're not afraid of growing old?"

"Not at all. To me it holds no fears, no terrors. I shall hold my head high as I bear the ugly scars of antiquity—"

She stopped suddenly, her eyes on his left cheek.

"Yes? What is it, dear? Why are you looking at me like that?" He knew. Here it was all over again. His teeth began to gnaw on his lower lip.

"Excuse me, but I'm a bit confused. I never knew one cocktail to go to my head, but—but I could almost swear my life away on the fact that your scar was always on the right cheek."

He smiled nonchalantly. "Don't swear on it, my dear, because you'd lose that precious life of yours."

"Isn't that odd? I didn't notice it all evening until just now, and it just struck me as being—oh, let's forget it."

Henry reached across the table and pressed her hand. It had been easier than he could have hoped. Once accepted, he would have no more explaining to do. At least not to her.

"Pardon, madame." It was the waiter with the dessert. "Does that not look delicious?"

"Yes, very."

They ate the dessert, as the ensemble began the captivating strains of Debussy's *Clair de Lune*.

"Oh," she said, putting down her fork, "I could die to this music."

"It is beautiful," agreed Henry. "My favorite, though, is Tchaikovsky."

"Mine is Deems Taylor."

"You prefer American composers? Well, at least you are loyal to your country."

"To say nothing about being loyal to the great clans of Taylors. After all, we must hang together, or we'll hang separately."

"Yes, that's right." Ah! He knew her name at last! Now he must try to find out her first name. After a moment he pulled out a cigarette and said, as if the thought had just struck him, "Speaking of names, I ran across a funny American game the other day. It combines a bit of handwriting analysis with a form of fortune telling."

"Sounds like it might be interesting. How does it go?"

"It's quite clever. Wait, let me see if I have a pencil. Oh, yes, here now. Have we any paper handy?"

"I don't think so. I haven't any."

"Never mind, I will use the tablecloth. First we write our last names. Now I will write Bartok. Under that I will write Taylor. Now you cross out the 'a' in my name, and the 'a' in yours. Then you cross out the 't' in my name and 't' in yours; then the 'o' in mine, and the 'a' in yours; then the 'r' in mine, and the 'r' in yours. What does that leave?"

"Not a hell of a lot!"

"Shush. It leaves the 'b' and the 'k' in mine, and the 'y' and 'l' in yours."

"Um hm. I follow you up to there. Now what do you do?"

"Don't be so impatient. That's only half. Now the first names are the key to the fortune. So, first I will write my first name. V-i-k-t-o-r. Now you must write your first name under mine." He smiled at her fondly.

"You write it."

"No, darling. That is not the game. How can I analyze your handwriting if I do the writing? It has to be in your own hand."

"Oh."

"Here."

"All right. This better be good."

"I can't promise anything. I only saw it done once. If it does not turn out, you will get a refund. That's fine. Now you cross out the 'v' in my name, and the 'v' in yours; then the 'i' in mine, but there are three 'i's' in yours, so we cross out that one, and that one, and that one. Now what else? Oh yes, the 'r' in mine, and the 'r' in yours. Anything else?"

"No, that's all I can see."

"Me too. So that leaves 'k-t-o' in mine, and the 'g-n-a' in yours."

"So?"

"So now you add them all up. You have left 'y-l-g-n-a,' 25 points for the 'y' because it is the 25th letter of the alphabet, see? All right, you have 25 and 12, and 7 and 14, and 1. That makes a total of 59. I have left 'b-k-k-t-o.' That totals up 2, plus 11, plus 11, plus 20, plus 15. That adds up to … 59! How do you like that! It's a tie! That's very unusual."

"That's astounding, darling. Now what do we give each other? A gold-plated mousetrap?"

"Oh, you are giving me the razzberry." He didn't blame her. He felt like a nitwit going through all that nonsense.

"No, Viktor, I'm not razzing you, darling. Don't be so sensitive. I think it's a cute game. But where does the handwriting analysis and the fortune telling come in?"

He had started something; he would have to finish it. Well, he had faked a great many things before, he could fake this too.

"Let me see … according to the way you make your 'r's,' you indicate a woman of extreme capabilities and a very fine appreciation of 'l'....."

An hour later Henry escorted his dinner companion to the entrance of the hotel.

"Oh, look, Viktor, it's raining!"

"So it is. Well, we'll get you a cab."

"Darling, it was a delightful evening. I enjoyed every minute of it. The dinner; 59 to 59; that wonderful handwriting analysis … my, I'm brilliant, aren't I, according to all those 'r's' and 'y's' and 'g's!' And I've even got a terrific future ahead of me too, haven't I? And here all the time, I thought the only thing I had that was sensational was my past!"

Henry laughed. "Not at all. You see you were saved from a very dull future by those triple 'i's.' Oh, there's a cab pulling up now. Doorman! Hold that cab!"

"Yes, doctor."

There was a hurried kiss, and in a moment she was inside the cab, talking through the lowered window.

"Goodbye, Viktor, darling. I love you. Please take care of yourself. Write me loads of letters, and I can't wait till you get back."

"Yes, dear, I'll write."

"Call me tomorrow before you leave—just to say goodbye."

"Yes, dear, I will."

"Goodbye, Viktor, darling. All right, driver. 1220 Lake Shore Drive...."

Henry smiled triumphantly; she herself had supplied that last link. "I'll call you tomorrow … Goodbye … Virginia!"

CHAPTER THIRTEEN

COLORADO SPRINGS
Wednesday
June 28th, 1939

"My darling Virginia:

"Tomorrow is my last day here. I will be home Saturday morning after one month of the most glorious vacation I have ever had. I am thoroughly rested, tan as a lifeguard, and feel like twenty-one. (If I can only live up to that!)

"In your last letter you said life had been dull and uninteresting since I went away. In one way this makes me happy—that is the selfish part of me—but in another way, it is wrong for you to make a female hermit out of yourself. Am I worthy of such loyalty?

"However, as long as I have never been out of town before, I think we have done very nobly under the circumstances.

"Of course there are women all over the place, but I have been too busy with the books and papers I brought with me to give them a glance. Isn't it just like a doctor—but I have really used the last 30 days to good advantage, going into further research. There is always room for improvement, you know."

"Thank you for writing so faithfully. I know I am not a good correspondent, but anyhow, a letter is a very inanimate object, and what I lacked in my letters, I will make up for in person.

"That is all for now. I will telephone you when I get in. Love and kisses from 59 to 59!

"Yours in adoration,
VIKTOR"

Henry threw down the pen, blotted the signature and placed the letter in an envelope. He didn't particularly relish writing these letters. He had not begun this most dangerous of ventures to acquire a mere sexual life. He had always had his full share of that without the nerve-wracking hazards that he was now facing. Money was his prime object. It represented to him the ability to bask in luxury, to associate with the people who had at one time found him socially inferior. He had vowed to himself on the day he was turned down by Phi Tau fraternity, that one day they would finish by eating out of his hand. There would be no resting, no sitting back, no resignation, until he had fulfilled that vow. It was not only a goal; it had become a driving, unrelenting necessity. Women were decidedly of secondary importance. They were all right as playthings, but they could not further promote his ambitions. And they all wanted to get married, which he did not have in mind. It represented nothing that could aid his forward trek toward power. He had tried it once with Carlotta. At the time, that had been a necessary step and definitely a marriage of convenience. Now he was in a position where he did not need marriage for convenience or anything else. He was quite self-sufficient. He would build up a defense against any plan of attack that might be launched by either of the two women he had inherited, or any other that might come into his life in the future. Romances? They were necessary. Marriage was not.

Suddenly Henry remembered that Evelyn Hahn's last words had been a request to drop a card if he found time. He had been here a month, and so far had failed to write her a line. This was not altogether his fault, since he hadn't the slightest idea of where she lived. Her address was not in Bartok's files. Bartok would have known, of course, and his failure to write could seem only neglect and indifference to her. He would have no logical explanation for his negligence, and if his aloofness had made her unhappy before, how miserable she must be now. If Bartok had fostered an office romance with Evelyn Hahn, and had declared his love (which Henry suspected to be true), then his failure to send any word was a painful slap in the face to her. Too bad, Henry sighed to himself, but there was nothing he could do, and for the moment he could think of no excuse that would justify his apparent indifference.

It was while he was going over the last cards of active cases in the file, preparatory to packing up, that he came across the briefcase he had shoved into a corner upon his arrival. In it he had stuffed a number of letters and notes from Bartok's desk. For a month he had busied himself studying his future patients and had completely overlooked the briefcase. Now he sat down and prepared to give the contents a careful perusal. For the most part, they were letters from friends and colleagues, receipts, and a number of private papers on theories and experiments in the neurological field. One paper in particular caught Henry's attention. It was dated February 10th, 1937; it seemed to be Bartok's treatise on a specialized theory; a theory of electric shock therapy. He read it carefully.

It is highly probable that in the last World War the ravages of shell shock to the central nervous system could have been considerably reduced by a type of electric shock therapy. This, which I would call electric sleep, would be given to a patient in impulses of fifteen to thirty seconds. The treatments would vary in length from three to nine weeks, depending upon the degree of shock, and would be administered once a day, along with intramuscular or intravenous injections of sodium amytal, luminal, or pentothal.

For other psychoneurotic problems arising from a soldier's fears in battle, wherein he becomes a distinct psychiatric case, I would experiment with a form of treatment that I have long considered the answer to this most baffling of army medical questions; i.e., how to rehabilitate the soldier suffering from war nerves. I think I have the answer in a swiftly administered and highly effective technique known as narcosynthesis. In this, the patient is put to sleep by intravenous injections of sodium pentothal. Then, in the synthetic dream-state which follows, terrors buried deep in the patient's subconscious mind come to the surface. He then talks freely with the doctor. Soon his most painful memories are robbed of their guilt feeling. The psychiatrist, knowing what is in the man's mind, can then work methodically to bring him back to normal stability.

In the case of traumatic neurosis, wherein the soldier, after recovering from his wound, is still suffering from the effects of the trauma, and constantly finds himself reliving his experience, I would recommend a combination of the first described treatment (electric sleep) plus the latter experiment (narcosynthesis). The alternate treatment of these two experiments should, in my opinion, have highly surprising results. First, because in the treatment of a traumatic neurosis, it is essential to bring the patient out of his physical fixation of continually reliving his experience in his dreams, as well as during his waking moments. This constant reminder of the trauma has unquestionably brought the patient to the highly neurotic state of hysteria, with its varying degrees of motor symptoms. In addition, we find very strong indications of subjective sufferings with marked signs of hypochondria, which are invariably followed by long periods of mental depression. Breuer and Freud both stated, in 1893, that hysterics suffer for the most part from reminiscences. Therefore, accepting this conclusion from two men of authority in the psychiatric field, I proceed on the theory that to bring about a cure in traumatic neurosis, we need but to banish forever the fears and their resultant effects upon the patient's nervous system. Only through sleep can we attack the subconscious mind and root out the disturbing factors that work insidiously to undermine and prevent the rehabilitation of the patient's mind to a state of peace and tranquility. This we would do with narcosynthesis, and proceed with the same treatment (as described in paragraph two) during the synthetic dream-state. The alternate treatments would be every other day; i.e., a fifteen-second application by electric shock therapy, followed the same day by the injections of sodium pentothal to induce the patient to fall into the completely abstract state of total subconsciousness, thereby offering a minimum of resistance to the psychiatrist's analytical probings. Discounting unforeseen complications, we should find the soldier suffering from traumatic neurosis returning to a state of happy normalcy within nine to twelve weeks.

My theories are based upon the actual results of patients I have attended. One was a Dutch airlines pilot, who, having survived a plane crash, developed the fear symptoms described in paragraph two. In six weeks at the Copenhagen clinic, I cured him by the narcosynthesis technique, so that he returned to flying, completely cured of his fears.

Also in 1930, while at the Copenhagen Institute, I was given the case of a young mining engineer who survived the underground explosion of a coal mine in Germany. He developed a distinct traumatic neurosis that had defied the best psychiatric heads on the continent. He came to me a complete hysteric, and suffering from frequent outbursts of maniacal anguish at real or imaginary sounds. The backfire of a motor car, or sudden clap of thunder, would send him into uncontrollable fits of terror and panic. I proceeded with the alternate treatments of electric shock therapy, and the injections of sodium pentothal for a period of eight weeks. At the end of this time, I found him to be completely restored to normal. The shooting off of blank cartridges without warning, the clap of thunder during an electrical storm, or the backfire of motor cars occasioned little more than the average reaction.

Both of the above cases, though civilian in method of acquisition, so closely resembled the reactions of wartime psychoneurotics, that I have every reason to believe that they could easily parallel the case of a flyer in battle, or a soldier wounded in the explosion of a shell. Therefore, in summary I would say that, technically, applied as cure for the several types of war neurosis, this treatise is purely theoretical, but I have complete confidence in my findings. None of these experiments has been tried under actual wartime conditions, but were I now in Spain during the present Spanish Civil War, I should very likely ask permission of the Loyalist Government to try out my theory.

Let us hope and pray, that here in America, I will never be called upon to perform my experiment on soldiers suffering from psychopathological disorders.

Henry paused to digest what he had just read. Then he reread the paper once more and sat for some time musing over the possibilities of Bartok's experiment and theory. If this treatment of electric shock therapy, with the narcosynthesis format of intravenous injections of sodium pentothal to induce synthetic dream-state, was as successful as Bartok reasoned, why, then here in his hand he held the answer to one of the greatest problems in the history of psychiatry. From numerous books that he had read, Henry knew that for years neurologists had sought desperately to find a successful treatment for war neurosis. This, then, was a hope for the future thousands of war-ravaged mentally deficients, a curative for the psychological scars left on the human brain in the never-ending struggle of man's efforts to destroy man.

Now there was peace—but not for long, Henry reasoned. Events across the Atlantic were moving swiftly toward a climax. War had been averted by a small margin of hours last spring when Chamberlain, apostle of appeasement, had handed the Sudetenland to Hitler on a silver platter. A few side dishes like the Ruhr, the Saar, the Rhineland, Austria, Czechoslovakia were thrown in as appetizers. And now Hitler was crying for Danzig and the Polish Corridor.

He folded the paper and slipped it back into the briefcase. To him it seemed a far greater discovery than Bartok's previous contribution of insulin shock treatment for schizophrenia, which had won the Nobel Prize in 1936. For a few minutes he felt pangs of conscience for having robbed the world of so gifted a brain. What could he give to humanity to justify his place in this vast scheme of things?

CHAPTER FOURTEEN

"Hello, doctor! Glad to see you back."

"Thank you. It's good to be back."

"My, you're tan! Did you have a nice vacation?"

"Yes, very restful, thank you."

"Here's your key, and there's quite a bit of mail in your box. There you are. Quite a handful, isn't it?"

"Yes. I didn't know I was so popular. But then, today is the first of the month, isn't it?"

"Yes, sir. July first."

"That probably accounts for at least half of my popularity."

The clerk laughed, and Henry went on up to his room. He looked over the mail. There was nothing of real importance, but one letter was a bit disturbing. It was from the University of Fort Dearborn informing Dr. Bartok that fall-term lecture classes were to start the second week in September, and asking if he would be available again this year for one lecture a week on psychiatry and neurology. It was hoped his schedule would permit, as they would be greatly honored to have so distinguished a physician on their lecture staff. It was signed by the dean of the medical school, Professor James T. Newcomb, and in the left-hand corner was a P. S. It said: "Don't let us down, Viktor, if you can help it. We need you! J. T."

Henry slowly put the letter aside and sat down to turn the matter over in his mind. This was a grave decision with which he was faced.

To turn the university down would be discourteous and unprofessional. If it had been some other school, he could decline, but at Fort Dearborn, Bartok had been a professor of neurology and had remained on the lecture staff at the end of the previous year. Henry Mueller was only a second-year medical student who had garnered his knowledge of psychopathology from textbooks, not from actual practice. Could he lecture once a week on psychiatry to a class of students, and be convincing? Did he have even sufficient textbook knowledge to step up on a platform and give an intelligent hour's talk? Could he direct the students in their studies, and tell them what strides were being made in the field of psychiatry? He would think it over.

That afternoon, after unpacking, he called Virginia Taylor and made an appointment to have dinner and spend the evening together. Henry looked forward to this engagement. Virginia was a very desirable woman, although no more so than Katherine Fitzgerald, with whom he had had a brief affair at Colorado Springs. An attractive divorcee, socially prominent in New York, she had been extremely receptive to Henry's attentions. By the time he left for Chicago he felt that his departure was all for the best, since the romance was becoming a bit more serious than he intended. Perhaps he had put too much fire and imagination into his love-making. He knew himself to be an ardent lover and magnetic with women, but he wished they were more like men in being satisfied with just having an affair. Why did they forever and always have to take their love so seriously, and start thinking of marriage? It was part of woman's nature, he concluded, and nothing would ever change the female psychology. Well, he would carry on with Virginia Taylor as long as she made it comfortable for him. After that—there were as many women from whom to choose as there were pebbles on the beach, and they were of little more significance.

Henry walked over to the record cabinet, took out a Rachmaninoff album, turned on the phonograph, and then prepared a hot bath. In the warm, soothing suds he relaxed at his ease, cigarettes and magazines at hand, as the strains of the beautiful Second Symphony in E Minor floated in through the open door. This was the way he had always planned to live, and now it seemed as if these luxuries had always been a part of his existence. Strange that his tastes and Dr. Bartok's should have been so similar. They liked the same things— music—beautiful surroundings—enchanting women—wealth, and lastly, freedom from marriage with its restraints and inhibitions. This feeling—of being absolute sovereign in his own little kingdom—

meant much to Henry. Bartok, too, had been fully aware of this greatest of all luxuries. From all indications, he had had no intentions of parting with his bachelorhood and his liberty.

At seven o'clock sharp he called for Virginia Taylor in the Cadillac which he had not driven since the night he had used it to dispose of the body of its rightful owner. Virginia, gay and beautiful, was extremely happy in the reunion. They had dinner in the exciting atmosphere of a swank Russian restaurant and afterward, they had their fortunes told by a palmist, who approached their table with an ingratiating bow. In a soft mystic voice, the yogi, dark-skinned and wearing a turban with a brilliant jewel in the center, told Virginia, "You are a woman capable of great love, but you are not happy. Yours is a false gaiety. You try to convince yourself of a happiness which you know does not exist. This is not your home in Chicago, is it?"

"No."

"Your home is in another city, in the east? Yes?"

"That's right."

"That is where your true happiness lies. Among your family, your friends—you left all that to come here to Chicago, but whatever you are seeking, you will not find here."

Virginia looked up, keen disappointment in her eyes.

"You are sure?"

"The palm does not lie, madame. The destiny of the soul is indelibly stamped in the lines of one's hand. A great power put them there. Not I nor anyone else could ever do anything to change them. I only read what I see. For the sake of my clientele, and because it is only natural for human beings to want to hear good things, I try to avoid discussing unpleasantries. You see, you are a very beautiful woman, and men are easily attracted to you. You have an interesting future ahead of you, and I see a marriage—but not the marriage that you envision now."

"No?"

"No, dear lady, that has complications—I mean your present hopes and desires will fail to materialize. But I see a life of far greater happiness for you elsewhere. A life of stability and peace which you do not now have."

"Is that all?"

"Yes, madame, only to remember that peace of mind is one of the most priceless of all possessions. And now, would the gentleman care to have his palm read?"

"No, I don't think so, thank you."

Virginia was too curious to let him off so easily.

"Oh, Viktor, yes. Please. I want to hear what he has to tell you. Why not?"

"Because I don't believe in this fortune telling business. It has become too commercialized."

The yogi smiled. "Excuse please, sir? I am not fortune teller, I am not gifted with the powers to foresee coming events. I practice no quackery, no fakery. I use no crystal ball. I am a student of palmistry. I only tell what I see written in the hand. That is your destiny. The lines in one's face can change according to age and manner of living. Even certain climates like the tropics will produce changes in the facial characteristics. But the lines in the palm remain unchanged and unaffected. From birth to death they are man's own chart of his happiness or unhappiness. It has been said that the eyes are the mirror of the soul. I would say that the eyes are the lens of the soul, and the palm is the photograph. Your eyes interest me. May I have the honor of reading your palm?"

Henry's reluctance made Virginia even more inquisitive. "Darling, now don't be an old cynic. You just found out all about me. My most private thoughts were scattered to the four winds, and my soul was laid bare and dissected into little pieces. But did I crawl into my shell and become morbid? No! I took it like a Spartan. That's your own expression for me. Remember? The last time we had dinner together you told me I had the courage of a Spartan. Now, where's your courage?" She did not know that Henry's reticence was prompted by his sense of inferiority; that he feared the Hindu's seeing that which others had failed to detect; that he was apprehensive lest he should be revealed in his true light. Still, that was sheer nonsense. How could the man know anything about him? He was Dr. Viktor Emil Bartok. He could prove it. He had all his identifications with him.

"Who says I have no courage?" He put out his hand in a gesture of nonchalance.

"Good for you, Viktor," Virginia laughed gaily. "I knew you wouldn't let us down!"

"The other hand, please," said the swami. "We read the right hand first."

He looked at length at Henry's palm, his findings cloaked in mystic silence. Finally, after a full minute he spoke. "The gentleman has one of the most interesting and unusual palms I have seen in many years. You are a man with many sides to your personality. It would be difficult to say which side is the one you assume today, and which one you will wear tomorrow. Your hand is the hand of a genius and a conqueror. You have a multitude of gifts. Your intelligence is that of a Socrates and your powers are that of a Caesar. You have a lust for life and a driving ambition that will not allow you to rest until you have attained your goal. The brilliance of your mind is capable of doing many things, both good and bad, and that will be determined by which of your several sides will predominate. Wealth and power will one day be yours. In your efforts to reach the heights, you will be victorious, but fame and fortune that is ill-gotten and procured at the sacrifice of self-respect and honor can bring to its possessor only the feeling of a triumphant emptiness."

Henry fidgeted. "Did you mean that for me? That's my future?"

The Hindu smiled again and his dark skin wrinkled as from under the thick bushy eyebrows his gaze slowly ascended. "Please to remember, kind sir, I am not a fortune teller. Shall I go on?"

Henry bit into his lower lip. "Yes, please do."

"Of course. Oh, Viktor, this is thrilling," said Virginia excitedly.

Henry was flattered by the comparison to Socrates and Caesar. He felt smug and pleased at the suggestion that he was a genius and a conqueror. He paid little attention to the insinuation of the reader that he had a split personality or to the prediction of the hollowness of his ultimate success. He only knew that he had heard the words power and wealth. Little else mattered.

"I also see in your hand the skill of one who might have been perhaps an artist, or an actor or even a doctor. Yours is a professional hand, artistic in its shape. The fingers are long and graceful and delicate. You are, of course, in one of the three professions I have just named?"

"Yes."

"I would say that had you selected the profession of medicine, you might have been a good doctor. As it is, I see that you wisely chose to become an actor."

Virginia gave way to laughter at this point. Henry kept silent.

"The lady seems amused?"

"Yes, please forgive me. I didn't mean to be rude. It was just the last thing you said struck me as being a bit humorous."

"You mean I was in error?"

Henry took over the question. "Rather. You see I am a … doctor."

"Oh, so sorry, kind sir. The hand showed a predominance for the make-believe, which is, of course, the most important asset in the art of acting. To have imagination and the ability to interpret various roles. To be able to express one's self so realistically that the actor finds himself actually living the part he is playing. It is unfortunate that you preferred being a doctor, as you have all the attributes of a great actor."

"Viktor, this is wonderful!" exclaimed Virginia. "Here I've been with a Barrymore all this time and didn't realize it! Although I had suspicions, because you know something? What's your name, please?"

"Shandru, madame."

"Mr. Shandru, I'll tell you a secret … he didn't fool me. He makes love like an actor!"

"To such a beautiful lady, I can well understand."

"Thank you."

"Now to go on. I see also in your hand a marriage…."

Virginia clapped her hands. "Oh, good, then he won't remain a sourpussed old bachelor. Well, as long as you don't see me in there, Shandru, tell us who it's going to be?"

"That I cannot, dear lady. Because, I do not see two marriages."

"Two? What do you mean? You just said that…."

"If the gentleman does not mind, the one I see is in the past!"

Henry withdrew his hand. "This is preposterous!"

Virginia narrowed her eyes, waved an admonishing finger in his direction. "Viktor Bartok! You old bluebeard! Holding out on me, are you? So, you have a skeleton in the closet!"

"Ridiculous!" Henry laughed it off.

Shandru rose. "Please to forgive, kind sir. You are through with my services? The party at the next table summons me."

"Oh, yes. How much do I owe you?"

"Whatever the gentleman cares to give."

"Here you are."

"Oh, thank you, sir. The gentleman is very generous, sir." He bowed deeply. "Excuse me, sir, excuse me, madame."

"Goodbye, Shandru," Virginia said.

Henry beckoned to the waiter. "Check, please."

"He was very amusing, wasn't he, Viktor?"

"Yes, amusing all right, but wholly a faker!"

A key turned the lock in the door of apartment 15-B of the 1220 Lake Shore Drive building and Henry followed Virginia Taylor into her smartly furnished suite. He tried to pretend that he was at home in these surroundings. The urge to exclaim "Nice place you have here" was difficult to repress. Instead, he said, "Your apartment looks more beautiful than ever."

"That's because you haven't seen it for a whole month, Viktor. You see, absence does make the heart grow fonder."

"Yes, I have missed you, Virginia."

"I've missed you, too, Viktor." She came close to him, looking up into his eyes. Henry enveloped her in his arms and drew her to him. Her lips quivered as his mouth pressed against them, and she swayed limply in his embrace. When she caught her breath, Virginia whispered softly, "Darling Viktor, I love you!"

"You do?"

"Yes, very much. And you know something?"

"What?"

"That month's vacation did a lot for you!"

"Really?"

"Definitely yes, if that kiss is any example!"

He laughed. "Yes, the rest made a new man out of me." He walked over to the lounge and sank down on its soft cushions.

"Some brandy, darling?"

"Yes, thank you, that would be fine."

She poured out two glasses from a decanter. "Well, here's to you, Viktor. To your success."

"And to your happiness, my dear."

She moistened her lips with the brandy, and sat there staring at the floor.

"What are you thinking, Virginia?"

"About Shandru."

"Oh? I wouldn't think too much about what he said. He has a wild imagination like all those Hindu fakirs."

"I'm not so sure there wasn't a great deal of truth to some of the things he said."

"You mean about me?"

"No, I was thinking about myself. He said I would never find peace or happiness here in Chicago."

"Do you feel inclined to agree with him?"

"I don't know, Viktor. I only wish I knew the answer."

"Have you been unhappy?"

"At times. I'm completely happy when I'm with you, but unhappy otherwise. Shandru isn't a faker, Viktor. You may have thought he outdid himself when he read your palm, and a lot of things he said about you did sound rather fantastic, I'll admit, but what he told me chilled me with its truthfulness."

Henry couldn't confess that he too had been chilled by the Hindu's revelations. He could only pretend to scoff at the incident.

"Really, my dear, I think you're taking him too seriously. After all, what could he tell you about yourself that you don't already know?"

"That's just it, Viktor. I'm fully aware of the things that he told me. That's what frightens me. He told me truths about myself which even you as a psychiatrist wouldn't tell me. He may not be a doctor with a great reputation, but he nevertheless gave me a psychoanalysis this evening that astounded me."

Henry sipped his brandy. "Well, maybe I should send my patients to him. Perhaps he could do a better job than I'm doing."

"I didn't mean it that way, Viktor. I've never been a patient of yours so maybe you never stopped to analyze me. I'd hate to think that I'd have to come to your office and pay you a fee before you would take the trouble to delve into my mind and see what makes the real Virginia Taylor tick!"

Henry looked up from his glass. He turned and saw that for the first time her eyes were moist and glistening. "Darling—you are actually disturbed over what took place tonight. I'm sorry that he upset you. If I had known, I would never have allowed him to join us."

She smiled and took his hand. "No, my sweet, I'm not unhappy that he told me what he did. Remember, Viktor, he said that the destiny of the soul is indelibly stamped in the lines of one's hand—and neither he nor anyone else could ever do anything to change them. We can't escape our destiny, Viktor, no matter how hard we try!"

"He did have an effect upon you, didn't he? You can even quote the words from his routine."

"Routine?"

"Of course, routine. He probably tells the same things to everybody."

"Somehow or other, I don't believe that. He struck me as being very sincere."

"That's your privilege, my dear. To me, he was an obvious charlatan. Talking about such nonsense as a triumphant emptiness."

"Yes, I wondered about that too. What do you think he meant?"

"Who knows? He was much too dramatic to be convincing. And the amusing part of it, he thought I was an actor!"

"Yes, that was rather funny."

"He did more acting for his fee than anyone else I've ever seen."

"Still, Viktor … I was terribly impressed with what he told me. My life in the last couple of years has been horribly mixed up. I haven't been able to find myself, and I haven't any idea where I'm headed. You do understand, don't you?"

He knew only too well. "Yes, I think I do, Virginia."

"You see, how our destiny takes hold of our lives. If I hadn't decided that I wanted to go to Virginia Beach two years ago, and had gone to Bar Harbor with my mother and father, as they wished, I would never have met you."

"Yes." This was the first he knew of their meeting place.

"But little Virginia had to be curious about the beach by the same name. She came, she saw, and she was conquered … by a handsome young doctor, who had a delightful continental accent, who made love to her, who was unattached, an eligible bachelor, and who was going to stay that way, by God, or else—!"

"You're convinced?"

"Of course I am. I was convinced two years ago when I gave up everything—my home, my family, my friends—to come to Chicago just to be near you—to have you when you wanted me—when you had time for me."

"That could be interpreted as an unkind remark."

"Forgive me, darling, I don't mean it to be. I came here with my eyes wide open. You didn't ask me to come. I followed you. I knew exactly what I was letting myself in for. Sometimes a woman will throw all reason to the winds … her intuition, her judgment, her entire perspective, all are completely dominated by her passions and instincts. Love is an awful thing, Viktor, it's a very devastating weapon, and few people have learned how to defend themselves against it. You're one of those few."

"I?"

"Yes. In a way you're extremely fortunate. You see, you don't love so deeply that you find it part of your body, of your soul. For you, that's great. It fits into your scheme of things beautifully. Love will never hurt you, although it's important to you, because it's not essential."

It was becoming more apparent to Henry each minute that Bartok's philosophy of life had followed the pattern of his own. He sat there listening to Virginia Taylor, seeing the counterpart of his own past being exhumed and reviewed. What a wild freak of nature it was, he thought, that had constructed two human beings so much alike in looks, in temperament, in personality.

"May I have a cigarette, Viktor, dear? Thank you. Would you like one?"

"Yes, thank you." He picked up the table lighter? "Well, as long as you're so thoroughly convinced that I am the way I am, what conclusions have you come to?"

She blew out a long thin trail of smoke? "None. Like Scarlett O'Hara, 'I'll think about that tomorrow?'" For tonight, I want to be made love to—violently, completely. And you know what?"

"What, my darling?"

She leaned over and whispered in his ear, "And you're just the guy that can do it, too!"

Henry smiled and his ego burst the dam of reserve that had held him in check and flooded his whole body with a triumphant feeling of greatness and power. The Hindu had likened him to Socrates and Caesar, but he was a Casanova as well. Women had always told him how irresistible he was! He took Virginia in his arms, turned her halfway round and kissed her the way she wanted to be kissed—violently.

"Yes," he said softly, "I'm just the guy that can do it, too!" He kissed her again and again, and the next few moments were intense with the excitement of two people caught in the ardent embrace of each other's arms.

"Whew! I'm warm," sighed Virginia as she rose from the davenport, "I'm going to put on something comfortable. Excuse, darling."

"Of course."

Henry walked about the room on a tour of inspection. Suddenly he noticed a picture of Bartok standing on a leather top drum table near the window. He picked it up and examined it closely. It was inscribed, "To my darling Virginia—Viktor." *It clearly showed the scar to be on the right cheek!* For a moment Henry pondered over the deliberate efforts Bartok had made to expose the scar in his pictures. He seemed to use it as a trademark. Ordinarily, when people have their picture taken, they prevail upon the photographer to minimize any unflattering blemishes on their faces, but it was evident that Bartok had gone to lengths to see to it that his scar was pronounced. There was no question but that he bore his saber wound with a deep sense of pride. Henry wondered whether Virginia had accepted the scar on his left cheek, or if she still thought it strange. Putting the picture down he strode over to the grand piano, seated himself on the cushioned bench, and with two fingers began to play chopsticks.

"That's very beautiful, darling, but I'd much rather hear you play *Clair de Lune!*" Henry stopped abruptly and whirled around. Virginia was standing over him clad in a black chiffon negligee with fuchsia trim. He tried to hide his surprise with a forced laugh and a gesture of nonchalance.

"Oh, I was just passing the time." Then hastily changing the subject, "Virginia, you look ravishing in that negligee!"

"Thank you, darling, you're very sweet." She bent over and kissed him. "Now I want to hear *Clair de Lune*. It's my favorite and you play it so well."

Henry was really in a spot. If he had known that Bartok played the piano, he would never have tinkered with the keys. That had probably reminded her of his ability. "I—I'm really not in the mood tonight, dear. Please forgive me—"

"Are you in a romantic mood?"

"Do you have to ask?"

"Then what could be more romantic than *Clair de Lune*?"

"Er … yes, I have to agree with you about the piece, but I … I'm just not in the mood to play tonight." He rose. "I'd much rather make love to you."

"But Viktor … every woman likes a little preliminary of some sort. And you know what beautiful music does to me."

"Yes, it's one of my weaknesses too, only I'd much prefer to listen than to play. Why don't we play the phonograph? There are dozens of beautiful recordings in the cabinet over there."

"But, darling, I can always play records when you're not here. When I'm with you, and that's not too often, I want to listen to you. Your playing thrills me. I don't know why, and don't ask me, because a woman can never give a reason for anything she does, but when you play for me and then make love to me, it's like being in another world. It's probably a foolish whim—but I know what it does to me."

Henry felt himself floundering about in a sea of vexation. Her request was so sincere, and her plea so touching, that he wished that for once in his life he could wave a magic wand and become a pianist. He wanted to say, "Of course, my darling, I'll play for you." Instead the words dribbled painfully out. "I'm … sorry … please don't ask me … to play."

Virginia turned, walked over to the davenport and sat down. She was disconsolate. Henry followed her a moment later.

"Darling—are you upset?"

Her voice was quietly indicative of her keen disappointment. "I'm hurt, Viktor. I didn't think you'd refuse me such a simple request. You never have before. You've always been more than anxious to please me."

"But I still am, my sweet. I'll do anything to please you."

"Except to play for me tonight. I suppose you think I'm being awfully difficult because of your refusal—"

"No, but I do think it's rather trivial to make an issue of it."

"Viktor—"

"Yes?"

"I don't know what it is, and at times I'm completely baffled by a lot of things you say and do, but for some reason or other you seem to be different from what you used to be. I can't quite put my finger on it, but there's something about you—I don't know whether it's my imagination or not—no, I'm sure it isn't my imagination—but in the past month you've been a changed man."

"In what way?"

"I can't tell you—I don't know. You're just different somehow. Different in many ways. You're like another man—"

"Oh?" Henry felt himself breaking out in a cold sweat. Now he would need to call upon all the reserve of calm and ingenuity he had stored up for just such an occasion. "I'm afraid I don't understand, my dear."

"No, of course not. How could you understand, when I don't quite understand the thing myself. It's just that I'm completely bewildered at times. You're Viktor and you're not Viktor. It's as if you suddenly got tired of being one personality and decided to be another. You're more sweet in a lot of ways than you ever were. You seem to be more articulate than you were before—you express yourself beautifully and easily, when you used to have difficulty in getting yourself to say all the things that a woman loves to hear. You were always afraid of committing yourself in some way. Now you don't have that reticence, for which I'm grateful—"

"For that I am also happy."

"But it was the suddenness of the change that baffled me—and there are things that I'm conscious of—like your incessant restlessness. You were the most composed creature on earth ... I always envied you for it."

"And now?"

"Now you give me the feeling that you're constantly ill at ease. There's an undercurrent of unrest and nervousness about you, as though something were always on your mind. You fidget a great deal, and in the last month you've developed a habit of biting your lower lip. You never used to do that."

"You're very observant, aren't you?"

"Forgive me, darling, but it's so obvious. You're doing it now."

Henry smiled uncomfortably. "First thing you know, you're going to make me self-conscious."

"Viktor! You, a psychiatrist, becoming self-conscious?"

"After all, I'm still human and subject to human frailties."

"I wonder, Viktor—I wonder if you really are."

"You don't think so?"

"I wish that I could think so. I wish that you were like other men, with other men's weaknesses—with other men's feelings, desires, emotions, instincts—"

"I always thought I was."

"No, you didn't, Viktor—not truly. You may like to think of yourself as being that way, but down deep inside you know you're not. And if you ever thought you really were, I'm sure you'd try to do something about it."

"You're quite a psychologist in your own right, aren't you?" Henry smiled.

"Two years of association with you have given me a much better insight into things than I ever had before. I can thank you for that, Viktor."

"On the contrary, the debt is on my side … for the privilege of knowing such a wonderful person as you."

"Darling! You see now what I meant when I said that you've suddenly developed a knack for saying the things I love to hear?"

"Didn't … I ever say things like that to you before?"

"No, my darling. You were always gracious and complimentary, but somehow or other you never could get yourself to put into words anything like what you just said."

"I don't know how I could have failed to, my lovely Virginia—I've felt this way about you for so long."

"Viktor, I know I've always been in love with you. Now I know I always shall be. Kiss me, my darling."

Again he took her in his arms and kissed her passionately. This time his hand found its way under her gown to her soft breast, and Henry felt confident. He had extricated himself from the precarious situation at the piano and had put a stop to her wonderings about differences in his personality.

"Would you like to change into something more comfortable too, dear?" Virginia inquired.

Henry swallowed hard and tried to appear casual. "Uh … yes, that's an idea."

"Well, your things are right where they always are. In the meantime, I'll put on some music."

Henry walked into the bedroom, noting with satisfaction the luxurious satin drapes and bedspread. One entire wall was mirrored, the bed itself, at least six feet wide, made of black walnut or ebony with a white quilted satin headboard. In one corner an emerald green chaise lounge yawned invitingly on a thick white rug. The dresser was the width of two and was black to match the bed. The vanity was unusual in size, entirely made of adjustable mirrors, and displayed a vast array of perfume bottles.

Henry walked over to one of the closets. There was nothing masculine to be seen in the profusion of silks and satins that hung in its well-ordered spaces. He closed the door and made his way across the room to another door; when he opened it a maze of dresses, suits and shoes greeted his eyes. Brows furrowed, he hastily backed out.

Gazing about the room further, he noticed another closet with sliding paneled doors. He rolled them back, and a smile came over his face as he perceived three lounging robes—one a silk in a gay paisley pattern, another of black satin piped in a soft pastel yellow, and the third a Chinese robe in mandarin red silk with a large monogram over the pocket. Below these were stacked fresh silk pajamas, in all colors and patterns. He counted an even dozen pair. Some had never been used.

Also hanging on the rack were three suits of clothes. He pulled open a drawer. Ties, handkerchiefs, socks and shirts. Henry clicked his tongue in amazement. No wonder there had never been any sign of Bartok's leaving the building; he hadn't needed to. No wonder Bartok had been a confirmed bachelor with a beautiful mistress in a luxurious apartment and an expensive wardrobe. And all of this at her expense. Bartok apparently had paid none of her bills; she was independently wealthy and probably could afford anything she wanted.

As he took out the Chinese gown and a pair of white silk pajamas, Henry smiled to himself over such an unbelievably made-to-order situation. He could take this kind of living the rest of his life! Where were the house slippers? Oh yes, there they were in the corner of the closet, two pairs. The red would match his robe.

In the white tile bathroom there was a glass-enclosed shower, and on the wall a large sun lamp that could be adjusted to any angle. Yes, it was plain that Virginia Taylor also had a taste for comforts, and the financial means to enjoy them. Henry noticed that there were two mirrored medicine cabinets. He curiously opened one. It contained a myriad of feminine creams and cosmetics. Then he opened the other. Inside were razor, shaving and bath soaps, men's bath salts, aftershave lotions, and several colognes. Henry whistled. Yes, sir, he told himself as he removed his coat and unfastened his tie, Bartok really did this up right!

Some minutes later Henry appeared in the doorway of the bedroom, white handkerchief flowing from the breast pocket of the dressing gown. Music from the phonograph softly filled the living room and dim lights threw grotesque shadows from the furniture across the beige carpet.

"Darling?" he called.

"Yes, my sweet?" was her reply, "I'm resting on the davenport." The muted nuances of her voice foretold exquisite intimacy.

"Oh, no wonder I couldn't see you."

Henry sat down beside Virginia, bent over, and a pair of white arms clasped around his neck. There was a long kiss and then in a whispered voice she said, "Darling, you smell so sweet and clean. What's more, you've even got on my favorite men's cologne, Beau Geste."

"Yes, that's right."

"Is that another of your inconsistencies?"

"What do you mean?"

"Don't you remember, when I bought it for you, you took one sniff and said you wouldn't be caught dead wearing that God-awful stuff!"

"Uh … I did, didn't I? Well, I … I … put it on just for you."

Virginia took a deep breath, exhaled with a long sigh. "Darling Viktor, you're becoming more puzzling to me by the minute." In the dimness her fingers slipped caressingly to his cheeks. "Your face is so nice and smooth, almost as if you just got through"—her voice stopped.

"What's the matter, my dear?"

"Forgive me, Viktor, it's that scar again."

"What about it?"

"Once I told you that it confused me. Remember? I said I thought it had always been on your right cheek?"

"Yes?" She couldn't see him biting his lower lip. "I just touched it with my … right hand."

"So?"

"But, Viktor, I've touched your face in the dark dozens of times, and always felt the scar with my left hand."

"That's impossible."

"No, darling. I'm not crazy. Please—I know what I'm talking about. For two years, I've touched your face and I know."

"But, my dear, I don't want to argue with you—it's really a bit ludicrous. Scars don't walk around, you know, and change positions!"

"No … of course not. Only it seemed so unnatural and different that I … I was bewildered. I mean—I still am …"

"The whole thing is rather silly, isn't it, my dear?"

"I suppose, but you know how a woman is—once she gets hold of an idea, it isn't easy to—" She suddenly sat up and felt for the switch on the table lamp.

"What's wrong, dear?"

"Nothing, I just thought of something."

"What?"

"We'll settle this once and for all." She got up and walked over to the drum table and returned with the framed picture of Bartok.

Henry watched her out of the corner of his eye, his brain working feverishly. Virginia held the photograph under the light.

"I knew I wasn't crazy. Look. There's the scar as big as life on your right cheek!"

"Left cheek!"

"What do you mean? That's your right cheek."

"It is, except in photography." He knew he was lying, that it happened only when a negative was intentionally reversed by the printer. "Don't you see, darling, when you have a photograph taken with a regular portrait camera, the image always appears upside down."

"Yes, I know that."

"Well, when the picture is printed, the negative is reversed and what is on the left appears to be on the right. See?"

"Oh, I didn't know that." Fortunately Bartok's breast pocket and handkerchief were not showing in the picture; Henry realized that no matter how much a negative might be reversed, a man's handkerchief is always worn in his left pocket and would unmistakably and inexorably identify the left side of the face.

"I'm sorry, dear—please forgive me." She put the picture down. Henry took a deep breath. What an evening, he thought! That made the third close call since they had returned to the apartment. He certainly had to be on his toes every minute!

"You didn't say you forgive me, darling," Virginia said putting her arms around him.

"Of course I do, my dearest." He pressed her close and they kissed again. This time there was an electricity that surged between the two tightly clasped bodies. When at last their lips parted, Henry whispered softly, "Shall we … go into the next room?"

"Yes, my dearest," she replied in a scarcely audible voice.

The lights were again dimmed, the music had come to an end, and with their arms entwined about each other they walked toward the bedroom. And Henry sensed triumphantly that her embrace would accord him complete assent.

CHAPTER FIFTEEN

"Step aside, please, and let them out."

It was the voice of the elevator operator as he stopped his car at the sixteenth floor and Henry stepped out behind another passenger.

Entering the reception room, he found a goodly stack of mail which had been dropped through the slot in the door and which was scattered on the floor. He walked back to the inner office to rid himself of the file box he was carrying and then returned for the mail. There was no time to look it over now, though; he had more important matters on which to spend the next thirty minutes. First of all, he wanted to know what patients had appointments today. He found the schedule book in Miss Hahn's desk. Monday, July 3rd, 9:00 A.M., Mr. Howard W. Richards; 10:15 A.M., Mrs. Mildred Schlesinger; 11:30 A.M., Mr. Kenneth Braun; 12:45 P.M., Mr. Russell B. Eckstrom; 2:30 P.M., Miss Margaret Gaines; 3:45 P.M., Mrs. Deborah Lewis; 5:00 P.M., Mr. George Holland. Seven patients. He took their cards from the file, refreshed his mind on their histories.

At five minutes of nine the reception door opened and closed. A few minutes later he heard the door open and close again. Then the buzzer sounded. He picked up the phone.

"Yes.

"Good morning, doctor."

"Good morning, Miss Hahn."

"How're you feeling, doctor?"

"Much better, thank you."

"Mr. Richards is waiting."

"Thank you. You may send him in."

The door opened and a well-dressed man in his early thirties entered the room. Henry rose and greeted his visitor.

"Hello, doctor."

"How are you, Mr. Richards? So good to see you."

"Thank you."

"Just have your favorite chair."

"I understand you've been on the sick list yourself."

"Yes, but all I needed was a month's rest."

"You look fine, doctor."

"Thank you, I feel fine."

"In fact, you look like a different person!"

"Really?"

"Oh, yes, doctor. It's amazing what a month's rest will do for a person. You look younger—more full of pep or something. You did look rather tired a month ago."

"Of course I was. We all need a vacation now and then to give us a new zest for our work. Now, then, how have you been getting along during my absence?"

"Not too bad, doctor. I've tried to keep in mind everything I've learned in my past visits with you."

"Do you feel more at ease, or are you still inclined to be jumpy and irritable?" Henry pursued.

"No. I definitely am more relaxed."

"How are you sleeping?"

"Much better. I only had to take a sleeping tablet once all last week."

"That's wonderful. Don't fight yourself, of course. If you feel that you're not able to fall asleep, by all means take one. I don't want you to break away suddenly from all the things you've been doing. Time is the great healer in psychiatry, you know."

"Yes, I understand, doctor."

"Now tell me, where did we leave off the last time?"

"I was telling you about how I met my present wife and the circumstances which preceded our first affair."

"Oh yes. Go on."

"Well, we went together for eight months and we saw each other five, six times a week. We had intercourse three or four nights a week; sometimes more, sometimes less."

"You completely satisfied her then?"

"Yes, doctor. I know I did. In fact, she told me."

"Did she make you feel the same way?"

"Yes. I was always satisfied."

"Did you use contraceptives?"

"Yes, that's why I never gave any thought to whether or not it was possible to have a baby."

"Naturally. Go on."

"Well, in August of that year, my divorce from my first wife became final and we got married the following month. Right from the very beginning Alice said she wanted to have a baby. She said that was probably what was the matter with my marriage to Connie, and she didn't want that to happen to us."

"Had you ever tried to have a baby with … Connie?"

"No. She never wanted one."

"I see. Go ahead, Mr. Richards."

"So we started in the first week. We tried continuously for a year and nothing happened. In the meantime, Alice went to a gynecologist, Dr. Rubens—"

"Simon Rubens?" interrupted Henry, brows arched in feigned professional curiosity.

"Yes."

"Very good. Go on."

"Well, Rubens examined her thoroughly and told her she was perfect. Then he told her he wanted a sample from me."

"Did you manage it?"

"Yes. Through her by way of a Huhner Test."

"Yes—go on."

"She came home and told me that Rubens said that the test showed my bugs were either dormant or dead, that under the microscope they weren't moving."

"So?"

"So I called Rubens and he told me to go to a G. U. man to verify and get his opinion."

"Did you?" Henry asked, leaning forward.

"Yes. I went to Earl Clinton, the best in town."

"And—?"

"He verified it all right. He told me I was sterile."

"Did the news affect you immediately?" asked Henry, pursing his lips pensively.

"No. I had relations with my wife two times afterward, but then it suddenly gave out altogether. I knew something was wrong the first night after he told me the news, and so did Alice. It was all over in a couple of minutes. Alice thought maybe I was just unnerved. We tried again the next night and the same thing happened. We waited a few nights and then tried again. But then I realized it was hopeless."

"How long ago was that?"

"That was in February of this year."

"Then you came to me in May," said Henry.

"Yes. You see I'm terribly in love with my wife, and I'm afraid that I'm going to lose her because of this. Either that, or I'm afraid she'll go out and have an affair with another man. After all, she's only human, you know, and it's been five months since we've had relations. How long can one expect a young girl to go on like that? Besides, she's very pretty and other men are easily attracted to her."

"If she's the right kind of woman, Mr. Richards, you won't have a thing to worry about. Women who really love their husbands don't run right out and have an affair with another man as soon as something goes wrong. And … if she does, I'm sure that's proof of the fact that she didn't love you in the first place."

"But, doctor, what has she got to look forward to with me? At the present time I'm impotent. She might have been willing to accept the fact that I was sterile, because sterility is not always a permanent thing. Dr. Clinton told me there are a number of different kinds of hormones and things that can be given to relieve a case of temporary sterility, although he wasn't sure that I would respond to that form of treatment. But what good is a man to his wife if he can't satisfy her at all? His life isn't worth a damn!"

A look of anguish came over Richard's face with his last statement. There was no question that this young man was in despair and experiencing profound humiliation. Henry felt a genuine sympathy.

"My dear Mr. Richards, I'm going to talk to you frankly and I want you to hear me out. First of all, you've got everything in the world to live for. Your life is not useless as you think, because, from what you've told me, this so-called impotency is a temporary situation brought about by a mental reaction to the news that you were sterile. Did you ever have a social disease?"

"Never."

"Then I'm more definite than ever that your present ... insufficiency—you see I do not use the word impotency, because you are not impotent—your present insufficiency is due entirely to a psychological reaction, the results of a profound feeling of inferiority which overcame you when you found you were sterile. You had always thought of yourself as very masculine, sexually capable of giving a woman everything she wanted. In fact, if I'm not mistaken, you even thought of yourself as superior in the art of lovemaking. Women always told you how good you were. Right?"

"Yes, sir."

"So, suddenly you are toppled from this pedestal you occupied; this feeling of masculine superiority is crushed by the word sterile. A word you had read or heard about in reference to other people, but which was not a part of your life. It could never happen to you. You could satisfy any woman. If she wanted to have a baby, you could make her pregnant. It was all part of your ego, your narcissistic personality which governed your whole sex life. When the news was given to you officially by Dr. Clinton that you were sterile, your entire world dropped from under you. You had visions of your wife leaving you, or going to another man who could give her a baby. You worried about it. You couldn't sleep nights. Pretty soon it was a fixation in your mind. In no time at all you had developed a first-class sense of inferiority about yourself. The word sterility became an obsession with you. You worried about yourself so much, and allowed so many purely imaginative things to creep into your mind, that it finally affected your sexual organs to the extent that you talked yourself into a temporary insufficiency. Have a cigarette?"

"Thank you, doctor. Here, I have a lighter."

"Thank you. Now that we know the cause, we can proceed with the cure."

The patient's face brightened. "Cure?"

"Of course, cure! Did you think for one minute there wasn't one?"

Tears came to Richard's eyes. "Doctor, I—I …"

"The first thing I want you to do is get rid of any ideas about yourself being impotent. You are not. I repeat emphatically: you are not impotent—furthermore, you are not even sterile!"

"But, doctor," said Richards with the first smile he had displayed since entering the office, "How can you be sure? You didn't even examine me!"

"I don't need to, my boy. Yours is not a physical insufficiency but purely mental. You are as good sexually as you ever were. You have just lost confidence in yourself. If I did not have faith in what I just told you, I would not have said it. Place yourself in my hands for six months and I will prove to you that all you need is to have confidence in yourself again. But you will not accomplish this by talking it over with your wife or anyone. You must not discuss this with a soul but me. I will start on your next visit with psychoanalysis, and you must see me no less than four times a week, and preferably five. All right?"

"Yes, doctor. I don't care how many times a week I come, if it will bring results."

"We will get results. First, we will try to give your wife a good bed-partner again. Give me at least six months for this. Then we will get around to the sterility. At that time I will probably send you back to Dr. Clinton for hormone injections, while I continue to work on you by psychoanalysis. A year from today, you will probably be fretting and worrying about your wife's pregnancy!"

The tears streamed down Richard's cheeks, and his joy was sincerely touching to Henry. "Dr. Bartok, besides your being a wonderful doctor, may I say something else?"

"Of course."

"You're a swell guy!"

At six-fifteen the last of the patients departed, and Henry relaxed in the big comfortable desk chair. This first day at the office seemed to have drained him of the last ounce of his energy. Keeping on his toes every second of the time was equal alone to a full day's work, without the added effort of administering intelligently to the mental requirements of seven people, each with an individual problem that had to be individually treated, and in a science in which he was far from professional yet. He had made up his mind that to the best of his ability he was going to handle Dr. Bartok's clientele the way Bartok himself would have handled them, and with as much consideration for the problems involved as if they were his own. That was the only basis on which he could possibly continue with the name and reputation of one of the country's leading psychiatrists. Henry knew that any quackery would soon lead to his undoing, and his ministerings must needs be as sincere as his knowledge of psychiatry would allow. He would continue reading and studying every spare moment. He would improve with time. This was a profession that paid well, but also one requiring a vast knowledge of human beings and a psychoanalytical comprehension of the workings of the mind. It was a vast responsibility and Henry was fully aware of his undertaking. He was determined to live up to the reputation established by his predecessor, and if possible to exceed it.

There was a knock on the door.

"Yes?" he called.

Miss Hahn entered. "Have you a moment?"

Henry rose. "Yes, yes, come in."

"You were so busy all day, I don't think I spoke a half a dozen words to you."

"That's right. Sit down. Have a cigarette?"

"Thanks."

"I've been hoping for a chance to talk to you all day."

"To ask me if I enjoyed those thick juicy letters that came three times a week?"

"Miss Hahn, you have every reason to feel this way, but—"

"It's even 'Miss Hahn' now. You once told me that the formalities would be reserved only for the patients, but I see you prefer it now all the time."

"Evelyn, please believe me, I wanted to write but I ... I couldn't."

She turned and faced him squarely. "Look, Viktor, before I listen to any thin-skinned, weak excuses about why I didn't receive even a postcard from you for a whole month, I'd rather you'd be the man I always thought, and come right out and tell me the truth. That you don't love me and never did! I won't hold you to any promises, any more than I held you to the promise that the next time you went on a trip I was to go with you. I didn't remind you about that when you left, did I?"

"Oh ... no." Henry was beginning to see the light.

"I hadn't thought, all this time that I allowed you to make love to me, that I was just your plaything—something to have handy for the time being. You told me I supplied the void in your life, I was more than just a secretary, I was everything you had always wanted in a woman but had never found. Not even in Virginia Taylor—"

So she knew about her! Of course, secretaries know about everything. Henry wondered if Virginia was aware of Bartok's affair with his secretary. Most likely not.

"I wouldn't be at all surprised if you had taken her with you instead of me."

"I went alone and I can prove it!"

"Maybe so. That's unimportant right now. The only thing that matters at the moment is that I've got an awful lot to live down. First, the fact that you casually told me to buy *one* ticket for Colorado Springs with not the slightest word as to why you suddenly changed your mind about taking me with you, and then the humiliation of not even receiving a penny postcard from the man I gave myself to for almost two years! And I always prided myself on my ability to tell when a man is sincere! Well, I'll admit you had me fooled. I had begun to trust you completely when you told me about Virginia Taylor—I really believed that you weren't in love with her … that when it came down to marriage, you could only see yourself married to a girl like me. I believed you. I even believed you when you said out next trip together was to be a honeymoon! Well, it was very nice. The most beautiful honeymoon a girl could ask for!" She burst into hysterical sobs.

Henry stood there, helpless and confused. Now he knew the whole story. It explained all of his secretary's peculiar actions—in a moment of anguish brought on by weeks of torturing mental conflict and pent-up emotions.

This was more than Henry had bargained for. His intrigue with Virginia Taylor was sufficient to keep his mind occupied, to say nothing of the responsibilities of his newly acquired practice, without the additional burden of having to placate a love-starved secretary. Still, he admired Evelyn Hahn and felt a real sympathy for her. He could hardly explain that his apparent formality and indifference had been the result of ignorance of the situation. She only knew that this was the man who had declared his love for her; the man to whom she had offered herself body and soul. Of course she felt humiliated, cast off. Well, there was nothing to do but make the best of his bargain. He had inherited Dr. Bartok's practice; he would have to take over his love life as well.

"Evelyn … darling." He put his hand on her shoulder. "Look at me. I know I've neglected you, but I haven't been myself lately. You know that. I didn't take you with me because I was afraid of what might happen. And I was right. It did."

She looked up, drying her tears. "What … do you mean?"

"I didn't want you to know it, but I suffered another attack on the train going down there. Had to be taken directly to a hospital … on a stretcher."

"Oh, my God! Viktor, darling!" Convulsive sobs burst forth again.

"That's all right, my dear. Don't cry. I'm all right now." He lifted her by the arms and she stood up, crying on his shoulder.

"Viktor ... I ... I love you so. I hadn't any idea you had been sick again. And here I said such cruel things to you. Forgive me ... forgive me, darling." She threw her arms tightly around his neck and Henry could feel the tears wetting his cheek.

"No, no, my dear. There is nothing to forgive you for." He silently applauded his ability to lie convincingly.

"How long were you in the hospital?" she asked with a little more composure.

"Almost the entire time I was there."

"Oh, Viktor, if I had only known...."

"For one thing, I didn't want you to know. Why should I cause you unnecessary worry?"

"Darling, how can you say unnecessary? I would have taken the first plane down there."

"I know you would have, my dear, but I didn't want you to. That would have been a nice vacation for you, wouldn't it? Sitting in a hospital!"

"Viktor, do you think for one minute I would think about my own pleasure with you lying in a hospital bed?"

"No, of course not. For another thing, I was too sick to even write a postcard."

"I understand, darling. Forgive me, I lost my head before."

He took his handkerchief and dried her eyes. "There is nothing to forgive, my sweet." He lifted her chin. "Kiss?"

Without a word she again flung her arms around his neck, not waiting for his lips to meet hers. She kissed him with more passion than he had thought her capable of. It was a kiss of release—of pent-up emotions—of total surrender. Henry felt his spine tingle. Yes, this was indeed far more than he had bargained for, and as their tightly clasped bodies swayed ecstatically, he could think of only one thing. Now he had *two* women on his hands! *Where in Christ's world would it all end?*

A few minutes later Henry took Evelyn Hahn to dinner. Afterward he made a point of escorting her home in order to find out where she lived. To his surprise, it was the Garland Apartment Hotel on Dearborn Street, not far from his own hotel. Henry said goodnight in the lobby, in no mood to further a romance with his secretary on this particular evening. He was genuinely fatigued. Even working at the tiring job of garage hand had not produced the exhaustion that he now felt. That had been physical tiredness, but this was a mental fatigue that seemed to have drained his entire being. He went home and slept the sleep of the dead.

Toward the week's end, he began to give thought to his neglected correspondence. Evelyn Hahn had responded to his attention, and Henry found his secretary in a gay and cheerful mood. He pressed the buzzer. The door opened.

"Yes, doctor?"

"I have some letters, Miss Hahn."

She returned with her notebook.

"How are you feeling today, my dear?" he asked.

"Wonderful, thank you. As I used to feel—happy and in love … with the world!" She laughed, and Henry joined her in a brief moment of gaiety.

"Now I have a few letters to answer. This first one goes to Professor James T. Newcomb, Dean of the Medical School, University of Fort Dearborn. My dear Newcomb: Thank you so much for your kind request to have me once again on your lecture staff for the coming fall term. I should be very happy and honored to serve in this most distinguished post upon so distinguished a rostrum. My only desire is that I may be of some service to the students of the university, the future doctors of our country. With kindest personal regards, I remain, cordially yours."

"That's a very beautiful letter, doctor, if I may say so."

"That's sweet of you, my dear."

"Not at all. You amaze me. You always used to have such difficulty dictating. Now you write beautifully without any trouble, instead of turning your letters over to me to answer for you."

"Uh … yes. Well, I'll … I'll tell you a secret. I've been studying English extra-curricularly."

"Oh, is that it? Well, I should say you've done very well. When do you find the time?"

"I'll tell you another secret. I don't. I'm doing it in twenty easy lessons by correspondence school. Tonight my lesson is, 'The lady is very beautiful—the lady is extremely charming. Would I were to have the good fortune of being the lady's love, so that I might spend every minute of every hour in her delightful company, hours that would forever remain the most priceless in the memory of a lifetime!'"

Evelyn sat there with her mouth open. "Viktor—I mean, Dr. Bartok—don't look at me with those eyes and say things like that."

"Why?" asked Henry casually.

"Why? With that voice, those eyes, and those words, how in God's name is a weak and defenseless girl going to keep sex from rearing its ugly head—and at 4:30 in the afternoon!"

Henry laughed. "Ah, my dear, that is the secret of controlling the libido. Sex is purely a state of mind, but you know something?"

"What?"

"In all my travels, it's the state I like the best!"

This time it was Evelyn who laughed, but her laughter was brief. "That's not hard to understand, and if I said I didn't agree with you, I'd be telling an untruth. It is the most beautiful state—the most tranquil state. I used to think of it as being something … indecent and immoral. You taught me otherwise; you showed me how it awakens the soul and lifts it to heights that are beyond the reach of anything else on earth." Her eyes grew soft with reverie.

Henry's voice brought her back to the world of realities. "You know, Evelyn, each day I'm discovering something new about you."

"After two years? I'm flattered."

"Don't be. I'm the one who should feel flattered—by all you have done for me—by the devotion of a girl of your character, with such real ideals, and that innate quality of understanding which, believe me, is a rarity among all humans."

She looked at him feverishly. "Viktor … darling, you've never said such things to me in all the time I've known you. You're not the same Viktor at all—you're someone who has me completely mesmerized— I'm hopelessly and helplessly in love, Viktor." Her voice choked.

Henry rose from the chair and took the two short steps that brought him to her. With the egocentric impulse of Henry Mueller, he took Evelyn Hahn in his arms and kissed her violently.

As he bent over and embraced her, she flung her arms desperately around his neck, and whispered, "Darling, darling, darling, I'm yours … all yours, now and always!"

She was hardly aware that the notebook and pencil had fallen to the floor.

CHAPTER SIXTEEN

The months of July and August passed quickly and Henry found scarcely a moment he could call his own. Seeing seven to eight patients a day, his nights divided between the university, Evelyn Hahn, and Virginia Taylor, and devoting any spare moments to reading professional material, his was no simple life of enjoyment and social activities. Catering to the whims of two women and keeping them ignorant of each other's romance seemed to Henry enough to drive anyone to desperation. He tried to analyze the situation and find a solution, but apparently there was none.

He was not in love with either of the two, he concluded. In fact, it was impossible for him to decide whether or not he wanted either one. He had simply inherited the two women, and there wasn't much that he could do about it. Of course, both were very desirable, but this dual affair absorbed too much of his time and prevented his branching out socially in other directions. Besides, he was not serious with either of them, and this was bound to cause trouble, especially with Evelyn Hahn, who had been given reason by Bartok to expect eventual marriage. Highly emotional, she gave of herself freely and completely, but her conception of love was sentimental and completely esthetic.

Virginia Taylor was more the sophisticate who saw love as a gay adventure—who would obligate to herself to no man, and would expect no man to be obligated to her. Not that she was merely promiscuous, or that she did not love Viktor Bartok with as much passion as did Evelyn Hahn, but she was much more resigned to his bachelor philosophy and her own inability to change his life.

If it came to a choice between the two, Henry leaned toward Virginia. She was more his type. She had the glamor, the sophistication, the background and the wealth, attributes which always had been important to him. Besides, he understood her reactions to life and love. He liked her willingness to accept him without promises and commitments. With her, he could take whatever she had to offer, without the feeling of having to give more than he wished in return and this was in keeping with his own self-centered temperament.

The morning of Friday, September 1st, dawned bright and warm, and as Henry left the hotel to walk the pleasant mile to his office, he was greeted by the cries of the corner newsboy.

"Extra paper, read all about it! Hitler—"

"Paper, sonny—"

"Yes, sir. Here y'are, mister."

Henry took in the headline at a glance: HITLER INVADES POLAND. So war had begun! This time the bloodless victories had come to an end. That would mean that Britain and France would soon be in if they lived up to the terms of their treaty with Poland.

Another world conflict about to unleash the merciless avalanche, yet no one seemed to care much. The motorists along Michigan

Avenue were concerned only with moving along as speedily as possible; the workers scurrying along the sidewalks were anxious only to be on time at their offices and shops; the taxicabs still cruised slowly looking for fares; the driver of the big milk truck across the street was thinking only of the nursemaid with whom he was flirting; no one gave the slightest indication that anything of unusual importance had taken place. Everything here pursued its routine course and yet four thousand miles away horror loomed inexorably.

That oncoming horror cast a pall over Henry's entire day. He detested war and all it represented. He hated Hitler and the whole Nazi Socialist Party. Though born in Essen and of German parentage, still he reasoned as he walked along, he was not much different from Hitler. He took what he wanted, be it by subterfuge or murder, the same as the Nazi dictator. And each aggrandized the worship of power and personalized glory. But fiercely he told himself that he regretted nothing. This was the road he had chosen of his own accord.

As winter came, Henry spent more evenings by himself. He found that to make his lectures at the university interesting, and equal to his reputation, he had to widen his scope of subjects. It was no easy matter to discourse for an hour on cases that he had never seen, and he had to conceal the identity of other neurologists in summing up their facts and conclusions. Sometimes he would take a case history of one psychiatrist, establish the patient as one of his own, and then formulate the theory and method of psychoanalysis that he had used. On other occasions he would talk freely about his experiences at the University of Vienna, and the more unusual psychiatric disorders he had encountered as chief of staff of the Copenhagen Institute. These were either cases which he took directly from Bartok's own books or figments of his own prolific imagination. Nevertheless, the lectures required more and more of his time for study and research.

These nights were provided at the expense of Evelyn Hahn. As long as he had to make a choice, he preferred to cut down on his evenings with her rather than on his time with Virginia Taylor, who was always gay and whose conversation never lacked sparkle. And of course her apartment was more luxurious and the conveniences to himself far more satisfying. He could languish well into the next day in her place if he chose, and she served him breakfast in bed. He catered to the regality of his tastes in the satiny trappings of her boudoir.

Evelyn's place was small, consisting of one room and a Pullman kitchen. The bed was an in-a-door and pulled down into the living room. The conveniences were very slight, and the luxuries nonexistent. In addition, he could never stay the night, for she guarded her reputation as well as his own, so he had to leave at all hours on the cold winter nights and make his way home chilled and tired. He saw her all day, which took the edge off being with her nights, and her conversation had become irritatingly sentimental. As a consequence she saw him hardly one night a week. This led her to discover that his nights were not all spent in study and research, and that Virginia Taylor was still very much upon the scene.

After the happy and gay mood that Henry had induced after his return from Colorado Springs, the end of the winter found Evelyn Hahn once again in a depressed state of mind. Henry's attitude toward her was now one of polite cordiality, and the rare evenings that he was with her were spent more out of sympathy than desire. He felt he had to be with her occasionally, that it would be a trifle awkward to drop the relationship entirely, so he continued to make occasional love to her with a feeling of apathy.

With the coming of spring, Henry discovered he had made considerable progress with his patients and had more new applicants than he could handle. He figured up his books and found that in six months of practice he had earned a little more than forty-eight thousand dollars. Dr. Bartok's fee for a case was $50 per visit. There were a few who were on the books at $25 per visit, but they were patients of long standing for whom Bartok had made special dispensations in their favor.

On numerous occasions patients had noticed little differences in techniques, in procedures, in digressions from Bartok's form of psychoanalysis, even in his manner of speech and other traits. But on the whole Henry concluded that he followed fairly closely his predecessor's pattern, and to his great satisfaction eighty percent of his patients claimed a definite improvement over the period of six months; ten percent said they noticed a slight improvement; and the remaining ten percent were not sure but were hopeful of the future. Several of the old patients had noticed the difference in the location of the scar, but Henry's alert mind and disarming manner invariably persuaded them that they had been mistaken.

Richards' case had Henry's special interest because of its unusual circumstances, and also because Richards had been his first patient. It was significant to Henry. He wanted this case to be his good luck charm—his inspiration for a long and successful career. For his own satisfaction he worked on Richards with intent purpose: *to prove to himself that he was not a quack.* He must justify his faith that he had the powers of a trained neurologist who could take a patient suffering from a case of psychasthenia and bring about a cure through psychoanalysis.

It was a great personal triumph for him when Howard Richards telephoned him at the Blake. It was eleven-thirty and Henry was just preparing to retire.

"Hello? Dr. Bartok?"

"Yes."

"This is Howard Richards."

Henry could detect a note of excitement.

"Yes, Mr. Richards, is something wrong?"

"Wrong! God, no, doctor! I just couldn't wait until tomorrow to tell you." Then, with a sob of emotion, "I'm okay again!"

"Marvelous! Wonderful! Come down tomorrow and tell me all about it."

"Yes, doctor. Please forgive me for calling you at this hour."

"That's all right, I wasn't sleeping yet. See you tomorrow at the usual time."

"Yes, doctor, goodnight and … God bless you!"

The last of the spring rains disappeared in the sunshine and warmth of May. One morning as Henry stopped to buy a newspaper he was greeted by the headlines announcing that Hitler had launched his blitzkrieg in the west and was proceeding to gobble up the low countries. There were dark days ahead on the European continent, and Henry's interest in world events became more acute. He had just finished reading *Mein Kampf* and realized its significance in predicting the end of democracy in Europe. Significant, too, was Hitler's picture of the United States. America was soft and its people weak, and soon it must succumb to its own cancer, which was gradually eating up the flesh of a nation that lived in demoralizing luxury and produced a population of degenerates, gangsters, and imbeciles!

Henry wondered. He automatically excluded himself from any such reference. Technically he was an American, but he had been born a German. *Hitler said that to be born a German was to die a German!*

All this was a part of him, Henry told himself. He couldn't help feeling one of them, in a subtle subconscious way, in spite of his overt hatred of Hitler's revolting program. He too was a Teutonic descendant born to a great destiny in his own private sphere. He had the stolid traditions of illustrious German names behind him. He himself was born Heinrich Mueller, as proud a German name as any in all the land between the Rhine and the Vistula from the Baltic to the Alps. But he was no longer a Mueller! Henry Mueller died the night Dr. Bartok's body plunged through the murky waters of the Desplaines River. He was now Viktor Bartok and a Czech, and Henry remembered vividly the vow that he took that grim and dismal night—never again to think of himself in terms of Henry Mueller.

The end of June brought Henry's lecture program to a welcome conclusion. He had given thirty-eight talks on neurology and psychiatry, and felt that he had done quite well, considering that he had been a practicing doctor for only twelve months. Yes, he actually had been Dr. Viktor Bartok for an entire year. Henry summed up his accomplishments with the feeling of a job well done. The body of Dr. Bartok had never been discovered and the chances were it never would be. He had established himself as the noted psychiatrist; had taken over his victim's practice, done a creditable job with the patients, and accomplished a steady increase in clientele. In addition, he had lectured to students, exchanged views with professors and doctors at the university, and no one had suspected the masquerade. He had increased his bank account by many thousands of dollars. His circle of prominent friends was a wide one in spite of the restrictions on his time, and altogether things had worked out far better than he could ever have anticipated.

So far as his love life was concerned, the situation remained unchanged. He still was with Virginia Taylor as often as time would permit, and the affair with Evelyn Hahn was allowed a minimum of nights. He hadn't noticed Evelyn's growing ever more depressed. In front of patients and friends she managed a gay and disarming exterior. In the sanctity of her room, she sat brooding over a lost love, taunted by thoughts of the woman who was replacing her.

During the last week in August, while Evelyn was on an enforced vacation, Henry received the startling news that he had been made Honorary Professor of Neurology at Wilmington University for his outstanding work in the neurological field. The Dean of the Medical School had written him personally, congratulating Dr. Bartok on his Nobel Prize-winning insulin-shock treatment for schizophrenia, which their experiments had shown was a highly successful form of cure. The letter concluded with an invitation to attend a ceremonial dinner in his honor on September 12th at Wilmington, Delaware, at which time the honorary degree of Professor of Neurology would be conferred upon him.

Henry read the letter and gave a soft whistle of amazement.

Another professorship! He had wanted fame, fortune, outstanding prominence. He had surpassed anything that he had ever thought possible in his life. But he was not yet satisfied. He was recognized as a man of distinction in the medical world, and the possessor of unusual ability in the field of psychiatry—now he must prove to himself that he had the power of ministering to the mental ills of an increasingly neurotic population, even though he had neither the training nor the experience of Viktor Bartok. Henry had long since decided that the treatment of psychosis was more within the psychological field than that of medicine. He knew that there were well-known lay psychologists operating flourishing offices who had never been inside a medical school. They were not quacks, nor did they make any pretense of being acquainted with the functions of the physical organs. Theirs was a thorough knowledge of the various forms of phobias and mental disturbances that upset the equilibrium of the individual.

Henry had read of one such psychologist in New York. This man who had never studied medicine was nevertheless an outstanding mental diagnostician numbering among his clientele some of the biggest and wealthiest people in the country. His income was between fifty and seventy-five thousand a year, and he was known for his large fees and discriminating clients. Therefore, Henry reasoned, to minister successfully to people suffering from mental disturbances, it was more important to have a complete knowledge of human characteristics than to have a complete understanding of the functions of human anatomy. Yet he himself was not altogether ignorant of medicine. He had had elementary medical schooling and was able to perform the elementary practices of medicine. Hence he believed himself to be more capable in carrying on with his clientele than his eastern colleague because he could tie up certain mental disturbances with possible organic disorders.

In short, Henry Mueller almost felt entitled to be called "Doctor."

Evelyn Hahn returned from her vacation the week after Henry received the letter from Wilmington. The day was an especially busy one, and he did not have time to chat with his secretary or to inform her of the new honor to be conferred upon him. When they had exchanged greetings in the morning he had told her he wanted to talk to her later.

At six-fifteen that evening, after the last patient had departed, Evelyn was just closing her desk when a very well-dressed, attractive woman opened the reception room door. Evelyn had never seen the woman before and thought her stunning.

"How do you do?" said the visitor with a pleasant smile. "Is Dr. Bartok busy?"

"I'll see," Evelyn replied with an equal politeness. "Did you have an appointment?"

"Yes, we did."

"The last patient just left—I didn't know Dr. Bartok had made another appointment."

"Oh, I'm not a patient, my dear. Dr. Bartok and I had a dinner appointment."

"Oh, I see." Evelyn's face fell. "Who shall I say is calling, please?"

She threw her sable jacket on a lounge and sat down. "Miss Taylor. Miss Virginia Taylor. I'm Dr. Bartok's fiancée!"

Evelyn felt her blood turn to ice water. "Oh, I see." She forced a smile. "Excuse me, please, I'll tell the doctor you're here."

She left the room, though she imagined her legs would not support the weight of her body. As the door to the inner office closed behind her, Henry was washing up at the little closet lavatory. He turned and greeted her with a smile.

"Well, Evelyn—I hardly saw you all day. How have you been? How was your vacation, my dear?"

She ignored the question. She spoke in a dull monotone. "Miss Virginia Taylor is waiting."

"Miss who is waiting?"

"Miss Virginia Taylor is waiting in the reception room."

"What is she doing here?"

"She says she has an appointment with you." There was still no inflection in her voice. "A dinner appointment."

"A dinner appointment? I don't know anything about any—"

"She's very beautiful, Viktor. I admire your taste."

"But I—"

"Congratulations."

Evelyn extended her hand. "Congratulations."

"Oh you mean on my—"

She interrupted the finish of his sentence. "Yes." He took her hand.

"Thanks. How did you—oh, Virginia told you."

"Yes."

"I wanted to tell you myself. I knew you'd be happy to hear the news."

"Oh, yes. I'm very happy for you, Viktor. When did all this happen?"

"While you were on your vacation. It was all so unexpected. It's rather wonderful, isn't it?"

Evelyn could contain herself no longer. "Yes," she sobbed out, "It's very wonderful! I hope you'll both be very happy!" She ran from the room, crying hysterically.

"Evelyn, wait! What do you mean—both? Evelyn! Listen to me!" The door closed and she was gone, leaving Henry in confusion. A second later, as his mind began to function, he started for the door, and as he pulled it open he was met by his caller.

"What's the matter, dear? Your secretary seemed upset."

"Where is she?"

"She's gone. She grabbed her purse and hat and practically bolted from the room."

"I don't understand. After you told her about my receiving the degree, she congratulated me and—"

"What are you talking about, dear? I didn't tell her anything about your degree."

"You didn't? Then in heaven's name, what did you tell her?"

"I … I didn't tell her anything."

"Don't lie, Virginia. She wouldn't have congratulated me unless you told her something. Did you tell her we were—"

"Now, darling, don't go getting so upset. I merely told her your fiancée was calling."

"Fiancée? Why? Why in God's name would you do such a thing?"

"Why? Viktor, I resent that. I can think of many things more unpleasant than becoming my fiancée!"

Henry gritted his teeth. "I'm sorry. At the moment I can't think of anything more revolting!"

There was a resounding smack as Virginia's hand fell across Henry's cheek. "You're a dog!"

"Thank you. It takes a dog to recognize a bitch!"

She slapped him again, this time on both sides of his face. "If I'm a bitch, I'm still true to only one dog at a time! You've been making love to me and your secretary for months, only I didn't discover it until this week. Tonight I said what I did because I wanted to find out for sure. Well, I found out all right. I found out that I've had the wool pulled over my eyes for so long that I've practically been living in total darkness. Not that I asked or expected anything from you—but at least I thought when you left *my* bed you went home to your own, and not to another one in the Garland Hotel!"

"You flatter me, my dear Virginia. I'm not that good. It was never on the same night. Since you seem to know my whereabouts so well, you should be more familiar with the schedule. If you recall, I usually put in my appearance at the Garland on Friday nights!"

Virginia walked over to the lounge and picked up her sable. "Thank you for reminding me, darling. By the way, Viktor, would you care to stop in at my apartment sometime? There are a lot of things that belong to you that you may have use for. You won't be using them at my place anymore."

"I'll pick them up."

"On second thought, don't bother coming up. I'll pack them up for you and send them to the hotel. That will be much simpler, and it'll avoid the … awkward pause?"

"Just as you say."

"Well, Viktor, this is hardly the way I thought it would all end. We've had some good times together, in spite of the fact that I was only one of several women in your life."

"I wouldn't say several."

"Modest to the last, aren't you, dear? All right. In spite of the fact that I was the other woman in your life. There's little compensation in knowing that there was only one other. Anyhow, no tears—no regrets. It's been fun while it lasted. Three years that I shall remember always. Three years of living by a man who missed his calling. You should have been an actor instead of a doctor."

"Seems to me I heard that before."

"Yes. I know. It was Shandru that night at dinner. He thought you should have been an actor too. In fact, he mistook you for one. I'm not so sure now that he wasn't right."

"What do you mean?"

"You're always acting, Viktor. You never stop. Everything you do, and everything you say, is for effect. You're vain, egotistical, and smug. You're concerned only with your own feelings and your own impressions. You're selfish and self-satisfied. You're successful and conceited as hell about your accomplishments. Your entire life revolves around Viktor Bartok and what pleases him. You've been so imbued with your own importance that you can't see the forest for the trees. You're so busy telling your patients how to live their lives that you've forgotten completely how to live your own. The Viktor Bartok that I met three years ago was a pretty grand guy. The Viktor Bartok that I've known for the past year is somebody else—a cheap imitation of the real thing!"

Henry winced. "What do you mean by that?"

"I mean for two years you were charming, genuine, and sincere. In the last year I've seen another side of you that I never knew existed. You're still charming, but the genuineness and the sincerity are gone. Even your charm now is a little bit on the oily side. It's a charm that floats only on the surface."

"Thanks again, You're very complimentary this evening."

"I just don't want you to think I have any false illusions about you. As I said before, I don't have any regrets about us, only I would have felt better after leaving Chicago if I could have still thought of you as being the same swell guy as the one I met at Virginia Beach three years ago."

"Oh? You're leaving Chicago?"

"Yes, Viktor, for good. Remember, Shandru told me I would never find my happiness here? That my only real happiness would lie elsewhere, among my family and friends? As it turns out now, Shandru was far from being wrong."

"Just a coincidence."

Virginia flung her jacket across one shoulder. "I don't think so. I think it was in the cards all the time. We can't escape our destiny, remember? What was it Shandru said about yours? Oh, yes, something about a triumphant emptiness …? Goodbye, Viktor."

Henry did not answer, but stood watching her with an immobile face, almost weird in its stoniness, for only the eyes moved as they slowly followed Virginia Taylor through the closing door.

That night Henry sat in his apartment, wondering how Virginia had found out about Evelyn Hahn. She must have become suspicious and trailed him. Well, there would always be others, only probably not with as many advantages. Virginia Taylor was unusual. She was beautiful, fascinating, and cultured. Her sense of humor was refreshing. She made love with complete abandon, and liked total unrestraint on his part. All these attributes, summed up, made for a rare combination. It would be a long time before he would again meet a woman with the qualities of Virginia Taylor.

So far as Evelyn Hahn was concerned, he would have considerable explaining to do. Although it would be easy to convince her that no engagement existed, he would have a difficult time explaining the fact that his romance with Virginia had not ended when she had supposed. That was going to take a great deal of soft-soaping and a bit of strategy, but Henry felt confident he would be able to bring her around as on so many previous occasions. He would not worry about that now. It was time for a brandy and soda.

The next morning Henry's first appointment was nine-thirty, so he did not arrive at the office until nine-twenty. He was surprised to find that his secretary had not yet arrived. That was unusual. Evelyn Hahn was always punctual. However, he paid little attention to the matter. She was probably still a bit upset from the day before. What if she was angry enough to quit? He hadn't thought about that—she might have been hurt sufficiently to leave her job. No, she wouldn't do that, she wouldn't be so vindictive. After all, he was now paying her sixty dollars a week. That was a good salary for a secretary and receptionist, but she was worth it. If she left, it would be a serious inconvenience.

Henry had just invited his first patient into the inner office when the phone rang. He excused himself and picked up the receiver. "Hello."

"Is this Dr. Bartok's office?"

"Yes, this is Dr. Bartok speaking."

"Oh. Well, Dr. Bartok, my name is Jennings. I'm the manager of the Garland Apartment Hotel where your secretary, Miss Hahn, lives."

"Yes."

"Can you come over here right away, doctor? It's very important—it's about your secretary. She's—well, I'd rather not discuss it over the phone, but I'd appreciate it if you'd come immediately."

"All right, Mr. Jennings. I'll be there in ten minutes. Thank you for calling."

Henry had a feeling of foreboding … he could tell from the man's tone that it was something serious. His patient could see that he was greatly upset.

"Something wrong, doctor?"

"Yes, you will have to excuse me, Mrs. Ellis, I just got an emergency call about my secretary. It seems she's ill or something. As you see, I'm terribly concerned."

"Oh, of course, doctor, I can wait—I do hope it's nothing serious."

"Thank you. I'll be back as soon as I can."

Henry left the building hurriedly and jumped into a cab. In less than ten minutes he was in the lobby of the Garland Hotel. The manager was waiting for him.

"Dr. Bartok?"

"Yes."

"How do you do. I'm Mr. Jennings. Would you step into my office, please?"

"Yes, of course."

Henry followed him behind the desk and into the small hotel office. The manager closed the door and spoke in a voice that quavered with nervous tension.

"Dr. Bartok, your secretary, Miss Hahn, is dead!"

"Dead?" Henry was stunned. He had expected from the sound of the manager's voice over the phone that she had done something desperate, but he hadn't expected this. He sank into a chair, staring blankly at the floor. "Tell me about it."

"Well, Miss Hahn leaves a standing call for seven-thirty every morning, and this morning the operator rang and rang and rang, and there was no answer. We knew she was in, because her key wasn't in the box, and anyhow she never leaves the building until eight-fifteen. When I came on duty at eight, the switchboard operator told me that she had been ringing every few minutes since seven-thirty, and suggested we ought to make an investigation and find out if something was wrong. So we took a passkey and opened her door, and we found Miss Hahn lying half on the bed, and half on the floor. I ran down to the third floor and got Dr. Bramson who lives here in the building and he came right up. He took one look at her and said, 'This woman's dead!'"

Henry was unconsciously chewing his lower lip. "Did Dr. Bramson find the cause?"

"Yes."

"What?"

"He found an empty bottle of sleeping tablets standing on the lavatory. He said she probably took an overdose, but that could only be determined by a chemical analysis of her stomach. But there's one thing Dr. Bramson said would never show up in a post-mortem."

"What's that?"

"Whether she took the overdose accidently or on purpose. Would you know whether or not she would have any reason to commit suicide? After all, Miss Hahn worked for you, and you saw her almost every day. You'd be in a much better position to answer that question than anybody else."

"Yes, that's right. Well, I'll tell you, Mr. Jennings, as far as I know Miss Hahn was a very happy girl and very much in love with life. This is a very tragic thing, and we've lost a girl who in my opinion was a jewel among jewels. The loss to me is irreparable. I'm deeply grieved."

"So am I, doctor. We all loved her. She was always so cheerful, and never failed to have a smile and a kind word." Jennings returned to the pertinent subject. "So, you don't know of any affairs of the heart that would have caused Miss Hahn to take her life?"

Henry thanked God that he had not come to the Garland Hotel more often, and that he had usually come late, after the few ground floor employees had gone off duty. "No, Mr. Jennings, I do not. It must be that she swallowed more than she could take. Of the pills, I mean."

"Yes, I suppose so. Well, will you notify her next of kin, or does she have any?"

Henry rose. "Yes, she has a mother and father in Galesburg, Kansas. I'll notify them when I get back to the office."

"Thank you, doctor. Incidentally, would you care to go up and see the … body?"

"No, thank you. I'd rather remember Evelyn as I last saw her … happy and gay."

CHAPTER SEVENTEEN

"Now, Miss Corbett, I'm going to leave everything in your charge. I'm sure you'll not have any trouble at all."

"Don't you worry about a thing, doctor. When you come back from your trip, you'll find your schedule all made out and waiting."

"Fine."

"I've had eighteen years of this kind of work, you know. I've been secretary, receptionist, and laboratory technician for five different doctors. I'd still be working for old Dr. Ziegler if he hadn't died. He was seventy-nine, going on eighty."

"Yes. By the way, if new patients call and inquire about the fee, there's only one price. Fifty dollars per visit."

She whistled. "Fifty dollars a visit! Gracious, that's more money than I'll be making in a week! That's twice as much as Dr. Janowitz gets and he's a psychiatrist in this building too."

"Yes, but he's on the 8th floor, and I'm on the 16th, so I'm twice as high!"

Miss Corbett laughed and her removable bridge showed. "Gee, for a doctor, you do have a sense of humor. I'll bet the ladies fall all over themselves going to you. Did you say you're a bachelor?"

"Yes. Now don't go getting any ideas, Miss Corbett!"

"Who, me? I wouldn't have the best man on earth." She took a dust cloth and began to clean the typewriter.

"I'm glad to hear you say that, Miss Corbett. Very glad. There's no man that's worth it!"

"You're tellin' me. When I was seventeen I was in love with a sailor—almost married him too, but then I found out from a friend of his that he had a wife and kid in Australia. Since then, I've never trusted a man. None except old Doctor Ziegler. He was seventy-nine, going on eighty—"

"Uh … yes, you told me. Excuse me. I have some matters to clean up in my office."

"Oh, sure, doctor, go right ahead. I'll just dust things off a bit around here. They sure can get dirty in a couple of days, but I'll have things spiffy in a jiffy!"

Henry closed the door of his office and, as he sat down, shook his head with a broad grin. He couldn't help being amused at the antics of his new secretary. She had been recommended to him by one of the other doctors in the building as a very experienced woman whose employer had just recently passed away. She bore a striking resemblance to Edna May Oliver, but, because of her long experience working with doctors and because he needed someone in a hurry, she was hired on the spot.

Earlier that week, Evelyn Hahn's parents had come from the small town of Galesburg, Kansas, to claim the body of their youngest child who had left her home town five years before to come to Chicago. She had wanted a business career and, after attending the University of Kansas, had headed for the great Midwestern metropolis. Evelyn had arrived in Chicago young, gay, full of ambition and hopeful of the future. Now, this very day, she was on her way back to Galesburg in the best coffin that her family could afford.

Henry had met them and their eldest son at the railroad station and had gone with them to the funeral parlor. The tragic mission proved too much for the mother, and she collapsed at the bier of her only daughter. They thanked Henry over and over again for his solicitous attitude toward them and his generosity and affection for their daughter. "All she ever wrote about was wonderful, wonderful Doctor Bartok!" they had told him, "you were her life, her God!"

All this made Henry squirm in discomfort. He got out of the undertaker's as quickly as possible on the pretext that he had an office full of patients. Before he left, he put a check for $500 into her father's hand "to help defray expenses." When the latter saw the amount, he cried on Henry's shoulder as if he were the member of the family that Evelyn's letters had led them to believe he would be some day.

Henry got out into the open air as fast as he could, with the satisfying feeling that he had been thoughtful and benevolent. He had purchased his freedom from conscience for $500.

As he sat in his office, Henry thought how strange it was that both of his romances had faded at the same time. He wasn't sure whether it was a stroke of good fortune or bad. One thing was certain, he would definitely have more time to devote to his work and to himself. Now he could really give thought to many things that the two women had caused him to neglect.

The more he thought of Evelyn's death, the less inclined he was to reproach himself. In his mind, he laid full blame at the feet of Virginia Taylor for pulling off what he considered a stinking trick. If she hadn't come flaunting herself in his office bent on a bitch mission, Evelyn would be alive today! But that was a woman for you. They were all alike: nasty, petty, possessive, garrulous—they only spelled trouble. Women were good to make love to, and then forget. Whenever they hung on with the tenacity of a bulldog, there were bound to be unpleasant situations. They took a lease on his days and a mortgage on his nights. As Henry pushed himself back in his big swivel chair and crossed his feet on the desk, he felt reasonably sure that all had been for the best.

Now he could start from scratch again. So many new adventures awaited him—there was too little excitement anyhow in being with the same woman week after week. He had given Evelyn and Virginia a year of his time: sufficient unto the day! The only real pleasure in life was the luxury of novelty. Nothing can be so dull as yesterday's love.

Henry looked at his watch. It was four-thirty. His train for Wilmington left at five-twenty. He looked forward to this trip. This was to be one of those new adventures he had been thinking about. He was going to receive the honorary degree of Professor of Neurology. That was different! Christ, yes! Of course, not for the real Bartok—he had known the thrill of being made professor—but for Henry this would be the first time he had ever donned the cap and gown and been handed the honorary certificate. That only happened to people important in the service of mankind. He now was to be one of them, one of the honored few! He had come indeed a long way from the squalid neighborhood in Pittsburgh. If only old Dr. Bauer, the family physician, could see him now! Old Dr. Bauer, who hadn't had a new suit of clothes in six years and who got two dollars for an office visit. If only the select little group of Phi Taus knew that he was soon to be given an honorary degree at fashionable Wilmington University! He would like to see the expression on some of their smug little faces. Those were the people who had turned their backs on him, by whom he had been given the cold shoulder and snubbed! Ha! Ha! Henry laughed out loud. In fact he hadn't realized it, but he had been laughing unconsciously for a couple of minutes. The buzzer suddenly sounded under his desk. He picked up the phone. "Yes?"

"What's the gag, doc?"

"Oh, Miss Corbett—"

"Sure, who did you think it was—Goldilocks?"

"What did you ask me?"

"I said what's the gag? You were laughing your head off."

"Was I laughing? You heard me?"

"Were you laughing? Are you kidding? I thought maybe you either just remembered a good one you heard last night, or else you just got it. If it's good and dirty, I won't want to hear it unless I close my eyes!"

"Ha, ha, you are very funny, Miss Corbett, and here I thought you were the very essence of primness and propriety!"

"Who, me? Don't be silly! You should hear the ones old Doc Ziegler used to tell me, and he was seventy-nine, going on eighty—"

Henry returned from his eastern trip on Monday, the 16th of September, having spent the weekend in New York City.

His brief vacation from the office put him in high spirits. Now he was ready to plunge into serious work. His clientele was clamoring for more time, yet there were only so many hours in the day. Of course, that problem could be solved by seeing patients at night, but Dr. Bartok had not given his nights to the office, and Henry saw no reasons for setting a precedent.

Miss Corbett proved to be an efficient secretary, and aside from her brashness and pixy sense of humor, she was working out very well. Henry soon resigned himself to her eccentricities, and eventually found her stimulating. She made the patients laugh, kidded them out of their troubles and worries and, with a nudge of the ribs, she quickly made friends with all his patients. And aside from the fact that she was in her forties and her looks did nothing to quicken the male pulse, Henry was satisfied.

One afternoon toward the end of September, Henry had an interview with his favorite patient, Howard Richards. He was still coming in for psychoanalysis, though he had long since been relieved of his impotency. Richards was in an excellent mental state, and he and his wife were very happy, both enthusiastically certain that Dr. Bartok was a "miracle man." To further Richards' aim of becoming a father in due course, Henry, while continuing his own treatment, had sent him back to Dr. Earl Clinton for hormone injections.

No sooner had Richards departed and the next patient entered the office than the telephone buzzer sounded under the desk.

"Yes?"

"Here's a call for you. Can you take it?"

"Yes, Miss Corbett."

"Just a second, doctor. O. K., go ahead."

"Hello, Uncle Vik?" The voice was young and excited.

Henry blinked. "Hmmmm?"

"This is Kris!"

"Kris?"

"Yes, Kris ! Your niece—or have you forgotten?"

Indeed he had. For a second Henry was thrown completely off balance. Where was she calling from?

"Oh, yes … how are you, Kris?"

"Fine. How are you?"

"Oh, fine …"

"I'm at the railroad station."

"Oh, you … are?"

"Yes, I just got in. I'm dying to see you, Uncle Vik. I'm coming right over. Just as soon as I can hop into a cab. Get rid of all those silly old patients because I'm taking over your time. I've got oodles to tell you and scads of kisses from Mom and don't you dare psychoanalyze me! Promise?"

"Uh … yes …"

"See you in fifteen minutes, Uncle Vik. G'bye."

"Uh … goodbye … Kris …"

He slowly hung up, still blinking in amazement at the suddenness of the situation. *Bartok's niece in Chicago! On her way over to the office at this very minute!* Now Henry remembered the letter that he had found on Bartok's body a year ago. It had been from his sister in California and mentioned that Kristina might come to the Art Institute to take a course in art work the next year. And now she had come. Her voice sounded youthful—she must be of high school age or thereabouts. Now he would have an adolescent on his hands— snooping around the office and prying into his affairs. Henry didn't like this—didn't like it at all. He went back to his patient, irritated at this unforeseen development.

One hour later, after the last interview was over, the phone buzzer sounded.

"Yes?"

"Your niece has been waiting for forty-five minutes, doctor."

"Oh, yes. All right … send her in!"

"She's some girl! We've been having the time of our lives here. We haven't stopped gabbing since she came in. Talk about personality plus—she's got it!"

"Well, I'm glad you two got along so well together. Tell the youngster to come in—"

"Yes, doctor."

Henry squared his shoulders and made ready for the entrance of his bobby-socked visitor.

The door opened.

"Hello, Uncle Vik—"

"Hello ... Kris ..."

Henry gulped and his eyes popped at the sight before him. Here was no adolescent, teenaged youngster, but a grownup young woman who looked about twenty years old. She was as bewitchingly and captivatingly pretty as a Petty model. She stood before him, dressed in a tailored traveling suit with a little sailor hat perched up on top of her upswept hair. Pink cheeks that were natural and a small, petulant mouth that fitted her heart-shaped face, blended with a petite turned-up nose to complete the perfect features that might well represent a photographer's dream.

During the split second that she stood in the entrance, Henry's eyes surveyed her from her head to her feet and back again. She was perfectly built, about five-feet-five, weighed about 120 pounds. Her hair was auburn, and her eyes blue with just a trace of violet. They were the eyes of innocence, eyes that envied sophistication and maturity, eyes that yet held some of the magic of childhood.

In another second she had darted from the door and was smothering Henry with hugs and kisses.

"Gee, I'm glad to see you, Uncle Vik."

"Yes, so am I ... Kris—"

"Golly, it's been ages."

"Let me look at you." He held her at arm's length. "You're beautiful—positively beautiful—and you're not a child!"

"Child? After all, you didn't expect me to stay an infant forever, did you?"

"Of course not. It's just that I became accustomed to thinking of you as the little girl in the picture on my mantel. The pretty little girl in the white dress and the long curls."

"Oh, that picture? Mother has one of those at home too. Gosh, I was about twelve or thirteen when that was taken."

"And how long is it now since we've seen one another?"

"Gee, Uncle Vik, I'm going to be twenty in a couple of months—I guess the last time you saw me was when Mother and Dad left Czechoslovakia to come to the United States. I was just a year old when they came over."

"So, I haven't seen my lovely little niece since she wore diapers!"

"That's right," she laughed. "But I'm thoroughly housebroken now!"

"Sit down, my dear, and tell me all about yourself."

Henry pulled up a large chair and Kris curled up comfortably in it. "Well, first of all, I'm here to take a course in advanced art at the Art

Institute. I got my B. A. degree at U. S. C. in June, but I need more work before I can do what I want to—fashion designing and illustrations for *Vogue* or *Harper's Bazaar.*"

"Sounds very interesting," said Henry as he reached for a cigarette. "Oh, do you smoke?"

"Yes, thanks."

He proffered his lighter. "So, you want to be a designer and illustrator of women's fashions?"

"Yes. Of course it depends on how good and original your ideas are. But my teachers all said I have a flair for that kind of work. I did designing for MGM on the coast for a whole year during my spare time."

"Well! You must be good! I'd love to see some of your work."

"I brought a lot of things with me but they're all packed in the trunk. Incidentally, I checked my suitcase and trunk at the station until I find an apartment. Do you know of something, Uncle Vik, that isn't too expensive?"

"Why, I think I can find you something."

"I don't want to spend over seventy-five a month, and I'd rather have something around fifty or sixty, if I can find it."

"I'm sure you won't have any trouble. In fact, I know of a place not far from my hotel. I know the manager. I'll call him and see what he has available."

"Oh, swell, Uncle Vik! I'll certainly appreciate that. I don't know my way around this town at all. In fact I should hire myself an Indian guide!"

"Well, my dear, I don't look the part, but I'll do my best to fill the role, if it's all right with you—"

"Is it! Gee, Uncle Vik, that would be wonderful. And you're much more handsome than any Indian I've ever seen. Gosh, I'll be the envy of every female in town!"

"Thank you, and I'll be the envy of every young boy in town!"

"Young boy? I can't stand young boys."

"My error. I should have said young men."

"Even young men bore me. They're crude and uninteresting and tactless, and if they don't talk about football, they're usually trying to paw all over you. Pooh!"

"What kind of men do you like?"

"I like men a little older. They seem to have more polish and dignity and are more worldly. I don't think a man can be interesting until he's at least thirty!" Henry was amused.

"Yes, I'm more or less inclined to agree with you," he said mock-seriously. "Experience and worldliness can only come with years. I didn't really feel my stride until I hit thirty."

"But you're unusual, Uncle Vik. You've probably been worldly and interesting ever since you came out of school. Weren't you already a professor at thirty?"

"Uh … yes. At Vienna University in 1927. That was thirteen years ago. I was just thirty then."

"And I was just seven, designing clothes for my dolls. Time flies, doesn't it?"

"It certainly does. Now look what the last thirteen years have done for you … transformed you from a child to a beautiful young lady who will soon be designing clothes for the fashionable women of America."

Kris laughed. "Maybe. If I'm lucky. But look what the last thirteen years have done for you. Brought you to America—the Nobel Prize, a reputation as one of the country's outstanding psychiatrists, fame, a great deal of money and success!"

"Yes, I'll admit that's true, but there's one thing I still haven't found—happiness."

"I've often wondered about that, Uncle Vik—I've often wondered why you never married."

"Maybe it's because we doctors become so absorbed in our work that we are blind to everything else." Henry enjoyed hearing himself implying that he had devoted his days to the benefit of mankind.

"But, Uncle Vik, you're still young and handsome. You probably could have any woman you wanted. Gosh, you're elusive, that's all. I don't think you want to settle down, and if you ever do, the woman that gets you has got to be a pretty smart cookie!"

"You're probably right. But speaking about cookies, I'll bet you're starved. When did you eat last?"

"I ate lunch on the train but that seems like four days ago. Why? Are you going to buy me a hamburger?"

"Hamburger, nothing! I'm going to buy you the biggest steak in town! We have to celebrate a reunion, don't we?"

"Swell! Oh boy, that'll be scrumdumtious! But I should change into something else first—I've had this suit on since early this morning."

"Well, I'll tell you what. I'll call my friend Mr. Jennings right now and ask about an apartment, and if he has something suitable, we'll go back to the station, pick up your bags and then you'll be able to freshen up in your new home before we have dinner. How does that sound?"

"Wonderful. You know something, Uncle Vik?"

"What?"

"Mother said you'd be much too busy to bother with me, and that I shouldn't make myself a nuisance." Kris looked demure and very young. "You don't think I'm a nuisance, do you, Uncle Vik?"

"Nuisance?" Henry walked over and tweaked her chin playfully. "Yes! I do!"

"You do?"

"Yes, you're probably the most delightful nuisance I have ever seen!"

"Mummmm, this is good!" exclaimed Kris as she tasted the thick juicy sirloin in front of her.

"Yes," replied Henry, "the food here is usually okay."

"It's a swell place—what do they call it?"

"The Gold Coast Room. I think it's one of the nicest places in town, but then I may be prejudiced, since I come here so often."

"And you live here?"

"Yes. I've lived at the Blake ever since I opened up my office."

"I'm crazy about my apartment. I can hardly believe it! Such a beautiful living room and bedroom for only fifty dollars! Gosh, rents are cheap in Chicago!"

"Uh … yes." Henry made a special point of the next statement. "Don't mention the price to a soul. You see, I know the manager, and he gave me a special price." The "special price" was the extra fifty dollars per month that Henry had told Mr. Jennings he himself would pay. Henry had made Jennings promise that he would never reveal the arrangement. "I want her to be happy while she's in Chicago," he told the hotel manager, "and she was so crazy about that apartment, I couldn't bear the thought of her compromising and taking another."

"Mother will be tickled when I write her and tell her that I found such a lovely place for so little money."

"Yes. By the way, how is your mother?"

"Well, as good as can be expected considering the fact that she has been almost an invalid for two years."

This, Henry did not know. "Yes, that was most unfortunate. I have been wanting to come out to California ever since I came to this country, but just never could find the time."

"Confidentially, Uncle Vik, mother has been quite hurt that her only brother has never come to see her. Two years ago you wrote that you were going to come, and then you never did."

"Yes, I know. Unexpected things crop up and ruin your plans."

"In the last year, we've only had three letters from you, and even those were typewritten by your secretary because you didn't have the time to write them yourself."

"That's right. I hope your mother will forgive me, but the last year has been such a hectic one, I hardly had time to think straight. You see, all last winter and spring I was on the lecture staff at Fort Dearborn and what with seeing forty or fifty patients a week, I've had very little time for pleasures or vacations. In fact I just came back ten days ago from the East, my first trip out of town in two years."

"Really, Uncle Vik? Your first trip in two years? Where did you go?"

"To Wilmington, Delaware. Another honorary degree—"

"Congratulations! I didn't know anything about that! Did you write mother?"

"Not yet," said Henry modestly, "I don't like to make too much fuss about those things." Then sliding back into the old Henry, "It was in all the papers, and even a newsreel photographer was there."

"Gosh, can I touch you? Golly Molly, that's really something! Have I got a famous uncle or have I got a famous uncle!"

"Now stop! Pretty soon you will be making me swellheaded!"

"Not you, Uncle Vik. Anybody else—probably, yes—but not you. We Bartoks and Dvoraks never allow fame to go to our heads. It never went to daddy's."

"No, that's right." Henry wondered who Kris' father was and how he was associated with fame. As he sat there trying to place the name, an elderly couple who were residents of the hotel stopped as they passed the table.

"Good evening, doctor."

Henry rose. "Good evening. How are you this evening?"

"We're fine, thank you, doctor."

"I want you to meet my niece from California. This is Kristina Dvorak, Mr. and Mrs. Hughes."

They exchanged greetings and after commenting on what a charming niece he had, passed on.

"They're awfully nice," said Kris.

"Yes, quite a lovely old couple. They've been married almost fifty years. They've been living here since the place went up."

"Gee, it must be wonderful for two people to live together for fifty years. I wish mom and dad had a chance to live together longer."

"Yes, it was too bad they couldn't." Henry wondered whether that meant he was dead or whether they had been divorced. He did not have to wait long for the answer, for Kris continued, in her reflective mood:

"Daddy was killed at the peak of his career. If he had lived, I'm sure he would have been one of the greatest pianists alive today. Before he died he was already being compared with Paderewski and Rachmaninoff."

Suddenly it dawned on Henry. Her father must have been Konrad Dvorak, the great Czech pianist who had been killed in a train wreck six or seven years ago. It had been in all the papers at the time. His wife had been seriously injured. Of course! He knew the name Dvorak sounded familiar. He had often listened to Konrad Dvorak's recordings while spending a quiet evening at home. He especially liked his rendition of Tchaikovsky's Piano Concerto No. 1 in B Flat Minor. So Konrad Dvorak was Kris' father!

"Yes," said Henry, "Your father was a great man and a great artist. He may be gone—but his talent will live always for millions to hear and enjoy!"

A trace of a tear glistened in Kris' eye. "Thank you, Uncle Vik."

"I've never listened to your father play without being thrilled by his magnificent artistry." Henry was not talking merely to ingratiate himself with this beautiful young girl. He was always sincere about music. He had a deep appreciation of fine music, for which he could thank his mother who had often bought gallery tickets to the concert or opera and taken her son with her. "Your father was one of my favorites," he continued. "Just a couple of evenings ago I listened to him play *Liebestraum.*"

"*Liebestraum?* That's rather queer," said Kris with a note of morbidity.

"Why?"

"*Liebestraum* was daddy's swan song. It was the last thing he played at Carnegie Hall before he and mom took the train back to California ... the train that was wrecked! To most everyone else, *Liebestraum* means life, and beauty, and love. To me it means only death—an ugly, horrible death!" She sat there staring emptily at the floor. "I hate it! I hate it!"

"Kris, please ... you shouldn't talk that way."

"It was daddy's favorite piece too. At the funeral, the organist in the church played *Liebestraum* and everyone cried. I hope I never hear it again!"

"Please, Kris ... we came here to enjoy ourselves. Let's change the subject ... yes?"

Her eyes shifted back to his. Suddenly, the twinkle was back. "Okay, Uncle Vik. I'll tell you what ... if you'll tell the waiter to have the orchestra play 'Stardust', I'd love to dance with you...."

"Fine! An excellent idea. I couldn't think of anything I'd rather do. Waiter!"

"Yes, sir?"

"Would you mind telling your orchestra leader that a very beautiful young lady would like to hear 'Stardust'?"

"Not at all, sir." The waiter headed directly for the bandstand where the leader stood arranging his music for the opening numbers. As he heard the whispered request, the leader turned and smilingly nodded in the direction of Henry's table. A few moments later the orchestra began to play.

"That's pretty, a dreamy tune," commented Henry. "What's the name of that?"

"'That Old Feeling'. It is pretty, isn't it?" Just then the music went into a repeat of the chorus and Kris began to sing the words. "I saw you last night and got that old feeling—when you came in sight, I got that old feeling—" Suddenly she stopped. "Come on, Uncle Vik, let's dance."

"But I'd rather listen to you sing—you have a delightful voice."

"Thanks, but I'd rather dance. Anyhow, I can hum it on the dance floor."

"Fine!"

Soon they were dancing to the lilting strains of the tune Kris had been singing a moment before. She picked up the melody as they moved slowly on the gradually crowding floor. "—And when you caught my eye, my heart stood still—Once again I seem to feel that old yearning—da da dada dum dumda is still burning—I don't know all the words—there'll be no new romance for me. It's foolish to start, 'cause that old, old feeling is still in my heart." The number came to an end and the dancers stopped and applauded. Soon the music started again.

"Oh! There's 'Stardust'," exclaimed Kris joyously. "I just love it, don't you, Uncle Vik.

"Yes, it's beautiful," said Henry as he took Kris in his arm and pressed her close.

They glided dreamily along and as they approached the bandstand the leader smiled and nodded.

"Thanks for playing my request," said Kris, looking up.

"Not at all." He was a handsome clean-cut young man. He gave Kris an admiring glance. "It was a pleasure."

They danced on. Soon Henry discovered Kris had snuggled up against his shoulder.

"You know something, Uncle Vik—" she murmured softly.

"What?"

"You dance awfully well."

"Oh, thank you, my dear. I never paid much attention to it."

"I like being with you, Uncle Vik. You're handsome and young—it's almost as if I was out with a new date."

"Really? I'm flattered. But you'd hardly call me young—after all I'm twice your age."

"That's nothing. You've got a lot more on the ball than anybody else I know. You bet! Out in Hollywood, they'd call you smooth."

"You mean I'm a smoothy?" Henry wasn't sure he should feel as complimented as he thought.

"No, Uncle Vik, not a smoothy in the sense of being licentious or lascivious—"

"Say, those are pretty big words for a little girl."

"Yes, I know, but when you've done work around the film studios, you soon find out that most men around Hollywood who approach that dangerous forty mark are usually members of the Four L Club."

"Four L Club? What's that?"

"Licentious, lascivious, lecherous louses!"

Henry gulped. Kris looked up and saw his surprised expression. "Oh, Uncle Vik, did I shock you?"

"Uh … rather …"

"Well, don't be. I just wanted you to know that I'm acquainted with that type of smoothy. They walk around dressed as men in the subtlest of disguises. Some hide behind the title of producer, some are directors, some publicity agents, camera men, actors, and even musical conductors. But you're safe—"

"I'm—safe?"

"Yes. I've never known one to masquerade as a doctor!"

"Oh!" He was momentarily ill at ease.

"But getting back to what I was saying. I meant you're smooth in a wonderful, clean, decent sort of way."

For once Henry was stopped cold. The words *clean* and *decent* held him at bay, like the uplifted sword-hilt before Mephistopheles in *Faust*. To this young, beautiful, innocent and idealistic girl, he represented all those things! She was still a hero-worshipper—and he was the hero. Yet he knew himself to be far from that. His life was founded on a hideous and despicable sham; he himself had destroyed the life of the very man who was actually her ideal. For the briefest of moments Henry was remorseful. He lapsed into a silence of deep penitence. Why was he not good, clean and decent? Why had he lived such a self-centered, cruel existence? Why couldn't he have been—

"You know, Uncle Vik—I never realized you had such big broad shoulders. You're built nice."

"Oh, do you really think so? Thank you, my dear. I work out at the gym two or three times a week." He suddenly found himself dancing straighter, inhaling deeper. His head lifted, his chin jutted forward; the period of penitence was over.

Henry was back in his stride.

CHAPTER EIGHTEEN

The next day was Saturday and Henry finished his work at noon. Kris came down to the office to meet him for lunch, after which they were going on a sightseeing tour.

"Uncle Vik's going to show me the town," she told Miss Corbett, "don't you think I'm going to have a handsome escort?"

"You sure are," the garrulous secretary replied, "but don't keep telling him that. This office won't be fit to live in!"

Kris laughed. "Oh, Uncle Vik's beyond that! He's not easily flattered. I think he's one of the most modest men I've ever met!"

Miss Corbett raised one eyebrow and gave vent to a deep sigh. "Ye gods! It's a good thing you're his niece, young 'un. You'd be duck soup for him!"

"What do you mean?"

"I mean that as far as your Uncle Vik is concerned, I think he's terrific. As far as being a good doctor, he's listed in *Who's Who* and he has the reputation of being the best in the business. The men patients swear by him, and the females who come up here bust their two-way stretches every time he looks at them. But as far as him being modest for all that, that I won't swear to!"

Kris walked up to her desk and leaned over. "You know something, Miss Corbett? I think you're crazy about him yourself!"

The secretary straightened up. "Who, me?"

Kris shook her finger. "Yes, you!"

Miss Corbett forced a laugh. "Why, I wouldn't be crazy about any man living. There's none of 'em worth it. The only man I've ever been crazy about was my last boss, old Doc Ziegler. He was seventy-nine—"

"Going on eighty!" Henry finished the sentence for her as he stood in the doorway of his office, laughing. Neither of the two had been aware of his presence. "What is she doing, Kris, telling you all about her love life?"

Miss Corbett flushed while Kris laughed gaily.

"Hello, Uncle Vik."

"Hello, my dear. Come, come, Miss Corbett, don't look so guilty!"

"That's not a guilty look, doctor. What have I to look guilty about?"

"Not a thing. I think it's wonderful to have a love life. I wish I had one."

A sly look came over the secretary's spinsterish face. "I wish I had one too!"

They all laughed. "Good for you, Corby," exclaimed Henry. "I'm glad to hear you're not a man-hater."

"I never said I was a man-hater. I just want to find one you can trust, that's all."

"Oh, there are lots of them, Miss Corbett," commented Kris. "Take my uncle for instance—"

Miss Corbett grunted.

"What was that 'hmpf' for?" inquired Henry.

"Just 'hmpf'—that's all," she replied good naturedly.

"That was a dirty 'hmpf' too." heckled Kris. "I don't think your secretary trusts you, Uncle Vik."

"Don't you think I'm trustworthy, Miss Corbett?"

She closed up her typewriter. "I'm not mentioning any individual names, but to me, the only trustworthy man is a dead one!"

"Wow! Let's get out of here, Uncle Vik, before she crushes all my faith in mankind." Kris reached for Henry's arm.

"Not mankind, youngster, just man—the kind doesn't matter!"

"Say, that's very good, Corby," Henry said, nodding his head. "Was that extemporaneous or have you heard that before?"

"How do you like that," she answered with her hands on her hips. "He doesn't even give credit for a good gag. Stick around, doc, I got lots more you've never heard."

"I'll bet you have. But don't ask me to stick around today. Today I have a date with a very beautiful young lady."

"Thank you, kind sir," said Kris with a curtsy. "Where are you going to take me?"

"First we're going to have lunch, and then we'll go to see the planetarium, then the aquarium and, if we have time, the Field Museum and the Lincoln Park Zoo!"

"Excuse me, Dr. Bartok—"

"Yes, Miss Corbett?"

"Is this going to be a date, or a session in astronomy, biology, and zoology?"

"Both," laughed Henry. "Those are very romantic places, Miss Corbett. Don't tell me you've never been kissed at a zoo?"

"No, I haven't."

"Oh, you don't know what you are missing. When I was a youngster, I kissed a girl once in front of the monkeys' cage. The next thing I knew the monkeys were all kissing one another. You know, they copy whatever they see."

"Really, Uncle Vik? This really happened?"

"Oh, of course, I wouldn't think of making up such a story. When it came time to eat, none of the monkeys ate a thing. They were all so much in love they had lost their appetites. They just sat around holding hands. Within a week, seven monkeys died from malnutrition. They had tried to live on love and starved to death! So you see what happened just from innocently kissing a girl at the zoo!"

"Oh, Uncle Vik," laughed Kris, "what a story!"

"It's a good thing you didn't kiss her in front of the bears' cage," injected Miss Corbett dryly.

"Why?"

"They probably would've hugged each other to death!"

"Come on, Kris," cried Henry. "Let's go. I can't top that!"

They left the office chatting gaily, walked up Michigan Avenue, and entered a restaurant.

The luncheon was excellent and they had an afternoon of sightseeing. They had dinner together and later Henry managed to pick up two good seats for a musical comedy.

Henry called for Kris early on Sunday to make a tour of the city in the big Cadillac. They drove along Sheridan Road past the city limits and into Evanston. He pointed out Northwestern University and continued northward into Wilmette.

There they saw one of the strangest and most beautiful buildings in the world, the Bahá'í Temple with its stone filigree dome hand-carved in intricate designs. After twenty years or more of labor and well over a million dollars in expenditures, the structure was still uncompleted.

"It's breathtaking!" commented Kris.

"Bahá'ís from all over the world have contributed to make this building possible," said Henry.

"What are they?" asked Kris.

"Well, as far as I know, they are all members of a movement that was started by a Persian named Bahá'u'lláh not much over a hundred years ago."

They strolled up the inclined walk and stood marveling at the magnificent edifice. A guide approached them and offered to show them about.

They made a complete circle of the building as they read the inscriptions over the nine entrances. "I've never seen anything to equal it in beauty," exclaimed Kris.

"Are services conducted by a priest of any kind?" Henry asked the guide.

"No, there are no services and no priests, ministers, rabbis, or leaders. Everyone who enters here prays in his own way, and according to the dictates of his own conscience. May I give you these pamphlets?"

Henry accepted the literature but handed it to Kris. They thanked their guide for his time and courtesy. As they slowly walked back to the car, Kris glanced at the small booklets she held in her hand. "It sounds like a very beautiful religion," she said reflectively.

"Yes, it does," replied Henry opening the car door, "if one is religious-minded."

"Aren't you, Uncle Vik?"

"Well," he said, settling himself behind the wheel. "So far, I've done pretty well without it."

He put the car in gear and they headed back for the city.

It was five-forty-five when Henry pulled up in front of the Blake entrance. "Come on upstairs for a few minutes, I want to show you my apartment. I think you'll like it."

"Oh, I'd love to see your place, Uncle Vik. I'll bet it's beautiful."

"I like it. It's nice and livable." He called to the doorman. "Fred, take the car and park it for me, please."

"You bet, doctor, be glad to."

A few minutes later Kris stood in the center of the living room of the apartment once occupied by her real uncle.

"Gee, Uncle Vik, it's simply magnificent! It's furnished like a movie set!"

"You like it?"

"Like it? I could move in tomorrow!"

"But it's not pretty enough for a pretty lady. After all, it is a bachelor apartment."

"I know, but I don't like a lot of frills and fancy feminine doodads. Give me something like this every time! I love studio apartments. They appeal to my Bohemian nature."

"And a true Bohemian you are."

"That's right. Born in Bratislava, Slovakia, and with a name like Dvorak, I could hardly be called anything else. Of course, the fact that I've been living in the United States for nineteen of my twenty years has had a tendency to Americanize me a bit, but I'm still proud of my Bohemian background and my Bohemian tastes."

"Naturally."

"Just like you, Uncle Vik; aren't you proud of being Czech?"

"Oh … of course, Kris … very much."

"Let's see the rest of the place. Golly, I'm wild about it—it's so modern and rich without being gaudy. I hope to own something like this someday … when my canoe comes in."

"I'm sure you will. I have a feeling you'll be very successful someday.

"Gee, I hope so, Uncle Vik. I want to do something useful, and feel that I've really accomplished things and done something with my life … like you have."

"Like me …?"

"Yes. Mummy and I are very proud of you, Uncle Vik, just like we were of daddy. You see, you're all we have left now, and we look up to you and are proud to be related to you."

"Aren't you giving me an awful lot to live up to?"

"I don't think so. You've already proved yourself, Uncle Vik. Your career and your achievements are not something in the distant future, they're definitely part of the record. You've attained them already, things like the Nobel Prize, and your honorary degrees at universities. Those things don't just happen; you have to work and earn that kind of fame and honor."

Henry did not answer. For once he could not find an answer to such misplaced faith, to such undeserved homage and loyalty.

"Here's the bedroom," was his way of changing the subject.

"Oh, it's darling. It's so restful-looking and dignified. Everything is just the way I'd picture my Uncle Vik living. It's you—it expresses your personality, your individuality."

"Thank you, my dear. And, oh yes, I must show you the bar."

"You have a bar, too?"

"Oh yes, of course." Henry strode over to the closet door in the living room and opened the automatically lighted bar.

"Golly be to Moses! Look at that! Uncle Vik, that's terrific. Everything from A to Z. From absinthe to a zombie!"

"Very cute," laughed Henry. "Would you like a zombie?"

"Can you make one?"

"Sure. Don the Beachcomber across the street showed me how to make them. They make the finest zombies in the country. At least the most potent. I had two there one night and I had to be poured into bed!"

"Really? Oh, Uncle Vik, you're fibbing."

"No, I'm not, honestly. The next morning I felt for my tongue and it wasn't there. It had turned into a cork!"

"Oh, you! You're getting to be a regular Baron Munchausen with your stories."

"Do you want me to make you one?"

"No, thanks, not on an empty stomach. I want to be able to register for art class tomorrow morning."

"Oh, yes, that's right. Well, speaking about empty stomachs, I think it's about time we replenished ours. Let's go over to Don's. If you like Cantonese food, you can't beat them."

"Wonderful. I love Cantonese dishes."

"Then Don's it is. But we mustn't stay there too long because the performance starts promptly at eight-thirty."

"What performance?"

"The Ballet Russe."

"The Ballet Russe? You have tickets?"

"Two in the sixth row center."

Kris closed her eyes and swayed. "This is too much—I'm going to pass out while I'm still happy!" She ran up and threw her arms around Henry's neck. "Oh, Uncle Vik, this is the most wonderful, wonderful weekend I've ever had in my life!" Henry could feel her cheek against his, and it was warm and glowing. He put his arms about her waist and pressed her tightly. This was nice, holding Kris like this. Her body was so supple and curvaceous. He could feel her round firm breasts pressing against him in the exuberant innocent embrace of her girlish delight. She left his clasp as quickly as she had entered it, but Henry knew that there would be repetitions. He felt a spark of something, as yet too infinitesimal to be detected, but strong enough in its impulse to register in the uncanny brain of Henry Mueller. Yes, there would be other times—other embraces. This was only the beginning.

"Come on, Uncle Vik," she said gaily as she picked up her purse. "I'm hungry."

The following evening Kris sat in her new apartment and wrote a letter to her mother:

"Dearest Mumsy:

"When I arrived, I wired you 'letter will follow,' so here it is. I'm writing this from my new apartment which is only a few blocks away from Uncle Vik. It's the darlingest apartment with a big living room and bedroom, and the cutest little kitchen, and guess what I'm paying? Only $50 a month completely furnished! Isn't that a steal? The reason I got it that cheap is because Uncle Vik knew the manager and he gave him a special deal. I'm not supposed to mention that to a soul, but aren't I lucky?

"I registered at art school today and was busy enrolling and buying things that I'll need. The Art Institute is a big place, and there are students here from all over the country. Met a few kids today who are awfully sweet and I know I'll like them. One is a girl from San Diego who used to go with Buzz Clayton. You remember Buzz from Cal Tech? So, here I am two thousand miles away from dear old Pasadena, and it's like old home week!

"Mumsy, I can't begin to tell you what kind of a time I've had since I arrived, but honestly, it was the most glorious weekend I have ever spent in my life! Every minute with Uncle Vik, and, Mumsy, he's the most wonderful man in the world! Whatever you said about your young brother wasn't half enough! Honest, darling, he's handsome enough to be in pictures. And charming—? He has enough charm to captivate any woman in Chicago—but he's not interested in women, he says; hasn't got time for them—too busy working on patients and lecturing at the University. I really believe Uncle Vik has dedicated his life to his fellow man—he's that engrossed in his work and his career. Too bad, too, such a gorgeous hunk of man going to waste, when he could be making some woman happy. But Uncle Vik had time for me! You thought I'd be a bother and a nuisance to him, but darling, he was happy to be with me. I really believe he was. He told me I was refreshing and made him feel young once again. Can you imagine that? Young once again! And Uncle Vik's only forty-three. Last night he took me to see the Ballet Russe. It was magnificent, and Tanya Baclavenska was superb. I loved every minute of it. Saturday night Uncle Vik took me to the Gold Coast Room of the Blake where he lives. After that we saw *The Student Prince* and had a midnight supper at the Petrushka Club. Uncle Vik has a big Cadillac and over the weekend he drove me all around and showed me Chicago and the suburbs. I can't rave too much about my attentive and gallant uncle!

"Take care, darling, and give my regards to Miss Danielson. I'm so glad she's with you. Hope she stays on indefinitely. I'll write soon again. Loads of love and kisses to the dearest Mumsy in the world!

Kris

"P.S. The doorbell just rang.

"Sp. P.S. (5 minutes later) It was Uncle Vik and he sends his love."

"Take this chair, Uncle Vik, it's nice and comfy."

"Thank you, Kris. Writing to your mother, huh?"

"Five pages. I told her all about what a wonderful time you showed me."

"Oh, but it was I who had the wonderful time. Don't forget, before you came, I was Chicago's unchallenged hermit."

"You mustn't ever allow yourself to get into a rut like that again, Uncle Vik. It isn't good for you. After all, you're young too."

"I shall keep it in mind from now on, Kris. I enjoy doing things with you. We seem to have so many things in common—strange, considering we're relatives!" Henry laughed heartily at his little sally.

Kris reached for a cigarette and Henry was alert with his lighter. "Thanks." She blew out a cloud of smoke and her face showed an expression of deep thought. "You're right, Uncle Vik. We do have a lot in common. I never realized it so much as I did today when I was at school."

"What do you mean, Kris?"

"I don't know, but I sat there waiting to register, and my thoughts were about you—about seeing you this evening. I was actually wishing it was eight o'clock so we could be together again."

"What a coincidence—I was thinking the same thing, during the hour I spent with my last patient. I was very grateful when she walked out and I knew that that ended my day."

"Honestly, Uncle Vik? That's wonderful, because I didn't know whether or not you might begin to think of me as a boring little nuisance."

"You—a boring little nuisance?" Henry laughed. "Heaven forbid! No, my dear Kris—" and his tone became softly serious, "you are to me anything but boring. On the contrary, you are the best thing that could happen to me. You are as refreshing as morning dew, as inspiring as a beautiful landscape. Nothing could compare with the thrill you gave me as you stood in the entrance of my office three nights ago, and I saw before me a young woman with all the bounties and beauties that nature could bestow upon her. It was a moment that I shall always remember."

Kris sat there as if in a trance looking at the man she believed to be her uncle. Finally she spoke. "Uncle Vik, that makes me feel we have more in common than just a few inherent traits that are in our blood. It seems you've always been there at my side to guide me and inspire me. Somehow or other, I don't think of you as being just my uncle and my being your niece. I think of you more as a great man whom it's a privilege to know and be with. I'm inspired when I'm with you. It's a strange bond that I can't quite explain. But, Uncle Vik, when I look at you your eyes tell me that you know exactly what I mean—what I can't seem to understand myself ..."

Henry took a cigarette also, and lighted it before he answered. "Yes, Kris, I do understand."

"It's a nice, clean, warm feeling," said Kris. "Like telling a person anything on earth and he would understand—like knowing that no matter how troubled you were, his counsel and encouragement could dispel all your fears—like just hearing that person's voice and knowing automatically that the world was beautiful, and exciting, and really a wonderful place to live in—"

Henry sat there hypnotized by the simple sincerity of this young, beautiful girl who possessed such an extraordinary attachment for her uncle. No, it was not for the dead Bartok that she had this unusual fixation, he told himself, it was for him, the live Bartok! Why? Because if the real Bartok were alive, he would be treating her with a politeness of kinship but nothing more. He would be conducting himself in the staid manner that blood relationship dictates; or else, having only a purely family interest in his young niece, he would have found only a few moments to spend with her. Therefore, all these years Kris had been in love with an illusion. If Bartok had lived, that illusion would have been dissipated by the normal reactions of persons related to one another. As it was, her idealistic conceptions were kept alive by virtue of the fact that the man whom she thought to be her uncle was not really her uncle at all. He was another man, a stranger who had entered her life, bound by no blood ties or kinship and possessing all the romantic qualities that appealed to her dream-filled world of fantasy and knights in shining armor.

Henry's special knack had always been the workings of the female mind, and he prided himself on having developed a genius for being able to psychoanalyze the feminine libido. He knew, from the first meeting with Kris, that when he had embraced her, even though she was conscious of being held in the arms of her supposed uncle, she was wishing that he was somebody else—someone to whom she could whisper how much she wanted to be kissed and loved. He had felt her body quiver as he pressed her to him, and Henry knew he had awakened something that had lain dormant all her life. Having studied much of Freud and being certain that sex governs human life, he sensed that Kris was unconsciously engulfed in a sexual conflict. He contemplated her.

Kris smiled at him and said, "I don't know what you were thinking,

Uncle Vik, but by the look in your eye, it must have been good!"

"Uh—I was thinking how nice and relaxing it is to sit with you across from me."

"Were you really? I like that."

"Yes, Kris, it's nice sometimes to sit and think—especially if you have a romantic imagination."

"I like to do that, too. It's no trouble for me at all to imagine myself doing all sorts of things, and traveling to the most romantic places. I've toured the world in my imagination. There's hardly a country I haven't been in." She laughed. "It's a wonderful way to travel! No budgeting yourself—no place too expensive to enter—no worry about passports or visas—you just pick yourself a place, and there you are!"

"Someday you will actually see all the places you've dreamed about," Henry said, glancing at her speculatively.

"I hope so, Uncle Vik."

"But it's no fun traveling all by yourself. Don't you ever think about going to all these places with a nice companion—a sweetheart or a husband?"

"Oh, of course! In all my dream travels there's always a handsome man by my side and we're strolling arm in arm, or we're leaning over the ship's rail watching the moon come up over the horizon."

"What does he look like? Or haven't you thought about him as having any particular outstanding characteristics?"

"Oh, yes, I have, Uncle Vik. I know exactly what he looks like. I've known for years—ever since I first saw your picture—"

"My picture?"

"Yes. You see, my lover, when he comes along, has got to look like my Uncle Vik."

"Like me? I'm flattered, my dear." Henry wished that it were possible to inform Kris that she need search no longer—that before her very eyes sat the one man in the world who really looked like her uncle, and yet actually was not. Here was her ideal, who could be everything she had always pictured, and who was not bound by blood ties that would make her love for him unholy and wicked. If only she could know.

"But," said Kris with a deep sigh, "I don't suppose I'll ever meet a man who has the looks and charms of my Uncle Vik."

Henry looked into her eyes with an encouraging smile. "I wouldn't be too sure of that, Kris … I wouldn't be too sure."

CHAPTER NINETEEN

As the days passed and the chill autumn winds gave way to the biting cold of December, Henry and Kris became more and more devoted to each other. They spent every available evening together—sometimes going to a concert, sometimes walking along the lake, or sometimes just sitting in Henry's apartment, listening to symphony recordings while Kris sketched and he sat watching her.

Henry often wondered whether he was actually in love with this young and beautiful girl, or whether this strange desire to be with her each night was prompted solely by physical urge. Could it be possible that finally, after so many years, he had at last met a woman who had found the secret passage into his heart and given him the feeling that he had always prided himself he would never know? He had said that no woman could ever get under his skin—make him quicken with love's pangs. Yet he was now experiencing that very feeling, and, ironically, he could do nothing about it. He found himself wanting to be able to love her in a normal, decent manner, as other men do when they meet a girl who arouses all of their masculine emotions. He wanted to be able to take her in his arms and say "Kris, I love you as I've never loved a woman in my life! You've awakened me to the beauties of life and romance—I've never truly been in love in my life, because I've never met a woman who inspired me as you do. You've told me that all your life you've worshipped me. You've been in love with an illusion ever since you were a child, but you need illusions no longer, because I'm here in the flesh, with each beat of my heart saying, I love you—I love you!"

Those were the words that Henry wanted to declare to Kris, but he knew he could never utter such phrases. For once, since he had assumed the identity of Viktor Bartok, he found himself helpless to realize the one thing that he now desired more than anything else—to possess Kristina Dvorak as Henry Mueller and not as her uncle. As Henry Mueller, he could have her. But as Viktor Bartok, her uncle, he could further neither his attentions nor his desires, for she would flee from his unnatural embrace.

Yes, for the first time since that macabre night when he buried Viktor Bartok, he had come to an impasse. Yet Henry felt intuitively that she desired him as much as he did her. He saw the look in her eyes, her quivering lips and dilated nostrils. He knew that inwardly she was a turbulent sea of self-conflict; that she had spent many hours by herself trying desperately to find a solution to this baffling situation. If only he could say, "Kris, I'm not your uncle, come to me, my darling—we're meant for each other!" Henry knew that he could never—would never—utter those words.

Nonetheless, it was not easy to resign himself to a pattern of restraint with Kristina Dvorak.

Henry and Kris spent a succession of holidays and events together. For her birthday, he bought her a solid gold chain bracelet with a large disk hanging from one of the links, which had engraved upon it: TO KRIS, WITH LOVE, UNCLE VIK. Then came New Year's Eve. Henry had made a reservation in the Gold Coast Room, and they had dinner there and saw the show. Kris was wearing an exquisite gown of pale blue net, with a bodice which flattered her already well-formed breasts. Her skin was radiantly white and flawless. Her swept-up, gathered coiffure added a touch of regality as well as smartness to her appearance. Never before had Henry seen her quite so lovely and alluring. Never before had he seen revealed such an expanse of her warm, white flesh. He stared at her, disrobing her visually.

"My orchid is so beautiful," she said, glancing down at it admiringly, "Thanks again, Uncle Vik."

"Don't mention it—I'm glad you like it, my dear. Orchids were made to make a lovely woman like you look even more lovely."

"You always seem to be able to say the things that make a girl want to hear more. I don't know how you managed to stay a bachelor all these years, Uncle Vik. I'm surprised some woman hasn't captured you with all those beautiful compliments you have at your fingertips. You know, you are positively irresistible."

"I am? Thank you, my dear, I didn't know—"

She flicked the ashes from her cigarette into the tray, and looked at Henry with a sidelong glance. "Yes, you do, Uncle Vik, you're not fooling me. I think you're fully aware of your charms, and I also think that you know you could have any woman you wanted."

"Maybe you're right, Kris—to an extent. Almost any woman, except one …"

"Except one?" She looked at him with an expression of keen interest. "Who, Uncle Vik? Tell me who she is?" Her eager eyes indicated her complete lack of knowledge of the real meaning back of Henry's words.

"That's a secret, Kris. A very deep secret."

She pouted. "Now, Uncle Vik! We shouldn't have secrets. I thought we could tell each other anything."

"Yes, Kris, I know. I feel that way with you, too. I feel that I could tell you just about anything and you would understand because—"

The blaring of trumpets and horns interrupted his words.

"It must be twelve o'clock," exclaimed Kris.

"It is," replied Henry, looking at his watch. Just then the orchestra began to play "Auld Lang Syne."

"Happy New Year, Uncle Vik," Kris reached for his hand across the table.

"Happy New Year, Kris … darling." Henry took her hand warmly, leaned forward. She turned her cheek to accept his kiss, making it one of formal well-wishing. They looked at each other; she, with a faint smile that belied her internal confusion, he with a still fainter smile and tightly compressed lips that did not quite hide the all-consuming fire that raged within him.

"You look so intense, Uncle Vik—what are you thinking?"

"I was just wondering what the new year holds in store for us— where we'll be a year from tonight—what we'll be doing.…"

"Golly, wouldn't it be wonderful if we could take a peek into the future and find out? We'd know what to do, and what not to do … perhaps save ourselves a lot of worry and disappointments.…"

"Yes, that's true," said Henry reflectively, "but personally I'm glad we can't do all those things. It would take all the romance and excitement out of it."

"That's right, Uncle Vik, and we're certainly both romantic, aren't we?

"Definitely. Beyond the shadow of a doubt." A drunk suddenly passed their table and blew his horn almost in Kris' ear. She jumped, startled.

"Gosh, he almost scared me out of a year's growth," she exclaimed with a gasp, "it certainly has become awfully noisy in the last few minutes, hasn't it?"

"Yes, it has. My head is buzzing from it. I have an idea."

"What?"

"Let's go upstairs to my place where it's quiet, and we can have something to drink and play a new album of music I just bought. How does that sound?"

"Wonderful, Uncle Vik. I've had just about enough of this noise for one evening anyhow."

Henry signed the check and they left. In a few minutes they were entering his apartment. "Don't turn on the lights yet, Uncle Vik. I just got a glimpse of all those winding lights along Lake Shore Drive. I want to look out the window for a moment."

"Oh, of course, my dear. Be careful you don't trip over anything."

"I won't," laughed Kris. "After all, I still want to use this neck for a few more years. I'm at the window now."

He followed her over in the dark.

"Gee," she said softly, putting out her hand to bring Henry up to where she stood, "look at all those street lights winding along the lake. They seem to go on for miles."

"Yes, it's quite a sight. Look at all the cars on the drive tonight. As if it were only six o'clock in the evening!"

"And look at all the lights in the apartment buildings. Hundreds of them! It seems everyone stayed home tonight and had a party."

"Yes." He slipped his arm about her waist.

They stood there for several minutes, gazing out. Finally Kris broke the silence. "Oh, I'm getting tired. Think I'll sit down."

"Just a minute, I'll light one of these lamps. There! Guess we can see our way around now."

She sank into the deep cushions of the lounge, "Mmm, it's nice and relaxing here after all that noise. Let's hear the new album you bought, Uncle Vik. What's the name of it?"

"Do you like Rimsky-Korsakov?"

"I'm mad about him."

"Then you'll like *Scheherazade*."

"Oh, Uncle Vik, did you really get *Scheherazade?* I go into ecstasies when I hear that."

"Well," said Henry moving toward the record cabinet, "be prepared to go into your ecstasies, because that's what you're going to hear."

"I'm crazy about that and his *Le Coq d'Or Suite.*"

"I have that too. We'll play that later." He placed the records on the automatic turntable, then sat down next to Kris. They lit cigarettes and leaned back comfortably, as the seductively melodic strains of *Scheherazade* floated through the quiet, smoke-laden atmosphere.

"It's magnificent," she murmured softly, her eyes closing. "What music like that can do to a person!"

Henry glanced at Kris out of the corner of his eye. "Yes," he replied knowingly, "it really does things to you, doesn't it?"

Her sigh was nostalgic, prolonged; her eyes were still closed as if spellbound. Having studied Kris over a period of weeks to learn her weaknesses and her vulnerabilities, his selection of this music had been fully premeditated. Now he turned toward Kris and watched the rhythmic heavings of her bosom, her closed eyes, her faint half-smile; and her full lips beckoned him to the point where restraint was maddening. His gaze returned to the low neckline of her gown, to the deep crevice between her enticing young breasts. The firmness of her nipples surged excitingly against her bodice. He sat there devouring the fascination of her smooth white skin until he was shuddering from sheer self-torment.

The music reached a crescendo of excitement. Kris' eyes flickered open. She saw Henry's face only inches away from hers; she saw his fiercely blazing eyes, his thick black wavy hair, his jutting determined jaw, his passionately quivering lips. She half-sensed his emotions, because her brain was in turmoil also. She saw Henry's face move closer, she again shut her eyes, her lips parted slightly. His mouth communicated to her the most violently sensual kiss she had ever received. It lasted until their breaths gave out, and then with tears streaming down her cheeks, she murmured over and over again, "Oh, Vik, Vik, Vik!" It was the first time she had omitted the word "uncle."

"My darling," he whispered, "my wonderful, beautiful, adorable darling. Oh, how I've wanted to kiss you like this!" He kissed her again, and her arms slid around his neck in a crushing embrace of full surrender. Even as he kissed her, Henry was jubilant to see that she did not revolt against his embrace. He had revised his original theory. From closer observations of Kris, he had psychoanalytically decided that she was sufficiently in love with him to allow her desires to overpower her logic and restraint. He sensed her ripe for his devastating inroads.

Kris was first to speak. "Uncle Vik—"

"Yes?"

"It seems funny to call you Uncle Vik … now … doesn't it?"

"Yes?"

"I always think of uncles as being sort of stodgy, elderly, and paternal-like. You're not any of those things. You're young, handsome and charming and not a bit uncle-ish in your conversation, mannerisms, or anything. In fact, Vik, you know what?"

"What?"

"I don't even think of you as being my uncle. For some crazy reason, I think of you more as a romantic stranger who's come into my life and—and …"

"And what, my darling?"

"Oh, I don't know. I'm all confused … I wish you weren't my uncle. God, how I wish you weren't!" She leaned her head back against the sofa and her eyes glistened anew with the freshness of more tears.

He saw before him the results of his deliberations and his handiwork, and his emotions were quixotically mingled. He leaned over to soothe her. "Kris, darling, please don't be sad, I love you, do you hear me? I love you!" He took her in his arms and smothered her face, throat and bosom with caresses. She held on to him desperately, weeping and crying, "God forgive me, I love you too, Vik … I love you … I love you!"

It was two hours later when Henry filled Kris' glass for the fourth time. They were listening to another album of symphony music, when she suddenly rose unsteadily from the davenport. "Scuse, please, gotta go somewhere."

"Where you going, dear?" He made a gesture toward aiding her.

"Thanks, Vik. I can manage."

"Can't I help you, darling?"

She swayed uncertainly. "Oh no, thanks. Can't help me where I'm going. Gotta go th' john." She took dubious steps that seemed to be treading on a curved floor, and made her way eventually toward the bathroom. "Gosh, it suddenly got warm in here," she exclaimed as she closed the door behind her.

Henry lit a cigarette and poured himself another brandy. He downed it, and stood for a minute staring at the empty glass. Then he placed it on the coffee table and glanced at his watch. It was two-twenty-five in the morning. He walked over to the mantel and examined himself closely in the mirror. He looked rather handsome, he thought. Yes, decidedly, he wore full dress with quite an air. Henry straightened his white tie and brushed the sides of his hair with the palms of his hands. Turning, he walked back to the coffee table and filled Kris' glass to the brim. Then he stood looking at the glass measuredly, until the sound of the bathroom door opening caught his attention. A second later, Kris, looking not too pert and a trifle disheveled, appeared. Her eyelids blinked slowly and she stood against the wall smiling childishly. Then, with an awkward attempt at coquetry, she waved her hand. "Helloooo!"

"Hello, Kris. How're you feeling? All right?"

"Oh, sure! I'm fine, but I'm awful warm. It's hot in here, isn't it?"

"No, I don't think so. I think it's quite comfortable. Come sit down. Shall I help you?"

"No, no, no, you stay right there. I'm comin' over t'you. Gee, Uncle Vik—I mean Vik—can't call you 'uncle' anymore—you sure look beautiful in tails—jus' like Paul Lukas, 'n' Charles Boyer, 'n'—" She staggered toward him and tripped against a chair. He caught her in his arms, "—'n' Ronald Colman!" She put her arms around his neck and clung there swaying unsteadily while she rested her head against his chest. "I'm dizzy, Vik—awful dizzy. That wine's gone t'my head. Think I better lay down for while."

"All right, my dear. Come, I'll walk you into the bedroom. Think you can make it?"

"Sure. I'm not drunk 'er anything—jus' li'l dizzy th's all."

Henry walked her slowly into the bedroom, and pulled back the satin covers of the bed. Then he eased her down gently until her head rested comfortably on the soft pillow, and raised her feet up on the bed. He sat down beside her. "Feel all right, Kris, darling?"

"Um hm." Her heavy eyelids had closed already.

"Here, I'll pull off these shoes and you'll feel more comfortable. There. How's that?"

"Fine."

He leaned over and kissed her lips. Her arms slid around his neck in a tight clasp. "I love you, Vik, I love you," she murmured.

"And I'm mad about you, Kris, you know that, don't you?"

"Yes."

He kissed her again. His hand, loosening the shoulder straps of her gown, found its way to her bosom. There was a protest as she pulled her lips away from his. "Don't, Vik, please—please—please, Vik—" Henry ignored her feeble protestations and kissed her again as his hand closed about her warm firm breast. Her struggles and remonstrations stopped altogether and she pulled him toward her in a violently ecstatic embrace. Then the only sound to be heard was her low moaning.

Henry awakened in the afternoon of New Year's Day. He had escorted Kris to the lobby of her hotel at six that morning and said goodnight to her. She was not only sleepy and bewildered, but strangely morbid. Henry had pondered over her sudden depression as he walked slowly home, feeling not too proud of himself. He had wanted Kris more than anything in the world, and now his triumph seemed empty and even a bit noxious.

He showered and shaved, and while waiting for breakfast to be sent up, decided to put in a call to Kris' apartment. To his amazement, the operator told him that Miss Dvorak had checked out with a suitcase several hours before. She had left no message, no forwarding address, simply said that she was going away for a while.

Henry hung up the phone, staring blankly at the floor. Going away? She had said nothing to him about going away. His guilt told him the answer. She was trying to run away from herself. Hastily, madly, blindly, she was trying to run away from her own conscience. She had only taken a suitcase; her trunk and other things were still there. It was a wild, frenzied departure, devoid of all sense and reasoning.

Where would she go? Where would she stay? She had no friends, no relatives within two thousand miles. She would be lost and confused. If only he knew where she was headed, where she might go, he would start after her immediately, but Henry knew it was hopeless to try to trace her. There was nothing he could do but wait for her return and hope that no harm would befall her.

The days wore into weeks and still Henry had no word from or about Kris. His deep concern showed in his work and his conversation. Miss Corbett was aware of Kris' disappearance, but had no knowledge of the events leading up to her departure. Her conclusions were purely that "you can't trust these irresponsible and impulsive youngsters." Several times, she had urged her employer to hire a private detective agency to try to find Kris, or else to notify the authorities. Both of these suggestions fell upon deaf ears, for Henry naturally wished to have no traffic with the thoroughness of law enforcement agencies. "It's only a young girl's whim," he told Miss Corbett. "She will return when she gets tired of traveling about."

His words belied his feeling of uncertainty.

Several times Mr. Jennings 'phoned Henry to inquire about the apartment. The manager's last call was received with belligerence on Henry's part. "I told you the last time you called me," he told Jennings caustically, "that as long as that trunk remains in that apartment, the place is rented! I'll send you a hundred-dollar check the first of every month, so let's have no more discussion on the subject!"

Late one afternoon in the last week of February, Henry was washing up at the small office lavatory when he heard the reception room door open and close. As he had heard Miss Corbett leave fifteen minutes before, he dried his hands and walked to his office door to investigate. He was met by a sight that jolted him into a state of shock.

"Kris!" he exclaimed hoarsely.

She did not answer, but stood there staring blankly. Her eyes were deep sunk and there were dark hollows beneath them. Her face was ash-gray, and the roundness of her pink cheeks had given way to bony sallowness. The smartly upsweep of her auburn hair had long since been forgotten, and it hung loose and unkempt about her neck. The dress she was wearing under her beaver coat was wrinkled and untidy. She had lost a good deal of weight.

"Kris!" he repeated, "for God's sake, where on earth have you been, and what have you done to yourself?" He hastily closed the door of his office and led her to a chair. But she continued to stand, looking at him with emotionless eyes.

"What difference does it make where I've been?" Her voice was dull and flat.

"What difference does it make? My God, Kris, how can you talk that way? I've been sick from worry!"

"Have you, Vik? You don't look it. You look pretty healthy to me."

"Kris, darling, don't say those things. I've worried about you night and day." He took her in his embrace and drew her to him, but her arms hung limply at her sides, and he released her at once, chilled by her lifeless tolerance of his caress.

"Here, Kris, sit down. Please. I want to talk to you."

She sat down slowly, her eyes away from his, focused on nothing in particular but the blankness and emptiness of the wall. "Remember the Bahá'i Temple, Vik?"

Henry stared at her quizzically. "The Bahá'i Temple? Yes."

"I used to sit there every day," she said, still looking at the wall.

"Sit there every day? You mean you've been in Wilmette all this time?"

"Yes, Wilmette," she replied calmly. "It's a nice little suburb, and it's so quiet and relaxing. You have time to think and be by yourself. So every day I would walk over to the Bahá'i Temple and sit there. It made me feel clean, and spiritual, and at peace with myself. They gave me a book and I used to read from it. There was one beautiful page I learned by heart:

"'In this hour of self-inquiry, I lift up my soul unto Thee, O God and Father, bowed down by the consciousness of my sins, I come into Thy benign presence, O most righteous Judge, and approach Thy holy throne. Thou hast given me understanding to distinguish between good and evil, and hast revealed to me Thy commandments that I may do Thy will. Yet I have pursued selfish purposes, and have done wicked things. Though Thou hast illumined my soul with the light of truth, yet I have chosen to walk in darkness. Whither shall I go from Thy spirit, O God, and whither shall I flee from Thy presence? Distance cannot separate me from Thee. Darkness cannot hide me from Thine all-seeing eye. But there is one refuge left for me, one hope to sustain me. I shall hide myself in the shadow of Thy mercy, I shall look for shelter under the wings of Thy grace; for Thy forbearance is everlasting, and Thy love endureth forever.'"

Henry was fidgeting nervously and his lower lip showed deep indentations where his teeth had sunk into the flesh. "Kris, for heaven's sake, why did you run away from me like this?"

"I wasn't running away from you, Vik, I was running away from myself, but I soon discovered conscience is a constant companion; you can never lose it or run away from it. I used to feel better, though, when I sat in the Temple. I prayed for you too, Vik."

"For me?"

"Yes, I prayed to God to give you strength too. You see, I was weak, but you were weaker. I looked up to you for counsel and guidance because you were older, and had lived longer, and had more experience. Your work in life was to correct the mental ills of people who had lost faith and self-confidence, and who needed someone strong to show them how to regain that lost faith and find themselves again. But you see, Vik, you're the most lost soul of all! You need more strength and faith than any of your patients. I'm not blaming you for what I did; everyone is responsible for their own deeds, and I must answer to myself. But you too, Vik, must answer to yourself. You've got to live with your conscience too. No one but you and I will ever know about this unholy relationship, but there's a day of self-examination, Vik, a day of reckoning when we must all face ourselves and answer for our sins. I'm answering for mine now. Yours haven't caught up with you yet. Maybe the shock will make you realize what we've done."

Henry looked at Kris with growing apprehension. "What do you mean, the shock?"

The words came with no emotion. "I'm pregnant, Vik."

His face blanched. "You're … pregnant?"

"Yes."

Henry was visibly shaken. "How … how do you know?"

"I've suspected it now for over a month. Today I came into town and had my second visit with Dr. Rubens. I remembered I had heard you mention his name as a very good gynecologist. So I went to see him. He told me today that the pregnancy test he took last week showed positive."

She turned and faced him for the first time since she had sat down. "Did that shock you into a realization of what we've done? Into the unholiness of an affair between an uncle and a niece? Quite a letdown from all the years of beautiful illusions and girlish dreams." She displayed the first signs of emotion since entering the office. "I gave myself to you in a moment of weakness—I lost all sense of decency and reasoning. You filled me full of wine and flattery and turned my head completely. Did you think for one minute that after something like that I could be myself again—ever live with myself again? You wanted me—I knew it; yet I was helpless to do anything about it. For weeks I was lost and confused and I wanted to be good, only I couldn't find the strength to fight back. You had me wrapped around your finger as much as if I were a puppet, and when you pulled the strings I danced. If you're proud of yourself for being able to accomplish all that, then—I hope you're satisfied with the results. I'll go through with this and present you with something to remind you the rest of your days of what a wonderful man you are—what a great lover you turned out to be!" She sobbed pitifully and Henry stood over her, watching her shoulders heaving convulsively.

"Kris … I … I'm sure there's some way out of all this …"

She raised her head and looked at him with deep bitterness in her glistening eyes. "Sure, there's a way out … I can always drown myself!"

"Kris, please, for God's sake, let's talk sensibly. I mean there's a rational way out of this. Just give me some time to think …"

"You'll have time to think, all right. You'll have the rest of your life to think … like I will …"

"In the first place, Kris, there is no need to think in terms of going through with this. In this modern day and age there are doctors and methods …"

"No doctor can treat my conscience," she hurled at him, "not even the great psychiatrist, Dr. Bartok!"

"It's not your conscience I'm thinking of now, Kris," he replied with an effort to placate her, "it's something more urgent. Please, Kris, let me handle this for you … will you?"

She dried her eyes. "Of course, why not? What have I got to lose at this point?" she replied sardonically. "Would you like to start psychoanalyzing me? Maybe you could convince me that I'm not pregnant … that it's just a state of mind!"

"No, I'm sure if Dr. Rubens said you were, his diagnosis was correct. I'll take his word for it. Did he ask you many questions?"

"Don't worry, I didn't tell him I was the niece of the prominent Dr. Bartok. I gave the name of Mrs. James Baker. That was the name of the old lady I lived with in Wilmette. She was wonderfully kind and sympathetic. She had a couple of rooms for rent. We became very attached. When I left she cried because she didn't want me to leave." Kris stared at the floor. "She told me I was the first young person in her house in fourteen years. Her own daughter died when she was only seventeen. She told me I reminded her so much of her. When I get through with all this … I'm going back and live with Mrs. Baker for the rest of the time I'm here. In the meantime …"

"In the meantime," interrupted Henry, "we've got to do something about you."

Kris rose from the chair. "I'm going back to the apartment and get off a letter to my mother. I wrote her several times from Wilmette, but I always came inside the city limits to mail them. I didn't want her to suspect anything out of the ordinary."

"Yes, yes, of course. Look? Kris, I … I know you have only bitterness in your heart for me now, but I want you to know that I'll do everything in my power to see that you are properly cared for and given the best treatment. There's no need for you to worry one minute. Trust me to leave no stone unturned to do whatever is necessary to rectify this … this situation."

Kris picked up her purse. "I'll leave everything to you, Vik," she replied cynically. "I'm sure a man who's been professor at three universities is smart enough to figure out a small thing like overcoming a pregnancy." She walked out without saying goodbye.

Henry stood staring after her, his mind a jumbled chaos of incoherent thoughts. He should never have permitted himself to become intimate with Kris; he should have known better than to start something that could only have dire results. He realized now that the indiscretions of one hour can mean the disaster of a lifetime. If only he had displayed a more avuncular attitude toward her, this would never have happened. He had been weak all these months. He had allowed her beauty and attractiveness to get under his skin, but he knew he never would have been satisfied to play the role of mere uncle to Kris. He would never have rested until he possessed her; it was his vanity which had taunted him to prove to himself that he could have any woman he set out to conquer.

Well, he had conquered Kris, but the victory was hardly worth the spoils. After all his vowed determination that a woman would never be his undoing, he had made a fool of himself because of an uncontrollable passion to have Kris. However, it was too late for self-remonstrations. The main thing now was to discover a way out of this predicament. Henry closed the door of his office and sat down at the desk to think. He had little desire to go out to dinner.

It was almost two o'clock when Henry finally got to bed that night. All evening long, he had paced the floor of his apartment trying to seek a solution that would take care of Kris and yet not reveal or endanger himself in any way. He well knew the perils and consequences of dealing with quacks, and the innumerable hazards of approaching a respected and recognized physician. Besides, there wasn't a doctor in Chicago that he knew sufficiently well even to hint at an operation. It would have to be someone whom he could trust and who was still a capable man. Such a person would not be easy to find. Yet he could not afford to allow too much time to lapse. Every day would count in a situation of this kind.

It was now almost two months since conception had taken place;

drugs or other devious methods would now have little or no effect. An abortion would be the only sure means of terminating Kris' present condition. But who could do it? That was the big question mark in Henry's mind as he tossed on a pillow that grew more uncomfortable with each shifting of his head. Kris' departing words taunted him as he tossed nervously from side to side. "Any man who has been professor at three universities should be smart enough to figure out a small thing like overcoming a pregnancy!" Yes, it was a caustic remark and he had had it coming, but suddenly it hit him with the force of a bolt of lightning. He knew a professor at a university—one who was an experienced gynecologist and obstetrician, Dr. Felix Marantz! He had forgotten all about him. There was the very man! He was now teaching at Midwestern University in Lowell, Iowa. But how could he be sure that Marantz would do such a thing for him— even listen to such a degrading suggestion? It was a long chance, but Henry knew that the time had come for long chances. Nothing ventured, nothing gained. Felix Marantz was an old friend and colleague of Dr. Bartok. They had known each other for years and had taught at the same university. He could approach him at least with the attitude of a confidant and divulge the story to him without fear of exposure. His niece had come to Chicago and gotten herself into trouble. He needed the service of a capable gynecologist and something of this nature could only be broached to an intimate friend of long standing. He was desperate and needed help. His niece was a very emotional and irresponsible girl who did things on impulse. She had become morbid and depressed since her indiscretion. Since discovering her pregnancy, she had fallen into an alarming state of melancholia which at times bordered on a suicide complex. All these symptoms caused him to fear for her life unless something was done. The only solution would be to give her mind a clean bill of health by ridding her of this pregnancy. Henry was sure such a story would not fall upon deaf ears.

Shandru had told him that he had all of the attributes of a good actor. Well, he would have opportunity to test his histrionic talents.

CHAPTER TWENTY

The Cadillac sedan sped along a wide cement highway and soon the driver could make out a church spire and several large chimneys in the distance. Presently the road signs warned: "Slow Down, Approaching City Limits." A mile or so farther on, a large black and white sign read: "YOU ARE ENTERING LOWELL, IOWA. POPULATION 18,264. PLEASE DRIVE CAREFULLY. THIS IS THE HOME OF MIDWESTERN UNIVERSITY, AND WE BID YOU WELCOME."

Henry slackened his speed to twenty miles per hour and gazed from left to right, as the quaint little town drew into sight. The weather was quite warm for a late February afternoon, and what snow remained on the ground was melting fast. The children playing in front of their houses scraped together the last few flakes of the previous week's light snowfall and hurled them at one another. The sparsely scattered homes of the city's outskirts soon gave way to solid rows of pretty little bungalows and white cottages. In a vacant lot alongside the highway another sign caught Henry's eye. "FOR THE BEST IN REST, VISIT THE LOWELL HOUSE—100 ROOMS, 100 BATHS."

He continued until he found himself approaching the downtown district, and soon the Lowell House itself appeared, with another sign extolling its profusion of rooms and baths.

Henry pulled up to the curb, parked the car and entered the quiet and dignified-looking hotel whose lobby was filled with ancient palms and ferns and giant rubber plants that seemed as old as the building itself. The tile lobby floor was cracked with age, and the leather chairs and couches were well-worn and pocketed.

After registering, he was shown to his room on the fifth floor. He picked up the phone and called information.

"I want to talk to Professor Felix Marantz of the Medical School of Midwestern University."

"Do you wish to call him at the university or his home?" the operator inquired.

"I—I think you'd better give me his home number," Henry replied.

"Yes, sir, just a moment, please."

She was back in a few seconds.

"The number is 512 J, sir."

"Thank you, will you connect me, please?"

"Mama, give Viktor some more meat loaf."

"Please, Felix, please—any more and I'll burst wide open. I've already had two helpings."

"Ach, two helpings! So what? So is there a law against three? Come, give me your plate."

"No, honestly, Felix, I couldn't really."

"But Viktor, you—"

"Papa, don't insist," interrupted the professor's plump little wife.

"You always want to stuff people. You think everybody has a appetite like you?"

"Like me, Mama? I don't eat so much."

"Did you hear that? He don't eat much! From what do you think I have to let out your pants from? Because you are getting blown up from air? *Nein!* It is from my good cooking. *Gott sei dank*, he has nothing wrong with his appetite, huh, doctor?"

Henry chuckled. "I would say Felix is doing all right."

Marantz took a deep sigh. "Ja, Viktor, eating with a good appetite is still one of life's blessings. I always make up my mind to cut down, but Mama constantly throws obstacles in my way."

"Obstacles? What kind of obstacles do I put in your way?"

"What kind? Dumplings! Meatballs! Blintzes! Strudels! Pot roasts! I have no defense against such weapons!"

Everyone laughed heartily, including Sara and Rachel, the Marantz' daughters. Sara was fourteen and pretty, with deep gray eyes and long brown braids that reached her waist and which were tied with small red ribbons. Rachel, who was twelve, was more quiet and reserved, with a face that was small and thin. Her skin was an almost transparent white, that color often associated with anemia which, judging from her delicate build, appeared to be present and of long standing. Her eyes were large and dark and the lashes long and sweeping. She too had unusually thick braids that trailed down the length of her back, only Rachel's hair was coal-black like her mother's. Both fortunately resembled their mother, as Felix Marantz with his squatty figure, squarish head, and large ears, together with his pug nose and thick lips, was unquestionably a homely man.

Henry looked about him at this contented little family and couldn't help feeling that here was true happiness in its simplest form. A man, his wife, their two daughters, a home—a respected position as professor of medicine at a leading university—a moderate income; none of the luxuries of life, but none of the heartaches either.

"You have a very nice place here, Felix," he commented.

"Ja, thank you. We like it very much. It is nothing pretentious, but it is home. I managed to buy this at a price. You know, I strike a hard bargain. We have seven nice rooms here and although it is only a frame house and not modern in its appearances, still it suffices very well for a man whose income is only $4,000 a year. We live well, we have plenty of food to eat, I have a wonderful family, thank God, and in a few more years, I make the last payment on this house." He took a slice of bread and soaked up the remaining gravy in his plate. "I am grateful for many things, Viktor. I have been in this country less than two years and I consider myself an extremely fortunate man. My job as Professor of Obstetrics at Midwestern has given me the confidence and faith in myself that I had almost lost when I was forced to leave Vienna with my family and live from day to day, from hand to mouth."

Mama Marantz took a deep sigh. "*Ach, Lieber Gott*, we should never know again such heartaches as we had trying to escape from those *verdammt* Nazis. *Ach*, I don't want we should talk about it. *Gott sei dank*, we now are over here where we can raise our children as Americans and they can open a book and read about Abraham Lincoln instead of Adolf Hitler."

"We studied about Lincoln today, Mama," said Rachel quietly. "He looks just like Grandpa Marantz."

"Ja, except Lincoln was tall, and Grandpa Marantz was small like your father."

"Short, Mama," interposed Felix, "but not small. A man can be short in stature and still be a giant mentally."

"Ja, Papa. I didn't mean small in that sense. Lincoln split rails, and you're splitting hairs."

There was again general laughter. "You know, Viktor," continued Felix, wiping his chin, "ever since Mama has been listening to this Fickle McGee—"

"Fibber McGee, Papa," corrected Sara.

"Ja. Well, ever since Mama has been listening to that program, I get gags for breakfast, lunch, and supper."

"Is that so?" replied Mama, shaking her head. "From gags you don't have that big belly!"

"Well, Felix," chuckled Henry, "that ought to hold you for the rest of the evening."

"*Nein*," said Mrs. Marantz, rising from the table, "that won't hold Papa for the rest of the evening. Not until we have apple-dumpling for dessert."

"Ah, my favorite—apple-dumpling," exclaimed Marantz gleefully. "Viktor, you have not lived until you have eaten Mama's apple-dumpling. It is like they say here in America, 'out of this world!'"

"Well, in that case, I'm glad I left a little room," replied Henry.

Mama Marantz took his plate. "You want coffee, Viktor, ja?"

"Black, please … Mama."

"Ah, it sounds good to hear you call me Mama, again. Always when we had our midnight *kaffee klatsch* in Vienna, you called me Mama; but you know something, Viktor?"

"What?"

"Since you have come to America, you have dropped all your

German and Bohemian expressions. Now you are a real Yankee."

"That's right. After all, I've been over here nine years now."

"My, how time flies," said Felix reflectively. "It seems like only last year that we were all together in Vienna."

"Ja, Papa. Now we are together over here, *Gott sei dank!* Sarah, help me to take in the kitchen some of these plates, ja?"

"Yes, Mama," Sarah replied, jumping from her chair. "Rachel, you can help us too!"

"I am still eating, Sarah. Mama, I am still unfinished."

"So sit and finish, *mein Kind*. Rachel is the slow one in the family." Rachel looked up from her plate, her dark eyes expressing a deep sensitiveness. "It is not wrong to eat slowly is it, Dr. Bartok? One should take much time to digest the food, is that not right?"

"Of course, Rachel, you are the only one among us who knows how to eat properly."

"Thank you doctor. I like to do everything slowly. To hurry tires me out and then I get sleepy."

The two men looked at each other in silence. Rachel's chronic anemia had left her delicate and with only a portion of the energy of normal children.

"So tell me how you are getting along at the university, Felix," said Henry, changing the subject.

"Extremely well, Viktor, thank you. You play a little politics; you use your *kopf*, and you soon learn when to talk and when not to. I get along fine with the dean and the rest of the board. I am the only Jew on the medical faculty, and it is not easy in a school that is traditionally Gentile. Not that there are any printed signs against Jews, but it does not take long to feel an undercurrent of anti-Semitism that makes itself felt every day. Several of my Jewish students have come to me complaining of religious intolerances that have made them feel bitter and extremely unhappy. There is no getting away from the facts, Viktor. There is a great deal of prejudice throughout this country against Jews. I did not realize that until I came to the United States myself. I always thought that in America everyone is a social equal, to go and come where he pleases, when he pleases. That is true only on the surface. There is a restricted section here in Lowell, where a Jew cannot purchase a house or a lot. Is that true of every community in the United States?"

"Yes, I'm afraid it probably is, Felix," agreed Henry. "Although in Chicago only certain apartment buildings are restricted."

"So, that bears me out. It is true not only of Jews, but Negroes as well. They are segregated and kept to themselves. Their opportunities are definitely restricted. The chances for improving themselves socially, politically, and economically are all against them."

Henry toyed with a fork. "You might as well make up your mind, Felix, that conditions like that will exist as long as the world exists. Whether you live in a country that is a democracy, a monarchy, or fascist in its form of government, you're going to have racial and religious intolerances. No government, no president, no king, no leader, can control the human mind. But here it doesn't mean that a policeman can come knocking at your door and ask you if you love your neighbor as much as yourself, and if you say 'no, he's a Christian and I hate his guts,' that you will be arrested and thrown in jail for obstructing justice."

"*Nein*, of course not," replied Marantz, settling back in his chair. "I see what you mean. This is a free country, and people are entitled to think as they wish. If some people prefer to have nothing to do with certain other groups of people, that is their privilege."

"Exactly. You can invent the most idealistic form of government with equalities and tolerance for all, but you can never control the individual's mind and heart. If he wants to hate his neighbor because he doesn't like the way he parts his hair, he will—that's all there is to it."

"Ja," sighed Felix as he clasped his hands on the table, "but it wasn't because of the way the Jews part their hair that they have been persecuted for five thousand years. It's because every century has had its Pharaoh, its Nero, its Philip, its Nicholas, and its Hitler. They tell their followers that the Jew is responsible for their poverty; their famine if there should happen to be one; their lack of opportunities; the war, inflation, depression, unemployment, world communism, and even the uneven distribution of wealth. They pick us as their scapegoat. In a world where there are over two billion people and only about fifteen million Jews, it stands to reason that the Jews could not be responsible for all those things, and intelligent, thinking people do not believe it. *Aber ja*, racial and religious intolerances are never fostered by intelligent, thinking people."

"Excuse me, Papa," interrupted Mrs. Marantz, "your apple-dumpling has been standing in front of you since the Declaration of Independence, and that was ten minutes ago. Even Rachel is through already."

"*Ach*, I get so carried away with myself, I forget to eat."

"And when you forget to eat apple-dumpling," she continued, "the world is in a pretty bad state. That's the first time, Viktor, that I have ever seen Papa allow Hitler to let apple-dumpling get cold."

Henry laughed.

The meal was finished without further discussion on world problems and, after sipping the last of his coffee, Felix pushed his chair back and rose. "So, we are all through. Now I get out my old briar, and have a few puffs. You want a cigar, Viktor?"

"No, thank you. I have my cigarettes."

"So come, we go talk."

Henry turned to Mrs. Marantz. "Mama, it was a delicious dinner. The best I have eaten since … since Vienna …"

"*Ach*, go away—you have had a lot better meals, I'm sure. This was nothing special, only what we would have any night. If I had known you were coming, I would have had steak or chicken."

"I'm glad you didn't. I hate steak and I detest chicken."

"Ho, ho, such a fibber. You try to make me feel good. Viktor is always the diplomat, huh, Papa?"

"Ja, always. So come, Viktor. While Mama and the girls do the dishes, we go up to my study and talk, eh?"

"Fine. Excuse us, yes?"

"Sure, sure, Viktor, go ahead. We see you later."

The two men left the dining room and retired to Marantz's upstairs study. Felix lit his pipe and directed Henry to a comfortable chair.

"Mind if I close the door first, Felix?"

"*Nein*. Nobody comes up here now. They are all busy in the kitchen."

"Well, I'll close it anyway just for security reasons," said Henry, moving toward the door.

They sat down and Marantz was first to speak. "Viktor, what is this all about? You seemed very nervous and upset when I talked to you on the phone."

"Yes, I know. It's … it's very important and very serious."

"I knew it. A busy man like you does not make a three hundred and fifty mile drive for pleasure."

"No, of course not. I … I … don't quite know how to begin …" Henry started his act by an over-display of nervous fidgeting.

"You're not in trouble, Viktor?"

"No, not me. It's … it's … my niece."

"Your niece? Meta's daughter …?"

"Yes. Kristina. You've never seen her, have you?"

"No. They live in California … ja?"

"Meta does. Kristina is in Chicago, studying at the Art Institute."

"Oh. The last I heard of your family was when Konrad Dvorak was killed. I was still in Vienna—and I think you were already in this country."

"Yes."

"Meta is still an invalid from the accident?"

"Pretty much so. Kris says she walks only a few feet. She has a housekeeper and companion with her."

"Is she able to get along … I mean financially?"

"Yes. They have their own home and Konrad Dvorak was heavily insured. He left a trust fund for his family that will take care of them the rest of their lives."

"So. Now what is wrong?"

Henry began the story that he had memorized word for word. As he unfolded the sordid details of a romance that was hatched in his imagination but which paralleled his own premeditated seduction of Kristina Dvorak, Felix Marantz stopped puffing on his pipe and sat with a grim expression on his face. Henry finished his story with a plaintive sigh. "So now I find she's two months pregnant."

"And you don't know who is responsible?"

"No. She refused to tell. Anyhow, that is unimportant. The main thing is, the damage is done."

"But I don't agree with you that it is unimportant and that any damage is done."

Henry looked up. "Why don't you?"

"Because if she loved this man sufficiently to give herself to him, she probably could love him sufficiently to marry him, and that would solve everything."

"Yes, but … but there are obstacles. He can't marry her."

"Why can't he?"

Henry had to think fast. "This man is … married!"

"Married? She told you that?"

"Yes. That's all she did tell."

"Um-hm. That throws a different light on it." He placed the unlit pipe between his lips, and sat staring at the floor. Slowly, he took the pipe from his mouth and turned his gaze toward Henry. "And what is it you come to me? For advice?"

"For more than advice, Felix … for help."

"For help? What kind of help?"

Henry swallowed hard. "I … I'd like you to do something for Kristina to … to help her get rid … of this pregnancy …"

Felix's expression turned to a look of horror. "Viktor, you're not hinting that you want me to … to perform … an abortion …?"

Henry lowered his eyes in abject humiliation. "Yes."

Felix rose from his chair. "Viktor! Are you out of your mind? Have you lost your senses completely?"

Henry knew the time had come for him to call upon all of the acting talents that he possessed; this must be the best performance of his career. He turned on the look of anguish; his eyes glistened with tears and his breast began to heave with emotional contractions. His voice quavered in a tremolo of sobs. "Felix—I don't know what to do, or whom to turn to. This is my sister's child, she's like my own flesh and blood She's desperate and says if she doesn't get rid of it, she'll kill herself. She's young, Felix, and talented, and beautiful. She has everything in life to live for. A girl shouldn't be asked to pay so much for one slip, Felix. She's human, and humans make mistakes. If anything should happen to Kris, I'd almost feel responsible myself, because as her uncle and a physician, I would never forgive myself if I did not do everything in my power to help this poor child. Not only that, Felix, but her mother is a sick woman and Kris is all she has. If this were to get to Meta, it would kill her, Felix … kill her!" At this point Henry drew out his handkerchief and caught the tears that ran profusely down his cheeks. There was a momentary pause while he wiped his eyes. "Now do you see why I've come to you, Felix?"

Marantz stood looking at him, his small beady eyes magnified grotesquely by the thick lenses of spectacles that made them look as though they belonged in the face of a gargoyle. Behind this almost mask-like countenance was a bewildered and seemingly petrified little man who tried vainly to call upon his powers of reasoning, who wanted to say something that would indicate his deep understanding, who wanted to express a profound desire to aid and comfort, but, like a deaf mute, could only show his emotions with his pathetic eyes. So, at a loss for words, confused and bewildered, suffering the hurt that one friend feels for another whom he loves dearly, stood Felix Marantz.

After what seemed an interminable length of time, the stillness of the room, broken only by the occasional sound of Henry's sobs, was interrupted by Marantz's hoarse voice. "You know I don't have a license to practice medicine in this country Viktor. I am a teacher. And even if I had a license, you know, as a doctor, that what you are asking me to do is against all the laws of man and God."

Henry did not answer, but buried his head in his hands.

Felix went on. "You know I love you, Viktor, and we are friends of long standing. There is nothing I wouldn't do to make you happy and relieve you of worry or trouble, but this kind of a request is beyond anything that a man should ask from any friend. There are certain things in life that we hold more precious than life itself, and that is our sacred honor. Never in all my fifty-two years have I ever done anything dishonorable. I have always been proud of my reputation as a doctor whose entire career has been devoted to the relief of human suffering."

Henry looked up pathetically through his tears. "But, Felix, this is a case of relieving the sufferings of a human. You'll be giving this young girl a new lease on life, where all that remains now is an apathy, a malignant melancholia that is slowly killing all her desire to live. She talks constantly of suicide."

Marantz walked toward the windows and stood staring out, his sloping back and bent head a picture of sorrow, indecision and fear … his thoughts a turmoil. He spoke without turning. "You know, Viktor, when you ask me to do something like this—you know you are asking me to destroy a life—?"

"Yes, but if nothing is to be done for Kristina, it may mean the destruction of two lives … she doesn't want to live, Felix." His tone became more anguished than before. "I can't go to anyone else, Felix; you're my sole salvation … my only hope … my one refuge. If you say no, I'll have to go back to Chicago defeated and beaten; I'll have to go back to Kris and tell her nothing can be done, that she must make the best of it alone and without any help or encouragement from those near and dear to her. It will mean that I have completely failed her when she needs me most, but it will also mean something else, Felix. It will mean that we've passed the sentence of death on her!" He once more buried his head in his hands, but through his spaced fingers, Henry kept his eyes on the forlorn little figure at the window who stood motionless, his hands behind his back, his thoughts cloaked in deathly silence. Henry watched from lowered eyes as a cat watches his quarry.

It was fully ten minutes later when Felix Marantz turned and walked toward the man he thought to be his bosom friend. His face showed the strain and anxiety of one who had been forced to make a decision involving a human life and a sacred trust. His answer was in the voice of self-condemnation.

"All right, Viktor, I do it!"

CHAPTER TWENTY-ONE

Henry returned to Chicago the next day and immediately called Kris. She had returned to art school. He came to her apartment that night and outlined to her in encouraging terms his journey to Lowell, Iowa, and his success in having procured the services of an excellent doctor, and old friend of his from Vienna. Dr. Marantz would be in

Chicago the coming Thursday, and Henry suggested she prepare herself for the operation. It would be a simple thing, there would be no pain or discomfort, she would be in bed a couple of days, three at the most, and the whole procedure could take place right in her own apartment.

Kris listened in cool silence while Henry talked in glowing terms of having driven seven hundred miles to obtain the best man in his field for the operation. Then he told Kris reluctantly that he had naturally been forced to change certain slight details of the story."

"… I told Dr. Marantz that I was not acquainted with the … uh … the man. That … er … the man was married, and that that had prevented any chance of the two of you getting married. You see, the reason I mentioned that was because Dr. Marantz thought there might be such a possibility, which would make the … operation unnecessary."

"You thought of everything, didn't you, Vik?" she answered with a cynical smile. "Did you tell him about the sleepless nights and the mental tortures you went through, worrying about your poor niece? That you were doing this all for her? I'll bet by the time you got through there were tears all over the place!"

"Kris, believe me, I—"

"Why should I believe you? Why should I believe anything you could ever tell me? You're a very clever man, Vik, far superior to any man I have ever known. But there's something very cruel about you … something diabolically cruel, though you keep it well hidden. It's behind that mask you wear, that mask with the personality and charm, that disarms people and coaxes them to trust you. That's the way I was for six months. I was completely in a daze, as though I had been drugged …" Her voice trailed off, not with emotion but as if the story no longer interested her. She came back to the present in a matter-of-fact tone. "Don't worry, I'll stick to this fantastic story that you gave the doctor, but not because of my own reputation. Because I'm protecting Viktor Bartok, the great psychiatrist. Of course, that's what you had in mind, wasn't it?"

Henry sat staring at the smoke curling its way up from the cigarette he was holding. There was nothing he could say; everything was his fault, the result of bad intentions. He had built a house of cards and then pulled it down upon himself. He knew Kris was telling the truth. "Thank you, Kris," he finally said. It was all he could think of to say.

The following Thursday morning, Dr. Marantz called at Henry's office. He carried a small black bag containing the instruments that he had not used since his departure from Vienna two and a half years before.

Felix Marantz had little heart for the task he had agreed to perform in behalf of his colleague. On the train coming down, he had been mentally nauseated at the thought of his mission. In all his years of practice and teaching he had never been called upon to do anything which he did not believe himself, and which would not have beneficent results either to his patients or his students. This, then, was his first deviation from the standards and principles which had always governed his life. He had told his wife that Dr. Bartok had invited him to Chicago to meet some important and influential people who could be of value to him in possible future connections.

Together the two men left the office and went straight to Kris's apartment in the Garland Hotel. There Henry introduced Dr. Marantz to his niece and, after a few words of polite formal conversation, took his leave and returned to his office.

Kris liked Dr. Marantz. There was something warm and trustworthy about the little squatty professor, whose homely face wrinkled into a wizened smile when he talked. Felix also took to her— he felt the confidence that she immediately placed in him when they met, and he admired the courage and the complete absence of fear that she displayed. He could see that she was wan and thin, and that, despite her loss of weight and the apparent evidence of sleepless nights and mental tortures, she was still a very beautiful girl.

There was a deep feeling of compassion for this young and attractive girl of twenty who so soon had to taste of the bitterness of life, and submit herself to the abomination of an illegal operation. It was as difficult for him as it was for her. Yet Kris was in no way made aware of Marantz's disgust for his undertaking as she lay in the bed smiling up at the white-gowned and gnomish-looking physician, as he returned from putting his instruments in the boiling water on the kitchen stove.

It was noon when Dr. Marantz pulled off his rubber gloves and sat down in the chair beside Kris' bed. He was worn out from his trip to Chicago, the strain of the operation, and the nervous tension. He looked at Kris, who had been an excellent and uncomplaining patient.

"I have given you something and you sleep now, ja?"

She smiled and nodded her head. Soon her eyes had closed and she was deep in slumber. He reached over and took her pulse. It was ninety, but that could be expected after something of this nature. In a few minutes, Felix Marantz had dozed off in the chair, and the heavy breathing of doctor and patient filled the stillness of the room.

At two in the afternoon Felix Marantz was awakened by a soft knocking at the apartment door. Opening it, he found it was Henry, who had returned to relieve him so that he could get a bite to eat. In whispers Felix explained that he was not hungry, that the operation had gone fairly well, and that Kris was now resting easily. Together they sat talking in low tones in the living room. Henry questioned him about his return to Lowell. He answered that he would not go back until he was assured everything was all right and Kris was out of danger. Henry offered him the hospitality of his own apartment, but Marantz declined, saying he would prefer to stay and watch his patient. He would sleep on the davenport in the living room.

As the conversation progressed, Henry cautiously broached the subject of expense money for the trip to Chicago.

"*Ach*, it was nothing," replied Marantz. "Do not even talk about it."

"May I show my appreciation, Felix, please? I want you to take this—" He took a check from his pocket and handed it to the professor. "Please, Felix, please accept this in the spirit that it is given."

The little man unfolded the piece of paper. "One thousand dollars! *Nein*, Viktor, I could not! Not that I do not appreciate your generosity, but neither a thousand nor a hundred thousand could pay me for what I do this morning. It is one of those things that money cannot buy. I betrayed all my teachings and all my principles by performing this abortion. Can I tell my students from now on to always be proud of their title of 'doctor,' and to never allow anything, especially the quest of gold, to lure them from the righteous and honorable path they have started out on? *Nein!* I will only be a hypocrite to them and to myself. A man must believe what he teaches. If he cannot, he is not worthy to teach. He is not worthy of the degree of professor." He handed the check back to Henry.

"Thank you again, Viktor, but I did this for you—as an act of friendship. For no one else on earth would I stoop to such malpractices."

"I … I'm deeply appreciative of that fact, Felix. I shall never forget your kindness and loyalty. It's through devotion like this in a man's hour of need that he learns what a wonderful thing true friendship is." He patted Marantz's knee as his eyes moistened and his voice became quaveringly emotional. "No, I'll never forget your kindness to me, Felix. Never."

Felix Marantz slipped his own hand over Henry's and squeezed it affectionately. "For those we love, Viktor, we do things even at the sacrifice of position, honor, reputation—even life …" Then he folded his hands and stared at the carpet. "There would be grave consequences for me if things were to go wrong. An illicit operation—no license to practice in this country—I could be sent to jail for twenty years and then deported as an undesirable alien. I would be disgraced and dishonored. My wife and children would suffer the agonies of my deed. I would be through forever as a doctor and a teacher. My life would be ruined—finished."

Henry prodded him good naturedly in the ribs. "Felix, for heaven's sake, stop thinking those things. The operation went well. Today is Thursday. By Sunday, Kris will be walking around good as new. You'll be back at Midwestern teaching, and all of this will be just a memory that will soon be forgotten."

"Ja," said Felix reflectively. "It's a funny thing … we'd sooner forget the pleasant things in life than the unpleasant things. They have a way of crawling out of the closet and reminding us of our misdeeds. I don't know about your life, Viktor, maybe you have never done anything to be ashamed of or to regret, but there's an old saying about reaping what you sow. It catches up with us sooner or later. It is the law of compensation, I guess."

Henry rose. This was touching on a subject that rubbed him the wrong way. He glanced at his watch uneasily. "Look, Felix, it's two-thirty. You haven't eaten all day. Why don't you go out and get a bite? I'll stay here with Kris until you get back."

"All right, Viktor," replied Marantz, lifting himself heavily from the lounge, "I go eat, but I have no appetite." A faint smile etched its way slowly across his face, "Mama should hear me say that!"

It was seven o'clock Sunday evening when Henry received a telephone call at his apartment. He had just finished dinner, not having spoken to or seen Felix Marantz since five o'clock in the afternoon of the previous day. He laid aside the fat Havana cigar he was smoking for a change from his daily cigarettes and casually picked up the phone.

"Viktor, this is Felix. Come over right away. I want to talk to you. I've been trying to reach you since four o'clock."

"Oh, I was out this afternoon. Nothing wrong, is there?"

"Come over. I tell you when you get here."

Henry put on his hat and coat and walked over to the Garland. He wondered what was the matter. Felix sounded a trifle nervous. Of course it was nothing, but then he should have been over hours ago to inquire about Kris and relieve Marantz so he could go out and eat. He felt a bit ashamed of his not having called all day. He would not mention that he had spent the afternoon at the home of one of his patients, Mrs. Clayton Rodgers, who had been entertaining at an afternoon tea.

As he rang the buzzer of Kris's apartment, Henry was met by a distraught-looking Dr. Marantz.

"Felix! What's the matter? You look as though you haven't slept."

"I haven't. Not all night. Come in, sit down, I want to talk with you about Kris."

Henry threw off his hat and coat. "What about Kris? She was fine yesterday afternoon."

"Ja, that was yesterday. Today she is not good." He sat down and his voice quavered as he spoke. "She spent a restless night and her head felt hot. I took her temperature at two in the morning. It was 100. At nine this morning it was 101½. Her pulse was 98. Now her temperature is 103 and her pulse is 110. There is an infection under way somewhere, Viktor. I don't know exactly what, and I hope to God I am wrong."

Henry showed the first signs of concern. "Wrong? Wrong about what?"

"Septicemia."

"Septicemia? But that's a blood infection. How could she develop something like that? You took all precautions, didn't you?"

"That you know. But after all, I was working in a hotel bedroom. One hundred percent asepsis is impossible anywhere except in a hospital operating room. I … I didn't tell you, but during the operation she bled considerably. Also, to start with, Kris' entire physical condition was none too good. She is thin and has evidently lost weight recently. Her resistance was low, and that would make her more easily susceptible to an infection. She has refused all food and has not had any nourishment except water in the last thirty hours. This is not helping matters any. She must keep up her strength if she is to fight this infection."

Suddenly from the next room came a plaintive cry that seemed heartrending in its appeal.

"Water! Water! Water!"

The two men jumped to their feet and Marantz was soon holding a glass to the parched lips of the fever-flushed young girl. Henry stood there awkwardly, fidgeting, with a feeling of utter uselessness. As Marantz lowered her head back on the pillow she murmured. "I'm hot, I'm hot!" Her eyes closed and her head tossed from side to side. She fell back into a fitful sleep, ignorant of the fact that Henry had even entered the room. Marantz took out his watch and counted her pulse. He looked up toward the man standing opposite him, whose face was blank and expressionless.

"Now it's 120," he whispered with a deep concern written on his features. He shook his head apprehensively. "I'm afraid," he muttered, "I'm afraid."

They walked back into the living room. Felix Marantz sank down with a heavy sigh into the nearby easy chair. "Viktor, my heart was not in this—I had a premonition—something told me not to do this thing. I was afraid from the beginning—"

"Isn't there something we can do? Something we can give her?"

"Only when you know what you are fighting, can you use the proper counteractives. In a hospital they could take a blood count—make tests—give her intravenous injections of sulfanilamide. Up here we are practically helpless. I have no idea what her white count is—I don't know what I am fighting. If she does not improve by tomorrow morning, I am sending her to a hospital."

Henry looked up sharply. "Hospital? Felix, are you out of your mind? You know what that means?"

Marantz shook his head slowly and his face seemed to age as he spoke.

"Ja, I know what it means. It means the end of me—"

"Felix, don't be crazy. We can't send Kris to a public hospital after something like this. It means definite exposure. They'll examine her and find out!"

"I know—"

"You know? And still you talk about hospitals—"

"Ja, Viktor. My heart does not pump ice water. Do you think I could sit here and see this girl suffer or die and do nothing just to protect myself? I am a medical man, Viktor, not a psychiatrist. You cannot cure blood infections by psychoanalysis!"

Henry did not answer but sat there biting his lower lip, as Felix stared coldly at him through his thick spectacles. "I don't know whether I admire you as much as I did, Viktor," he went on. "I don't know but what your last remark gives to me the feeling that I have never known the real Viktor Bartok. Any doctor who would think of self-preservation before the life of his patient is not worthy of his profession!"

Henry fumbled for words. "Why? Because I was trying to save you from—"

"Not me! You're thinking of yourself, Viktor. You're thinking of your own hide and your own reputation."

"That's not true, Felix. I was merely trying to protect you!"

Marantz's attitude had taken on a sudden coolness toward this man he thought to be his old friend and colleague. There was something more than coolness in his voice. There was an unmistakable revolt that Henry sensed immediately and which stung him with the sharp prick of a needle. "Trying to protect me!" said Marantz bitterly. "Thanks for your thoughtfulness! This is a fine time to speak of protection, with a human life lying at stake. In that room, racked with high fever and a blood infection, is your niece—your sister's child. To me, she is a stranger, and yet I am willing to sacrifice myself to save a life. You, who cried in my home about this young girl who was like your own flesh and blood, you said, who should be given every opportunity to live and enjoy life, for whom you would never forgive yourself if you did not do everything in your power to help her—now you talk about leaving her to rot in that room while blood poison slowly eats her up! Viktor, I am ashamed and disgusted with you. You call yourself a doctor! In my estimation, you have lost the right to call yourself a doctor! You are a selfish, self-centered, cowardly vulture, living off the flesh of wealthy neurotics who pay you big fees to tell them in honeyed words what they want to hear. You are not the same man who worked side by side with me at the clinics in Vienna, who was not interested in how much money will he be able to earn, but in how much good he will be able to do the world! That man is dead. The man that took his place is evil, devilish and coldblooded—a cheat and a fraud!"

Henry jumped up from his chair, his eyes blazing in rage. He stood with clenched fists and glared hate at the little man who had at last seen through his transparent skin and bared his soul for what it was worth. As he glowered at his antagonist, Felix Marantz returned the gaze, unflinchingly, imperturbably, with a defiant challenge that seemed to erect a barrier of truth between himself and the man who towered over him. Without further words, Henry picked up his hat and coat and left the apartment.

Professor Marantz sank back against the chair, disheartened and weary. In this moment of trial he had been deserted by the very man he had sought to befriend; for whom he had gambled his honor, his reputation, his whole career as a doctor. Now he was alone, left by himself to face a verdict that would be self-accusing and damning, which would crucify him before the world as a quack and a charlatan, a murderer of the unborn. Yes, that would be the charge hurled against him. His plea that he did it out of friendship would be scoffed at and derided. Besides, if Viktor Bartok wanted to turn into a complete scoundrel, he had in his pocket a check for one thousand dollars which he could say was the fee agreed upon. No, he would never do that—Viktor could not stoop so low, be so vile, so base. Still, any man who would be willing to allow his niece to die rather than chance exposure by sending her to a hospital, might go to any lengths to protect himself. His thoughts became a montage of self-condemnations as he sought desperately to blot out from his mind the repercussions of the step he was about to hazard. Whatever resulted from such a move, Felix Marantz could come to only one ultimate and inescapable decision: if Kristina Dvorak was removed to a hospital, regardless of the outcome, whether she recovered or died, he would have to pay the penalty that the law exacts for committing a crime against man and against God's commandment: "Thou Shalt Not Kill."

All through that night the faithful little doctor sat in the dim light of the bedroom and watched the tossing of the pathetic young girl he was helpless to aid. He watched the look of pain and agony, the dry tongue that tried vainly to moisten the parched lips, the face that grew more crimson as the temperature mounted. He sought to reduce the fever with ice packs, but he knew that this would give her at least only a brief respite—that his only means of attacking the infection was with a powerful counteractive that would go to work immediately and destroy the bacteria that were fast multiplying and spreading over her entire body. To take a smear, he would have to have a microscope— here he had nothing—no means of identifying the virulent bug he was combating.

At quarter of five in the morning Marantz again took Kris' temperature. It was 104.2 and her pulse was 128. He knew now without a trace of a doubt that his patient was steadily growing worse and that her chances of throwing off the infection without hospitalization and potent drugs were impossible. He picked up the phone and called the night operator.

"What is the nearest hospital, please?"

"There's one about six blocks from here. St. Benedict's."

"Thank you, and will you do me a favor, please?"

"Certainly."

"Will you call an ambulance service right away?"

"Of course. Is something wrong with Miss Dvorak?"

"Ja, I'm sorry to say she's very ill. This is her doctor speaking."

"Oh, I'm so sorry. I'll call right away, doctor."

"And operator—"

"Yes?"

"If Dr. Bartok should call, please leave a message for him that his niece has been removed to St. Benedict's Hospital."

A white-gowned interne walked into the spotless laboratory and approached a technician bent over a microscope.

"Can you make it out, Lou?"

"Yep. Can't mistake these frisky little fellows. They're having a helluva time. So damn many of them it looks like they're having a convention. Want to take a look? Let's see how good you are on your bacteriology."

The interne leaned over and squinted into the microscope. "Well, the pigment is not orange to white, and the bugs are not formed into grapelike clusters, so we'll eliminate staphylococcus."

"Right so far," came the reply.

"The bugs seem to divide in one plane, occur in chains, but not in packets and do not form zoogloeal masses—did they ferment in insulin?"

"Nope."

"Then, I would say, my friend, that these are what are known as the genus of nonmotile, gram-positive bacteria of the family of Coccaceae, more commonly known as streptococcus—species Beta Hemolytic, and that correct diagnosis would be puerperal septicemia."

The bacteriologist slapped him on the back. "Right on the button, Irv. Ah, your old professors at Northwestern would be proud of you, m'boy. Calling off those cocci as though you'd been playing with them all your life. What did your mother buy you when you were a baby? I'll bet instead of a rattle you had a 'scope!"

"Go 'way," chuckled the interne. "You don't have to be a genius to figure that out. She's been here three days now. Her white count had gone from 14,000 to 26,000, her last reading was 104.6 temperature, and a pulse of 130. From the history of her case, how could I miss?"

"Say, you're O. K., Irv. All you Northwestern medics turn out to be good doctors. I predict a brilliant future for you, m'boy!"

"Quit giving me the rib, will you? You Illinois guys are just jealous, that's all."

"Not me, pal. I'm a Wisconsin man myself."

"That's still worse," laughed the interne. "Well, excuse me, Lou, I've got to make out this report and give it to Doc Ferrin. He'll probably want to push more sulfa since the blood cultures showed strep. She seems to be in a bad way."

"She an old dame?"

"Uh, uh. Young—about twenty or so and darn good-looking. Too bad she's down with this. I hope she comes around all right. Maybe she'll fall for the interne, who can tell?"

"There you go again. Now I know why your last name's Wolff!"

"You said it. See you, Stinky."

The interne finished his report and took them to the office of the chief resident physician.

"Here's the lab report on the patient in 402 who was brought in Monday morning, doctor."

"Thank you." The middle-aged gray-haired physician studied the diagnosis. "Hmm. Strep infection developing into puerperal septicemia. White count 26,000, red 3½ million. Are you still pushing fluids?"

"Yes, doctor. She's received 2,000 cc's five percent glucose in distilled water, plus 1,000 cc's five percent glucose in normal salt by slow intravenous drip."

"Very well, continue the fluids. Now, beginning immediately, administer sulfanilamide intravenously in the usual ampoule doses."

"Yes, doctor. Incidentally, did you make a thorough diagnosis of this patient?"

"Yes, Wolff. This strep infection is due to a septic abortion."

The interne seemed a bit surprised. "Septic abortion, doctor?"

"Yes. Upon examination, I found the lower part of the abdomen elicited acute tenderness. The uterus was enlarged and extended ¾ cm. above the symphysis pubis. Blood was observed on the vulva and in the vagina. Many blood clots were present in the cervical outlet. Also there was marked tenderness in both parametria, and all indications pointed to the fetus having recently been removed by surgical operation. It was a neat job, evidently done by someone who knew his business, but he didn't count on his patient developing a septicemia."

"What are you going to do, doctor—I mean about the abortion?"

"Well, first of all, we'll see if we can clear up this infection. The patient is our first concern. After that, I'm not sure exactly what I'm going to do. You see, Wolff, this is rather an unusual case."

"Unusual, doctor?"

"Yes. Miss Dvorak, the patient, is a niece of Viktor Bartok."

"Viktor Bartok, the psychiatrist?"

"Right!"

The interne whistled. "Boy-oh-boy, this thing is getting more complicated every minute. How did you find that out?"

"From the girl herself. I called Bartok this morning but his secretary says he's out of town. Won't be back until the end of the week. I doubt very much that he knows anything about this. Miss Dvorak told me her home is in Pasadena."

"So she's all alone—no relatives, no friends, nobody except that little man who brought her here and who comes to see her every day."

"Oh, yes, I've seen him. He's the one with the thick glasses and the large head. Who is he?"

"He told me he was a friend of the patient's. I think he said his name's Marantz."

"Marantz? Rather an odd name," commented the physician. "Have you talked with him?"

"Yes, several times," replied the interne, "and it's a funny thing—"

"What is?"

"He's asked me a number of medical questions, and when I started the glucose injections he said he was glad that she was to get 2,000 cc's of five percent distilled water and 1,000 cc's of the same percent in salt. I thought it was certainly unusual for a layman to know all about that, and besides, every day he's been asking me about her white count. In fact, the first day she was here, he hinted that he was pretty sure she had a puerperal septicemia. He's evidently read a lot of books on medicine."

The physician leaned back in his chair and scratched his chin. "Um, hm. I'd go a step further than that, Dr. Wolff. I'd say that our friend is not only well read in medicine, but he's also practiced it!"

"You mean you think he's a doctor?"

"Yes, and the one who performed the abortion!"

"Well, I'll be! Of course, I begin to see it now. He brought her here when she developed the infection."

"That's right."

"But, Dr. Ferrin, wasn't he taking an awful chance of exposure?"

"Certainly. That's why I'm quite sure he's no quack. Quacks wouldn't risk being caught by bringing their patients to a hospital. I don't think he's a Chicago doctor. At least I don't recognize the name. Marantz. That's an unusual name. The only Marantz I've ever heard of was the well-known gynecologist, Professor Marantz, who taught at the University of Vienna. Wonder what ever became of him? Well, better get going, Wolff, on that sulfanilamide."

Felix Marantz returned to Kris' apartment in the Garland, where he was staying. The little professor had aged ten years in appearance in the past week and he verged on a collapse from nervous exhaustion. He fell upon the bed and soon was in a deep slumber disturbed by haunting dreams. When he awoke the following afternoon, he found he had slept sixteen hours, his first real sleep in five days. Picking up the phone, he called long distance, and in a few minutes was talking with his wife.

"—And so don't worry, Mama, I called the University Monday and told them it was impossible for me to be there this week. After all, I am entitled to a vacation after two years."

"Ja, Papa. Are you having a good time?"

"Ja, Mama, wonderful. I'm seeing nightclubs and shows—"

"That's good. Enjoy yourself, Papa, you deserve it. You've been working hard. How is Viktor?"

"Viktor? He's … he's fine, Mama. He's been showing me around all over …"

"Give him my love, and, Papa …"

"Ja?"

"When you think you will be coming home?"

"Well, today is Friday. I be home about Sunday."

"All right, Papa. Take care of yourself. Sara and Rachel are lonesome, so we look for you the end of the week. Ja?"

"Ja. Goodbye, Mama, the time is up now."

"Goodbye, Papa, goodbye."

Felix shaved his three-day beard and, after a hot bath, dressed himself and went to the hospital. As he entered Kris' room he was met by Dr. Ferrin and the interne, Wolff. He nodded and greeted them anxiously.

"How is the patient today?"

Dr. Ferrin answered him. "Not very good. She's not responding to the sulfa as well as we expected."

Marantz's face fell. "Oh."

"Would you mind stepping into my office with me … doctor."

Felix looked up with a not too surprised look. Then quietly, "Ja."

The three men walked to Dr. Ferrin's office. "Sit down, please, doctor." The physician directed him to a chair.

"Thank you."

"Now, Dr. Marantz, we'll have a little talk. It's needless for me to tell you your patient is suffering from a septic abortion. You performed this abortion, didn't you?"

"Ja." He lowered his head in a feeling of shame.

"You also know that she has developed puerperal septicemia and that at the moment her condition is very precarious?"

"I knew about the septicemia but I didn't know her condition was that bad. I thought the sulfa would bring her around."

"Unfortunately, as you know, sulfa is not a cure-all. Although her blood stream has responded temporarily to the sulfa, there are regions where the streptococci cannot be reached and where they cannot be rendered sterile. In the last forty-eight hours we have discovered strains of anaerobic streptococci in the pelvic vessels which have become thrombosed and which cannot be sterilized by the sulfa. These areas remain as a constant source of the bacteremia, and are potential feeding grounds which we are helpless to combat. There is every possibility that the patient will not be able to fight this infection successfully. Unless there is a decided improvement within the next forty-eight hours, I'm afraid she won't last over the weekend."

Felix did not answer, but sat staring at the floor. He felt a futility and a weakness that rendered him incapable of finding words, yet he wanted to cry out his innocence, his unwillingness to perform the abortion; his revolt at the thought of degrading and dishonoring his profession and himself. He wanted to cry out his condemnation of the man who brought all this upon him. He wanted to cry out his sorrow for this young girl who lay in pain and agony, who was suffering needlessly, who should be out laughing and dancing, enjoying her beauty and her youth, instead of being racked with a burning fever from a morbid infection. But Felix Marantz could find no words for these thoughts.

"I do not doubt that the patient contacted you for this abortion," continued Dr. Ferrin, "but I am forced to remind you, doctor, that you will be held responsible for this girl. If she dies, I hesitate to think what the penalty will be."

"I know," replied Marantz with a deep sigh, "I know."

"Dr. Bartok, the patient's uncle, is a well-known psychiatrist. He's been out of town on business all week and I can well imagine his feelings when he returns and discovers what has happened in his absence. For Dr. Bartok's sake, I would be inclined not to press this publicly in order to spare his reputation, but if Miss Dvorak should die, this becomes a criminal case and completely out of my hands. you … you understand that, don't you, doctor?"

"Ja, I do."

"Incidentally, I see you speak with a foreign accent. Marantz is not a common name. But if I'm not mistaken, there was a Professor Marantz who used to teach obstetrics and gynecology at the University of Vienna. Were you acquainted with him?"

"Ja, the last I heard of him he had come to the United States and was teaching at Midwestern University in Lowell, Iowa."

"Oh, is that so? And where do you live, doctor?"

"Lowell, Iowa."

It was one-forty Sunday morning when the night nurse called the interne on the floor and told him she didn't think that the condition of the patient in 402 was very satisfactory.

"Her pulse suddenly dropped from 130 to 40, doctor."

The interne hastened into the room and applied his stethoscope to her chest.

"The beat is very faint," he told the nurse. "What's her respiration?"

"It was 46 a few minutes ago."

"Must be around 50 now." He felt her pulse. "Seems to be very weak. I think I'd better call Dr. Ferrin. I don't like the looks of this."

In a few minutes, Dr. Ferrin was in the room. "She's slipping fast," he said softly. "Nurse."

"Yes, doctor?"

"Call Dr. Marantz at the Garland Apartments. He asked me to phone him if anything should go wrong. Tell him to come immediately. Also phone the Blake and see if Dr. Bartok returned."

"Yes, doctor."

Then he turned to the interne. "It's too bad, Wolff, too bad we couldn't save her."

"Yes, it is, doctor," Wolff replied quietly. "I'd like to have known her … when she was well … she's a very beautiful girl … isn't she?"

"Yes, I have a daughter just about her age. I know how I'd feel…."

"Isn't there something else we can do, doctor?"

"I'm afraid not, Wolff. We've tried everything. Sulfa, 10,000 units of anti-toxin, nothing seems to work. I understand there are experiments under way with a new drug called penicillin which is supposed to be more potent and has more therapeutic powers than sulfanilamide for certain types of bacteria."

"How about Beta Hemolytic septicemia?"

"That's one of the infections that according to experiments responds beautifully to penicillin. If we had had 100,000 units here, Wolff, I think we would have had this strep infection licked." He sighed. "But, unfortunately, it's still in the experimental stage. Someday, Wolff, we'll probably have a hundred million units in our vault right here, and young girls like this won't slip out of our hands."

Suddenly from the white Dresden-like face on the pillow, lips that had been still began to move. The voice that emanated from them was weak and scarcely more than a whisper. "Mumsy—mumsy—mumsy! Here … I … am … mumsy … where … are … you … mumsy?"

"God! And her mother two thousand miles from here," said the physician ironically. "Not one person that's near and dear to her even here to comfort her!"

The feeble voice continued to call futilely. "Mumsy … mumsy … mumsy …"

Felix Marantz arrived by two A.M. and stood anxiously outside Kris' room. He looked pitifully haggard and his eyes were bloodshot from sleeplessness and strain. The nurse came to the door and admitted the professor.

"She's been calling for her mother," she said disconsolately. "In the last few minutes she's called for Vik."

"That's her uncle," replied Marantz bitterly. "He's out of town."

As he entered the room he whispered a forlorn greeting to the two doctors who stood at the bedside in profound silence. Neither acknowledged the greeting but condescended a nod of the head.

"Vik … Vik … Uncle Vik … where's … mumsy?" came the plaintive murmur.

Felix turned to the men with a searching expression on his face. "Please, doctor," he whispered. "May I sit with her? She calls for her uncle who is away. Maybe I can pretend to be her uncle, and that will give her some comfort. Please, doctor, ja?"

Dr. Ferrin nodded his head and motioned for the nurse to leave. Then he and the interne followed her out.

Felix walked with a heavy heart to the bedside of the dying girl and sat down. He took her pale hand in his, and stroked it tenderly. "Kris," he called gently, "Kris, I'm here…."

She stirred feebly. "Vik …? Uncle Vik …?"

"Ja, it is Uncle Vik … Kris, darling…."

"Vik … can't call you Uncle Vik …. anymore … Not … now …. anymore … don't tell Mumsy … will … you … Vik … I wanted to be … good … Vik … why didn't you … help me … to be good … I loved you … Vik … I loved you….."

Felix Marantz listened bewilderedly to the girl's delirious ramblings as, between the quick short gasps, she uttered continuously the same phrases. "I … wanted to be … good, Vik … wanted … to be … good … I'm going back … to … Bahá'i Temple … Vik remember … Bahá'i … Temple … Vik … Pray … for … you … too … Vik … Darkness … cannot hide … me from … Thine all-seeing … eye … Oh God … and Father … bowed … down … by … the conscious … ness … of … my … sins … we have … both … sinned, Vik, both of us … will God … forgive us … Vik … He knows … we … did … but … Mumsy doesn't … don't tell … Mumsy … will you … Vik … what … what did … they do … with … the baby … Vik … you … didn't … want it … Vik … too bad … we … couldn't … keep it … Vik … Maybe … it would … have … looked like … you … here's … Bahá'i Temple … Vik … got … to go … in and … pray … got to leave … you now … Vik … time to … go in … and pray … I shall … look … for shelter … under … the wings

... of ... Thy grace ... for Thy ... forbearance ... is ... everlasting ... and Thy ... love ... en ... dur ... eth ... for ... ever...."

The eyelids ceased to flutter and the lips were stilled.

A cold drizzle wet the face of Felix Marantz as he made his way slowly along in the damp night, his eyes those of one who walks in his sleep. Behind them glowed furious hate, and the face was grim and the lips set. He had left the room ignoring the two doctors waiting outside in the corridor who made no effort to stop him as he brushed silently by. Steps had been descended without feeling of descent—streets were crossed without knowledge of crossings—Felix Marantz trudged into the night, hating with all the venom that his body and soul could muster, hating with a vengeance of which he had thought himself incapable, for never before had Felix Marantz hated as he now did the man whom he had once known as his friend.

His thoughts raced through his befuddled brain and brought the vision of a blurred picture into the sharp focus of clarity and reason. He had been tricked into performing an abortion by the very man who was responsible for it! A man who had seduced his own niece! A man who sought to avoid suspicion by inventing the story of another man, and who was cold-blooded enough to leave a young girl to die alone in a hospital room without a word, a gesture. And Dr. Ferrin had said he could imagine Dr. Bartok's feelings when he returned and found what had happened to his niece!

Marantz knew he had no leg to stand on. Bartok would deny all knowledge of the abortion and his word as a reputable physician would be accepted. Furthermore, Marantz also knew that he had admitted the abortion to Dr. Ferrin in front of the interne, and that very little else mattered. Ferrin had reminded him that regardless of who did the contacting, he would be held solely responsible.

His thoughts went back to Viktor Bartok. It was difficult to believe that a man with whom he had worked for years, whom he had once loved, respected, and admired, whom less than two weeks before he had entertained in his home at dinner, could be the object of so much of his loathing, so much of his vitriolic abhorrence; could be so despicable and vile as to make incestuous love to his own niece!

The very thought of the word incest caused Felix Marantz's stomach to constrict, and, with it came a feeling of nausea. He not only felt a violent hatred for Viktor Bartok, but his own act had taken on a rottenness that sickened him. On and on he walked, little caring in which direction, utterly oblivious of the hour. The deserted streets appeared like dark, yawning chasms between the mountains of buildings that threw weird and grotesque shadows across the wet pavements. His thoughts drifted toward home, and his wife and children. He had promised Mama he would be home Sunday. This was Sunday morning. It had been ten days since he left, ten days that were hard to remember, days that seemed lost in a maelstrom of human conflicts that were without parallel in his stormy life. Even his flight from Vienna and the voyage to America loomed up in his mind with more freshness than the events of the last ten days. He ran his hand across his eyes as if to brush aside the film of unreality that had blotted out the logic, the normal, the believable, and in its place had left this haze of incredibility, this nightmare that was born of fantasy and delusion. Was it all a bad dream? Felix Marantz could not grasp the full meaning, could not gear his brain to the acceptance of the events of the past ten days. It was all a figment of his imagination, an invention of a disordered mind. Yet, this was not Spring Street on which he was walking. The buildings did not look familiar, there was no church on the corner, there was no little white frame house in the middle of the block in which he lived.

This was a strange street in the city to which he had come to perform an abortion, and the girl had died. He was now a murderer, an outcast, a fugitive from justice, an ex-doctor, an ex-university professor, dishonored and disgraced! No, no, that couldn't be! His mind was playing tricks on him—he was Dr. Felix Marantz, Professor of Obstetrics and Gynecology at Midwestern University! Yesterday he had said, "Now, gentlemen, tomorrow we discuss the uterus." Only yesterday he had walked home and Mama was waiting with a hot bowl of soup. And Rachel had gotten him his house slippers, and Sara, his pipe. Yes, that was only yesterday. Then where was Spring Street, and the church, and the white frame house? No, no, it was not all a bad dream. It had happened. Only fifteen minutes before, he had held a dying girl's hand. Had heard her gasp her last breath. Had seen her eyes flutter and close in death … a death that *he* had caused by an illicit operation that he had performed—a death for which *he* would be held responsible and for which *he* would have to pay the penalty. Only fifteen minutes before, he had walked out of St. Benedict's Hospital, out into the street, to walk alone with only his shadow as his companion, a shadow that trailed his every step as surely as the law would trail him for the murder of Kristina Dvorak.

CHAPTER TWENTY-TWO

"Come in, Dr. Bartok, come in." Dr. Ferrin stood up, greeted his visitor and showed him to a chair. "I don't believe we've met before, have we?"

"No, I don't think we have," replied Henry, extending his hand. "Sit down, won't you?"

"Thank you." Henry fingered his hat nervously.

"Now, Dr. Bartok, you know of course why I phoned you?"

"Yes, I learned of the tragedy this morning when I arrived. I've been in the East for a week."

"First of all, please accept my sincere sympathy."

"Thank you."

"We did everything humanly possible to save her, doctor, but she had a Beta Hemolytic streptococcus infection which, as you know, is an extremely virulent bacteremia."

"Yes."

"Your niece was brought here last Monday morning with a temperature of 104 and the infection well under way. Even large doses of sulfa failed to check the poison. I hope you can stand hearing the truth, Dr. Bartok—"

"Truth?"

"Yes, I see no reason why any facts should be withheld. I called you down here to inform you of the reasons behind the death of your niece, and it's my duty as a physician to give you the facts without trying to gild them or make them sound pleasant to the ear. You see, Dr. Bartok, your niece died of puerperal septicemia as a result of an abortion."

"Abortion?" Henry decided if he were going to play innocent, he might as well go all the way. "Abortion … doctor?" He gave it the touch of incredulity.

"Yes, doctor. I knew this wasn't going to be easy on you, but in a case of this kind I can't spare feelings. You … er … didn't have any knowledge of her pregnancy, did you?"

"Certainly not." He could tell from the way Ferrin talked that Felix had not mentioned his name, and that so far he was free from suspicion.

"I didn't think you did, doctor. There are quite a few unusual angles about this case. The man that brought her here was the man who performed the abortion."

"Oh, I see." So they knew Marantz did it.

"Yes, there was no attempt on his part to deny the operation. When I tell who he was, I think you'll have quite a surprise. It was no quack. It was a man who knew his business and an expert on obstetrics."

"Really?"

"Yes. The fact that an infection set in was not his fault and not because he didn't do a good job—it was just one of those unfortunate things. Well, I'm here to give you facts, so here they are. The man who performed the abortion on your niece was Dr. Felix Marantz, Professor of Obstetrics and Gynecology at Midwestern University, and formerly a professor at the University of Vienna. Did you know him?"

"Er … yes, quite well. In fact, I often mentioned his name to her."

"Well, that's the man. She must have contacted him without your knowledge. The thing that I don't understand is how Marantz would become involved in something like this. In the first place, I can't see why he would have jeopardized his entire reputation by performing such an operation. Then, on top of everything else, he put his neck in a noose by bringing his patient here where he was subject to immediate exposure. I detected the abortion upon my first examination. All I can say in favor of Dr. Marantz is that he's an extremely honorable man, and that he proved that his first obligation was to the welfare of his patient. Very few doctors would have sacrificed themselves by bringing the girl to a public hospital and turning the case over to a staff physician. That was practically signing a death certificate for himself."

Henry was a bit concerned at this point. "Why? What do you intend doing, doctor?"

"Well, in spite of the fact that I said Marantz had done an honorable thing by bringing her here and subjecting himself to exposure, that still does not change the fact that he performed the abortion. I admire the professor as a great man and a great physician, and I'm sorry that he became involved in something of this nature, but I must do my duty as Chief of Staff of this hospital. If your niece had recovered, even though that would not have lessened the crime any, I nevertheless might have been willing to look the other way because of the circumstances … your reputation, doctor, I mean…."

"Thank you."

"But the fact that your niece died makes this an out-and-out case of criminal abortion resulting in death, and something that's out of my hands completely."

Henry did not like this. There were bound to be repercussions that would have disastrous results for him. There would be a trial. Marantz would accuse him of being the instigator, of coming to Lowell, Iowa, to procure his services. It would be difficult to deny those things—difficult to deny his ignorance of Kris' pregnancy. Of course, no one knew that he was the father of her child, but still he would become involved and named as an accessory for contacting Marantz. Felix would be sent to jail, and there was no telling what his own punishment would be. Maybe he would be found guilty too and given a sentence. Then they would take his fingerprints, discover his record and prove he was not really Dr. Viktor Bartok at all, but Henry Mueller, ex-convict No. 147963. Then where was Dr. Bartok? They would theorize that he probably had murdered him and assumed his identity—they would prove it. He would be headlined in every newspaper in the country—the biggest hoax of the twentieth century would come to light and Henry Mueller would face the electric chair. There were the thoughts that sped through his brain as he heard Dr. Ferrin utter the last statement.

"You say it's really out of your hands completely, Dr. Ferrin? I … I hate to see this happen to Dr. Marantz. I … I … find myself at this point rather sorry for him. It means the end of his medical career … he'll be through at Midwestern—or any other university, for that matter … my niece is gone—prosecuting Dr. Marantz won't bring her back. I … I'd hate to think of ruining his life too...."

Dr. Ferrin leaned back in his chair. "Yes, I agree with you, Dr. Bartok, and I think it's very noble of you to feel that way about a fellow physician. But, as I said, this is not just a case of abortion, this is murder, and where I might have been willing to look the other way as regards the first offense, I can't turn my back where murder is concerned. I referred the case to the coroner's office this morning and the police are already out to pick up Dr. Marantz."

Henry's heart skipped a beat. "Oh," he said quietly. "Well, if there's nothing else you want of me, I think I'll run along." He rose. "I've got a number of people waiting for me at the office."

"All right, Dr. Bartok. Sorry we had to meet under such unpleasant circumstances."

"Yes. Well, thank you for all your efforts on behalf of my niece. I know you did everything you could. Mail the bill to my office, and I'll send you a check."

"Thank you, doctor. Incidentally, if you care to view the body, we sent it over to the undertakers."

"Oh … Uh … yes. Which one?"

"The Crawford Funeral Parlor."

"The Crawford Fu— oh, yes. Thank you."

Henry knew the name sounded familiar. It was not long ago that he had been there when Evelyn Hahn's parents came to view the last remains of their daughter. Would he have to face Kris' mother, too? Oh no, she was an invalid. She would not be able to come to Chicago. He took a deep breath of satisfaction. "Goodbye, doctor."

"Goodbye, Dr. Bartok."

Dr. Ferrin watched Henry as he left his office. Then he shook his head slowly from side to side. "Too bad," he muttered to himself. "Too bad things like that have to happen to a fine man like him."

Twenty-four hours later two men stepped from the train and stood gazing at the wooden railroad station where a sign hung that read: "Lowell, Iowa. Elevation 246 ft."

"Well, this is it, Harry. Got that extradition paper with you?" "Yep," replied the other. "Looks like a nice peaceful little place. Reminds me of my home town in Indiana. Just about the same size."

"Zat so? You come from Indiana? And here I always thought you were a Chicago boy."

"Me? Hell, no. I was born and raised in New Castle, Indiana. Well, let's get goin', we gotta job to do."

"Yep."

"What's that address again?"

"426 Spring Street."

"Shoudn't be hard to find in a town this size."

"Naw, we oughta be back on our way to Chicago tonight. Let's see, there's a schedule up there. There's a train outta here at 6:10 and another at 9:14. I'd like to catch that 6:10. That'll get us back to the city about two in the morning."

"What's the rush? We can stay over. The chief said we can come back anytime between now and Thursday."

"Not me. These small towns gimme a pain. Anyhow, I gotta go shoppin' tomorrow with my wife. We're gonna pick out a baby carriage."

"No kiddin'? When she expectin'?"

"The end of the month."

They started moving toward the heart of town. "Well, that's swell. That'll make four for you, huh?"

"Hell, no. That'll make five. That's why we gotta go shoppin' for a new buggy. The other one's busted through already!"

Professor Marantz left his classroom, started walking home slowly. There was the church on the corner and in the middle of the block was the white frame house where he lived. Yes, this was real, this was believable … this was home. But for how long? A few days? A few hours? A few minutes?

"Hello, Rachel. Hello, Sara. How are my little girls?"

"Fine, Papa," they said, hugging him.

"Oh, such a squeeze! Rachel, you are getting more muscle every day. What are you doing, exercising in the gymnasium?"

"No, Papa," she laughed. "That comes from eating lots of meat and potatoes! That's what you told me to do. Remember?"

"Ja. You are a good girl. Pretty soon you will have more red corpuscles than you know what to do with. Where is your Mama?"

"In the kitchen," Sara answered. "Mama! Papa's home! Rachel and me are going outside and play."

"All right," she called back. "Papa, come to the kitchen."

"Ja, I come. Mmmmm. What is this I smell?"

"Pot roast. And does it *schmeck goot*, Papa, ja?"

"Like ambrosia from the gods, Mama!"

"Ja? Well I bet theirs wasn't as good. I make this with garlic!"

"*Ach*. Then there is no comparison. So, what is new, Mama?"

"Nothing," she replied, lifting the lid of one of the pots on the stove. "You had a couple of callers."

"Callers? What kind?"

"Two men from Chicago."

"Oh." Felix breathed a sigh of resignation. "What did they say?"

"They asked for you and I told them you were still at the University. Then they asked what time you would be home. I tell them usually you come home around five o'clock, so they leave and say they come back at five."

Felix looked at his watch. It was four-twenty-five.

"You know these men, Papa, you were expecting them?"

"Ja, Mama, I … I was expecting them … any day...."

"You want a nice hot plate of soup, Papa? The soup is done."

"*Nein*, Mama … thank you, I'm not hungry...."

"What's the matter, Papa....? Always you eat soup."

"Ja, I know, but I just remembered. I left a book … an important book that I must have for some reference work. I forget to take it with me.... I go take a walk back to the University and pick it up...."

"Can't you get it tomorrow, Papa? Today it must be?"

"Ja, Mama … today...."

"So … all right."

Felix walked upstairs to his study and went directly to the writing desk. He opened one of the drawers and placed a bluish-looking object in his pocket. Then going back downstairs he returned to the kitchen. He stood for a moment in the door unobserved, watching his wife as she busied herself straining vegetables. Suddenly she caught sight of him.

"So, Papa, you are still here? I thought already you were gone."

"*Nein*, I … I go now … goodbye, Mama...." He walked over and put his hand on her cheek. "A little kiss, ja?"

She leaned toward her husband and Felix kissed the woman who had been his companion for sixteen years, borne him two children, loved him in sickness and in health, in poverty and in time of strife. "You have been a good wife, Elsa … a good wife...."

"Thank you, Papa," she said simply. "It is not hard to be a good wife to a man like you. Always I have been proud to be married to Dr. Felix Marantz."

He kissed her again. "I hope you will always be proud, Elsa.... Always...."

"Now hurry up and go, Papa. All of a sudden sentimental you are at four-thirty in the afternoon. I don't want you should be late for supper. Pot roast is no good cold."

"All right, Mama, I go."

"And don't stop to *schmoos* with Mr. Greenspahn at the bookstore. Whenever you do, my supper gets like a lump of paste."

"Ja, Mama, I go right now." Felix walked to the vestibule and put on his hat and coat. Outside he found his two daughters playing a sidewalk game.

"Where you going, Papa?" Sara inquired.

"For a walk, Sara. I … I forget something at the University."

"Can we walk with you, Papa?" asked Rachel anxiously. "We like to walk with you, don't we, Sara?"

"Yes, can we, Papa?"

"*Nein, Kinder* … I must go alone today. You will not be angry with me?"

"No, Papa. We thought maybe you'd like company," said Rachel. She began to hop on one foot from square to square in the chalked design they had drawn.

"Come, give your papa a hug like before, ja?"

Rachel and Sara ran up to him and he caressed them both. Neither saw the tear that coursed its way down his cheek. "Be good girls now, ja, my children?"

"Yes, Papa," they replied.

"Don't be late for supper," called Sara. Felix did not answer as he trudged wearily away from the little home that would have been bought and paid for in four more years. He glanced once again at the little white Methodist church that had stood at the corner of Market and Spring for fifty years, and which he had passed every day since he took up residence in Lowell. He turned down Market and walked by the many familiar landmarks that he had grown to know and love—the Lowell Public Library, the Klinger Dairy Company, the Scully Lumber Yard, Ed Roper's Harness and Saddle Store. Soon he found himself on Canal Street and he was passing the Foster Shoe Store, Rinkmeyer's Emporium and Greenspahn's Book Store. He waved to Joe Greenspahn who was busy with a customer, and Joe waved back. He would have liked to ask Joe if that copy of *John Brown's Body* by Stephen Vincent Benét had come yet, but Joe was busy. On he strolled past Pfeiffer's Barber Shop. Karl Pfeiffer was cutting the Finley kid's hair while his mother sat there watching scrupulously to see that he didn't take too much off the top. Jimmy looked forlorn and unhappy. Suddenly a voice greeted Felix.

"Good afternoon, doctor."

"Oh, good afternoon, Mrs. Dickson."

"Nice day for a walk, isn't it?"

"Ja, Mrs. Dickson, very nice."

"How is the family?"

"They are all well, thank you."

"Nice to have seen you, professor."

"Thank you, Mrs. Dickson. Good afternoon."

Felix replaced his hat and walked on. He crossed Center Street and paused to look in the window of Henderson's Hardware Store. He stood there for a couple of minutes, gazing at the different items that he would have liked to have had. Puttering around a work bench in the basement had always been a weakness of his. For years he had wanted to own a small lathe and a drill and a vise.

Then his eyes fell upon another object. Yes, there it was! That pair of pliers that he was going to get. He needed it very badly. And a new hinge for the cellar door. The old one was rusty and corroded. That "T" hinge on display was just the kind he needed. Every time Mama went down to the cellar to get some preserves, she had trouble with that door. Then his eyes returned and looked longingly at the pliers. Ever since he had moved into his home on Spring Street he had been needing a good pair of pliers, but somehow or other he just never seemed to be able to get around to it—not until today. He walked into the store and the clerk approached him.

"How do you do? Something for you, sir?"

"Ja. I want a pair of pliers like you have in the window. A good pair."

"Yes, sir. Step over here, sir." The clerk slid back a showcase window. "Here's our best household pliers, sir. A dollar seventy-five."

"That's the kind, ja." Felix turned them over in his hand and maneuvered the jaws back and forth. "Ja, I take this pair."

"Yes, sir."

The clerk wrapped them up and Felix walked out with the package in his overcoat pocket, which he unconsciously rubbed affectionately as he ambled along. His wanderings took him past Kessner's Five and Ten Cent store. There was a peanut machine out front and he inserted a few pennies and retrieved a handful of peanuts which he put in his other pocket. He crossed Sherman Street and as he passed Lindstrom's Bakery, the aroma of fresh bread and rolls caught his nostrils. Lindstrom's was crowded, as they usually were around five. He remembered all the times he had stopped in Lindstrom's and brought home a Vienna rye, and coffee cake, and lady fingers or cream puffs for Rachel and Sara. He gazed into the window. They had a whole cheese cake on display. He loved fresh cheese cake.

Marantz walked on past Chestnut Street toward a familiar sign that hung over the sidewalk, "Judd's Tobaccos." He always stopped in Abner Judd's Tobacco Store to buy a jar of tobacco. He remembered that he owed Abner Judd thirty-eight cents from his last purchase, when he gave Abner a ten-dollar bill, and Abner didn't have change. Abner had told him to stop in any time and pay. That was last week. Now would be a good time. The little bell tinkled as the door opened.

"Hello, professor, nice to see you."

"Thank you. How are you, Abner?"

"Fair to middlin'. What can I do for you? A jar of Royal Mixture?"

"No, thank you, Abner. I still have plenty. I just wanted to pay you that thirty-eight cents I owe you."

"Oh, you didn't have to come in specially for that. You could've waited until you came in to buy something. After all, you're not going anywhere!"

"Ja. Well, anyway, I was just passing and I happen to remember. Let's see. Twenty-five, thirty-five, and three pennies. There you are."

"Thank you, professor. Nice day out, isn't it? Almost like spring."

"Ja."

"I think our winter is just about over. And none too soon for me. I'm anxious to get a rod and reel into my hands. Expect to do some fishing up at Paradise Lake this summer. You oughta come with me, professor. You'd be crazy about the place. When you go up there, you feel like you haven't got a care in the world. No wonder they call it Paradise."

"Ja, it must be beautiful. Well, nice to see you again, Abner."

"Same here, professor. I'll look for you next week."

The bell tinkled again and Felix found himself once more making his way along the quaint little thoroughfare that had become part of his everyday life. He turned onto Grant and then up Cedar which took him out of the business district and through the residential section. Here were the fine homes. The president of the bank lived in Cedar Hills, and the mayor and Mr. Bonney, owner of the Bonney Manufacturing Company where they employed two hundred people, and Mr. Klinger of the Klinger Dairy Company and Professor Burton, Dean of the Medical School, and Thomas Blackstone, President of the University—and all the rest of the town's social element. This was the restricted section of Lowell, where not all could purchase a lot or a home. But there were no restrictions on walking, and Felix strolled on, oblivious of time and cares, strolled on till the mansions and homes gave way to a park, and a lagoon, and a thick grove of trees. This was Gage Woods, where the picnickers brought baskets in the summer, and played games and watched ducks swimming in the water.

Felix walked over to his favorite bench on the gravel path and sat down. From his overcoat pocket he took his old briar pipe and filled it full of tobacco. He struck a match and in a second heavy blue smoke came pouring forth. Smoke that was pleasant and relaxing, smoke that for the moment spelled peace and contentment. A squirrel darted down a tree and sprang down the path. Half a dozen feet away it stopped and stood looking intently, first in one direction, then the other. It inched forward toward Felix and paused again.

"Well, what do you want? You think I got something for you, eh?" The squirrel looked at him as if understanding every word. Closer it edged until it came almost to Felix's shoe.

"So! You want something to eat, huh? All right, you little beggar!" Felix's hand went into his pocket and fished out a few of the peanuts he had got from the vending machine. He scattered them before his little friend who bounded eagerly after them, devouring each nut as quickly as his sharp little teeth would crush it. A flock of pigeons atop the conservatory joined in the proceedings. One by one they circled down until there were a dozen or more walking about looking for a handout.

"Well, what is this? I see you have competition now, eh? So. We see how far this goes around." He threw some more peanuts on the path. There was a wild scramble by all to snare the tiny morsels. The squirrel edged within arm's length of his provider. "Ho ho, you are getting smart, huh? All right, out from the hand you take it, eh. Felix held forth a handful of the nuts at a tempting distance, chuckling as the squirrel seized one, then darted away to eat leisurely as he stood upright on his hind legs.

Fifteen minutes later Felix threw the last of the peanuts to his busy little friends and knocked the ashes from his pipe. There was a decided chill in the air now as the early March sun quickly sank in the west. As he replaced his pipe in his overcoat pocket, his hand fell upon the small package he was carrying. He withdrew it and opened it up. For a moment he worked the pliers about in his hand and then carefully wrapped them up again and returned them to his pocket. He rose from the bench with a resigned dignity and walked slowly but with unfaltering steps toward the shallow lagoon. For a while Felix stood there gazing at a few wild geese which had settled on the water in their northward migration. Then he headed toward the thick grove of trees on the opposite bank. Soon he was lost from sight in the dense foliage.

A moment later a sharp report rent the quiet atmosphere and the startled geese rose from the water in wild flight.

CHAPTER TWENTY-THREE

"Can you take a call, Dr. Bartok?"

The voice was Miss Corbett's over the office phone.

"Yes."

"Just a second, please. All right, go ahead."

"Hello, Dr. Bartok? This is Dr. Ferrin."

"Oh, yes, Dr. Ferrin. How are you?"

"I just received a call from the state's attorney's office."

"You did? What ... what about?"

"There'll be no need to prosecute Dr. Marantz—"

"I'm afraid I don't follow you, doctor ..."

"Dr. Marantz committed suicide in Lowell, Iowa, yesterday."

"No!" Henry was shocked and relieved at the same time. "Dr. Ferrin ... don't know what to say, I'm stunned beyond words ... it's been a terrible affair...."

"I guess there is nothing to say, Dr. Bartok. That just about closes the case."

"It does?"

"Well, it does as far as I'm concerned. How about you?"

"Oh, yes, yes, of course...."

"I'm naturally sorry that Professor Marantz took such a drastic step.

He must've taken this thing pretty hard."

"I imagine so."

"Did he have a family, Dr. Bartok?"

"Yes … I … I … think he had a wife and one or two children if I'm not mistaken. It's been years since I've seen him...."

"Well, it's too bad. A thing like this always upsets me—particularly when it has to do with a member of our profession."

"Yes."

"I'm going to call the state's attorney's office again and request them to quash the whole case so that the newspapers don't get hold of the thing. As far as they know now, Professor Marantz was a suicide, but they don't know why. It's quite obvious to me that he wanted to spare his family the shame and disgrace that would follow his arrest, so I'm going to do all I can to spare them."

"Yes, I agree with you heartily, Dr. Ferrin. No need of letting the innocent suffer."

"Well, that's all, Dr. Bartok. I just wanted to let you know. Drop over and see me sometime when you're in the neighborhood and we'll have a chat."

"Yes, I'll be glad to, and thanks for calling me."

"Not at all. Goodbye, Dr. Bartok."

"Goodbye … sir."

Henry hung up the phone and a trace of a smile crept across his face. *Now he was in the clear!* Now he had no reason to be apprehensive. From now on it would be smooth sailing once again. If only he didn't start getting soft—if only his conscience didn't start getting the best of him as it had last night. He couldn't get Kris' mother out of his mind; he hardly had had an hour's sleep all night. Now there would be two women haunting his conscience—Kris' mother and Mrs. Marantz. No, he wouldn't think about them— tonight he would sleep peacefully, knowing that he was in the clear. Dr. Ferrin said he was going to call the state's attorney's office to quash the case. That would be the end of that. He had all the unpleasantness in back of him now. The wire to Kris' mother informing her of the death of her daughter due to a strep infection had been sent two days ago—he had worded the telegram as tactfully as possible—the body had been shipped west the same day. It would be a blow, naturally, but that couldn't be helped. He had informed her that he had done everything possible—had hired the best doctors, but unfortunately nothing helped. Yes, it would be a blow all right—Kris was her only child, but Meta Dvorak had lived through misfortunes before—her husband had died in a train wreck and she had managed to survive through those dark days. People always find a way to rise above their tragedies....

His thoughts were interrupted by a knock on the door.

"Yes?"

Miss Corbett. "Here's a telegram that just came, doctor."

"Oh. Thank you."

She handed it to him and left. Who was sending him a wire? For a moment he held it, feeling it contained something that he would rather not learn. Finally, with a deep sigh, he tore open the envelope. What Henry read caused him to pale, and his teeth sank once again into his lower lip.

REGRET TO INFORM YOU OF SUDDEN PASSING OF YOUR SISTER META FROM STROKE AS RESULT OF LEARNING DEATH OF KRIS I KNOW THIS IS MORE THAN SHOULD BE ASKED OF ONE PERSON TO ENDURE BUT GOD GIVE YOU STRENGTH IN YOUR HOUR OF TRIAL.

BERTHA DANIELSON

So now she was gone too. That rounded out the Dvorak family. No, people don't always rise above their tragedies. Sometimes things like this happen—like what happened to Felix Marantz. He wasn't able to rise above his tragedy either. He wasn't able to face the shame and disgrace that he had brought upon his family—the possibility of deportation or prison, so he had taken the only means that he knew to prevent having himself and his loved ones shipped back to the Nazi-dominated land from which they had fled. At the moment, Felix Marantz was anything but a coward in the eyes of Henry Mueller. Rather, Henry Mueller felt the insignificance of his own life compared with Marantz' goodness. And he thought of his own selfish existence and the complete uselessness of his life. What had he accomplished? If he had killed himself, no one would have mourned, no one would have missed him. Marantz had left a wife and two daughters, all of whom loved him dearly. They were left alone to face a world that was harsh and unfriendly. Who would support them? Marantz had probably left very little. Their home was still unpaid for. All of this because Henry Mueller had become Dr. Bartok. This entire series of tragic events was of his design! He had begun with the killing of Viktor Bartok. Then came Evelyn Hahn's death, then Kris, then Marantz and now Kris' mother. Yes, he was responsible for the deaths of five people and Kris' unborn child! Quite a parade of faces to haunt him in the darkness of his room—in the delirium of his dreams.

He used to be a sound sleeper; lately he found it difficult to loll off to sleep in the easy carefree manner of times past.

There was a knock once more on the office door.

"Come in."

Miss Corbett entered.

"Pardon me, Dr. Bartok, I got to thinking, after I walked out of here, about Kris' mother. How is she taking all this?"

Henry handed Miss Corbett the wire. She knew that Kris had died of a strep infection, but that was all. She sank into a chair, crying. When she had composed herself, she turned to Henry as she dried her eyes.

"Excuse me, Dr. Bartok—things like this usually don't get me down, but I was so crazy about that kid, and now this has to happen."

"That's life," said Henry philosophically.

"Yes, that's life," she replied. "But some people deserve better breaks, and you're one man who's entitled to them!"

A week later, Henry received a letter from a firm of attorneys on the West Coast stating that he was the sole beneficiary to the estate of the late Mrs. Meta Dvorak, and that one of their representatives would be in Chicago to read him the contents of the will and settle the estate. Strangely, he did not relish this unexpected part of the proceedings. He did not want the money; he did not need it, but whether he did or not, there seemed to be no alternative.

Several days later, a Mr. Seymour Pollock, of the Los Angeles law firm of Coulton, Pollock, Fowler & Harris, called at Dr. Viktor Bartok's office. Henry received Mr. Pollock cordially and together they closeted themselves for the better part of an hour. The attorney read the will to him, and for the first time in his life, Henry found himself reluctant to accept money. He was thinking of Mama Marantz, and the home that was not paid for. He wasn't even listening to the lawyer as he waded through the long legal-sounding document.

"Whereas it is my desire—"

He was thinking of Kris and the money that belonged to her—

"Whereas it is my desire—"

He was thinking of Sara with her long brown braids—

"Whereas it is my desire—"

He was thinking of Rachel with her pale esthetic face and her deep black penetrating eyes—

"Whereas it is my desire—"

He was thinking of Elsa Marantz—*"Thank God we are now over here where we can read about Abraham Lincoln instead of Adolf*

Hitler—"

"Whereas it is my desire—"

He was thinking about Felix Marantz—*"For those we love, Viktor, we do things even at the sacrifice of position, honor, reputation—even life...."*

"I do hereby bequeath my entire estate to my daughter Kristina—"

"Kris, I'm mad about you ... you know that, don't you?"

"—but in the event she should precede me in death ..."

"It's as though you've always been at my side to guide me and inspire me, Uncle Vik—"

"I do hereby bequeath my entire estate and all my worldly possessions—"

"I sat in the Bahá'í Temple, Vik. It made me feel clean and decent and at peace with myself—"

"—to my dear brother Viktor—"

"I prayed for you too, Vik—"

"And that's it. The estate comes to quite a tidy little sum—"

"—because you're the most lost soul of all—"

"In exact figures it comes to eighty-four thousand seven hundred sixty-eight dollars and forty-three cents—"

"I'm answering for my sins now, but you've got to answer for yours too, Vik—"

"You see, Konrad Dvorak carried a hundred-thousand-dollar insurance policy—"

"You've got to live with your conscience too—"

"—so that naturally swelled the estate—"

"You'll have time to think all right—you'll have the rest of your life to think—"

"Now if you'll please sign this paper, doctor—"

"Hm? What did you say?"

"I said if you'll please sign this paper—"

"Oh. Yes, yes ... of course. There you are."

"And our check for $84,768.43 will be mailed to you after the estate's been probated. Doctor, it's been a pleasure meeting you."

Henry shook hands and rose mechanically as the attorney gathered up his briefcase, coat and hat. He stood looking after him as he disappeared behind the closing door. Slowly he lowered himself to the chair and sat staring ahead of him, his eyes lost in a world of past recollections. He recalled the attorney's words:

"Our check for eighty-four thousand seven hundred sixty-eight dollars and forty-three cents will be mailed to you, after the estate's been probated."

Suddenly, from out of the past, the words of another voice floated through the still atmosphere. A voice that had reminded him that there was no escape from one's own destiny, a voice that seemed to echo the plaintive cries of all who had suffered and died through his evil machinations:

"You have the hand of a genius and a conqueror. You have a driving ambition that will not allow you to halt until you have attained the goal you have selected for yourself. Wealth and power will one day be yours. In your efforts to reach the top you will be victorious, but fame and fortune that is ill-gotten, and procured at the sacrifice of self-respect and honor, can bring to its possessor only the feeling of a triumphant emptiness...."

The weeks slipped by and soon another summer had come and gone. Henry thought little of vacations or social activities. He wanted only to work and forget. The harder he worked, the less time he had to think—and thinking was not good. It made him morbid and depressed.

During the rest of the year, he drove himself as he had never before in his life. For the first time since taking over Dr. Bartok's office, Henry began evening hours, seeing three to four patients a night on three evenings a week. On the other nights he surrounded himself with books and plunged into deep psycho-pathological study. He wanted only to improve his mind so that he could administer to the ever-increasing types of nervous disorders of his ever-increasing clientele. He now had patients coming from all parts of the country, recommended to him by doctors in a score of cities. His fame for accomplishing results through psychoanalysis was known to the medical profession, and on more than one occasion he had been described in leading medical journals as possessing the most fertile mind in the neuropsychiatric field. One article in particular revived his dormant ego. It said that "even without a knowledge of medicine, the psycho-analytical mind of Dr. Viktor Bartok would have made itself known and come to the fore. His innate intelligence and vast knowledge of the workings of the human mind would have labelled him as a great and gifted psychologist, although he might have become anything but a doctor. As it is, the medical profession can be proud of having in its ranks the psychiatric genius of Dr. Viktor Emil Bartok."

Plaudits such as that made Henry feel he had done something worthwhile with his life. If he had been a fake, he would have been doomed long before. His practice would have fallen off instead of increasing; the patients would have complained of feeling worse instead of praising his work. He had managed to maintain his record of eighty-per-cent cure or improvement sufficient to dispense with psychiatric services.

During these months of intensive work and study, Henry never once felt the necessity for the companionship of a woman. It was the first time since taking up his role as Dr. Bartok that a woman had been absent from his everyday life, but now it was a welcome respite. On too many occasions women had almost been his undoing and now he wanted neither their love nor their attentions. He realized only too well the disastrous results of feminine entanglements, and he had made an irrevocable vow never again to become involved with a woman. Nor were the times propitious for an *affaire d'amour*; December 7th, 1941—day of infamy—was at hand....

The next twelve months saw the people of an aroused America celebrate the first anniversary of Pearl Harbor with quiet dignity and grim determination. There were no speeches, no parade, no demonstrations. In office and factory the men and women throughout the land went about their daily tasks with a "business as usual" attitude. There was a job to do and Americans were doing it. Already the machinery set up by the draft boards was grinding out soldiers from the steady flow of waiters, cooks, salesmen, clerks, taxi-drivers, actors, musicians, plumbers, carpenters, architects, draftsmen, mechanics, and the thousand-and-one other workers in non-essential jobs. Only if he was vital to war production or home-front existence, was "Civilian Joe" kept from being "G. I. Joe."

On a hot summer day some eight months later, Henry came down to his office. As he entered the reception room, he was greeted by his secretary.

"Good morning, Dr. Bartok."

"Good morning, Miss Corbett."

"Here's your mail, doctor."

"Oh, thank you. I can always tell when the first of the month is here."

Miss Corbett laughed. "Yes, and here I thought it was your popularity."

Henry walked into his office and sat down. First he tore off a sheet from his calendar pad. "Today is July 1st, 1943," it said. Then he looked over his schedule for the day. His first appointment was at 9:30. As he shuffled through the dozen or more letters in the morning mail, his eyes suddenly fell upon a large envelope. In the left-hand upper corner were the words WAR DEPARTMENT, THE SURGEON

GENERAL, WASHINGTON, D. C. Underneath in black type was printed OFFICIAL BUSINESS. Henry pondered for a moment until it suddenly dawned on him what the contents might be. He lost no time in verifying the correctness of his hunch. The letter read:

"Dear Sir:

"The Surgeon General has directed me to inform you that due to the great needs of the Army Medical Corps for all types of specialists in the neurological and psychiatric fields, you are being called up for active duty to serve in the Medical Corps of the Army of the United States in the probable grade of Lieutenant Colonel.

"You will therefore kindly take steps to close your civilian affairs. In the meantime further instructions will be sent you where to apply for your physical examination, pending the approval of your promotion in the above stated grade by the Surgeon General.

"Thanking you for giving this matter your immediate attention, I remain

Yours very respectfully
WILLIAM J. SCHOFIELD
Brig. General
Asst. to the Surgeon General."

So, there it was. He was being called up for active duty as a psychiatrist in the Army Medical Corps. And they were going to jump him from the rank of captain to lieutenant colonel! That was quite a promotion, but it was not unusual for the army to give high ranks to outstanding doctors, and he was one of renown. Lieutenant Colonel Bartok! He liked the sound of his new title. It sounded impressive. In conversation the lieutenant is almost always dropped, and he would be called "Colonel." Colonel Bartok! That certainly was a long way from Henry Mueller, ex-convict No. 147963. Then it dawned on him. The Armed Forces take only men who have no criminal records. No man who has ever been convicted of a felony can wear the uniform of the United States Army or Navy. But as far as the Surgeon General's office was concerned, he was not Henry Mueller, he was Dr. Viktor Bartok, eminent psychiatrist, citizen of the United States, and captain in the Reserve Medical Corps. Luckily, he wouldn't even have to be fingerprinted, as Bartok himself must have gone through that procedure when he applied for a reserve commission in 1938. That was indeed fortunate, as Henry knew that if the army took his fingerprints, they would be sent to the central fingerprint files in Washington, and the F. B. I. would know in a short while that his prints were the same as Henry Mueller, ex-convict! That would be the end of him. No, Henry was quite sure he wouldn't be fingerprinted again. What bothered him most at the moment was the thought of having to give up the profitable practice which he had built up over a period of four years. However, the war would not last forever and some day he could return to his Michigan Avenue office and take up where he had left off.

On the 17th of August, Henry received a notification to appear at the Headquarters of the Sixth Service Command, General Dispensary, where he was to undergo his physical examination. He spent some two and a half hours undergoing examination in every phase of army physical requirements and was told by the examining officer that he was an unusually healthy specimen. To his relief, he was not re-fingerprinted.

"That'll be all, doctor, thank you," the major told him.

"What? Don't I get an opportunity to spend a few moments with the army psychiatrist? I understand that everyone is interviewed by a psychiatrist before the physical is considered complete."

The major laughed. "No, I don't think that'll be necessary, doctor. When two psychiatrists get together, it's difficult to tell who's interviewing who!"

"I see what you mean," chuckled Henry. "Before he got through talking to me, I would probably be telling him that I don't think the army could use him!"

"Exactly," chortled the major. "Either that or he'd probably tell you that you're not Dr. Bartok at all. That you just think you are!"

"Uh ... yes ..." Henry's laugh trickled off weakly.

On September 6th, Henry received the official news of his acceptance in the form of a letter from the Adjutant General's office:

In reply
refer to:
201—Bartok, Viktor E.   O-647963
SUBJECT: Temporary Appointment
TO: Lt. Colonel Viktor E. Bartok, Army of the United States

1. The Secretary of War has directed me to inform you that the President has temporarily appointed and commissioned you in the Army of the United States, effective this date, in the grade shown in the address above. Your serial number is shown after

O above.

2. This commission is to continue in force during the pleasure of the President of the United States for the time being, and for the duration of the present emergency and six months thereafter unless sooner terminated.

3. There is enclosed herewith a form of oath of office which you are requested to execute and return. The execution and return of the required oath of office constitute an acceptance of your appointment. No other evidence of acceptance is required. This letter should be retained by you as evidence of your appointment.

EDWARD F. DELANEY
Adjutant General

He looked at his instructions:

"Lieutenant-Colonel Viktor E. Bartok O-647963

"To report on the 9th of October, 1943, to the Commanding officer at Medical Field Service School, Carlisle Barracks, Pa. approx. six weeks."

Suddenly Henry stiffened. *The last five numbers of his army serial number were the same as his prison number at Mohawk!* And now he was Army Serial No. 0-647963. Was fate playing tricks on him? Out of millions of numbers assigned to soldiers, he had drawn one almost identical to his prison number! He dismissed it from his mind as being purely coincidence. He pushed the button on his desk. Miss Corbett entered.

"Well, it's happened, Miss Corbett! I'm in!"

"Congratulations, doctor. That's wonderful. What is it now, Captain Bartok or Major Bartok?"

Henry smiled smugly. "Lieutenant Colonel Bartok, if you please!"

Miss Corbett whistled. "Ain't that something! Good God, with a rank like that you'll be making life miserable for everybody in the army! I'd sure hate to be a buck private under you!"

"Oh, come now, Miss Corbett—you know I'm not that bad. You make me sound like an awful tyrant."

"No, you're not that bad, doctor. I'm glad you got such a high rank. After all, a man of your reputation is entitled to it. When do you leave?"

"I have to report at Carlisle Barracks, Pennsylvania, on the 9th of October. That's a little over a month. Well, call up all the patients and tell them Uncle Sam wants me to do my psychoanalyzing for him for the duration."

"Oh, dear, Mrs. Feldman will have a fit—and so will Mrs. Moody, and Mr. Crockett, and Miss Becker, and Mrs. Higginbotham will just die without her dear Dr. Bartok to hold her hand and tell her she looks wonderful today!"

Henry snickered. "That's just too bad, but tell them their neuroses are not as important as the ones some of our boys develop from shells bursting around them." As long as he was going in and had no alternative, he might as well sound noble.

"I'm proud of you, Dr. Bartok," said Miss Corbett as she extended her hand.

"Thank you." He took her hand and clasped it warmly.

"And now you know something else, doctor?"

"What, Miss Corbett?"

"When I first started to work for you, I wasn't sure I was going to like you, but now I want to say I think you're one of the finest men I've ever met."

"Oh. Thank you, Miss Corbett. That's very sweet of you to say that. I like you too—and I'll tell you a secret. When you started to work for me, I wasn't too sure I was going to like you either."

"Really?"

"Cross my heart. I thought it was only a question of time before I wound up lying alongside old Dr. Ziegler. You remember him—he was seventy-nine—"

"Going on eighty!" She finished the sentence for him and they both laughed loudly.

The next day Henry began making preparations to draw his civilian affairs to a close. One thing he felt he should do was to make out a will—just in case. He consulted with a lawyer and they drew up a will dividing his $260,000 estate into two parts. Half to the University of Fort Dearborn and the other half to be divided equally between the families of Evelyn Hahn and Felix Marantz. Elsa Marantz was still living with her two daughters in Lowell, Iowa. She had been managing to earn a somewhat meager livelihood. The last he heard she had been employed as librarian at the Lowell Public Library. This position was obtained largely through his own action after Felix's death. He had contacted the library officials and in memory of his good friend and colleague, Dr. Felix Marantz, expressed a desire to endow the institution with a sizable gift. In view of this generosity, he had intimated that he would deeply appreciate any aid they might tender the wife of this dear friend. They offered Elsa Marantz the position of assistant librarian, which she gladly accepted. Henry had taken this roundabout way to make up in some small measure for the cruelty of his deed. He knew he could not go directly to Mama Marantz with an offer of money. He could not face her after the death of her husband—the death which he had caused as much as though he had pulled the trigger of the gun. Besides, she was much too proud to accept money, and anyhow he did not want to answer the questions which she was certain to put to him. He was relieved that she had not sought him out in Chicago to ask questions about the strange death of her husband in relation to his visit to Chicago.

Henry had attempted to salve his conscience further by paying the balance of the mortgage on Marantz's home. This he accomplished by informing the mortgager that he was an old friend of the Marantz family and that he wished to help them in time of need. He gave the man his check for $2,500 and he received the promise that the secret would never be divulged. The cancelled mortgage, signed, and sealed was to be delivered to Mrs. Marantz with the statement that her husband had paid off the indebtedness before his death. The man was to end questions by saying only that Marantz had given him the money and that it had not been his concern how it had been obtained. Thus Henry felt he had ingratiated himself with the God of Love and Forgiveness with whom Kris said she had made peace in the Baha'i Temple, and to whom she had said he too must eventually answer. Thus, by willing part of his estate to the families of those who had suffered his crimes, Henry sought to escape the wraiths which, in the darkness of his room and the limbo of his subconscious mind, sometimes paraded past his bed as he tossed restlessly in broken sleep.

After three weeks of hard work and intensive preparations, Henry began to clean out his office. Everything was to go in storage— apartment furniture, office furniture, books, files, and all. He gathered together whatever papers he thought might be of value to him in the army. He picked up the old briefcase which had belonged to Dr. Bartok, and which he had not handled since his return from Colorado Springs four years ago, when he had locked it in the bottom of his desk. Cleaning out the contents, he once more came across Dr. Bartok's treatise on war neuroses and the suggested cure for shell shock by the narcosynthesis treatment. He had forgotten all about that paper. For over six years that possible cure for suffering mankind had lain there, undisturbed—waiting patiently to be rediscovered. Henry read again the thesis which ended with the phrase: "Let us hope and pray that, here in America, I will never be called upon to perform my experiments on soldiers suffering from psychopathological disorders."

That had been written in 1937 when America was at peace. Now it was 1943 and America was not at peace; soldiers were suffering from psychopathological disorders. Henry sat for a long time pondering over the valuable document. Finally, he put it back in the briefcase along with the other papers he thought he might need. There would be ample time to think about the mental disorders of soldiers after he had seen some. In the meantime, he had an appointment with the military outfitters for his several uniforms, which were to be custom-made.

That afternoon Henry stood looking in the mirror of the military store where he had purchased six hundred dollars' worth of uniforms. On his shoulders were the silver leaves of a lieutenant colonel.

"Fits you like a glove, Colonel," the tailor said proudly.

"Think so?" Henry examined himself admiringly.

"Yes, sir, and everything you ordered will fit you the same way. Would you care to try on the other things? The gabardine topcoat or the winter overcoat?"

"No, thank you. I'll take your word for it. Send the other things out along with my civilian clothes. I'll keep this on."

Henry walked out on the street toward his office, his shoulders back, his head held high. Toward him sauntered an enlisted man who was more interested in the girl by his side than in the struggle of nations locked in a deadly war. At Henry's approach, he straightened up and his hand snapped to his cap in a meticulous salute. Henry smiled and his arm flashed upward in recognition.

Lieutenant Colonel Viktor Bartok had performed his first official act as an officer in the Army of the United States.

CHAPTER TWENTY-FOUR

Henry finished his indoctrination course at the Medical Field Service School at Carlisle Barracks on November 23rd. His orders were to report at Fitzsimons General Hospital at Denver, Colorado, on the 1st of December, which gave him a seven-day leave. New York seemed a likely place to spend his week's vacation. After six weeks of intensive study and training, he wanted to see some life and gaiety. It would be a long time between leaves. He arrived in New York with several other officers who were also going to take advantage of the big city's night life, and checked in at the Admiral.

One of the officers who had gone through the six weeks course at Carlisle with Henry was Captain Livingston, a native New Yorker. He and Henry become friends at Carlisle, and as they parted at the railroad station, they planned to get together before the week was up.

A couple of evenings later, Henry had dinner at Sardi's and managed afterward to get a good seat to see *Oklahoma!* After the show he dropped into the Stork Club and had a few drinks at the bar. The place was jammed with laughing, fun-seeking people trying desperately to escape themselves and the war. Men in uniform, some spending their last furlough in this country before being alerted, were very much in evidence. Henry looked about him at a sea of unfamiliar faces. Suddenly, in a corner, he spied a lone man in a uniform sitting at a table. It looked like—yes it was—Livingston! He drank up the remaining liquor in his glass and edged his way through the throng toward the small table.

"Stan!"

Livingston looked up. "For God's sake! Bartok!" They shook hands and the captain pulled up a chair for Henry. "If this isn't a coincidence! I phoned you at your hotel this evening."

"You did? That must've been after I left."

"Yes. I wanted you to join us this evening."

"Us?"

"My wife and I. She's in the powder room now. Be back in a minute. Gosh, it's good to see you, Vik."

"Same here, Stan. Believe me. I didn't think it was possible to be surrounded by people and still be lonesome, but a moment ago I felt like the lonesomest man on earth."

"I thought you might be. That's why I told my wife we'd have you over for dinner some night this week."

"Oh, that's very nice of you, Stan."

"Not at all. There's always enough for one more. How about Thursday night?"

"Thursday? Fine."

"I'll pick you up at the Admiral at six in my car."

"It's a date, Stan."

"Here comes my baby now." The two men rose as the captain's wife approached the table. "Honey, I have a surprise for you. Of all people, I ran into the colonel right here. Small world. Colonel Bartok, my wife, Mrs. Livingston. Viktor, this is Carlotta. I call her Carlotta the Beautiful."

Henry felt his heart momentarily stop as he gazed into the eyes of his former wife. He could see the color leave her cheeks as she looked at him and nodded. "How do you do, Colonel," she said quietly as her husband seated her.

"It's a pleasure, Mrs. Livingston." Henry did not bat an eyelash, but held his composure and his dignity. She could not know it was he. For one thing, his name was Bartok: he also spoke English with a slight flavor of a European accent, and there was a large scar on his cheek. Henry Mueller had none of those things. Besides, he was now a doctor and a lieutenant colonel in the army. She would never suspect that the man who had walked out on her almost five years before, whom she had called shiftless and a parasite, was the same person who now sat opposite her. Nevertheless, Henry could see she had been startled by the resemblance. Her husband, too, detected the sudden change that came over her.

"What's the matter, dear? You act as though you'd seen a ghost!"

Carlotta forced a smile and rubbed her fingers over her forehead. "If … if you will forgive me, that is exactly what happened. For a moment, thought the colonel was … I mean … looked like someone I used to know …"

Henry nonchalantly lit a cigarette. "Really? In that case Mrs. Livingston, I resent your husband referring to me as a ghost!"

The captain laughed. "Listen, Vik, if you look like someone Carlotta used to know, you can bet your life it's nothing you need resent. My wife knew the nicest people."

"Thank you, darling," said Carlotta, taking her husband's hand in hers. "Colonel, I have the sweetest husband in the world. He never fails to say nice things to me."

"Can you blame me, Vik?" He kissed her fingers. "Wouldn't you do the same if you were married to a beautiful woman like Carlotta?"

"I … I certainly would," said Henry with a feeling of envy. Carlotta looked older, she was now about thirty, but she was also more beautiful than ever. There was a depth to her eyes—a softness and an understanding which radiated the mellowness that comes from having lived happily. Henry could see that now she had found herself —now she was truly happy. He watched as they held hands and gazed adoringly into each other's eyes. "How long have you two … lovebirds been married?"

"It will be three years this Thursday," said Carlotta joyously.

"Thursday?" exclaimed her husband, "That's the night I invited Vik over for dinner."

"Wonderful," she replied, "then you can help us celebrate our anniversary, Colonel."

At this point Henry felt a little like an interloper. "I … I really think you two ought to be by yourselves on that occasion. I can make it some other time."

"Nonsense, Vik." The captain slapped him on the shoulder. "I can't think of anyone I'd rather have at my wedding anniversary. Besides you'll be leaving soon and I want you to meet Terry and Sandra."

"Oh? You have two children?"

"Yep. Terry's my stepson. He's nine, and Sandra's our very own. She's a year and a half."

"And such a pretty little baby, Colonel," said Carlotta.

"I can well imagine, if she looks anything like her mother," replied Henry as he searched her eyes.

Carlotta lowered her gaze in modesty. "Thank you. The colonel is very kind."

"The colonel is also very dry at the moment," laughed Livingston. "Waiter! Another round of drinks. Vik, what'll it be?"

"I'll have some Black Label, please, with a dash of lemon peel."

Carlotta looked up sharply and her eyes froze as the blood once more drained from her face. Henry immediately realized his blunder. *Of course, that was Henry Mueller's favorite drink—the dash of lemon peel his own particular little idiosyncrasy!* How could he have been so stupidly forgetful? He pretended that he did not see her deathlike stare, that nothing unusual had taken place.

"So, Stan, where do you go from here when your leave is up?"

"For the time being I'm to be stationed at England General in Atlantic City. Fortunately, that's not too far away from home. Where do you go?"

"To Fitzsimons General in Denver. I'm looking forward to it. You see, I've never been West."

"You haven't?"

"No," and this was to offset his blunder for Carlotta's benefit. "I haven't had the time. Ever since I came to this country ten years ago I haven't had time to leave Chicago. For two years I was Professor of Neurology at the University of Fort Dearborn, and afterward I went into private practice but still continued at the University on the lecture staff."

"Well, no wonder you haven't seen any of the country. You've been so busy psychoanalyzing people you've forgotten that there's a lot of interesting things in this country to see."

"Yes," replied Henry, "that's right. But I hope to see something of the United States now."

Carlotta turned to her husband. "Did you say … psychoanalyzing?"

"Yes, honey. Vik's a psychiatrist, didn't I tell you?"

"No. That's very interesting," Carlotta said, glancing at Henry curiously. "Psychiatry is delving into the human mind—studying the underlying thoughts of people, is that not right, Colonel?"

"Uh, yes … in essence, that is correct."

"And psychoanalysis is analyzing that which takes place in the person's mind—in other words, being able to figure out the thoughts which are creating a disturbance?"

"I would say, yes—that's a fair interpretation."

Carlotta smiled. "Could you … analyze my thoughts? I mean could you psychoanalyze me at the moment and tell me what I'm thinking."

Henry returned the smile. "Yes. You're thinking of your past and your present. You're thinking how much happier you are now than at any time in your life, and how proud you are to be married to Captain Livingston."

"Thank you, Colonel," Carlotta said quietly. "May I compliment you on possessing such a gifted mind. Your analysis was perfect—almost."

"Almost?"

"Yes. The only other thing that I was thinking is that you don't look like the person I at first thought you did."

"Oh?"

The drinks arrived and Henry raised his glass. "May I drink to the health and happiness of Captain and Mrs. Livingston?"

"Thank you," they both replied.

"And I would like to drink to the colonel," said Carlotta. "An officer … and a gentleman."

The next day Henry packed his bags and left New York. He wasn't sure whether or not the incident of the night before had prompted his sudden departure. Anyhow, he knew definitely that the one thing he did not wish to do was to spend the occasion of his former wife's anniversary in her present husband's home. Then, there was Terry, who had never liked him. Would he recognize or remember him? He did not feel that he wanted to dine with the family group of the woman he had once forsaken. If she was ignorant of the fact that she had spent an hour in the company of the man she had once loved, to whom she had given freely of her devotion and possessions, only to have the one trampled upon and the other accepted greedily, then better to let sleeping dogs lie. Carlotta was happy now. For once Henry felt that he had visited enough misery upon the people who had crossed his path. He did not want Carlotta to suffer any more hurts. Besides, why run an unnecessary risk? Enroute to Denver, he would send a telegram with his apologies and wish them happiness.

He arrived in Denver three days ahead of schedule and registered at the Palace Hotel. He spent the remainder of his leave sightseeing and resting. On the 1st of December, he reported to the adjutant at Fitzsimons General Hospital and was assigned to his office and duties.

His routine from then on was fixed. He was to have periodic interviews with the disabled soldiers, endeavoring to eradicate unhealthy after-thoughts about their experiences and misgivings about their future as civilians in a world that had been quick to praise and would be quicker to forget. Some of those who were aware that their physical handicaps were permanent required skillful daily psychotherapy to prevent their slipping into a mood of self-pity, bitterness, or depressive melancholia. Others were cheerful and very receptive of the physiotherapy, one of the army's important methods of physiological rehabilitation, wherein the soldier patient relearns the use of his arms, his legs, and his hands. Special machines had been devised to teach the recuperating soldier how to use the incapacitated member, and bodies that twenty-five years ago would have been bedridden for months while the injured part slowly and painfully healed were put to use by these devices of modern science. Many men began exercising their limbs forty-eight hours after an operation, an unheard-of procedure in the last war, when, from months of inactivity, the injured organ became inert and stagnant, muscles became atrophied because of long periods of immobility, and many more months of painful efforts were required to bring about restoration to a point of partial usage. Now almost normal function of the disabled part was attained in the same length of time required for healing.

Henry walked through the physiotherapy section and watched the men as they were given whirlpool baths of air, heat, and water, each of which were used to stimulate skin growth. He marveled at the special exercise equipment to develop and restore the inactive muscles. Men were working special pulleys designed for knee and arm joints and a small finger ladder to limber hands.

In another section he found men engaging in occupational therapy which, like physiotherapy, made use of their arms, hands, and legs; but here the disabled soldiers were actually building or making something of use. Here more normal activity had been attained, in so far as the men had a feeling of working at a civilian trade. One was using his legs to operate a bicycle-type jigsaw, and at the same time exercising his ankle and knee joints. Another, was operating a printing press which restored motion to his injured elbows. Still others were engaged in carpentry, leather work, cord knotting, pottery making, wood carving, typing, and using hand tools. He came across one man walking slowly along in the center of a steel walker, a device made of tubular steel which had rollers on the bottom. With this, he was able to walk short distances holding on to the sides, much as a toddling infant learns to walk. The apparatus was equipped with a seat to allow him to rest if he found the strain too much or became tired. Thus science and medicine had combined to deplete the ranks of the wheelchair soldiers who had thought they were sentenced to perpetual helplessness and inactivity.

It was several days later, when Henry was making one of his periodic visits to the wards, that he stopped to chat with one of the bedridden patients who had had both of his legs shattered by a land mine in the North African campaign. Henry had been informed by one of the orthopedic surgeons that Private Caruzzi in Ward 6B was evidencing signs of deep depression and incipient melancholia. Henry approached the bed with a smile and an informal greeting.

"Good morning, Joe."

Joe Caruzzi looked up from his crossword puzzle with a marked lack of cordiality. He knew that Lieutenant Colonel Bartok was the chief psychiatrist in the hospital and that he was going to sit down and make efforts to probe and snoop into his innermost thoughts. He wanted to be left alone—he did not want to be psychoanalyzed as a guinea pig for these army psychiatrists. He was prepared to resent any intrusion into his private self. "Good morning … sir," he replied coldly.

Henry pulled up a chair and took out a pack of cigarettes. "Have one, Joe?"

Joe went back to his crossword puzzle. "No thanks," he said curtly. Henry lit one for himself and sat for a couple of minutes smoking in silence. "What's the word you're stuck on, Joe?"

"Oh … a word beginning with 's' and ending with 't' that means standing still."

"Let's see—I think the word is … stagnant, right, Joe?"

"Yeah, that's it. Fits in perfect. S-T-A-G-N-A-N-T. I should've known. That's me all over—stagnant!" He sat staring at the bed with a look of apathy.

Henry saw that his patient was beginning to open up. "Why? Why do you think you're stagnant, Joe?"

"Why? Because I lay here day after day stagnating, that's why—laying here helpless—useless—working crossword puzzles till I'm blue in the face. When I get tired of crossword puzzles I have my choice of basket weaving or rug making or playing checkers or cards with the other guys who're stagnating up here. It's not much of a future to look forward to when you know your legs are all shot to hell and that you'll never walk again—that you'll spend the rest of your life laying in a bed or sitting in a G.I. wheelchair working on baskets or crossword puzzles!"

"That's not your future, Joe. Wherever did you get that idea?"

"Where? From the fact that that's all I've been doing for nine months now. For nine months I've been on my back weaving baskets or working crossword puzzles that end up with a word like stagnant. That's reason enough, isn't it?"

"Yes, Joe—it's reason enough if you're going to allow your mind to stagnate while your body is inactive. But your mind, Joe, is as active and healthy as it ever was. You see, the chart on your case says: 'leg injuries.' There's nothing on the chart that says your mind was wounded. With your mind, Joe, you can create a lot of things that your legs never could. Your legs only do what your mind tells them to. Your mind is your master, the legs are only the servant. Nobody ever did his thinking with his legs. What did you do before you went into the service, Joe?"

"I was a mechanical draftsman."

Henry thought for a moment. "How would you like to do mechanical drafting now?"

Joe looked up and his eyes brightened. "Are … are you kidding me, sir?"

"No, I'm not kidding you, Joe. Would you like that?"

"Would I? After being here like this for nine months? I'll say I would, sir. A chance to do something really worthwhile again—but where you going to get a drawing board, and a T-square, and all the instruments? The army doesn't go out shopping for little things like that for every guy that wants them...."

Henry got up from his chair. "Don't you worry, Joe. That's my worry. I'll see that you get whatever you need to start doing mechanical drafting. So long, Joe. I'll be seeing you."

Joe smiled. "So long … Colonel."

A few days later Henry took a bus from Aurora, the suburb of Denver where the hospital was located, and went to the downtown section of the city. There, in a large office supply house and with his own money, he purchased a complete set of drafting instruments and a portable table that would fit across the bed and against which Joe could rest the drawing board.

"I want a lot of thumbtacks, and drawing paper, and pens, and pencils, and ink, and whatever else is necessary."

"Yes, sir," said the salesman. "I'll take care of everything for you, sir. And to whom do you want this sent?"

"Here's the name and address. Send it out right away."

"Yes, sir. That's C-A-R-U-Z-Z-I?"

"That's right."

"Do you wish to put in any sort of card as to who the sender is?"

"Yes … put in a card and write on it: 'From Uncle Sam.'"

Within a week's time Joe's happiness over his new-found interest was evident in his complete mental change. He no longer sat listlessly in bed with dull eyes and a feeling of utter uselessness. His moods of depression completely disappeared. He was gay and cheerful, and spent ceaseless hours working over his drawing board. In addition to the instruments, Henry had brought him several reference and text books on mechanical drafting which gave him the opportunity to study up further on his profession.

Henry stopped by Joe's bed several days later on one of his routine inspections through the wards. Joe was sitting propped up, his drawing board stretched across the bed, one of the books open, as he peered into it, apparently puzzled over a mechanical problem.

"Hello, Joe …"

"Oh! Hello, Colonel Bartok." He smiled cordially and appeared eager to receive his visitor.

"How're you coming along?"

"Oh, fine, sir. I'm just trying to figure out a problem here. Gee, these books are a great help. I've found out an awful lot about mechanics that I never knew before." Then he turned to Henry. "Thanks again, sir, for … everything. I know you were the 'Uncle Sam.'"

"Don't thank me, Joe. One of these days I'll be thanking you for giving me an idea."

"What sort of an idea, sir?"

"Oh, an idea on how to make a lot of the boys in here a great deal happier."

Henry took his idea to the Commanding General, Brig. General Forrester.

"I've made a study of the bedridden cases in here, General, and I've talked to most of the boys who are forced to spend all of their time lying in their cots. They're all agreed on one thing—they want to do something worthwhile. I told you about Caruzzi and the psychological stimulus he received from being able to work at his own trade once again. We've got machines for occupational therapy for our ambulatory cases, and those men are materially benefited by being able to exercise their bodies and occupy their time advantageously, but I think we could make some of our bedridden cases a lot happier by adding to the type of occupational therapy we now give them. Along with basket weaving, and leather working, and wood carving, suppose we offered them the opportunity to do a healthy man's job—something that doesn't give them the feeling of being an invalid—that doesn't remind them of their helplessness and inability to perform the kind of work they did as civilians. It's my contention, General, that basket and rug weaving and leather working and wood carving have a psychological tendency to remind the patient of his incapacities—that he's still being treated as an invalid."

"Yes, I see what you mean, Colonel Bartok, but how are you going to go about instituting normal occupational therapy to men who aren't able to leave their beds?"

"By giving them something to do that won't require their leaving their beds. Ninety percent of those men sitting propped up in their cots have their hands free. With their hands they can do many things besides playing games or basket weaving. Give them something to do to make them feel they're still in there fighting—doing their share toward winning the war. With their free hands they can put dozens of little parts together that go into our war weapons. There are all kinds of small fuses, and caps and little gadgets that women put together in war plants. These men could do that here, too, right while they're sitting in bed. They'd welcome it as a relief from the monotony of the card games they play every day, and at the same time they'd have the feeling that they're still in there pitching—"

"Um hm. I think you have something, Colonel—"

"I know I have, sir, because I've talked to the men. As a matter of further stimulus, we could even institute competition among the boys by offering a prize or an honor rating for the wards that turn out the most production every month. In that way the men would take a personal pride in their work."

The general leaned back in his seat. "Colonel Bartok, I think your idea is splendid. I'm all for giving it a try."

"Thank you, sir. If it works out, I think it's something that probably could be attempted in other of our hospitals, because men are the same all over. They must occupy their minds at something. Are you familiar with Blaise Pascal?"

"He was a French philosopher, wasn't he?"

"Yes, sir. He once said, 'nothing gives man more of a feeling of utter futility than complete repose of the mind, without passion, occupation, amusement, care. Then it is that he feels his nothingness, his isolation, his insufficiency, his dependence, his impotence, his emptiness.'" Henry spoke Pascal's words with a feeling that was at once ironic and poignantly sincere.

"You … you seem to be quite familiar with the quotation, Colonel…." The general peered intently at Henry.

"Yes … I also know that feeling that comes over a person from long periods of inactivity."

"Oh, were you once confined to a room yourself?"

"Yes, General, I … I was once confined to a … room myself.…"

It took a month of red tape for Henry's idea to bear fruit, but finally he had the satisfaction of seeing his plan in operation. By early spring, it had definitely taken its place on the list of occupational therapies for bedridden patients. In popularity it replaced the rug weaving, basket making, and wood carving among the convalescent soldiers. The entire staff of physicians noticed the mental change in the men, and unanimously agreed that the psychological effect of working at a healthy man's job, especially one which had a bearing on the war effort, had produced a remarkable degree of self-confidence in the patients.

The plan was not without its disadvantages. The problem of transporting the small mechanical parts that the men worked on to and from the hospital required special handling, but the beneficial results to the patients more than made up for the difficulty of keeping the trucks going and coming. As problems go, this was a small item in the army's vast program of logistics, where millions of tons of supply were transported all over the globe each day. If America's disabled soldiers could be made happier by instituting a new type of occupational therapy, then from the standpoint of army psychology, it was well worth the effort.

On the 21st of April Henry received telegraphic orders of a very secret and important nature. He was to be assigned on a special mission which would be revealed to him within twenty-four hours. The next morning Brigadier General Forrester sent for him and showed him the orders which had just arrived from the Surgeon General's office in Washington. He was to leave Denver immediately by special plane and be flown by the Army Transport Command to Miami, Florida. There he was to change planes for one leaving for Trinidad, thence to Natal, Brazil, where they would stop only long enough for refueling, and then across the South Atlantic via Ascension Island to Accra, on the Gold Coast of Africa, and then on to his destination which was the American Base Hospital at Naples, Italy!

Henry was stunned by the news of his orders. In a few hours he would be on his way to Italy!

"This is a very important mission, Bartok," said the general.

"They've heard about your good work here and are quite satisfied that you're a man of ideas. Besides, they haven't forgotten that you won the Nobel Prize a few years back for one of your scientific discoveries. I can't tell you the nature of this mission, because I don't know myself. You'll find out when you report to General Hartlett in Naples. All I can tell you is that it's something important or they wouldn't be flying you there. I have a lot of confidence in you, Bartok, and I know you're the right man."

"Thank you, sir." Henry smiled awkwardly. "Well, I … I guess I might as well begin to pack up...."

Forrester rose. "Yes. Well goodbye, Colonel, and good luck."

"Thank you, sir." They shook hands, and Henry left the general's office fingering a large white envelope. He walked down the long corridor, lost in thought, a faraway look in his eyes. He paused to reread his orders. Yes, there it was—American Base Hospital, Naples, Italy, on or before the 25th of April, 1944. That was Tuesday—and today was Saturday. Within seventy-two hours he would be in Naples! He put the orders back in the envelope and quickened his step. His plane would be waiting at the airport.

CHAPTER TWENTY-FIVE

Henry slept like the just after his long tiresome journey. The room to which he was assigned in the mayor's residence at Naples was not luxurious—the best ones had been taken by the general staff—but it was comfortably furnished and the bed was better than many he had slept in since entering the army.

At nine the next morning, Henry reported to General Hartlett and was immediately shown into his office.

"Welcome, Colonel," the general said cordially as he rose and extended his hand.

"Thank you, General Hartlett, it's a pleasure to meet you, sir."

"Sit down, Colonel. Have a cigarette?"

"Thank you."

"How was the trip?"

"Very smooth, sir. Had no trouble whatsoever."

"Understand you came from Fitzsimons?"

"Yes, sir."

"How is my good friend Forrester?"

"Excellent, sir. Incidentally, the general sends his regards to you."

"Oh, thanks. Forrester and I used to be together in the Surgeon

General's office. Great fellow."

"Yes, sir. One of the finest."

"Well, Colonel, I suppose you're curious why we sent for you...."

"Rather, sir."

"I cabled Washington a few weeks ago that I wanted a top man here to see what he could do with our N-P cases. We've got quite a few, and I don't want to ship these men back to the States because we need every man we can spare. If it's possible to cure them, I'd like to do it right here, so they can be sent back to the front as quickly as possible. In the last war, shell shock meant the man was off the active list for good. But you know we no longer believe it's necessary to send a man back home as a total loss to himself and the army. However, we haven't been very successful here in finding a method of treatment for these boys. We're developing too many neuropsychiatric cases. They have been on the increase for some time now, and we've got to do something to stem the tide. I cabled the Surgeon General to send me the best man in the Medical Corps to see if he couldn't handle this situation. They cabled me back that they were dispatching you, so I guess that means you're the best in the business."

"Thank you, sir, I'm flattered."

"No need to be, Colonel. I've had a copy of your past record. That's a good enough recommendation for me."

"Thank you, sir. I might say that someone in Washington seems to be a bit psychic in picking me for this assignment. You see, General, it so happens that I've done considerable research in the past on war neuroses. In fact in 1937, during the Spanish Civil War, I wrote a treatise on this very thing that seems to be an army problem right now."

The general's mouth opened in amazement. "No!"

"Yes, General. In fact, I have the treatise with me in my briefcase. I brought it along with me when I left my civilian practice, thinking that sometime in the future I might need it for reference work."

General Hartlett leaned forward with an eager expression. "Let's see it, Colonel, let's see it."

"Yes, sir." Henry opened his briefcase and pulled out Bartok's own theory on a treatment for war neuroses. "Yes, here it is, sir."

Hartlett reached excitedly for the treatise. His eyes widened as the skimmed rapidly through the typewritten document. As he approached the last few paragraphs, he was beaming, and it was evident that he was fascinated by what he had read. He looked up at Henry, "By God, Bartok, this sounds terrific! And you've actually tried this narcosynthesis technique on civilians and had success?"

"Yes, sir." Henry knew that if Bartok wrote that he had treated civilians successfully, he could safely reply in the affirmative. "It's never been attempted on soldiers, but as you can see from my past experiences, these civilian cases so closely resembled army neuropsychiatric symptoms that I have every reason to believe the technique will work on soldiers as well. We have nothing to lose by experimenting anyhow."

"Certainly not, Colonel. By God, Bartok, I'm as pleased as punch. I certainly didn't expect to get action this soon. Imagine cabling Washington and getting the right man the first time!" He chuckled heartily. "That, Colonel, constitutes what is commonly known as a major victory!"

Henry laughed along with the general. "Let's call it a piece of luck, sir. The major victory doesn't come until we've actually cured these men."

"Right! But by God, Colonel, I've got a feeling it's going to work. Not only that, but we might be able to kill two birds with one stone. I see you have a suggested treatment for traumatic neurosis as well as the functional disturbances."

"Yes, sir, I think the combination of the sodium pentothal and the electric sleep will do the trick in traumatic cases."

"Well, we'll give it a try. Anyhow, at the moment, I'm more interested in curing these psychoneurotic cases than anything else. We have far more of those. Men with battle fatigue, war nerves, fear and anxiety reactions, and plain ordinary shell shock—even though the Surgeon General's office says we mustn't use the nasty word. You can dress it up with a fancy name like psychoneurosis, but to me, it's still plain ordinary, garden variety shell shock, like they had in the last war. Words change, but men don't and these boys have the same symptoms as their fathers had in 1918. They go into hysterics, cry on the slightest provocation, tremble at the sound of a plane flying over, and manifest all sorts of hysterical symptoms. Generally speaking, there's not much wrong with them physically, they just have to be rid of their fears, that's all."

"I think this narcosynthesis will do it. While the man is in a synthetic dream state, we can get at the root of his trouble. For the acute cases, the electric sleep."

"It sounds like the best thing yet, Colonel. But damn it, there's not an electric shock machine in Naples. I'll have to cable Washington for a couple right away. They can fly them over."

"It's too bad I didn't know the nature of my mission before I left. I could have brought them along with me."

"Yes, but while we're waiting for the machines to arrive, we can get started on the narcosynthesis treatments."

"Yes, sir. I'll start right in today." Henry rose from the chair. "Is that all, General?"

"Yes, Colonel."

"May I … uh…. have the … treatise back, sir?"

"Oh, yes, yes, of course. May I say that I'm happy that Washington sent you, Colonel Bartok, and also that I have a world of confidence in you and the outcome of this experiment?"

"Thank you, General Hartlett. I shall try to justify that confidence." He started for the door.

"Oh, Colonel!"

Henry turned. "Yes, sir?"

"Do you like good spaghetti and ravioli?"

"Yes, sir, I certainly do."

"I'd like you to be my guest at dinner tonight. I know of a nice little place where the food is good and the wine is heady.…"

Henry smiled. "I'd be delighted, sir."

"Very well. Meet you at six."

"Thank you, sir."

"And by the way, Colonel, I think you'd better take a copy of this with you. After all, you're going to be here in Naples for some time." He handed Henry a small booklet. "I think this'll get you around fairly well."

Henry looked at the cover. It was an Italian guide book, explaining Italian customs and necessary words and phrases for dealing with the people of Naples.

"Thank you, General. This will come in quite handy."

"Yes. I think you'll find it an invaluable aid in going about Naples. And, Colonel—"

"Yes, sir?"

"Just in case you happen to meet a pretty Italian signorina—"

"Yes?"

"Don't bother to look in the book. It isn't in there!"

That night after dining with General Hartlett, Henry sat in his room pondering over the treatise that Bartok had written on war neuroses. It was strange that after all this time the paper should offer a suggestion for combating a problem that had long puzzled army psychiatrists. He had no qualms about his ability to carry out Bartok's narcosynthesis treatment. The procedure used to place the man in a narcosis—in a synthetic dream-state—was not in itself an extraordinary discovery. Henry knew that the same thing could be accomplished with intravenous or intramuscular injections of sodium amytal as well as the sodium pentothal. The test would be in his own ability to probe the soldier's mind after he had been put to sleep. Then everything depended on the psychiatrist's ingenuity in rooting out the disturbing factors in the back of the patient's mind and eradicating the cause of the psychosis. Any doctor could put a patient to sleep— that required no skill. The trick was in being able to apply the proper psychology afterward to bring the patient back to a state of happy normalcy. That was where Henry felt he excelled. He knew he was sufficiently talented to handle his patient properly and accomplish results. He had successfully psychoanalyzed hundreds of people in the last five years. Of course, he was willing to concede that Viktor Bartok had made an important discovery in the narcosynthesis technique, and particularly in the electric sleep method of using electric shock therapy, but he was not overlooking or underestimating his own talents as a psychiatrist in bringing about the final cure. He was sure that the success of Viktor Bartok's discovery lay in his own ability to put it in force. In fact, it was with a feeling of genuine pride that Henry gave to the Army Medical Corps and suffering mankind, *his* treatise on a suggested cure for war neuroses.

With the arrival of two electric shock therapy machines the following week, Henry plunged into serious work on his psychoneurotic cases. The first patient to receive the electric sleep treatment was a Corporal Butler who had survived the African and Sicilian campaigns, but had suddenly gone into hysterical fits and outbursts of weeping during the heavy bombardments of the Salerno beachheads. He was finally brought to the Naples hospital after several unsuccessful attempts had been made to quiet him with sedatives in front-line aid stations. Henry studied the case. When brought into the hospital with a number of other patients suffering from neurotic disorders, he showed signs of a complete mental breakdown. It was an accumulation of strains, both mental and physical, of great intensity—bodily danger, continuous physical exertion, loss of sleep, insufficient and irregular meals, perpetually recurrent bombardment, and the sight of comrades being killed around him.

His clinical picture was the forerunner of those of a number of soldiers to be brought in after him, all surprisingly uniform in symptoms. First, the signs of physical exhaustion—thin, fallen-in faces, pallid or sallow complexions. The expressions and the whole attitude of the body was one either of tension and anxiety or of a listless apathy. In addition there were usually present neurological signs of a functional nature. A coarse irregular tremor of the hands was exceedingly common. Reflexes were usually exaggerated, occasionally sluggish. Mentally the patients complained of the common symptoms of the acute anxiety state: sleeplessness, terrifying bad dreams, a feeling of inner unrest, and a tendency to be startled at the least noise but particularly at the sound of an airplane flying overhead or the backfire of a motor outside the hospital. In the case of the corporal, his hysterical fits would be repeated intermittently throughout the day. On occasions, he would suddenly shoot up in bed, throw his hands over his head and give a series of loud groans. Sometimes he would awaken in the middle of a bad dream in which he saw his buddies being mowed down by machine gun fire, and cry uncontrollably.

Henry started treatment on the sixth of May with thirty-second impulses of electric shock therapy every other day together with intramuscular injections of sodium amytal. In this state of hypnosis, he was able to probe Butler's mind. The corporal talked freely and exposed a deep-rooted feeling of cowardice and guilt regarding an incident at the front when he allowed two of his buddies to be cutdown by a withering fire of machine guns when he could have saved them by calling out at the expense of exposing his own hiding place and subjecting himself to the deadly fire of the guns. Afterward, this feeling of guilt had become an obsession. That, together with the terrific bombardment of the Salerno beachhead, had proved too much for him and he had cracked up completely.

Within one week Henry noticed the change in his condition. The hand tremor diminished in intensity, as did the general attitude of tension. Planes flying over the hospital no longer produced fits of hysteria and weeping. The patient slept better, and his appetite increased. In addition, he talked freely with Henry and seemed anxious to converse. At the end of three weeks of electric shock treatments, he was taken off the machine entirely and Henry continued with the narcosynthesis technique.

At the conclusion of the sixth week, Corporal Butler left the hospital smiling, fifteen pounds heavier than when he had come in, and ready to rejoin his company at the front. Every trace of psychoneurosis had disappeared completely. This rehabilitation was the beginning of Henry's success in curing a vast number of soldiers of neurotic conditions through the electric sleep and narcosynthesis treatments.

As the days wore on, Henry worked untiringly on his patients. Here in this hospital some sixty miles behind the front lines he came face to face with the stark, real picture of war in all of its most horrible and gruesome aspects. Here was the unglamorized, the stripped, unvarnished bleak panorama of suffering humanity as Henry had never conceived it in even his prolific imagination. Each day brought its new cargo of demoralized and dismembered beings that a few hours or a few days ago had been men sound in mind and body. As the fight for the Italian capital became more intensely ferocious, the casualty lists grew in proportion. Henry walked among the cots of men who had lost an arm or a leg, or in some cases, both, and found it difficult to comprehend their apparent cheerfulness. They were not the psychotic cases. Strangely, most of the neuroses were found in men who had very little wrong with them physically. Yet, these were the ones who suffered untold mental agonies and tortures, who required the utmost tact and skill of psychiatric treatment. But Henry felt a deep sense of admiration for these other men who, knowing that they were no longer whole in body, could laugh and joke and smoke with an amazing calm. Their philosophical acceptance of their fate gave him a feeling of inadequacy. It was here, working among men in their misery and their pain, among the blood and the sweat of soldiers and doctors, that Henry came to realize the complete futility of his own life; he comprehended at last his acceptance of false values, his life-long quest for the pot of gold that here was so meaningless, his desire for the fame and the recognition of a world of vanity whose plaudits were as empty as his own existence.

Here was no select, wealthy clientele. Here were only suffering men who were not concerned with whether the doctor attending them had a reputation or belonged to a country club. Most of the time the soldier did not even know the name of the doctor who sewed up his wound or amputated his shattered stump. These were men. Men who sang a song to bolster their courage while a piece of shrapnel was dug out of their flesh, or who cried like children from pain and fear. Here were only men—glad to be lying between white sheets and eating hot food, glad to be away from the muck and the mud and the stench of decayed, rotting flesh, the ear-splitting, brain-hammering din of the battlefield, the cries and the groans of dying men, and the weariness of bodies that were too exhausted to sleep. And they were men who gave Henry a sense of utterly profound emptiness and sheer uselessness; a feeling of shame and degradation that shocked him into realization of his rapacious and egocentric self. It was impossible to live and work among men such as these casualties of battle and go about with any feeling of smug self-importance. Henry found himself undergoing his daily tasks with humility, grateful that he was still sound in mind and body, thankful and willing to help those who were not so fortunate.

The hot summer days dragged on and Henry worked feverishly on the psychoneurotic patients who came in ever increasing number to the Naples hospital. Many were suffering from traumatic neurosis as the result of physical injuries, and he had the opportunity to work out Bartok's theory on them. Some were extremely difficult cases that required expert care and handling, and Henry approached each with a renewed interest. He had been assigned to a job, and he would do it to the best of his ability. Now there were no fees involved, only the satisfaction of seeing accomplishments. Henry labored unceasingly, foregoing sleep, skipping meals, forgetting completely about himself and his own health. By the end of October he had made the remarkable achievement of having cured all but two of the soldiers who had entered the hospital with psychoneuroses. These two men had been found to be suffering from organic conditions as well as the functional psychosis and were shipped back to the United States for discharge. Henry himself was pale and thin, but he never considered rest if there was still a patient to be seen or a new theory to be examined.

It was then that he was summoned to the office of Brigadier General Bartlett. The general was fingering a white piece of paper as Henry entered. He rose and greeted his visitor.

"Good afternoon, sir," Henry said cheerfully.

"Good afternoon … Colonel." Hartlett sat down in his chair. "Colonel Bartok, you've been here six months now, and you've done a very creditable job for the Army Medical Corps....."

"Thank you, sir."

"Everything that you said your narcosynthesis technique would do, it has done. Along with your idea of using electric shock therapy, it has proved to be the most successful treatment ever devised for psychoneuroses. You've cured dozens of men brought into this hospital as total mental wrecks, and by your efforts and patience sent them back to the front in a healthy frame of mind and made them once more efficient fighting men. This salvaging of human material that would otherwise have been a total loss has been a gigantic step in the progress of mankind and medicine." The general sat back, puffing slightly from the effort of the speech.

"Thank you, sir," Henry replied with a feeling of genuine modesty.

"Your government is proud of your work, Colonel, and in appreciation of your ceaseless efforts to restore these men to health,

I received this communication from Washington today. I'm happy to inform you that you have been promoted in rank and that you may now wear the eagle insignia of a full colonel."

Henry was completely surprised. He had thought nothing about promotions or honors. He had been too absorbed in his work to think in terms of himself.

"I'm pleased beyond words, sir," Henry said quietly.

"Not only that, Colonel, but I personally have recommended you for the Legion of Merit for your service to your country. I'm sure the Secretary of War will approve the citation."

Henry swallowed the lump in his throat. "Thank you, sir … that's very kind…."

"Not at all. You deserve it, Bartok. You've earned recognition from your country. I've watched you work since you came here. Half the time you've gone without sleep to help these men. In psychoneurotic cases, medicine and machines can only do so much. Nothing can supplant the human element. I realize this narcosynthesis technique and the shock machine were important steps in combating these cases of neurotics, but I still feel that half its success is due to the genius of your mind, Colonel, in knowing how to handle these men and probe into their innermost thoughts. No machine can do that. You were born with a gifted brain, Colonel Bartok. A brain that God gave you and ordained to be used to benefit your fellow men and relieve him of his mental ills. Maybe someone else wouldn't understand my philosophy, but I believe that certain gifts are ordained by God!"

Henry straightened up in the chair and his eyes opened wide in a seemingly fixed stare into space. *No, he was not a fake, he was a great doctor in his own right!* The words came from General Hartlett, a man high in the ranks of the Army Medical Corps—one of the few doctors in the army to reach top rank. He had just been told he was a great doctor, ordained by God to administer to the ills of suffering mankind!

"Thank you, General," Henry answered softly.

"After this war is over, Colonel," continued Hartlett, "Your great work should continue with this particular type of psychiatric disorder. The world will need men like you. Literally thousands of people who cannot afford your services will need them. Men in government hospitals, people in mental institutions, people who through your efforts and your gift can be rehabilitated and made useful citizens once more. Forgive me, Colonel, for mentioning these things, and I know that it's a deviation from the professional standards for one doctor to advocate or suggest what another physician should do in his private practice, but I'm so proud of you, Colonel Bartok, that I'm willing to chance being considered unethical to bring out the moral and spiritual aspects of this discussion." He looked down at his desk, then at Henry again, "You see, I'm an idealist, Colonel, and I'm quite sure you are too. I have a strong conviction that Divine Providence has guided you, and that this is the type of work that has been cut out for you. I've often heard it said that only the rich can afford to be sick, and that only the extremely rich can afford to be psychoanalyzed. I'd like to see you, Colonel Bartok, after you leave the army, refute that statement. There's a world full of the mentally sick, the frustrated, the helpless, waiting for you after your country has said to you, 'well done!' You have a mission in life, Colonel. You are destined to be one of the great doctors of the twentieth century!"

"Thank you, sir." Henry's voice was scarcely audible as he rose from his chair and saluted the general. He walked from the office scarcely conscious that he did so. He passed nurses and orderlies and doctors and patients, but saw none of them. He had suddenly been transcended into the nebula of a new world, a new self.

Henry walked upstairs to his small room and sat dazedly upon the edge of his bed. He sat there, his mind whirling, the words of General Hartlett echoing and re-echoing through the caverns of his turbulent brain. He sat there, unaware that the shortening day had given way to the twilight of evening. Soon darkness came and the Italian night descended over the war-torn city of Naples. Henry fell back on the pillow, and a cloak of satisfaction spread over him such as he had never before known. He folded his hands behind his head and lay there with a feeling of beatific bliss. Slowly he was overcome with a profound sense of worship—self-worship that caused him to think once more of his achievements and his goal. Could it have been that his goal, his destiny, was as a savior and a healer? Yes, of course that was it! If he did not have curative powers, he could not have accomplished the unbelievable. But now it was understandable. He, Henry Mueller, the ignominious Henry Mueller, who was once not good enough to be admitted to Phi Tau fraternity, was destined to be one of the great doctors of the twentieth century!

He had always wanted to be a great doctor. His mother and father had always hoped he would be one. At last he was beginning to achieve it. The general had recommended him for the Legion of Merit. He had earned the eagles of a full colonel, and soon he would be wearing the ribbon of an honor award for having served his country and his fellow man. Yes, Henry Mueller had come a long way. Henry Mueller was at long last beginning to achieve the fame he had always sought. Fame in his own right as a doctor. He might have stolen the treatise on war neuroses from Bartok; the narcosynthesis technique was not his own idea, but he had perfected it. Machines and medicine can only do so much. General Hartlett had said that himself. It was his own genius that brought about the cures of these men. Half the victory belonged to Henry Mueller. Henry Mueller was the one who was destined to be one of the great doctors of the twentieth cent—

Suddenly the truth hit him with the force of a landslide, crushing him with full realization: *Henry Mueller was non-existent.* He was Viktor Bartok and he would always be Viktor Bartok. As Viktor Bartok he had won the fame he had always sought for Henry Mueller. He had achieved nothing in his own name. As Henry Mueller he could not practice as a psychiatrist. *Henry Mueller was nobody—a nonentity.* To whatever heights he would climb, it would be as Viktor Bartok! Viktor Bartok had won the eagles of a full colonel. Viktor Bartok had been recommended for the Legion of Merit. The man that he had killed lived on to rob him of *his* glory—*his* achievements—*his* success—*his* fame—*his* entire identity. He had done away with Viktor Bartok, but ironically Viktor Bartok had also taken the life of Henry Mueller. The dead had had the last laugh! Viktor Bartok was laughing uproariously from the depths of his watery grave! He could well laugh. His name was being perpetuated—his work was being carried on—he was achieving recognition from his adopted country for his contributions to medical science.

It was *Bartok* who would be hailed as one of the great doctors of the twentieth century! It was *Bartok* who would be cited for distinguished service! Henry Mueller must remain forever the ghost of Viktor Bartok. Henry Mueller was the slave—he would be doing all the work and Bartok would get all the glory! He was chained for the rest of his days to a corpse that would laugh derisively at all of his future accomplishments—accomplishments that could have only the hollow ring of an empty triumph. *Empty triumph!* He had heard those words somewhere before … Yes, he knew—it was long ago, and from out of the past came the haunting words of Shandru to remind him of his destiny: *"In your efforts to reach the top, you will be victorious, but fame and fortune that is ill-gotten and procured at the sacrifice of self-respect and honor can bring to its possessor only the feeling of a triumphant emptiness...."*

CHAPTER TWENTY-SIX

On the gray, foggy morning of Saturday, December 16, 1944, Field Marshal Karl Gerd von Rundstedt launched his stinging counterattack against the American First and Third Armies and pushed his armored divisions fifty miles into Belgium before they were finally halted. Behind them on the frozen muddy ground lay the bodies of men who died with knives clenched in their fists, having run out of ammunition. In American base hospitals throughout France and Belgium, the wards were piling up with all forms of casualties. On Christmas Day Brig. General Simon Hartlett received a communication from Lt. General Alexander Swift, ordering that Colonel Bartok be sent immediately to the American base hospital in Antwerp, since there were battle casualties with psychiatric disorders who required his immediate supervision. He was to be in complete charge of all psychoneurotic casualties on the western front.

After a brief conversation in which Hartlett gave him final instructions and wished him well, Henry departed from Naples the following day in a fast bomber for the 860-mile flight to Antwerp. Less than three hours after leaving the Naples airfield, the speedy Douglas A-26 attack bomber circled a small field outside Antwerp and landed on a soggy airstrip.

Henry was taken by jeep to the American hospital and then reported to General Swift at military headquarters. The next day he took over duties as chief of the psychiatric ward. He found the cases there similar to the Italian campaign casualties in the Naples hospital.

They were the psychoneurotic results of Von Rundstedt's surprising and devastating blitz attack which had caught the tired American forces completely by surprise and without adequate supplies to repel the twenty fresh divisions of fanatical young Germans, spearheaded by 75-ton King Tiger tanks and sworn to die for their Fuehrer rather than allow one allied soldier to set foot across the Rhine.

There was no celebration of the new year as the men attached to the American Base Hospital at Antwerp worked throughout the day and night on the endless stream of casualties that came in on foot and on litters. One man who was ranting and crying hysterically on his cot, suddenly broke into a wild frenzy of shouts and groans as a squadron of British planes flew low over the blackened town. Henry, who was standing nearby, ran to the cot in an effort to soothe the soldier, who was completely out of control. Seeing that it was impossible to subdue or calm the man's violence alone, Henry called to an orderly who was working on a patient several beds away.

"Yes, sir. Coming, sir," he answered quickly.

As the orderly approached the cot where Henry struggled with the hysterical soldier, Henry noticed that he had stopped a few feet away and was staring at him with mouth open.

"Well, come, soldier, give me a hand here," Henry called to him, "what are you standing there …" His words were cut as though by a knife, and a cold chill raced up and down his spine. *It was Turk!* In a flash Henry had recovered from the unexpected shock. "Well, dammit, soldier, don't stand there like a statue, help me with this man!"

"Yes … sir." Turk swallowed and came forward, his eyes ready to pop out of his head. "Hold him down by the arms while I give him a hypo," Henry commanded.

"Yes, sir."

A hypodermic injection of morphine was given to the pinioned arm of the patient and within a few minutes Turk was able to release his firm grip as the soldier fell into an exhausted sleep. "Thank you, orderly, that will do for now," Henry said curtly.

"Yes, sir," Turk answered, still looking completely dazed.

Henry turned on his heels and walked away, leaving Turk standing there frozen in a state of bewilderment and uncertainty. Henry walked upstairs to the small room he had been assigned and sat down. *So, it was a small world after all! Christ! He had traveled half way around the earth and then been assigned to the same hospital where Turk was stationed as an orderly!* He was sure Turk had recognized him; he had stared at him as though he had. Or maybe he had just been struck by the resemblance and decided it was the real Dr. Bartok. Turk would not think it humanly possible for his old pal Henry Mueller to be wearing the eagle insignia of a full colonel in the Medical Corps and be in charge of all the neuropsychiatric cases on the western front! Then, too, he still spoke with the slight foreign accent and had the large scar on his cheek. Would none of these things be sufficient to fool the man with whom he had lived and roamed the country for three years? But, Henry began to wonder why he had pretended he did not know Turk. It was part of his defense, he decided. It was part of his fear of being associated in any way with the past that he had relinquished. Fear of having anyone share his secret—even his old pal Turk. He trusted no one. He had come a long way and there was no sense in chancing anything at this stage of the game, not even for an old friend like Turk. Yet, it was good seeing an old-time pal, a familiar face. It would be nice to sit down and reminisce, to talk over the old days. But that would mean he would have to explain to Turk that he had actually gone ahead with his plan to do away with Bartok, and he remembered Turk had told him that if he was contemplating cold-blooded murder, he wanted nothing to do with him. All right, that was still okay with him. He would continue to go his way and Turk his. It was just as well. Officers and enlisted men are not supposed to fraternize anyway. Then it came back to him again as on that night in Naples. It wasn't he who had come a long way, it was Bartok! Maybe Turk was only a buck private, but he had something that Henry didn't have, and that was his own name and identity. Yes, Turk was richer than he. Turk probably would not change places with him for anything in the world. Henry was tired of this masquerade, of this living of another man's life. He wanted to be free of the corpse to which he was chained—a corpse that had never died and which laughed at him—which mocked him and derided him at every opportunity. It was clear now that Bartok had never died, because wherever Henry Mueller went, whatever he did, it was as Viktor Bartok. Bartok would always rob him of his identity, his work, his achievements, his glory! The phantom followed everywhere—even to his room. He was laughing at Henry even now. Henry could hear Bartok laughing in this very room—jeering at him, laughing uproariously. Why didn't Bartok stop? Why must he follow everywhere and laugh, laugh, laugh! But the laughing did not stop, it increased, it grew louder and louder, filling the room and bursting his eardrums. He threw himself down upon the bed and tried to bury his head in the pillow, but that grisly laughter would not let him sleep. He tossed deliriously from side to side, always the leering, taunting face of Viktor Bartok before him. Then it dawned on him! He had quieted the hysterical soldier with a shot of morphine, why wouldn't it work for him too? Of course it would! In that way he'd be able to sleep; sleep and forget Viktor Bartok. He went downstairs and returned with a hypodermic syringe and a quantity of morphine. In a little while, the hypnotic powers of the potent drug had taken effect, and for the time being, the laughing corpse of Viktor Bartok returned to the silence of his murky tomb.

Henry awoke from his deep slumber the next morning and tried vainly to pull himself out of his lethargy. Throughout the day, his mind seemed sluggish and slow to respond with its usual alertness. His efforts to work on the psychotic cases met with little response and he had a feeling of frustration. Several times he passed Turk in the corridors, but he held his head high and made no attempt at recognition or even casual friendliness. That night, as he threw himself, weary and distraught upon his bed, the fateful vision once more returned to remind him that there was no peace of mind or rest for Henry Mueller. The laughing, taunting, vision of Bartok was ever present. Only a soothing, grateful shot of morphine would allow peace and sleep to comfort him. Soon the narcotic carried him off to a land of beauty and tranquility, a land where dwelt the Kingdom of the Great, and there, in a many-towered castle, he ruled. He was king and master of all he surveyed, and his court paid him homage, and bowed and fawned over him. His subjects likewise did his bidding and as he passed among them they fell upon their knees in abject humility. In his travels throughout the land, he stopped at an inn, and the keeper served him food and drink. He lifted the goblet of deep red wine but as he drew it to his lips, he saw the sparkling liquid was *human blood*, and glancing at the food, he became aware that it crawled with *maggots*. He ran from the inn and made his way back to the castle, but where the castle had stood was now only a deep abyss, black and bottomless. He tried to flee from its brink, but suddenly he found that he was engulfed in immobilizing chains. He cried out against the chains as they began to draw him toward the edge of the chasm, but only laughter met his ears. Loud laughter that he had heard before! Slowly, slowly the chains dragged at him, and the laughter grew louder. He was going over the side now—one more second and he was over—hurtling through space—twisting and turning—over and over, falling and falling, while from the depths of the abyss came the loud laughter echoing from the very bowels of the earth!

Henry awoke from his delirious sleep with a cry, his heart palpitating. Cold sweat drenched his body and his mouth was parched from the effects of the morphine. He tried to go back to sleep but his mind was a chaos of violent and disturbing thoughts that would allow no relaxation, and he tossed restlessly until daylight came. As dawn broke over the cold gray January sky, Henry dragged himself feebly from the bed, and with a pounding head that seemed on the bursting point, managed to get himself dressed for his daily duties.

That afternoon, one of the doctors, Major Gibbs, noticed that Henry was acting peculiarly and going about his work in a seeming daze. He called the matter to the attention of another doctor, Captain Sloan, who concurred with his opinion that Bartok looked sick. They noticed the deep, dark circles under his eyes, the sallowness of his skin, and the almost drunken movements of his body.

By the end of the week, Henry found, to his distraction, that each night his room held terrifying apparitions, and that his only escape was increasingly larger doses of morphine to carry him off to sleep. Soon he discovered that his days required the stimulant as well as his nights, and before long his appearance took on the very aspects of the psychoneurotic patients on whom he was attempting to work. Each day that passed, his peculiar actions were noted by one or another of the doctors or nurses, and finally Henry's strange behavior became a matter of discussion and concern to those about him. When he was questioned, Henry's troubled eyes took on a suspicious expression and his defenses sprang into immediate action. Instead of a smile or a pleasant response, he would snap at his inquirer, "Of course I'm all right, what makes you think I'm not. This attitude toward his fellow officers did not help matters. Turk too, noticed the gradual decline in Colonel Bartok's appearance. On one occasion, as Henry barked antagonistically at one of the nurses for being tardy in summing up one of her reports, Turk thought he detected a tone of cruelty in the voice of Viktor Bartok which, despite its foreign accent, reminded him of the voice of another man who long ago had seized him by the throat and almost snuffed out his life.

Then it broke—a rumor that spread throughout the hospital. *Colonel Bartok was cracking up*—overwork—strain—mental fatigue—war nerves. Two nurses swore they had seen Colonel Bartok slip morphine into his pocket from the hospital vault, an orderly had found a hypodermic syringe in his room when cleaning up. In spite of all this, Henry worked night and day on his patients and paid little attention to his observers, who could see the day-by-day disintegration of their chief psychiatrist.

Soon the rumors reached the ears of General Swift who conferred with several of the doctors in the hospital. All agreed unanimously that Colonel Bartok was an N-P case.

"In my opinion, General, Colonel Bartok is as much a neuropsychiatric as any of his patients," said Major Gibbs. "I've observed his actions for two weeks now, and I would say that at times he's definitely irrational."

"Is that your opinion too, Captain?"

"Yes, sir," replied Sloan. "There's no question about it. He's in a state of narcosis half the time from morphine. He's been working eighteen to twenty hours a day for months and I believe he should be given a rest before he cracks up completely."

"Thank you, gentlemen."

The next day, General Swift summoned Henry to his headquarters. He was surprised at how haggard Henry had grown since reporting four weeks before. He tried to be as tactful as possible.

"Colonel Bartok, you've been working quite hard since you landed over in the European Theater of Operations last April. For nine months now, you've worked night and day on these battle casualties, and I think you've earned a well-deserved rest."

Henry did not quite know how to accept the general's statement. It had a suspicious ring, like the actions of all the others who worked around him. For days Henry had been aware that whispering and plotting were going on behind his back. He was surrounded by people who were jealous of him. Jealous of his rank and authority. He was in charge of all the N-P cases on the Western Front and nobody was going to take that job from him. It was his: he had earned it; worked for it!

"I … don't think I follow you, General. I only arrived here a little over a month ago. You sent for me. The hospital is full of NT cases. These men need me. I'm not asking for any leave. I don't want any leave."

"I appreciate your attitude, Colonel, and it's very admirable of you to want to stay here and work, but I really think you deserve a nice long vacation back in the States."

"The States? You mean you want to send me back to the States? That means I'm being relieved! I see it now. You think I'm not fit to work on these men—that I'm sick—that there's something wrong with me! There's nothing wrong with me—they're all plotting against me—it's politics—they want to get my job, want to get credit themselves for my narcosynthesis treatment! It's mine. I perfected it—I cured all those men in Naples. General Hartlett knows that. Ask him!"

General Swift remained calm and made an effort to placate his irrational visitor. "Of course, Colonel, we know all that. I'm fully cognizant of your accomplishments in Naples. If I weren't, I wouldn't have sent for you. But that has nothing to do with the present situation. We're still of the impression that you've worked too hard and are deserving of a long vacation."

"Long vacation!" Henry sneered. "Why don't you come right out with it and say you're sending me back because you think I'm slipping! Well, I'm not. I'm just as good as I ever was! I won't go back to the States! My duty is here with these men—they need me. I gave the army something they never had before! General Hartlett recommended me for the Legion of Merit. Besides, he told me I was one of the great doctors of the twentieth century!"

Swift's patience had reached an end. He rose from the chair and his eyes blazed. "Colonel Bartok! General Hartlett is not in command of this area! We will have no further discussion on the subject. You will pack your bags and prepare to return to the States. You will receive your orders when to leave."

"I won't go back!" Henry shouted defiantly. "I won't go back! *God has ordained me to cure those men!*"

The last statement was sufficient to convince General Swift that Colonel Bartok was definitely a psychotic case himself; he walked to the office door and opened it. "Sergeant!" he called to his aide.

"Yes, sir!"

"You will escort Colonel Bartok to his quarters, and if necessary, you will call the Military Police!"

"Yes, sir." The sergeant gestured to Henry, who walked contemptuously from the room.

That night, Henry paced up and clown in his small room, tortured by a variety of taunting thoughts. He was being relieved of his duties—sent back to the United States as a psychotic case himself! They weren't fooling him—this was no vacation. He would he sent back and discharged from the army as unfit for military service; branded as neuropsychiatric! What an ironic stroke of fate! He, who had done so much to cure others of their mental illnesses was mentally ill himself. At least he was as far as the army was concerned. He knew differently. He wasn't mentally ill. It was just that Bartok had a habit of visiting him each night and laughing at him and wouldn't let him sleep. Then there was Turk. Turk knew he wasn't Bartok. Turk would be around soon and.... Yes, he would get Turk transferred; that's what he would do. No, no. He had been relieved of his command and he couldn't order anyone around. Oh! God, if he could only sleep. Yes a little shot of morphine in the arm would make him sleep beautifully, make him forget. That's what he needed now. He was tired and weary. He opened the drawer, but the hypodermic syringe was gone! Somebody had taken it! He decided to go downstairs and get another. He walked to the door and opened it. A sentry was posted there!

"What're you doing here?" Henry demanded.

"You've been confined to your quarters, sir. General Swift's orders, sir."

"But I ... I want to go downstairs for something. I ... forgot it this afternoon...."

"Sorry, sir. Orders."

Henry slammed the door shut and threw himself down on the bed. Confined to quarters! They were treating him like a criminal! He,

Colonel Viktor Bartok, the noted psychiatrist who had given to the army medical corps the narcosynthesis treatment for war neuroses; who had been recommended for the Legion of Merit, was being treated like a cheap ordinary criminal!

"Well, aren't you?" The voice came out of nowhere and Henry looked up, startled and trembling. It was a voice that was very much like his own. One that had a slight accent. He knew that voice. It belonged to Viktor Bartok. Bartok was returning to taunt him again. *Noted Psychiatrist!* Legion of Merit! "These things belong to me," the voice said deridingly, "along with the narcosynthesis treatment that you told everyone was yours! No, those things are all mine. The only way they would belong to you is for you to be Henry Mueller—to tell the world that you're Henry Mueller and not Viktor Bartok. But you wouldn't do that, would you? No, of course not. That would mean giving yourself up—confessing that you murdered Viktor Bartok, and then all your little castles would fade into thin air—all the fame you have acquired would be meaningless, and you would face the electric chair. Of course, your fame is meaningless anyway, you know that, don't you? Whether you give yourself up or not, *I'll still be the one to get all the credit for whatever you've accomplished. You can't win! YOU CAN'T WIN!*" The taunting voice began to laugh. It was the same jeering, tantalizing laugh that he had heard so often before. If only he had some soothing morphine, he could banish the face and laughter of Viktor Bartok. They always disappeared like magic a few minutes after he took the shot. But now he had none and Bartok was there— he could see him plainly by the window, leering at him and goading him on. If he could only get at him to crush him and silence that laughter once and for all. He found himself rising from the bed and walking toward the window where the mocking, sneering figure of Bartok stood framed in the casement. He walked slowly, deliberately, menacingly, toward the guffawing specter of the man who would allow him no peace of mind. As he drew closer, his outstretched hands twitching to clasp themselves around the throat of his nemesis and silence it once and for all, the laughter suddenly grew louder and the face more taunting. Henry's teeth were gnashed together in a viselike grip and his eyes were the glassy, distorted eyes of a man in the throes of hate, fury, vengeance, murder … insanity! Henry sprang at the laughing, derisive apparition in a powerful lunge that sent him hurtling through the window to the street below.

A thin stream of blood coursed unevenly between the cobblestones, and Henry Mueller's crumpled body lay in stillness where it had fallen.

The crash of broken glass was heard simultaneously by the sentry outside Henry's door and another posted outside the hospital. They rushed to the spot where he lay, and a moment later Henry was being carried on a stretcher to the first-aid room. They laid his broken and bleeding body on a table and attempted to stop the flow of blood from his head injuries. Then he was taken to a small private room and there one of the doctors gave him an injection of the precious morphine, which a few minutes before he had craved so intensely. This time, it was used to kill the excruciating pain of his shattered bones and internal injuries.

Henry remained unconscious most of the night, but toward dawn his eyes fluttered open and his lips began to move. A few moments later, a nurse was seen to leave the room hastily. She encountered Major Gibbs in the corridor on the way to the room.

"He's conscious now, Major," she said quietly, "but seems to be very low. He's calling for someone, sir."

"Let's go in," he replied quickly.

They returned to the room and from the anguished look on Henry's face, Gibbs could see that he was in pain.

"Give him another morphine injection … a quarter grain."

"Yes, sir."

"Turk … Turk … Turk …" Henry called faintly.

"That's who he's been calling, Major. Turk."

"Turk. Who can that be?"

"The only person I can think of, sir, is a Private Turkel. He's an orderly here. Everyone calls him Turk for short. Do you think it's possible the colonel could mean him?"

"It's possible," said Gibbs with a puzzled expression, "but I can't understand why he'd be calling for him. I'll see if I can get the colonel to tell me. Are you through with that injection?"

"Yes, sir."

Gibbs stepped up close and leaned over Henry, who still called weakly for Turk. "Colonel Bartok, this is Major Gibbs. Do you hear me, Colonel?"

"Yes," Henry gasped. "Hear you … Want Turk. Get Turk."

"Turk who? Do you mean Private Turkel, the orderly?"

"Yes … Turk … Order … ly … want … to … see … Turk … alone … don't … want … to … die … with … out … Turk."

"Nurse, bring Turkel here immediately," Gibbs directed.

"Yes, Major."

She left the room hurriedly, and Gibbs stood at Henry's bedside looking down with a mixed feeling of compassion and wonder at this man who was hailed by every doctor in the medical corps as one of the most brilliant minds of the generation—a man who had risen to the heights and then fallen apart completely, a victim of the very thing he had so successfully cured in others. Now he lay broken and dying, a suicide from psychoneurosis and morphine! Gibbs stood there shaking his head and trying to decipher the reason back of Bartok's mental crackup. War nerves? Physical and mental strain? Fatigue? Worry and fear? He pondered in silence the problem of what had so suddenly snapped in the colonel's brain since his arrival a short month ago. When the colonel had reported to take charge the day after Christmas, he had seemed to be in good mental and physical condition. Now, it was only a question of hours or perhaps even minutes before he would breathe his last. And in view of his fearful injuries, the death that seemed so imminent would be merciful.

In a few moments the nurse returned with Turk, who entered the room looking bewildered and awkward.

"I … just heard about the colonel, sir," Turk said haltingly. "I … uh … I'm awfully sorry." His confusion over his summons to the room was written on his face.

"The colonel has requested to see you, Turkel. We'll leave you alone. Come, nurse. We'll be right outside. And, Turkel …"

"Yes, Major?"

"Don't talk to him too much if you can help it. He's pretty weak."

"Yes, sir."

The door closed and Turk stood there, perplexed and frightened. He made his way over to the bed and as he approached, the face turned toward him and a faint half-smile appeared on the lips.

"Hello, Turk…." came the whisper.

"Hello … Henry," replied Turk with a grin, feeling more at ease.

"You … knew … it … was … me … all … along … didn't you … Turk….?"

"I was pretty sure, Henry, but you had me fooled the first couple of days. 'Course, you froze me like a hunk of ice right from the beginning, so I figured with them chickens on your shoulders you didn't want to take up with the common people, so I just minded my own business from then on."

"I … apologize … Turk … I … wasn't … trying … to give … you … the … go-by … I … was … just … afraid … to … have … anyone … know … my … secret … that's … all."

Turk pulled up a chair. "Why did you do it, Henry? I mean, why did you want to kill yourself?"

"I ... guess ... I ... kind of ... lost my ... head ... Turk. Ever since ... I ... came to this ... hospital ... my ... mind has ... been playing ... tricks ... on ... me ... Bartok's been ... catching ... up ... with me ... I ... I'm ... all ...washed up ... Turk."

"So you really went ahead and knocked him off, huh?"

Henry was now breathing with difficulty and his face showed that his life was drawing to a close. "Yes ... Turk ... I ... killed ... him ... and I've ... been ... living a ... lie ... for ... six ... years ... living ... a ... masquerade."

"So it was you who became the great Doctor Bartok and cured all those soldiers, and got to be a colonel? I don't know how you did it, Henry, but you sure climbed up there. Well, you always wanted to amount to something, Henry. You always wanted to be important and famous, and you did. I guess you got to be just about as famous as anybody in this war. And you did good, Henry. You cured a lot of guys and sent them back healthy and fighting. You can be proud, Henry. You did a lot of good for your country."

"Yes ... Turk .... I ... did a lot ... of good ... but ... I've done ... a lot of ... bad ... too ... a lot ... of people ... suffered ... through me ... I killed ... a ... man and ... four others ... died ... on ... account ... of me ... just as ... much ... as if ... I ... killed them ... myself ... I always ... wanted to ... be somebody ... im ... portant ... but ... I ... have ... nothing ... now ... because ... Bartok ... gets ... all ... the glory ... I stole ... the cure ... from him ... Turk ... it ... was ... his. Henry Mueller ... is nothing ... Turk ... nothing ... when ... they bury... me ... I ... don't ... even ... get ... my ... name ... on ... the grave. Bartok ... wins ... there ... too. He ... gets ... a... decent ... burial ... after ... all ... Henry Mueller ... the ... smart guy ... ends ... up ... with ... nothing."

"I know what you've done, Henry, and you'll always be a great guy in my book—a guy who went places—and did a lot of good."

"Thanks ... Turk ... you're ... one in a million ... yourself. You always ... did overlook ... my faults. You're the ... only real ... friend ... I ever had ... and I ... kicked you ... around too."

"Aw, that's all right, Henry," Turk answered with an affectionate smile, "I never held it against you."

"Sure ... Turk ... that's because ... you're ... built ... that way ... Will ... you do ... me a ... favor ... Turk?"

"You know I will, Henry. Name it."

"Hold ... my ... hand ... will ... you ... Turk?"

"Sure, Henry."

"I ... want ... to feel ... close ... to ... some ... body. I've ... got ... Nothing ... else ... nothing ... nothing."

Henry closed his eyes and Turk sat there holding the hand of this strange paradox of a man—this man whom he could never understand—who was mean, tough, and hard, and yet who always could wrap Turk around his little finger. It was a great liking that he had always had for Henry Mueller. Henry drew like an electromagnet and people clung to him, but also with the ease of an electromagnet that suddenly shuts off its current, he could drop them like so many pieces of scrap iron.

Turk sat there holding Henry's hand till he felt it slowly growing cold, and as the first streaks of daylight filtered in through the latticed window, Turk knew that Henry Mueller had died.

They buried Henry in the American cemetery which was located on a little wind-swept knoll outside Antwerp. Turk stood unnoticed among the small group of enlisted men and officers who gathered at the grave while a chaplain read from the book. Before them stood the flag-draped coffin of a man they had known only a short while, but whose accomplishments with the mentally sick were already legendary.

"Colonel Bartok was a man whom it was a privilege to know," the chaplain said quietly. "He gave unselfishly of his time and energies to his fellow men, he gave to the last ounce of his strength and his death took from this earth a life that was destined to go on to great heights as man's benefactor. His loss is a loss to our country as well, for it was he who restored to health many of our boys who might otherwise have been doomed to helplessness and a life of mental anguish. Untold others have been robbed of his genius and the fruits of his knowledge. Viktor Bartok will live always in the hearts of those who knew him, as a great doctor and a great man. It was a strange stroke of fate that the approval of the Legion of Merit which he so richly earned in life should be received from Washington a short time after his death. General Swift, will you make the presentation, sir?"

The general stepped forward and two enlisted men standing nearby removed the flag from the coffin and opened the lid. Then in a dignified and well-modulated voice he said:

"Colonel Viktor Bartok, on behalf of the President of the United States, I have been authorized to award you for your tireless efforts in the rehabilitation of your fellow man, and for the distinguished service you have rendered your country. Therefore, before your body is laid to rest, I present to you posthumously the Legion of Merit. May God grant you a happy life in Valhalla, the home of heroes."

From a small black box, the general took the medal and pinned it over the left breast pocket of Henry's uniform. Then he stepped back one pace and saluted. The coffin was closed and the chaplain spoke again:

"Lord, what is man that Thou takest cognizance of him?
  The son of mortal—that Thou regardest him?
Man is like a breath,
  His days are like a passing shadow.
In the morning he blossometh and is changed;
  In the evening he is mowed off and withereth.
What man is there that shall live and not see death?
  That can deliver his soul from the power of the nether world?
Thou turnest man to contrition and sayest;
  Return, ye children of men!
Let us know how to number our days,
  That we may obtain a heart endowed with wisdom.
If they were but wise they would understand this,
  They would consider their latter end.
For when he dieth he can take nothing away;
  Observe the perfect man, and behold the upright,
For there is a future for the man of peace.
  But God will redeem thy soul from the power of the nether world,
For He will take away.
  The Lord redeemeth the soul of His servants,
And all that trust in Him shall not incur guiltiness,
  But shall repose forever in the Kingdom of Paradise."

A signal was given and the coffin lowered away.

"Almighty God, we herewith consign to this hallowed ground the last mortal remains of Colonel Viktor Emil Bartok. May he rest in everlasting peace. The Lord giveth and the Lord taketh away; blessed be the name of the Lord. Amen."

As the casket touched bottom, an officer barked a command. "Detail attention. Present arms. Ready, aim, fire!"

There was a loud report as six rifles cracked.

"Load, aim, fire!" There was another blast and still another, and as the bugler sounded taps, Turk stood at silent attention with his hand to his helmet in rigid salute. Henry Mueller had had a burial worthy of a man who had risen to glory and fame—a burial that—and suddenly it dawned on Turk, too. *The cross would not bear the name of Henry Mueller.* Now it was clear to him what Henry had meant.

Bartok was the winner; Henry was the loser. He had succeeded only in erecting a monument to the man he had murdered. *Henry Mueller had died the night Viktor Bartok was killed!*

That night Turk and another orderly sat in a little wineshop not far from the hospital. A barmaid approached their table.

"Cognac for me," said Turk.

"Two cognacs," replied the other, holding up two fingers for emphasis.

"Two! Understand? *Comprenez?*"

"Certainly she understands," said Turk laughingly. "Whaddya think, she's dumb? She's probably been around as many G.I.'s as you have."

She brought the drinks and Turk raised his glass. "Well, here's to the colonel, God rest him—"

The other raised his glass, "Yeah, too bad."

They drank the brandy in a gulp and for a moment there was silence.

"I understand the colonel sent for you before he died, is that right, Turk?"

"Yeah."

"You mean to tell me you knew the colonel that well that he'd send for you?"

"Yeah."

"Where'd you know him from? The States?"

"Yeah."

"They tell me that at times he could be a regular sonofabitch, is that right?"

Turk picked up his glass and drained another drop of the brandy. "Yeah, he was just about the most magnificent sonofabitch I ever met!"

THE END